Sent to Watch

David J. Lebenstein

DORRANCE
PUBLISHING CO
EST. 1920
PITTSBURGH, PENNSYLVANIA 15238

The contents of this work, including, but not limited to, the accuracy of events, people, and places depicted; opinions expressed; permission to use previously published materials included; and any advice given or actions advocated are solely the responsibility of the author, who assumes all liability for said work and indemnifies the publisher against any claims stemming from publication of the work.

Dorrance Publishing Co
585 Alpha Drive
Suite I03
Pittsburgh, PA I5238
Visit our website at*www.dorrancebookstore.com*

ISBN: 978-I-6491-3792-0
eISBN: 978-I-6491-3980-1

This book is dedicated to the revival of the memory of a great statesman, whose opportunity to serve his country and leave his mark in history was cut short.

I would also like to thank and acknowledge my wife and my son for helpful suggestions and editorial assistance, as well as help with the cover design.

Prologue
The King's English

"I believe you have had quite enough to drink, Lieutenant," admonished Major Weatherby.

Even in the dim light of the crowded pub, the concern on the major's face was as unmistakable as the large scar on his left cheek. Major Robert Weatherby was the sort of man who attracted attention. He was six feet tall with deep blue eyes, dark brown hair, and a large forehead that gave him the appearance of a born leader. Together with the gravity of his persona, his serious expression and his robust physical condition, the major commanded respect by his very presence.

Weatherby was youthful, only twenty-five years of age, and was reputed to have purchased his rank, although he never spoke of his family or the source of his moderate wealth. The major was handsome by any method of accounting, that is, when viewed from the right side. The Battle of Waterloo, fought just months before, had left him scarred for life. The marks of battle on his left shoulder and upper arm were covered by his uniform, but the mark on the left side of his face could not be hidden.

"No need to worry about me, Major. I know when I've had enough," Lt. Greenhill retorted. "And as I said, I'll have another pint."

Lt. William Greenhill bore scars from Waterloo of a different kind. Ever since that awful day, he had begun to consume more and more beer and ale. Everyone in the regiment had hoped that leaving the Continent and returning to England would do Greenhill some good. Greenhill was a bright young officer with a promising future in the Royal Army. He was as tall as the major, with dirty blond hair and brilliant blue eyes, but with a more jovial disposition, at least before the battle.

It was well known that Major Weatherby and Lt. Greenhill were close friends. They were from the same town, and it was said they grew up together. They were both left-handed. Like Weatherby, Greenhill spoke little of his past. One thing was becoming increasingly apparent: Weatherby was covering for his friend. It was time for Greenhill to pull himself together and get the better of his drinking.

The waitress had been sitting at the next table with other soldiers. She got up, went to the bar to get the pint and brought it to Greenhill. As she placed it on the table, Greenhill reached up and stroked her face. "You're a pretty one, you are."

She drew back. Someone at the table shouted, "Hey there, lieutenant boy! Keep your bloody rich boy 'ands off of 'er."

"That is no way to address an officer in His Majesty's Army," Greenhill shot back indignantly.

Usually officers and noncommissioned soldiers did not mix, but the town was small. There was only one pub.

"Step over 'ere and I'll show you what for!" the soldier challenged Greenhill.

"May I remind you that striking an officer is a flogging offense," Weatherby warned the soldier. "And as for you, Bill, I think it's time to leave. I'll walk you back to quarters."

"Can't I finish my pint?" Greenhill protested.

"It's time to go, old friend," Weatherby stated solemnly.

Weatherby and Greenhill stood and proceeded to the door. Greenhill's gait left little doubt that he was under the influence of strong drink. The cool air of the autumn night met them as they turned left and proceeded down the street.

"That was just in time, Bill," Weatherby remarked. "We have little time to spare."

The two of them turned left once again down an alley and were soon outside of town. They walked silently down a country road past farmland. The crops had already been harvested, and the fields were vast.

Weatherby truly loved the English countryside. He loved all four seasons. He loved it in the day and the night. The vista, the scent of the air, and the tranquility of the green hills had a certain charm, even a power over him.

Weatherby secretly worried it would soon be taken away from him forever, or more aptly, he would be taken away from it.

After about twenty minutes, Greenhill pointed to the right. "It should be over there."

Weatherby and Greenhill left the road and vaulted over a short stone fence. Greenhill stumbled and fell. "Let me help you up, Bill," Weatherby offered.

"I don't need your help, thank you," was the impetuous reply.

The pair climbed a small hill. As they went over the top and looked down across the field, they could see a dark red glow.

"By George, look at that!" Weatherby exclaimed. "You were right."

As they made their way across the field toward the glow, it became clear that the dim light was coming from the underside of a round disk shaped like an upside-down bowl. The object was large, about forty feet in diameter and about twenty feet high at its center. It was dark, but shiny and metallic, suspended over the ground about ten feet in the air. The red glow was coming from underneath it. As they drew closer, it became apparent that the object was supported by six evenly spaced columns or legs protruding from its flat bottom, forming a circle.

Weatherby and Greenhill began to walk more quickly, directly toward the object. Weatherby was walking faster than his impaired companion and reached the object first. He stepped under it, past one of the six supports. There was a circular opening at the bottom about three feet across and a silver ladder extending from the opening toward the ground. Red light was coming from the opening.

Weatherby ascended the ladder. His face broke the plane of the floor, and he saw a round metallic room with small lights on some of the walls, but the main lighting on the ceiling was a circle of red lights around the periphery of the room.

Directly in front of him were silver boots. He looked up and saw that the boots were part of a person standing before the hatch he was entering. The person was female, with a slight frame, moderately short in stature, clothed in a tight-fitting silver suit. She was wearing silver gloves; only her head was not covered in the silvery fabric. From the angle of his gaze he could only see that she had dark brown hair, cut somewhat shorter than most English women.

She reached out her hand and helped him to his feet as he emerged through the hatch. In an instant, he was face to face with his hostess. She had a fair complexion, deep blue eyes, a prominent nose, and a smooth, round forehead. She greeted her guest, "Good show, Captain Weatherby, jolly good show."

"You speak English?" he asked incredulously.

"I should hope so," the woman replied. "I worked at it for nearly two years, and I dare say it was not an easy task."

Weatherby wanted to reply, but he suddenly remembered his comrade below. "Hurry up, Bill. Do you need help?"

"No, I do not. I'm fine."

"Your fellow officer does not appear to be fine at all," the woman observed.

Weatherby turned to his hostess. "I must apologize. I am afraid that my fellow officer has had a bit too much to drink."

"Oh, stop it," Greenhill protested as he pulled himself up into the room. "And is this the King's English I hear?"

"Yes, indeed it is," Weatherby replied.

Glossary

Persons

Zahanper Duvass - Field agent assigned to France under the alias Jean-Pierre DuBois.

Arjus Ferrute – Dictator of a totalitarian faction on Earth 5.

Major Hortu - Confederation military, pilot of an Atmospheric Entry Vehicle.

Ustipas Keepetta – Subdirector of the Interplanetary Intelligence Service.

Gutsatal Leka – Analyst.

Lorch Lorbank- Field agent assigned to France under the alias Louis LeBlanc.

Agent Lorku – Field agent without an alias in several support roles.

Sreedro Metchavork - Field agent assigned to Prussia under the alias Friedrich von Mecklenburg.

Agent Mlai – Field agent without an alias in several support roles including posing as a beggar.

Saibert Ortees - Field agent assigned to the Spanish Empire under the alias Sebastian de Leon.

Vlevlan Qlat – Field agent assigned to the United States under the alias Stephen Galt.

Lt. Squeem - Confederation military, copilot of an Atmospheric Entry Vehicle.

Urelt Sraymlat - Field agent assigned to the British Empire under the alias William Greenhill.

Huha Srot - Field agent assigned to the Spanish Empire under the alias Juan Ortiz.

Huha Svortomit - Field agent assigned to Prussia under the alias Dieter Dehrmann.

Grugar Tekalta – Analyst.

Orishackt "Ori" Svavapass - Field agent assigned to the British Empire under the alias Robert Weatherby.

Sral Vlaris – Team Leader for Earth 48.

Unni Vlaytork – Analyst and field agent assigned to the British Empire under the alias Jennifer Carter.

Places

Botvrayt – A nation on Earth 19 in the northeastern Zarfixu where Unni Vlaytork and Sreedro Metchavork were born.

Confederation of Civilized Planets – A confederation of twenty-seven autonomous planets whose interplanetary trade and security are regulated by commissions. Laws governing interplanetary relations are binding if agreed upon by three-fourths of the member states.

Dufa Da – The capital city of Grelland and the principal city of Earth 2.

Grelland – A nation in northwestern Malefora whose language and culture became dominant on Earth 2, and whose language, Grellish, became the international language of Earth 2 and the interplanetary language of the Confederation of Civilized Planets.

Malefora – An equatorial continent on Earth 2, whose nations became technologically advanced and colonized the rest of the planet.

Mraznia – A nation on Earth 1 whose language and culture became dominant and whose units of measure and calendar were adopted for interplanetary communication in the Confederation of Civilized Planets.

Olistoss – A nation on Earth 19 in western Zarfixu where Ori Svavapass was born.

Omtvumx – A nation on Earth 19 on the continent of Svartolk whose language and culture became dominant on Earth 19; a former colonial power that once occupied Olistoss.

Ropalb – The principal city on Earth 43.

Svartolk – An equatorial continent on Earth 19, whose nations became technologically advanced and colonized the rest of the planet; former rivals Omtvumx and Urgst are located on this continent.

Tlat Mlang – The capital city of Mraznia and the principal city of Earth 1 and the administrative center of the Confederation of Civilized Planets.

Urgst – A nation on Earth 19 on the continent of Svartolk; a former colonial power that once occupied Botvrayt.

Yoilafa – The capital city of Botvrayt and hometown of Unni Vlaytork.

Zarfixu – A temperate continent in the southern hemisphere of Earth 19 where Olistoss and Botvrayt are located. Zarfixu was once colonized by the powers of Svartolk. The natives of Zarfixu bear a close resemblance to Europeans on Earth 48. Almost all of the field agents serving on Earth 48 come from Zarfixu.

Time

The Confederation of Civilized Planets has agreed to use the calendar of Earth 1, which circles its sun in 380 days. Its calendar consists of ten months, each thirty-eight days in length. Dates are written by the year, month, and day. For example, June 18, 1815 was 37527.4.1, and November 13, 1819 was 37531.6.14. The week is ten days long with seven workdays. The day is divided into twenty hours, but a day on Earth 1 is almost the same length as a day on Earth 48. Thus, an hour on Earth 1 is approximately seventy-two minutes in length using the minute of Earth 48.

1.

Interplanetary Confederation

Tens of light-years away there was a planet that called itself Earth, at least in most of its major languages. Most of the surface of the planet was covered by oceans. Some of its continents were inhabited, and the isolated people had adapted to the climates of their homelands. On the several continents, the people competed with one another for resources, territory, and markets. Sometimes the competition was peaceful, but more often than not, there was war. Empires rose and empires fell. New inventions were devised and neighboring nations eventually obtained them, with technology moving forward at differing rates among the isolated continents.

One such continent, called Malefora, straddled the equator and spanned one-third of the circumference of Earth. On the western side of the north coast was a large peninsula shaped like a large oval pointing north, joined to the continent by a narrow, mountainous isthmus. The peninsula was divided into nine warring kingdoms. Over several centuries, one of the kingdoms began to prevail through military victories and strategic royal marriages. That kingdom was Grellyrort, but for the ease of the reader, it will be referred to in this treatise as Grelland; its language will be called Grellish. The capital of Grelland, Dufa Da became a great city and was the capital of the peninsula.

Some of the nations of Malefora advanced in the field of navigation and these nations began to sail the oceans. The Maleforans discovered that Earth was round, and they discovered the other continents. It seems that the warmer climate on Malefora had allowed them to advance more rapidly than the

1

people on the other continents. Soon Grelland and the other Maleforan empires were competing with one another to colonize the other continents and subjugate their peoples.

With the rise of industrialization in Malefora, the people congregated to the cities. Some philosophers noted that often the rich get richer and the poor get poorer, and they devised alternative economic systems that would redistribute the wealth or the market shares or both. The competition of the monarchs of Malefora eventually led to war fought on all of the inhabited continents. Millions died. The people of the defeated nations became impoverished and desperate. These nations turned to the alternate economic systems.

Governments strong enough to redistribute the wealth had the means to confiscate it from the fallen aristocracy and middle class. Unfortunately, governments powerful enough to confiscate wealth and control the flow of goods were also able to restrict their citizens' rights. Dictatorships abounded. It was tragic that the men who rose to the top in the totalitarian nations were the most ruthless and also ambitious for conquest. Millions more died.

Earth was divided into three camps: the free countries where people retained their freedom of speech, worship, and private ownership; the totalitarian socialist dictatorships where freedoms were extinguished; and the nationalistic corporativist dictatorships where freedoms were curtailed and ethnic minorities were persecuted. It should have been obvious to all that the competition between the three economic systems would be decided militarily.

The Grellish people were fortunate. Their country had been on the winning side of the previous war, and their people retained their freedoms through a constitutional monarchy. But to protect their rights and freedoms, the Grellish and their allies had to fight a costly mechanized global war in which civilians were subjected to aerial bombardment.

The three groupings of nations fought, two against one, and one of the totalitarian systems was eliminated. By then, weapons of mass destruction had been invented, and direct military confrontation became impossible. The Free World looked to Dufa Da for leadership. Grelland and its allies competed with the other totalitarian system for more than a generation until the dictatorship collapsed under its own rottenness.

Colonialism ebbed and the nations on the other continents became independent. This led to smaller wars as ancient grievances among these nations surfaced.

As all these things were occurring, Grelland continued to make techno-logical progress and eventually landed men on both moons. Young people from all over the world flocked to Grelland's universities to study. Academic journals were now requiring authors to submit their papers in Grellish. There reached a point where half of the people on Earth spoke Grellish either as their mother tongue or as a second language.

Scientists had set up arrays of dish antennae to send and receive messages from other civilizations to determine if there was extraterrestrial life. After two generations of sending patterned pulses and patient listening, the people of the planet called Earth received a message from a solar system five light-years away. That the message came from an intelligent extraterrestrial source was undeniable.

Over the years, the two planets worked out a code of communication and expanded their arrays to allow for more sophisticated messages. It became ev-ident that the aliens were similar to themselves, with two eyes, two hands, ten fingers and ten toes. Their planet was similar in size and had oceans of water and an oxygen-rich atmosphere, just like Earth, except that it had three moons instead of two.

With time, it became possible to trade photographs. To everyone's sur-prise, the aliens looked just like themselves; they were human! Like Earth, the alien planet had multiple races with different skin colors and physical traits. Audio transmissions followed, and audio-video clips. Many of them were themed to assist the other planet in learning their alphabet and language.

The aliens began to learn to speak and write Grellish, and the people of Earth began to learn Mraznian, the language of the aliens. As communication improved, it was learned that both planets called themselves Earth in their own languages. To avoid confusion, it was agreed that they would refer to each other as Earth 1 and Earth 2. The Mraznian speakers were Earth 1 and the Grellish speakers were Earth 2.

It turned out that the two planets had similar histories, with Mraznian culture becoming dominant on Earth 1. As on Earth 2, the people on the warmer continent on Earth 1 had developed more quickly from a technologi-cal standpoint and had come to dominate the people on the colder continents, where conditions were less favorable for development. Eventually both plan-ets had moved away from colonialism and racism, but the languages of the first continent to develop navigation were among the major languages on the respective planets. Neither planet was politically unified; both planets still had nations, but warfare was less common and on a smaller scale than it had been in the past.

After a century, the scientists and engineers on Earth 1 invented an interstellar radio by which messages could travel faster than light. They sent the specifications to Earth 2. Within ten years, the two planets were conversing. At that time, an agreement was made. The language of interplanetary communication would be Grellish, using the Grellish phonic alphabet; but the Mraznian system of measurement would be used, including units of length, mass and time, as well as the Mraznian calendar.

Both planets had days and years that were approximately the same. Earth 1 circled its sun in 380 days. Their calendar had ten months of approximately thirty-eight days based on the time between the alignment of their two larger moons. Because of the ten months, ten fingers and ten toes, Mraznian mathematics was base ten, their units were decimal, and their circle had one hundred degrees. For the ease of the reader, in this treatise all measurement will be translated into English units at an equivalent level of precision. Idioms in the dialogue will be translated as well to make for smoother reading.

After another generation, the principles of the interstellar radio were expanded to develop spacecraft that could travel faster than light. Thus, interstellar travel was possible. Ambassadors were exchanged, as well as science and culture. Before long, there were interstellar trade, interstellar commerce, interstellar lawsuits, interstellar romance, interstellar marriage, and, of course, interstellar mixed-race children. Even horses and dogs from the two planets were mixed in breeding. And existing breeds were traded. Children on Earth 1 were seen playing with loyal Ortivian retrievers from Earth 2, and cute little bossy lapdogs from Earth 1 were seen in the homes of the people on Earth 2. And heard.

Interstellar commissions were devised to regulate commerce, travel, and health. The latter commission prevented the spread of plagues. In the center of the commissions was the High Commission. This body passed laws governing interplanetary matters. Each world had one vote, and both had to agree for a law to become binding.

After two centuries, three more Earthlike inhabited planets were discovered in rapid succession, designated Earth 3, Earth 4 and Earth 5. Space stations were placed in orbit of the planets whose crews included linguists to learn the major languages of each world. After two years of surveillance, the visitors sent a transmission to the major governments announcing their presence and requesting permission to land and meet with the leaders of the major nations on these worlds.

The assimilation of Earth 3 went smoothly. The people there were at technological and cultural levels that were comparable to Earths 1 and 2 at the time they made contact. Earth 4 required more work because they were at a lower level of technology. The visitors from space lavished new science and technology on their hosts, and Earth 4 made the transition to membership in what was coming to be known as the Confederation of Civilized Planets.

But on Earth 5, things went terribly wrong. Earth 5 was at an earlier stage of its development. It still had a major totalitarian state, replete with unwilling allied satellite states. Arjus Ferrute, the dictator of that state, tricked the Confederation into giving him advanced technology that he could use for military means. When Ferrute launched a war of conquest, the Confederation felt obligated to aid the other nations. Before long, the High Commission was recruiting military forces and sending them into the global war on Earth 5.

Ferrute claimed that his country was fighting to repulse an "alien invasion" and that the allies of the Confederation were "collaborators." In this way, Ferrute was able to win allies from states that had previously opposed his form of government. The ferocity of the war and the tenacity of the resistance was beyond anything that the people of the Confederation had anticipated.

There was sentiment among the people of the four planets to simply withdraw from Earth 5. But others were concerned about the fate of the Confederation's friends on that planet who had trusted them. Not only so, but there was concern that Earth 5, once unified into a global totalitarian state, might pose a threat in the future to the other four worlds. The High Commission made the decision to fight on despite protest and division among its citizens on all four planets.

After eight long years of fighting and tens of millions of people dead, the nations backed by the Confederation prevailed. In some parts of Earth 5, an insurgency continued for nearly a century. Divisions at home caused by the debate over the war took a generation to heal. At long last, Earth 5 became a normal member of the Confederation. But a painful lesson had been learned.

Henceforth, the Confederation would never again try to influence the development of the course of history of any planet. They would never again reveal themselves to the natives of a new world until the Exploration Commission certified that the subject planet was ready.

It was with this view that the Interplanetary Intelligence Service was created. Its mission was to discover and study planets with intelligent life, to learn their languages and culture, and to help the Exploration Commission decide when and whether to make formal contact.

The Interplanetary Intelligence Service conducted this work in a stepwise approach. First, yellow nonbinary stars were visited by starships to determine if there was an Earthlike planet. If so, the second step was to determine if there was intelligent life. If the planet was populated with intelligent beings and the natives were at Technology Level 10 or higher, they would possess radio. A space station manned by agents of the Service could be inserted into orbit to monitor radio and television transmissions, learn the major languages, and follow events on the surface.

If the planet was not yet at Technology Level 10, then specially trained agents of the Interplanetary Intelligence Service would be sent to the surface to blend into the population and learn what they could. To make the best use of resources, they agents were placed in the nations or cities that were the most advanced or expected to emerge as the leading civilizations on the planet, as Mraznia and Grelland had on their respective planets. Once a planet reached Technology Level 10, field agents could be withdrawn and surveillance could be carried out from orbiting analysts listening to radio broadcasts.

Agents were given intensive training and much latitude to carry out their mission. But there was one very strict rule that all agents of the Service had to obey at the cost of their lives: never to intervene or interfere in any way with the normal development of the planets they were surveilling. Their motto was "Sent to watch but not to affect." It rhymes in Grellish.

To hide the fact that they are from other worlds, field agents carried very little equipment that could be identified as "otherworldly." They had emergency medical kits in thin packages sewn into their clothing. Agents were usually supplied with precious metals that they could use to purchase everything else they needed. For communication, each agent had an implant in his or her upper left arm. It acted as a transponder so that an orbital spacecraft could track their movements. It also served as a means of communication. When the Interplanetary Intelligence Service wanted to communicate with a field agent, it would send a series of three pulses, with one to ten beats in each pulse. The message would be repeated multiple times. Field agents were required to memorize the meaning of at least one hundred such messages. A common message was a recall message, instructing an agent to proceed to a pickup point where a transport would pick them up.

The field agents with long-term undercover assignments were supported by short-term agents who performed very specific missions, such as acquiring papers for forging and creating aliases for their long-term colleagues, and "arranging" jobs and housing. Using gold and silver from the prolific mines of Earth 4, these agents could obtain large amounts of local currency, which could be conferred to an agent's alias.

In the century after the war on Earth 5, nineteen more inhabited planets were identified, numbered Earth 6 to Earth 24, but only five were added to the Confederation. Four others were watched from orbit, and the other ten were the workplace of field agents.

Eventually the number of "Earths" reached 51.

One of the most interesting of the civilized worlds was Earth 48. It only had one moon, but that moon was one eightieth the mass of its parent planet, and of the perfect size and distance to create total solar eclipses. Another unusual aspect of Earth 48 was that its colder continent developed technically before the warmer continents. The people on Earth 48 were also unusual: most of them were right-handed, as many as ninety percent of the population. One consequence of this remarkable anomaly was that most of their languages are written from left to right!

Over the eight centuries since its discovery, Earth 48 has had approximately a dozen agents of the Interplanetary Intelligence Service operating at any one time. The spies served for a five-year tour of duty, and many of them volunteered for multiple tours. At first, localities of interest included places on four different continents. Agents learned Chinese, Mayan, Hindi, Arabic, and Greek. Eventually, it was realized that the portion of Continent 1 called Europe was becoming the most technically advanced. For a time, Portugal was considered the nation most likely to emerge as dominant. Later Spain, France, and the Holy Roman Empire were given much attention.

Most field agents on Earth 48 were from Earth 19, one of whose continents, Zarfixu had a race that most resembled Europeans. The match was not perfect: their blue eyes were a very light but deep blue that differed from

7

the eye color of the natives. However, that minor difference did not seem to interfere with the ability of the field agents to blend in with the natives.

By the year 37512 (which was 1800 using the natives' calendar), the factions of greatest interest on Earth 48 were called England, France, Prussia, and Spain. The Exploration Commission was reasonably certain that one of these nations would become dominant, as Mraznia and Grelland had on their respective planets, and one of their languages would become the international mode of communication. But which one?

2.

The Conference

Agent Unni Vlaytork rose from her seat the moment the spacecraft landed on Earth 48 in a place the natives called England. The upper deck was a round room about thirty feet in diameter with twelve seats fastened to the floor. Two seats were at the controls where two military men were seated, Major Hortu, the pilot, and Lieutenant Squeem, the copilot. Unlike the field agents, the pilot and copilot were dark in complexion and would not pass among the natives for Europeans.

The pilot and the copilot were dressed in silver suits, as was Agent Vlaytork. Four of the seats were occupied by field agents of the Interplanetary Intelligence Service that had just been picked up, two from outside of Magdeburg in Prussia, and the other two from a field outside Paris. They were still in native clothing.

But this was the pickup that Agent Vlaytork had been dreading. The transponder of one of the agents assigned to England had become still during a major battle they had witnessed from orbit; it had not moved in over one hundred days. Its owner, Agent Orishackt Svavapass was therefore presumed dead. Everyone on board the spacecraft expected Agent Urelt Sraymlat to board shortly and confirm the grim news.

Sraymlat's transponder was showing on a small screen between the pilot and copilot in the front of the vessel.

Major Hortu pointed at the screen and said, "He should arrive momentarily."

9

"I'll go down below to meet him," Vlaytork replied solemnly.

"I had better go with you," Agent Svortomit offered. Like Agent Sraymlat, Svortomit was youthful, only a year into his assignment to Earth 48. He had been Sraymlat's roommate at the Academy.

"That won't be necessary," Vlaytork said as she began to descend ladder to the lower deck.

"Oh, yes, it is necessary, and I'm coming too," Agent Duvass declared. "Sraymlat has company."

Vlaytork stepped back onto the upper deck and swiftly made her way to the forward console, where an infrared image showed two figures walking toward their vehicle. One of them had a gold dot signifying his transponder.

"It looks like we have a curious native to contend with," Lt. Squeem confirmed.

"Yes, and he is closer to the ship than Sraymlat," Duvass pointed out.

"Sraymlat is having a hard time keeping up," Svortomit said. "The terrain must be rough."

"Then why is the native moving so well?" the copilot wondered. "Unless Sraymlat is injured."

Vlaytork peered at the infrared silhouettes. "I'd recognize that gait anywhere!" she declared excitedly. "That's Agent Svavapass!"

"It can't be," Squeem said. "There is no transponder."

"Please control your wishful thinking," Agent Lorbank admonished the youthful agent.

"It *is* Svavapass," Vlaytork insisted. "I've got this."

She quickly made her way down the ladder to the lower deck. The room was dark, lit with the red lights used during a night pickup. The hatch leading to the planet's surface had been mechanically opened by the pilot just after landing.

Vlaytork stood at the open hatch to receive the men below.

The first man's face broke the plane of the floor, and Vlaytork recognized him at once, even in the dark lighting. It was Agent Svavapass! As he continued to rise, she could see his native costume, the uniform of an officer in the British Army.

Vlaytork reached out her hand and helped him to his feet as he emerged through the hatch. In an instant, she was face to face with her fellow agent. "Good show, Captain Weatherby, jolly good show," she greeted him.

"You speak English?" Svavapass asked incredulously.

"I should hope so," Agent Vlaytork replied. "I worked at it for nearly two years, and I dare say it was not an easy task."

Svavapass wanted to reply, but he suddenly remembered his comrade below. "Hurry up, Bill. Do you need help?"

"No, I do not. I'm fine."

"Your fellow officer does not appear to be fine at all," Vlaytork observed.

Svavapass turned to his hostess. "I must apologize. I am afraid that my fellow officer has had a bit too much to drink."

"Oh, stop it," Sraymlat protested as he pulled himself up into the room. "And is this the King's English I hear?"

"Yes, indeed it is," Svavapass replied. "Agent Vlaytork speaks English now."

"And you can call me Jenny," she quickly interjected. "Jenny Carter."

"Well then, you had might as well call me *Major* Weatherby. The natives promoted me after an important battle I took part in."

Agent Orishackt "Ori" Svavapass was rather proud of the fact that his alias, Robert Weatherby had earned a promotion.

"And since when does an analyst get a native alias?" asked Agent Urelt Sraymlat, a.k.a. William Greenhill, breaking into the Grellish language.

The main lighting came on as the lower hatch closed. The light stung the eyes of the two recent arrivals, as they had been adjusted to the darkness outside.

"I have been accepted for field work," Vlaytork replied.

"What?" Svavapass seemed surprised. "Field work?"

"Hurry up down there!" Major Hortu boomed from the main cabin above. "I have another pickup to make. We need to get going."

Svavapass turned to grab the ladder to climb into the main cabin. It was then that Vlaytork first noticed the scar on the left side of Svavapass's face.

"What happened to your face?" she asked with concern.

"A battle scar," Ori replied.

"We know about that battle," Agent Vlaytork affirmed. "We saw signs of it from orbit. Quite honestly, I have been very worried about you for months, and I am quite happy to see you alive."

Svavapass, Sraymlat, and Vlaytork proceeded up to the upper deck. Svavapass was surprised to see four agents seated there, but the team leader, Special Agent Sral Vlaris, was absent.

Whenever there was an unscheduled pickup, their team leader would be on board the transport to confer with the agent or agents. The absence of the team leader could only mean one of two things: the mission was being aborted and Agents Svavapass and Sraymlat were being extracted, or a major conference was about to take place on the orbiting space station. The presence of four other agents seemed to suggest the latter.

Svavapass and Sraymlat recognized their four colleagues. Agents Sreedro Metchavork and Huha Svortomit were dressed in military uniforms of a nation of natives known as Prussia. Agents Lorch Lorbank and Zahanper Duvass, who were assigned to France, were in native civilian clothes. The agents were visibly relieved to see Svavapass alive, especially Svortomit.

Agents Svortomit and Sraymlat had been freshman at the Academy the year Ori Svavapass was a junior. The two had been friends with Svavapass back then.

"Look at you, Svortomit in that sharp uniform!" Sraymlat exclaimed. "You look like a real Prussian soldier. *Eins, zwei, drei, vier; eins, zwei, drei, vier!*"

"Is he drunk, Svavapass?" Svortomit asked.

"I am afraid so," Svavapass replied. "And I ran out of sobriety pills weeks ago." He stroked his uniform over the concealed pocket where agents kept their hidden stash of medical supplies.

"You had better take this," Vlaytork offered, passing Sraymlat a small pill.

"The things I do for the Service," Sraymlat sighed.

Immediately after he had swallowed the pill, the transport took off.

"Svavapass made me feign a drinking problem as part of my cover," Sraymlat continued. "That native brew is awful! They call it 'beer.'"

"Maybe the English beer is bad," Svortomit agreed. "Obviously, you have never tried German beer."

"Say, where are we going?" Ori asked Unni.

"To pick up Ortees and Srot," she replied.

"But Spain is that way," Svavapass said, pointing. "They are assigned to Spain, aren't they?"

"Indeed they are, but their transponder shows them to be on Continent No. 3."

"*Amérique du Nord,*" Lorbank said.

"A small village in a sparsely populated area," Squeem the copilot interjected. "It's called Sinant... Sanint...I can't pronounce these weird alien names."

"Flash it to me in the alien alphabet," Vlaytork volunteered. She looked at the small screen on the armrest of her seat. "San Antonio de Béjar in a colonial province of the Spanish Empire called Tejas."

"Like I said," the copilot muttered, "weird alien names."

"What are Ortees and Srot doing all the way over there?" Sraymlat asked.

"You can ask them when we get there," Major Hortu said without humor. The military men did not hold the spies in very high esteem. They saw them as a coddled elite.

Less than an hour later, the transport touched down at the prearranged spot south of San Antonio. Major Hortu was pleased that Agents Ortees and Srot were already in place and that they promptly boarded the transport. It was still daylight in Tejas, and Hortu hated daytime landings. Like all pilots operating on alien planets, Hortu did all he could to avoid being sighted by natives. No sooner were Agents Ortees and Srot seated in the cabin, Hortu took off, ascending at a sharp angle.

Ori Svavapass recognized Agent Saibert Ortees right away. Ortees was an older agent and had spent more than twenty years on this planet. Although Ortees hardly knew the younger agents, he was a bit of a legend among them as were the exploits of his alias, Col. Sebastian de Leon. He was looking old and a bit haggard. Having spent a little more than three years on the planet himself, Svavapass could understand how the assignment could have aged Ortees. The other agent, Huha Srot, was young, and Svavapass did not know him very well. Both were dressed in a type of native clothing with which Svavapass was unaccustomed.

The transport headed for Space Station 48-3, a space station that was in geosynchronous orbit over the largest ocean on the planet. Hortu accelerated continuously. When they were halfway to the destination, he flipped the vehicle around and began to decelerate. It was a terrible waste of energy to fly that way, but it created enough artificial gravity to keep his passengers comfortable. Transporting weightless passengers entailed the risk of someone vomiting, and it would be the military personnel who would be tasked with the cleanup.

By that time, Sraymlat seemed to have recovered much of his sobriety. He asked Agent Ortees how he got to be in New Spain. Ortees explained that he felt it profitable to leave Spain when it became politically unstable after Napoleon had been defeated in that country in 1813. He manipulated his superiors to transfer him to New Spain on the North American Continent. But the colonies were also becoming violent with different parties favoring monarchy, a republic, and even independence. He volunteered to go to the province of

Tejas in 1814. Even that remote and sparsely populated province was shaken by unrest. Through all of the upheaval that began with Napoleon's invasion of Spain, he had gone through four partners, and his present partner, Agent Srot, had said he was not interested in staying when his tour of duty ended next year.

A little over an hour and a half later, the transport reached Space Station 48-3. The space station was shaped like a wheel with an elongated axial hub. The spinning of the wheel gave much of the station artificial gravity from centrifugal force. Station 48-3 had six docking ports on one end of the axial hub. The transport docked and its crew and passengers disembarked through the hatch at the bottom of the vehicle. They were temporarily weightless as they made their way to a tube leading to the wheel.

All eleven persons had to pass through the decontamination chamber to avoid bringing any diseases onto the ship. Attendants confiscated their native clothing. After they were fully cleansed, they were given uniforms of the Interplanetary Intelligence Service.

The eight field agents were given a meal and escorted to their temporary cabins. They were to write a report of their activity since their last communication, about one and a half years for most of the agents. After that, they were instructed to get some sleep. While they rested, the analysts, both human and android, would analyze their reports. After that, the agents would be fed breakfast and hold a conference with their team leader.

Svavapass sat down at the console in this cabin and placed his hands into the two hand-shaped indentations that constituted the keyboard used for typing. A form came up on the holographic screen monitor. He entered his name, his serial number, his alias, and the date. Svavapass was about to check the box indicating the report type when he received an error message on the date. He had written "October 14, 1815." He felt momentary embarrassment. Svavapass quickly corrected it, "37527.7.5." He supposed it was a combination of tiredness and of being too long on assignment.

Agent Svavapass poured out his report over the next hour and a half. When he was done, he got into the comfortable space station bed. As he was falling asleep, he asked himself, "Did Unni Vlaytork really say she had been worried about me?" He did not ponder the thought long. He soon settled into a deep sleep.

The next morning, the eight field agents were in the conference room eating their breakfast with two analysts including Unni Vlaytork and Grugar

Tekalta. On the left side of the table from the front were the two agents assigned to Prussia, Sreedro Metchavork (Oberst Friedrich von Mecklenburg) and Huha Svortomit (Lt. Dieter Dehrmann). Next to them were the two agents assigned to France, Lorch Lorbank (Col. Louis LeBlanc) and Zahanper Duvass (Lt. Jean-Pierre DuBois). On the right side of the table were the agents for England, Orishackt Svavapass (Major Robert Weatherby) and Urelt Sraymlat (Lt. William Greenhill), and the agents for Spain, Saibert Ortees (Col. Sebastian De Leon) and Huha Srot (Juan Ortiz). The analysts were at the foot of the table. There were two empty seats at the head of the table.

Everyone was telling stories of their experiences down below on the planet's surface and funny things that occurred at the Academy. Some attendants came in and removed the plates and cups. Then the team leader Sral Vlaris came in, took a seat at the head of the table, and called the meeting to order.

Vlaris was an older man with gray hair balding at the forehead. He was over six feet tall and broad-shouldered. Like the field agents in the room, he had a fair complexion and deep blue eyes. When he was younger, he had served for nearly twenty years performing field work on the surface of the planet. Everyone at the table was from the continent of Zarfixu on Earth 19. Only the other analyst, Agent Tekalta, was from a different planet, Earth 16.

"Gentlemen, before the Subdirector calls in, there is a certain matter that needs to be resolved among us."

Vlaris pressed a button on his console and a photograph appeared on the main screen behind the team leader. It was taken from space, and showed a section of the planet's surface. Roads, hills, and trees were visible. Smoke could be seen from a source in the center.

"Do you gentlemen recognize this place?" Vlaris asked.

"I'd rather forget that place," Lorbank rued.

"That is Belgium, and the figure centers on a town called Waterloo," Metchavork responded.

"It was taken on date 37527.4.1," Vlaris went on grimly.

"It is easier on the agents if you convert to the native calendar," Agent Vlaytork suggested. "That would be June…"

"June 18, 1815," six of the agents said in a cacophony of English, French, and German.

"Right," Vlaytork agreed.

"I suppose there is a good reason that you all seem to remember the date so well," Vlaris remarked dryly. "Probably because of this."

Vlaris magnified the photo showing much smoke and signs of military units. "I don't believe one needs to be an experienced analyst to interpret this photo," Vlaris continued. "A military engagement of major proportions, Technology Level 8."

"Uh, yes, sir," Agent Svavapass began to explain. "That is the Battle of Waterloo, sir. It will probably go down in history as one of the most important battles in the history of the planet."

"Yes, a victory of planetary proportions," Metchavork agreed.

"Or more accurately, a catastrophe of planetary proportions," Lorbank opined.

"Seriously, Lorch, you don't think a victory by Napoleon Bonaparte would have been good for that planet, do you?" Agent Svortomit asked incredulously.

"Yes, I do. His defeat was a setback for Earth 48," Agent Lorbank replied. "Napoleon was a force of justice, unity, and progress…"

Lorbank was cut off by protests from six agents, who all at once rebutted him. "Napoleon was a tyrant!" one said. Another said, "He was a greedy warmonger!" Others ascribed additional unflattering attributes to Napoleon while Lorbank and Duvass argued back.

"Gentlemen, Gentlemen!" Vlaris called for order. "The issue here is not the merits of one native ruler or another. We can discuss that later. My problem is this."

Vlaris clicked and six dots appeared on the screen in close proximity. "Do you know what these dots are?"

The agents were silent. They knew too well, but Vlaris answered his own question. "These dots are your positions based upon the transponders in your bodies. You will note that at this instant, the six of you were within sixty yards of each other participating in combat on both sides of an intense battle!"

"Our cover, our roles on that planet are military," Svortomit tried to explain. "Military men obey orders. Or else."

"Your role on that planet is to study the natives on an alien planet and their development, culturally, technologically, and politically. And your orders come from me!"

"What would you have had us do, under the circumstances?" Svavapass asked.

Vlaris glared at him. "And you, Svavapass. We thought you were dead. Your transponder stopped moving. It is still at Waterloo even now."

Ori Svavapass blushed and stiffened in his chair. "Well, yes, the military surgeon who stitched up my shoulder mentioned that he had taken out a piece of shrapnel. I figured it was my transponder when I stopped getting any more signals…"

"And why was a native military doctor operating on you at all? Look at you, your face! You men are too highly trained to get killed in an alien war."

The agents dared not say another word.

Vlaris gave the concluding remark. "NEVER let this happen again!"

"Yes, sir," the agents affirmed in muffled voices.

"Oh, and by the way," Vlaris added. "Excellent work, men. I read your reports. Truly great intelligence work."

"We have the Subdirector," Vlaytork announced.

"Put her on," Vlaris commanded.

A hologram appeared at the head of the conference table.

"Good day," Ustipas Keepetta greeted the agents from her seat light years away in the interplanetary capital city of Tlat Mlang. Subdirector Keepetta was an older woman whose white hair, pulled back in a bun, was accented by her black complexion.

She looked down at her tablet. "Earth 51 at Technology Level 7 and Cultural Level 6: it appears that the situation on Earth 51 is very grave: volcanic eruptions and earthquakes in the primary continent, the threat of famine…"

The arm of a younger man briefly entered the hologram and tapped her on the shoulder and whispered to her.

"My apology," she said with a brief wide grin. "Earth 51 is my next meeting. I had the wrong file.

"Oh, yes, Earth 48 at Technology Level 8, Cultural Level 6. This is the one with all those wars on its primary continent, and that fierce native warlord, Napoleon Binnaypart. Did I pronounce it correctly?"

"Close enough," Lorbank offered.

"The Service summoned you here to help us assess the political situation on Earth 48," the Subdirector began. "According to your reports, you concur that Napoleon's career is over. We would like to go over the implications of this fact, as it ends an era. We have entered your reports into predictive models and have been running probabilistic simulations for hours. But we would like to hear your analyses, given your unique points of view as persons embedded in the society of the most powerful factions on the planet."

Each agent gave his view of the present situation in Prussia, France, the British Empire, and the Spanish Empire. After that, the agents were asked to venture a prediction as to which nation on Earth 48 would ultimately triumph as the strongest and most important.

The "French" went first. Agent Lorbank made the presentation. "Recent events have been disastrous for the French people, who have lost their recent territorial gains and their overseas colonies. But France has emerged from this defeat with its home territory intact. Its capital Paris is still a center of the arts, science, and mathematics. Even now, three great mathematicians are working, even a fourth until recently, and they have made great advances in multidimensional partial differential equations.

"I believe that France will rise from defeat and soon resume the mantle as the leading nation on Earth 48. Given time, the French language will prevail as the international language of science, commerce and diplomacy."

The Subdirector motioned to the analysts. "What do the simulation models say?"

Vlaytork looked at her tablet. "The models concur that France will recover from this defeat and will be an important power on this planet for the foreseeable future. However, few of the simulations show France prevailing as the leading nation on the planet. This is a change from what we were predicting even five years ago. A lot has changed."

The Subdirector extended her holographic hand to the two agents assigned to Prussia. Agent Metchavork predicted that Berlin would one day be the leading capital on the planet. "The German people are divided into dozens of petty states orbiting two great capitals, Berlin and Vienna. But Agent Svortomit and I are convinced that nationalism will prevail over the religious disputes of the past. In the coming decades, Germany will be unified into a single empire. Its capital will be Berlin and the king of Prussia will be its Emperor, or Kaiser as the natives say."

Metchavork got up from his seat and went to the screen, which displayed a map of Europe. "This Empire will stretch from the North Sea to the Adriatic, from Meuse to East Prussia. The Germans are leaders in science, engineering, mathematics, literature, and music. They possess a strong work ethic and a proud military tradition. They are also keen to liberal ideas and social progress.

"In summary, I see Prussia uniting the German people into a single mighty nation in the midst of the most advanced continent on the planet. Within a century or two, German will be the international language of science, commerce and diplomacy. Earth 48 will be German!"

"Thank you, Herr Oberst von Mecklenburg," Vlaris said with some degree of sarcasm.

"A different interpretation of the status of the planet," the Subdirector observed.

Agent Duvass shook his head. "It must be in the water."

"Or perhaps the beer," Agent Sraymlat quipped, looking at his friend Agent Svortomit.

"What is beer?" Agent Tekalta asked.

Agent Vlaytork brought the meeting back on point by giving an analysis. "In most of our simulations, many of the German states unite behind Berlin, and the resulting nation becomes a force to be reckoned with. But the matter of the German state becoming the dominant faction on the planet, while plausible, does not occur in the majority of the simulations."

The Subdirector motioned to the two agents assigned to the British Empire. Agent Svavapass gave the report. "The British Empire has no need to emerge as the world leader; they have already done so. They possess territory on all of the inhabited continents. The British have the greatest navy on the planet and can project their power anywhere in their world. Their skilled diplomacy complements their military might to put forward their interests. The British are leaders in commerce, engineering, science, and culture.

"My colleagues have emphasized the achievements of the factions to which they are assigned, but I would like to call to the attention of the Subdirector that the British discovered the seventh planet in this solar system, the first discovery by the natives of a planet not visible to the naked eye."

Svortomit suddenly interrupted Svavapass. "Pardon me, but you have failed to mention that the discoverer of the planet in question was Friedrich Wilhelm Herschel, a German."

"Frederick William Herschel is a subject of the King of England!" Sraymlat retorted.

"German is his mother tongue," Svortomit argued. "He emigrated from Hanover."

"Agent Svortomit, you are out of order," Vlaris declared. "I would admonish you to keep silent and let your fellow agent complete his report."

"My apology," Svortomit replied.

"The British people have a sound government, a constitutional monarchy that is poised to begin making the substantive reforms that will allow for a better life for its citizens and open the way for further technical progress. In summary, the British Empire will prevail as the leading civilization on this planet and English will become the international language."

"Well, Special Agent Vlaris, it would appear that your agents are enthusiastic about the native factions they have infiltrated," Subdirector Keepetta remarked. "While their immersion into their roles is refreshing, I question their objectivity."

Agent Vlaytork replied before Vlaris. "Actually, there is merit to Agent Svavapass's assessment. Our analysis confirms that the British Empire is indeed the greatest on Earth 48, and most simulations show its continued growth."

Vlaris nodded to Vlaytork, in part expressing his appreciation for her turning the discussion from a seemingly embarrassing questioning of his agents' objectivity.

The Subdirector's holograph motioned to Agent Saibert Ortees. The older agent began, "The Spanish Empire covers half of Continent 4 and half of the habitable part of Continent 3. Its vast territory is rich in natural resources, and some cities in its overseas colonies have relatively well-developed infrastructure. Therefore, I would say that the Spanish Empire is the prevalent faction on this planet."

Everyone in the room gasped, and Vlaris slapped his hand on the table in exasperation.

Ortees immediately grinned and said, "Only joking."

Everyone in the room laughed.

"You have lost none of your reputed sense of humor over the years on that harsh planet, Saibert," the Subdirector remarked.

"Seriously, the Spanish Empire, though vast in extent, is on the verge of collapse," Agent Ortees continued. "The aftereffects of Napoleon's invasion have seriously weakened Spain. This empire might have had a chance of survival with strong leadership, but the present king is ill-suited to the task. The people of Spain are divided and the colonists are in rebellion. I predict that most if not all of Spain's colonies will completely break with Spain in the near future, and Spain will be reduced in status to that of an ordinary nation not worth the effort to keep under surveillance."

"That matches the model simulations," Vlaytork concurred.

After a brief moment of silence, the Subdirector asked Agent Ortees if he had an opinion as to which nation on Earth 48 might emerge as the primary power. "After all," she said, "you appear to be the most objective field agent in the room."

Agent Ortees replied, "Given time, I believe that the strongest and most influential nation on Earth 48 will be the United States of America."

Everyone in the room burst into laughter that was louder and longer than the previous round. Only the Subdirector remained serious. Vlaris quickly caught himself and pounded on the table for order. "Agent Ortees, I exhort you to cease your jesting, at least so long as we have the Subdirector with us."

But Agent Ortees denied that he was joking. "I honestly believe that the United States of America will indeed prevail to be the most prominent nation on Earth 48."

"I honestly believe you need a vacation, Saibert," Agent Lorbank remarked.

"Better yet, retirement," Svortomit agreed.

Svavapass also disagreed with Ortees's assessment. "The Americans are a disparate collection of farmers, hunters and trappers, few in number, spread out over a vast territory with little infrastructure and limited in their access to culture and education."

"And these farmers just routed a larger force of professional soldiers from your British Empire at New Orleans," Agent Ortees countered. "From my viewpoint in Tejas, I have been watching the Americans as they advance to the West. They are a determined and hardworking people, a free people, a people motivated by ownership of their own land and businesses, a people unshackled by despotism and willing to fight for what they believe in. I have read their constitution and their declaration of independence. They have established an excellent republic that is very advanced for a planet at Cultural Level 6.

"Their population is climbing due to immigration from Continent 1. In just forty years, they have added five states to the original thirteen, and you can expect many more within the next several decades.

"In my opinion, our entire surveillance program of Earth 48 will fall short if we do not pay more attention to this new republic that has been founded on Continent 3," Ortees concluded.

Vlaris was incredulous, but he did respect Agent Ortees too much to completely dismiss his view. He checked with the analysts.

Tekalta spoke first. "Agent Ortees's analysis is not completely without foundation. As we were building our model, the first few simulations showed the United States of America expanding to the west coast of the continent and becoming a major power."

"Really?" Vlaris asked with surprise.

"But those runs were preliminary," Vlaytork clarified. "The Americans are beginning to have sectional troubles. Our model predicts that there is a ninety percent probability that the states will divide into two or more nations."

Tekalta continued, "If the northern states secede, the southern states can defeat them and force them back into the union, but as time goes on and the north industrializes, that will become increasingly difficult to do."

"And once that nation splits in two, it will continue to fragment," Vlaytork concluded.

"In one of the models, a general like Napoleon emerges and reunites America as an empire, but not with the ideals of the present republic," Tekalta added.

"And in most models, at least one faction rejoins the British Empire, which only adds to Britain's global dominance" Vlaytork pointed out. Based on our computer simulations, I have to concur with Agents Svavapass and Sraymlat that the British Empire is the best place to invest our personnel for surveilling this planet."

There was more discussion about conditions in the various nations of Earth 48. Because it appeared that the primary continent was entering a more peaceful epoch, it was decided that it was no longer necessary to infiltrate the militaries of the subject factions. The Service was to go back to placing agents in the universities and diplomatic circles. The Subdirector was persuaded that the British Empire was the best place to invest its personnel. The operation in the Spanish Empire was to be terminated.

As Subdirector Keepetta prepared to end the transmission, she added, "And I will talk to the Director about funding for two agents to observe these United States of America. In the interim, have agents Ortees and Srot emigrate there, to the new state called Lis-yana. Did I pronounce it correctly?"

"Close enough," Lorbank replied.

After the holograph of the Subdirector disappeared, Vlaris commended his agents for a productive round of discussion. Then he asked the agents if they had any questions or suggestions as to how to complete their respective tours of duty on the surface of the planet.

Agent Ortees asked if he could pose as his partner's uncle when they moved to Louisiana. "And I would like to change my alias to Sebastian Ortiz. You know, I was rather disappointed not to get the name Ortiz as my alias given that my real name Ortees."

"Yes, let us do that," Vlaris agreed.

"Does that mean we can stay on this space station for a few months while we learn to speak English?" Srot asked.

"Of course not!" Vlaris replied. "We will drop you back in Tejas, and you can walk to Louisiana and learn English on your own, just like real native immigrants."

Lorbank was next to make a request. "I have an opportunity to join the diplomatic service in the restored Bourbon government. In view of the present discussion, I would like to have Col. Louis LeBlanc leave the army and join the civilian government."

"Permission granted, but proceed with caution," Vlaris responded. "I have my doubts about the long-term viability of the Bourbon monarchy."

"Anything else?" Vlaris asked.

Svavapass and Sraymlat exchanged glances. "Dare we?" Svavapass asked his partner softly and in English.

"It is now or never, old chap," Sraymlat replied.

"Before we adjourn, Agent Sraymlat and I would like to make a special request," Svavapass began. "Especially in view of the new interest in civilian roles for the agents."

"Yes?" Vlaris appeared interested.

"There appears to be an enormous opportunity for us," Svavapass began. "During the Battle of Waterloo, the commanding general of British forces was in the vicinity of our regiment when the French charged our position with heavy cavalry. We "formed a square," a standard defensive tactic against a cavalry charge. General Arthur Wellesley, the First Duke of Wellington was inside our square."

"That was when Svavapass got these wounds," Sraymlat interjected. "Our regiment saved the general's life."

"Since that time," Svavapass continued, "the general and I...Wellington appointed me to his staff."

"Interesting," Vlaris commented.

"In the past, Wellington was in politics and I believe he intends to run again for a seat in Parliament. Being a war hero, it is only a matter of time until he is prime minister," Svavapass continued.

"And Svavapass, that is, Major Weatherby could become one of his aides," Sraymlat added.

"Yes, an excellent intelligence opportunity," Vlaris agreed.

"There is more," Svavapass said. "King George III is old and infirm. His son is his regent and successor. But the crown prince has no legitimate sons. His only heir is Princess Charlotte, a young lady more interested in music than statecraft. She will still be young when she ascends to the throne. That is projected to occur in about ten to fifteen years."

"Right about the time when Wellington will become prime minister," Sraymlat interjected.

"No doubt, the young queen will need some sort of assistance…"

"Wellington would be more than influential," the excited Sraymlat interrupted again.

"And Svavapass would be in his inner circle gathering intelligence on the most important nation on the planet," Vlaris concluded. "I will discuss this with the Subdirector. This is aligned with her strategy for Earth 48."

"And who knows?" Svavapass commented. "I could even influence him here and there to accelerate the progress and development of the planet."

"Is that legal?" Lorbank gasped. "Given the regulations against intervention in the development of other planets…"

"We are only allowed to observe the course of events, not change them," Metchavork agreed. "Sent to watch but not to affect."

"It wouldn't really be interference," Svavapass explained. "Just a little influence. The natives would be doing everything themselves."

"I am not sure I could approve even a little influence," Vlaris explained. "The rules are very explicit on that matter. Remember Earth 5."

"But this is different," Sraymlat protested. "It would not be interference. Just a little nudge…"

"No, I cannot allow that," Vlaris declared.

"Could you at least bring it up to the director?" Sraymlat asked.

"I suppose, but…" Vlaris paused. "Years ago, when I was a field agent on Earth 48, I was posing as a Frenchman, a diplomat. I spent a considerable portion of my time in that native settlement called Vienna. As part of my assignment to study alien culture, I used to frequent the concert halls. There was a young native musician there at that time who composed the most excellent music. Whenever he was performing, I made it my business to attend the concert. And, of course, it enhanced my cover as a diplomat.

"Then one day, I heard that the musician was seriously ill. From what I could gather, it was an infection, and you know the primitive medical practices down there."

"And you had your Service-issue medical kit, and the means to save his life…" Sraymlat surmised.

"Yes," Vlaris continued. "I never told anyone this before, but I went to his dwelling with a small antibiotic pill. I contemplated going up to visit him, putting it in a cup of water and giving it to him to drink."

"So, did you?" Vlaytork asked.

Vlaris bit his lip. "I stood there outside his dwelling torn between two choices. I remember it being cold. It was very cold. But I could not do it. I remembered the Noninterference Protocol and turned around and went to my hotel. He died three days later."

Vlaris cleared his throat. "On my next trip to Vienna, there was a performance of one of his compositions—the aliens have an intricate and elaborate musical art form called the 'symphony'—and he had written three more in his final days. The performance was one of those last three, Symphony Number 40. I can never forget that beautiful music."

Tears were forming in the team leader's eyes. His voice became softer. "It was the most beautiful… If only I could have…"

Vlaris choked up. The agents sat in tense patience as Vlaris composed himself.

Then the team leader barked gruffly, "We are only there to observe. Remember our motto. We are 'sent to watch but not to affect.' Any kind of influence is against the rules!"

After the meeting, each team had an hour of consultation with the team leader. The team working in France went first while the agents stationed in Prussia were given a thorough physical examination by the ship surgeon. Then the two teams traded places. During that two-hour interval before their turn with the team leader and the surgeon, the teams working in England and Spain were sent to separate rooms to watch training videos.

Agents Ortees and Srot were very pleased when they saw the title of their video, "The Fundamentals of the English Language of Earth 48." Vlaris had a heart after all, they thought.

But agents Svavapass and Sraymlat were immediately irked by the title of their video, "Remedial Training: The Lessons of Earth 5—Why We Are Sent Only to Watch."

"Remedial Training?" Sraymlat complained. "We know this stuff already, Ori. Why is Vlaris making us see this?"

"Why do you think?" Svavapass shot back.

Four hours later, Svavapass and Sraymlat found themselves back in their British uniforms on a transport with Ortees and Srot on their way back to Earth 48. The transport, or "Atmospheric Entry Vehicle" as it was technically called, had just returned from dropping off the other agents at points outside of Paris and Magdeburg.

Sraymlat commented that Major Hortu and his copilot Lt. Squeem would have been flying for six straight hours by the time the two roundtrips were completed. "That is a lot of work for one day," he said, trying to get the humorless and reticent pilot to open up.

"I enjoy flying," Major Hortu responded tersely.

"He certainly must," Ortees added after a brief silence. "I read that Major Hortu is one of the best. He has flown over four hundred orbit-to-surface missions without a single native abduction."

"487," the pilot stated dryly. "This trip is number 488."

"You make that sound like a major accomplishment, Saibert," Sraymlat remarked to his older colleague. "Really, how hard is it to pick up agents and not accidently abduct a native?"

"You spies really have no idea of the risks we take to shuttle you around, do you?" the copilot replied. "Most of our pickups are in the dark. Your spy agency has its personnel masquerading in native clothes, and your protocols do not allow you to speak Grellish until the hatch is closed. How are we to know if we are taking on agents or curious natives?"

"The task is even more difficult when one of the agents has lost his transponder and the other shows up drunk," Major Hortu added.

Sraymlat knew not to reply to that incisive remark. Svavapass still had a sore shoulder from the spot where the surgeon had inserted his new transponder. Now his pride was wounded as well.

Eventually, Ortees broke the silence. "So one of the analysts is going into the field."

"Yes, that would be Agent Vlaytork," Svavapass explained.

"She's a little crazy if you ask me," Srot opined.

"She has a lot of courage, I'll give her that," Ortees observed. "Earth 48 is at Cultural Level 6 and is still mostly agrarian. Women's rights have not progressed very far in Spain, and I doubt they are much further along in England."

The transport landed in England to drop off Svavapass and Sraymlat first. The pair was relieved to get away from that dour pilot. It was cool and dark in the field where they had been left. The two had been away for almost twenty-four hours.

Agent Svavapass took a deep breath of English air. He found it refreshing.

They were sure no one would ask them where they had been. No doubt the natives would think Lt. Greenhill was sleeping off a hangover and Maj. Weatherby was covering for him.

3.
New Leadership

The winter passed slowly for Agent Svavapass. Very little was happening, he almost never saw Wellington, and he felt he was not accomplishing anything for his real employer, the Interplanetary Intelligence Service. Although he was somewhat bored, he was enjoying the winter weather.

Orishackt Svavapass had grown up in a country called Olistoss on the cold continent of Zarfixu on his native planet, Earth 19. He was an only child. His father was a nuclear engineer at a fusion power plant. Just before Ori was two years old, his father received an accidental exposure to radioactive material and died. His mother never handled the loss of her husband well and was never able to work a full-time job. Young Ori was very intelligent, but he had had to work odd jobs ever since he was in his teens, trying to save up to go to a good university. During that time, he avoided girls; he simply had no time or resources for dating. He was accepted to go to one of the most prestigious institutions of higher learning on his planet, but he could not afford it. Ori was in excellent physical condition and his grades were outstanding, so he applied to the foremost military academy in the Confederation which was located on Earth 1, and he was accepted. The Academy was on a tropical continent where he never saw a real winter.

During the second semester of his freshman year, his mother became engaged to remarry. The wedding date was set during the week of final exams. Ori declined to go, and his mother's new husband took great offense.

At that time, the Service was looking for people who could pass for Europeans for assignments on Earth 48. Ori was recruited and majored in Interplanetary

Espionage. By the time of his graduation, he was fluent in four languages, two from Earth 19, as well as Grellish and English. He also knew some basic German and French. Months after his graduation, Ori found himself in the role of Captain Robert Weatherby, in the Royal Army in the middle of the Napoleonic Wars.

Ori was three and a half years into a five-year deployment. He knew he would be strongly encouraged to accept a five-year extension as Robert Weatherby. He would gladly accept. He had lost his relationship with his family when he was at the Academy, and he was not sure what else he could do. And he loved spying. Or was he falling in love with Earth 48?

Sometimes he would think about Agent Unni Vlaytork and her kind words to him the past October. He would quickly put those thoughts out of his head. Good intelligence agents were not to think about women in that way.

As spring began to manifest itself, there were rumors in the regiment that they were going to be sent to India. On other days, they were going to Canada or the Caribbean, or to Egypt. Or maybe they were just going to stay in England in case France destabilized.

One day in May, Ori felt a pulse in his shoulder. It was repeated several times. He knew what that meant. He was to set up an alibi to disappear and go to a pickup point to rendezvous with a transport in three days.

On the appointed evening, he went into a freshly planted field and boarded the transport. Lt. Greenhill was not with him. As he entered the vehicle, he was surprised to see Agent Ortees on the lower deck in a silver travel uniform.

"I don't know where Agent Sraymlat is," Ori informed Ortees.

"I didn't summon him," Ortees explained. "I wanted to talk to you alone. There have been some changes in the Service hierarchy. Some of the senior officers have retired, and others were promoted to fill their positions. Vlaris has been promoted to a desk job in Tlat Mlang. I was appointed team leader in his place."

"Congratulations, Agent Ortees," Svavapass said.

"Thank you. Only that's *Special* Agent Ortees now.

"Of course, sir."

Ortees reminded Svavapass that the Service wanted more agents in civilian roles, or at least non-combat roles. He had "arranged" for Major Weatherby to be given a teaching job at the War College.

"Do you mean that new school, the Royal Military College in Sandhurst?"

"That's the place. I want you there for a reason. Analysts agree that your friend the Duke of Wellington will soon be reentering politics. When he does, I don't want you in India or Canada or some other distant place. I want you right there, near London, where he can see you, see your battle scars and re-member you. If you can be in his entourage as he rises to high office, you will be in a position to gain the best intelligence."

"You realize that as Wellington rises to higher office, it will become more difficult to discretely slip away for these, uh, meetings."

"Correct," the new team leader affirmed. "I will assign an agent to work nearby you. You will pass your reports to this agent, and it would be that agent's responsibility to get the information to me. Your main job is to do whatever it takes to stay close to that native general."

"This sounds like a long-term assignment," Svavapass observed.

"Indeed," Ortees agreed. "But I didn't take you for a one-termer. Think it over, because if you agree to this assignment, you are committed to stay on this planet for another eight years and probably more."

"I don't need to think it over," Svavapass replied. "I accept."

"I will check with you again in about one month."

"Any other changes?" Svavapass asked.

"Yes, a big one, but I do not feel to discuss that right now…Oh, why not? That 'little nudge' you suggested a few months ago—I am carefully working with my superiors to obtain a broader definition of 'watching' and a narrower one of 'affecting.' But please do not repeat this to anyone."

Svavapass was elated as he walked across the dark field back to his quarters. His idea of guiding the natives to faster social progress was under considera-tion. And he would be spending a lot of time in England.

Ortees and Svavapass met again in late June, and Svavapass reiterated his deci-sion to accept the long-term assignment. Not too long after that, Major Weatherby was informed of his appointment to the War College in Sandhurst. Weatherby would be teaching mathematics.

From the very onset of his assignment at Sandhurst, Major Weatherby forged a positive relationship with his direct superior officer, Lt. Colonel George Keaton. Keaton was quite a bit older than Weatherby. He had a kind disposition and immediately took a liking to the young major. Keaton was aware of the fact that the twenty-six-year-old officer had never taught in a class-room before. He dropped in on some of Weatherby's lectures and was impressed with his quick adaptation to the role. Keaton was amazed at the professor's depth of mathematical knowledge and his ability to communicate it to the cadets.

Shortly into the fall semester, Weatherby was in the administration build-ing when he saw a familiar face among the female secretaries: Agent Vlaytork posing as Jenny Carter. Their eyes briefly met. The normally stoic agent could barely hide his pleasure at seeing her familiar face. Any doubt was quickly dis-pelled that she was the agent to whom he would be supplying information.

Ori Svavapass could not but ask himself why he was so delighted that the agent he was to work with was Vlaytork.

As per his orders, Svavapass went to London in full dress uniform whenever there was an opportunity to cross paths with the Duke of Wellington. He found himself invited to certain balls and social functions, and speculated that the Duke himself had placed his name on the invitation list. At these functions, Svavapass tried to get acquainted with the rich and the powerful. He also tried to learn the details of British politics, the issues, the key persons, and where they stood.

As a good spy, Svavapass was an excellent listener. He was also observant of small details. After each social event, Svavapass would meet privately with Agent Vlaytork to pass on what he had learned.

Later in the fall, he was invited to a banquet at Apsley House, the res-idence of Sir Arthur Wellesley's older brother Richard, who was a Marquess. The Duke of Wellington was there. Svavapass especially wanted to hear the Duke's political views.

On that evening, an older major general and his wife, Alice, greeted him in social talk. Alice was somewhat overweight with a round face wrapped in gray hair. She had an outgoing, jolly disposition, and was very talkative.

Alice remarked about the scar on his face and asked if he had received it at Waterloo. When Svavapass affirmed that he had, her husband, the general, asked, "You wouldn't happen to be Major Weatherby by any chance?"

"Yes, I am Major Robert Weatherby."

"This is the young officer the Duke was referring to at the last ball, the one who saved his life," the general told his wife."

"Actually, it was the regiment that saved the Duke's life," Svavapass stated modestly. "I was only one of its officers."

"Whose bravery and gallantry kept the unit from routing," the general continued. "If that square had faltered!"

The major general liked to go off into a separate room with other officers to smoke and play cards. Smoking was a disgusting habit among the natives of Earth 48 by which dried and ground leaves of tobacco, grown on and around the continent of North America, were rolled into a cylinder bound by paper into "cigars" or "cigarettes." One end of this cylinder was lit on fire and its user would inhale smoke through the other end. One element in the smoke, nicotine, would enter the bloodstream and stimulate pleasure centers in the brain. The problem with smoking is that tiny particles of the smoke would enter the lungs, bringing with them dozens of chemical compounds that were cancer-causing. The exhaled smoke left a fine brown film on the walls, curtains and furniture in any room in which smoking took place. The smoke also had a decidedly foul odor. Not only did smoking shorten the life of most of its participants, but the nicotine was addictive, making it very difficult to break the habit.

Alice found smoking to be repulsive and would not accompany her husband into rooms where this activity took place. She had an ear for gossip. Svavapass found Alice to be treasure-trove of information. Because it was difficult to get a word in once she built up her verbal momentum, many of the guests avoided her. But Svavapass sought her out.

From the Duke's discourses at the long and elaborate dinner table, Svavapass learned that Sir Arthur Wellesley was a Tory, the more conservative of the two major political parties. He wondered if that would make it somewhat more difficult to "nudge" public policy in the direction of technological and social progress. But there was another side to Wellington's political views.

The Interplanetary Intelligence Service was long aware of the religious schism in Europe between Catholics and Protestants and its political implications. The British Empire was Protestant, and Catholics did not have the right to hold public office or public employment, and could not graduate from certain universities. This disability basically disenfranchised most of the population of Ireland. Svavapass learned that Wellington was born in Ireland and had some sympathy for the Irish Catholics. He wondered if this feeling would blossom into a public stand in favor of Catholic emancipation, and, in turn, toward other reforms.

Agent Vlaytork would linger at the office at the end of her workday. If Agent Svavapass showed up, they would talk together for a few minutes. Then he would walk with her toward her dwelling about half of the distance. During the walk, the two would be careful no one was listening and would change the conversation to the weather or some other light subject whenever they thought someone was listening. But they always spoke in English. It was believed that the use of Grellish or any foreign language would lead to their being accused of spying for an enemy power.

In turn, Vlaytork met weekly with Ortees aboard a transport. She would convey all that she had learned and bring back instructions to Svavapass from the team leader.

Ortees was delighted with the work Svavapass was doing. Wellington was the perfect politician to align with. He was a war hero, destined for higher office. But even more, he was a conservative with an open mind.

"Wouldn't it be better if Ori worked to align with a reformer, like William Wilberforce?" Vlaytork had once asked her superior officer. Wilberforce was the member of Parliament who had championed the abolition of the slave trade just nine years before.

"No, I would prefer we worked with the conservatives," Ortees replied. "The reformers will always advocate change. But it is our experience that true change occurs when it is embraced by the more conservative elements of a democratic society. Wellington is a conservative, but his potential support of Catholic emancipation indicates that he might be an unstoppable instrument of progress if "nudged" in the right way. He might be especially useful in the areas of science and technology."

Vlaytork conveyed this information on to Svavapass one snowy evening as they walked together. Svavapass could not help but take notice of Vlaytork's cozy winter coat, gloves, hat, and scarf. How well those native garments portrayed his fellow agent!

During his trips to Apsley, Svavapass observed that the Duke was rarely seen with Kitty, his wife. They were always on opposite sides of the room. At first, Svavapass thought nothing of it, but after several social occasions, Agent Svavapass was forced to conclude that there was a problem in the Duke's marriage.

Alice confirmed Svavapass's conclusions. She told him that Wellington had been close to Kitty's brother, General Edward "Ned" Pakenham. They served together against the French in the Iberian Peninsula. Pakenham had often served as a mediator in the troubled marriage between his sister and close friend. But Pakenham had been killed fighting the Americans in the Battle of New Orleans in 1815.

Svavapass began to wonder if Wellington might harbor a special resentment toward the United States, with whom British relations were quite poor already.

When Vlaytork brought this matter to Ortees's attention, he also was concerned. "Our models project that Wellington is likely to become prime minister at about the same time Andrew Jackson reaches the office of President of the United States," Ortees explained.

"Andrew Jackson? Isn't he the general who led the American forces at New Orleans?" Vlaytork asked.

"Yes, he is," Ortees replied. "When and if Wellington reaches the office of prime minister, one of our little "nudges of influence" will be to prevent a war between the United States and Great Britain. Such a war would not be in the interests of either state and may be contrary to our interests on Earth 48."

"Does the Confederation have interests on Earth 48? Aren't we just 'sent to watch'?"

"Well, yes," Ortees answered. Then he hesitantly added, "For now."

Agent Vlaytork wondered what Special Agent Ortees meant by that. She pondered his cryptic remark all the way home from the transport rendezvous site.

She and her fellow agents would find out soon enough.

4.
Unni Vlaytork and Jenny Carter

The system agreed upon between Ortees and his field agents was that Agent Vlaytork would go to the small office shared by Svavapass and one other professor, Captain Haywood. Vlaytork knew the teaching schedule of all of the staff, so she could choose a time when Agent Svavapass was alone. But in practice, it was Agent Svavapass who would visit Vlaytork in the late afternoon. It seemed awkward under the social norms of England at that time for a woman "of Jenny Carter's station" to be seen visiting the workspace of an officer of means such as Major Weatherby.

But Svavapass began to visit the administration building more often, even to pass on intelligence of trivial importance, including sundry developments in tactics and ancient weaponry. Svavapass would even visit Vlaytork's desk during regular working hours. He was careful to time his visits so that the other members of the secretarial staff would be away. If another secretary returned from an errand, Svavapass would quickly move on to pick up or drop off papers or meet with an officer in an adjoining office.

Sometimes he would talk about himself and about his work, or about his youth on Earth 19 in metaphorical speech that did not betray his extraterrestrial origins. For example, the "countryside" was their home continent of Zarfixu in the southern hemisphere of Earth 19. Other times, he would get Agent Vlaytork to talk about her family and youth, again in metaphorical speech. The more he learned about Unni Vlaytork, the more fascinated he became with her.

Agent Vlaytork was born on Earth 19 in Yoilafa, the principle city of Botvrayt, a country on the east side of the north coast of the continent of Zarfixu. Unni was the second of two children. Her brother Maykot was ten years older than she, and Unni hardly knew him growing up. Her parents were employed by a major luxury hotel and sometimes brought young Unni to their place of employment. Mingling with the guests, Unni began to show a talent for learning other languages. By the age of twelve, Unni was fluent in three languages: her mother tongue of Botvraytish, as well as Urgstish, and Omtvumxian, which was the predominant language on Earth 19. That year, she began to study Grellish with the thought of a career in interplanetary commerce.

In addition to languages, Unni was an excellent musician and earned top grades in school. Unni graduated early and was accepted to a university in Yoilafa. The Vlaytork family was short of funds, so Unni applied for several scholarships.

By that time, it was well known in the Interplanetary Intelligence Service that the fair race of the continent of Zarfixu on Earth 19 bore a striking resemblance to the people of the continent of Europe on Earth 48. That made Zarfixians an excellent choice for field agents on Earth 48, where the European empires were the dominant nations on their planet. Young Unni Vlaytork was given an excellent scholarship by the spy agency in exchange for seven years of service upon graduation.

Unni graduated near the top of her class and was sent to Earth 1 for training. Her parents were told that she was given a job in marketing for a major interplanetary corporation.

At the Academy, Vlaytork became acquainted with some of the cadets from her own planet, including Orishackt Svavapass, Urelt Sraymlat, and Huha Svortomit. But contact between the sexes was regulated, and Unni, being the conscientious young lady that she was, adhered to the rules.

After graduation, Vlaytork became an agent and was assigned to a starship that patrolled Earths 46 to 51. She spent most of her time on Space Station 48-3, an orbiting outpost that circled Earth 48. After a year, Vlaytork began to entertain the idea of field work, even though the culture on Earth 48 was male-dominated. She decided to study English, French, and German. Her analysis of the situation on the surface of the planet led her to emphasize English, which she learned to speak accent-free.

The Interplanetary Intelligence Service created the alias Jenny Carter, a young girl from the countryside who had gone to London to seek opportunities besides farming. Vlaytork was sent back to Earth 1 to study survival techniques and skills for daily living in a Technology Level 8 society. One day in late August 1816, Agent Vlaytork was dropped off in a transport outside of London dressed in native clothing befitting a poor country girl, with two positive letters of recommendation written by the Service. Vlaytork was hired for secretarial work at the Royal Military College in Sandhurst.

Vlaytork rented a room in the home of a widow together with two other young women with whom she split the rent. One of her roommates was a nanny and the other worked as a maid. The three women did not share much conversation. They merely coexisted. Vlaytork found her roommates to be contrary and difficult to like. She simply tolerated them.

The room was hot in the summer and drafty in the winter, heated by a small fireplace. The living conditions were less than ideal, but the dwelling was less than two miles from the Royal Military College. That was important because she had to walk to work every day, and her work hours were long. She also had a long walk of several miles every Saturday to the meeting place where Ortees would land in the transport to meet her. Fortunately, the Interplanetary Intelligence Service had fabricated comfortable shoes for her that had the appearance of native footwear.

Several days after Vlaytork started to work at the Royal Military College, she saw Svavapass. Seeing a familiar face was quite a relief to Unni, but she exercised her training and self-discipline not to show her joy at seeing him.

The first six months of her deployment at Sandhurst went very smoothly. Svavapass was producing excellent intelligence. Information was being passed on to Ortees with little difficulty. Ori was also performing well at his cover. His students liked his classes and he had a good relationship with his superior officer, Lt. Col. Keaton. Although her hours were long and her work was exhausting, Agent Vlaytork was enjoying her field assignment. She felt like she was accomplishing something, making a difference for the Confederation.

Every time Ori came to visit her office, Unni was comforted just to see someone from her world. So, when Ori began to pursue any excuse to visit the administration building, often without notes to pass on to Ortees, it was difficult for Unni to speak any sort of word of caution. Sometimes he spoke with Unni three times in the same week.

Ori seemed unable to control the frequency of his visits to see his fellow agent. After he left her presence, he felt a joy within that made any visit to Unni the top event of the day. Despite his training and self-discipline, Ori was totally oblivious to the fact that his actions were generating gossip among the secretarial staff.

By March, Unni decided to bring up the matter with the team leader. But Special Agent Ortees was not concerned in the least. He was rather delighted about the gossip. "What an excellent cover! Let them think there is a romantic angle to your meetings with Agent Svavapass."

But Agent Svavapass had another superior to whom he was accountable who was not pleased about the growing relationship. Or, more accurately, Major Weatherby had a concerned superior. Lt. Col. George Keaton did not approve of the budding relationship between one of the professors and a common farm girl like Jenny Carter.

Lt. Col. Keaton liked Major Weatherby. He was not only pleased with Weatherby's work as a professor, he was impressed with the stories he had heard of Weatherby's bravery at Waterloo. It was also known that Weatherby had a source of wealth.

In part, Keaton wanted the young major to achieve his full potential. But this was outweighed by a personal motive: Keaton wanted Robert Weatherby as a son-in-law.

In March, Keaton began to invite Ori to his townhouse to cultivate a friendship and to put him in front of his daughter Katy. The townhouse had an impressive dining room with a long, elegant table. The Keatons had a butler, a footman, several cooks, and other servants. Whenever Ori was invited to dinner, he would always be seated across from Katy to make it easy for them to converse. Just about anything Ori said would result in a huge smile from Mrs. Keaton.

Keaton started calling Weatherby by his first name and asked Weatherby to call him George. He began inviting the major to go fox hunting and bird-shooting with his other friends. Afterward, they would return to the Keaton residence, where Katy would be waiting.

Katy was a fine young lady. She had brown hair that was so dark it was nearly black, and warm brown eyes. Her face was round, and she was a somewhat above normal weight. Katy was cheerful and outgoing, but giggly and not very sophisticated. She had her father's kindness and her mother's charm.

Ori had a positive opinion of Katy. But it was unlikely that Major Weatherby would end up marrying her even if he were not actually Agent Svavapass from another world. She simply did not match him.

It seems the feeling was mutual. Katy liked the young officer. She even admired his battle scar. But she did not see him as a future husband. Major Weatherby's conversation seemed to be beyond her understanding. And Katy was aware of the fact that her parents were doing everything they could to arrange a marriage with the dashing young officer.

There was another obstacle to Ori falling in love with Katy. There was something deep in his being that was reserving him. It was something besides his sense of duty to his real mission. But Ori was still blind to what should have been obvious, that his heart was reserved for Unni.

Lt. Col. Keaton and his wife were beginning to notice that their machinations to capture a prize for their daughter were not working. Keaton decided to address the matter in a more straightforward manner. He invited Weatherby to go hunting. It was a misty morning in early April. Keaton and Weatherby were closing in on a fox when it suddenly turned and ran.

"A spunky little creature, that fox," Keaton observed.

"I suppose we were stalking the wrong animal," Ori agreed.

"Are you sure you aren't stalking the wrong young lady?" Keaton asked.

Ori was puzzled as to what Keaton meant by that question.

"Or are you perhaps the prey and she is the hunter?"

"I am not sure what you are talking about," the befuddled young major replied.

"It is well known in the office that you and Jenny Carter are, well, rather friendly."

"She takes care of my papers," Ori admitted. "Jenny does excellent work."

"I am sure she does, Robert. But she is below your station. She is a farm girl who struck out for the big city to try to escape the toil and poverty of her youth."

"How do you know she is of low station? Perhaps her father sent her away to London to get her away from a suitor of whom he did not approve."

"To work for long hours and low wages and live in a wretched flat? Robert, use your intelligent mind. And have you not noticed that Jenny is left-handed?"

"Is there something wrong with that, sir?"

"Indeed, there is. It is a window, a clue to the real Jenny Carter. Why, if she were really from a proper home, she would have had a tutor as Katy has

41

had. No proper tutor would let her take on such a ghastly habit as writing with the wrong hand!"

Ori now saw a way out of this awkward discussion. "It would be hard for me to look down on someone for being left-handed. Surely, you must have noticed from watching me lecture that I am also left-handed."

Keaton blushed with embarrassment and began to compose an apology. But Ori grinned and let Keaton know that no offense was taken.

In the carriage back to Sandhurst, Ori began to ponder why Lt. Col. Keaton would think he was pursuing Jenny Carter. Ori did not believe he was pursuing any kind of romantic relationship. That would be unprofessional.

The Keatons were becoming desperate to win Major Weatherby for their daughter. Mrs. Keaton suggested that her husband use his high position to get Katy hired into the secretarial staff. He could promote her to be the leader of the group within several months. Once Katy was the leader of the group, she would assume any and all assignments to assist Weatherby with his papers.

"If that Jenny Carter gets in the way," Mrs. Keaton declared, "I will counsel Katy how to deal with her."

Lt. Col. Keaton did not agree at first. He was too much of a gentleman to entertain such a plan. But Mrs. Keaton could be quite persistent.

In the meantime, Unni was having a harder time believing that the attention Ori was giving her was merely an excellent act by a skilled spy. Her instincts were telling her that Ori might have a genuine interest in her. This was troubling to Unni. She admired Agent Svavapass, but she was not ready for anything beyond a professional friendship. Besides that, Unni was not sure that Ori was the person she would want to spend the rest of her life with. He seemed too focused on his mission, on the Service, and on the Confederation.

Once again, Unni took up the matter of Svavapass with Special Agent Ortees. At first, Ortees dismissed her belief that Ori was interested in her. But Unni explained the situation in more detail. Eventually, Ortees agreed that Ori's actions were baffling. He was highly out of character, potentially posing an unnecessary risk to the mission.

"Try to get with him alone and explain to him how his actions are causing gossip. Try to find out what is going on with him," Ortees concluded the discussion.

As the transport lifted off into the dark sky, Agent Vlaytork knew what she needed to do.

Late one afternoon, Ori happened to visit the administration building at a time when only Unni was present in the large area where the secretarial staff worked. Unni suggested that they go on a picnic the following Saturday. Ori quickly accepted the invitation.

"Except that by English cultural norms, the man is supposed to invite the woman," Unni reminded Ori.

"Oh, yes. Of course," Ori agreed. He quickly extended the invitation to Unni.

"Let me think about it," she replied. Ori's countenance fell. "Only joking; of course, I accept."

Saturday was a beautiful sunny day, but cool even for April. Ori was alone at his wooden desk in the small office he shared with another professor, writing study notes that were due to the printer that Monday for distribution to the cadets. It was taking the major longer than expected to complete his study guide on geometry.

Just then Unni arrived. Ori was willing to drop his work and leave immediately, but Unni suggested he finish his work first.

"I know what I will do," Ori said with a smile. "I will work at double speed."

Ori took a second sheet of paper and found a second quill pen and began to write with both hands simultaneously. Unni bit her lip. She gazed in awe as her fellow agent threw caution to the wind. Within minutes, he was done.

As Ori picked up his coat, Unni broke her silence. "What were you doing? No one on this planet can write with both hands at the same time, much less plan where the flow of the text will be on the second page. How would you have explained it if you had been caught?"

"But I didn't get caught, did I?" Ori replied with a grin.

The two found a spot by a pond under a large tree whose branches were covered with small buds ready to explode with the coming of spring. They spread out the humble picnic blanket and opened the basket and began to eat.

Unni was now clear that she was dealing with a man who was fully beside himself. She also perceived that he might not even realize his own situation. She carefully considered what she was about to say and chose her words carefully.

"Major Weatherby," she began.

"Call me Robert," he insisted.

"Robert, I have something I have been meaning to tell you," Unni said. Unni began to speak of his frequent visits to her desk in the administration building.

Ori could hear what she said, but was only partially listening. He gazed at her warm, caring face, her flowing brown hair parted at the middle, her strong blue eyes, her smooth round forehead, her prominent nose and chin, her slight frame so warmly bundled up.

"You understand what I mean, right?"

Just then Ori realized that he had not been paying attention to what Unni was saying.

"Yes, Jenny, yes," he agreed.

"This entire situation has left me confused, not knowing what to do," Unni continued. "The other women in the office are talking about this."

"Perhaps I ought to be more careful about how often I visit you," Ori suggested.

Unni was carefully trying to caution Ori about the appearance of a romance, but in Ori's mind, he heard it as a cautionary word about their cover as agents.

"But the natives on this planet, I mean the English people surely have contact, I mean discourse between men and women," Ori continued. He recalled what Keaton had been saying. "If the natives think that is the reason I am visiting you, would that not be a great cover for our actual mission?"

"I suppose."

When the two parted ways at the end of the afternoon, Unni realized she had accomplished little. She knew this issue could not properly be addressed until her fellow agent came to understand his real feelings. She decided she needed to seek further advice from her team leader.

Ori left the picnic in a state of elation. But he still did not admit to himself why he felt that way.

It was difficult for him to do so. For many years, Ori had put dating and the opposite sex aside. As a teenager, he had worked hard on his studies and on making money for school. As a student, he spent all of his energy on his coursework and other duties. Then as an agent, he had put his private life on hold. His strong self-discipline was now translating into powerful denial. The longer Ori remained in denial, the more energetic his denial became, and the more powerful his love for Unni Vlaytork was becoming.

At first, Ori sharply decreased the number of his visits to the administration building. But after a few weeks, he began to go there more frequently.

When Unni next met with the team leader, the subject came up again of Agent Svavapass and his visits to see her.

"I believe it is time for me to have a word with Agent Svavapass," Ortees said. "I have an important tactical decision to make and this matter of Svavapass might affect the logistics."

One day near the end of the semester, Svavapass was having tea in the faculty dining hall with two of his colleagues, Captain Robert Helm, a professor of mathematics, and Major William Anson, a professor of science. Captain Helm finally asked Weatherby how long he was going to put off proposing marriage to Jennifer Carter.

"Propose marriage?" Weatherby was stunned. "What are you talking about, Robert?"

"We all know how often you go to visit her," the captain went on. "I can see how you feel by the way you look at her. Why put it off?"

"You are mistaken," Weatherby protested.

"Don't pester the man," Major Anson advised. "Perhaps his family objects to his marriage to a woman below his station. Leave Weatherby to sort out his own dilemma."

Ori did not reply. He pondered why everyone around him seemed to think Weatherby had an eye for Jenny Carter.

But that evening, as he was grading an examination, an emotional dam burst in Ori's constricted soul. "That's it!" he declared to the table laden with examination papers. "I love Jenny Carter! Yes, I am in love!"

Then he broke a major protocol in the Interplanetary Intelligence Service. Even if totally alone, it was against to rules to utter a word of Grellish or any other language not of the planet an agent was surveilling. But Svavapass said in Grellish, "I love Unni Vlaytork!" Then he said it once more in Olistossian, his mother tongue on Earth 19. "I am in love with Unni Vlaytork!"

After he extinguished his candles, Weatherby went to bed in ecstasy. The storm in his being was over. There was no denying it. And he was determined to marry her.

Certainly, a marriage between agents would change the way their mission was carried out. They would need the blessing of the Interplanetary Intelligence

Service. Ori desperately wanted to see Special Agent Ortees to discuss the matter. But how could he arrange the meeting?

While Ori pondered these things, he fell into a deep sleep.

Ori was no longer self-deceived about his real feelings for Agent Vlaytork. But he still was in the dark as to the difficult position he had put her into. Unni was indeed in a difficult position, and the mission as well. That was without factoring in the plot Mrs. Keaton had hatched, of which both Unni and Ori were unaware.

5.
Tactical Decisions

The inevitable meeting between Svavapass and his team leader took place shortly thereafter. Ori began with the usual intelligence update. He informed Special Agent Ortees that Wellington was purchasing Apsley House from his brother Richard.

"I heard Richard say that Wellington 'needed a London base of operation.' This can only mean that Wellington is about to become politically active once again," Ori surmised.

"This is an important development for our mission in the British Empire," Ortees acknowledged.

Ori sought permission to spend a large sum of money to purchase a townhouse in London. It would give him a place to stay on the weekends and whenever he was going to London to attend social gatherings and meet with political figures.

"The thirty-mile trip from Sandhurst is quite long using Technology Level 8 transportation. With Wellington moving to town, I believe this home will be very useful." Ortees agreed. Of course, Ori had another reason for desiring a nice place to live.

After several more minutes of discussion about various important persons whom Ori was following, the subject came to the personal matter that Ortees was anticipating. Although Ori had rehearsed in his mind what he was going to say to his team leader, he still fumbled for words as he struggled to inform him that he wanted to marry Agent Vlaytork.

"How does Unni feel about this?" the team leader asked.

"I am not really sure," Ori admitted. "I suppose she is open to the idea."

"Here is what you need to do," Ortees advised. "Go to her right away and tell her how you feel, and find out how she feels about this. I will be back in seven days and we can talk about what happens next."

The team leader told his agent that there were several possibilities as to how to use Agent Vlaytork's talents, and his decision would depend on how Unni reacted to Ori's proposal.

"Is it common for agents to marry?" Ori asked.

"Oh, yes," Ortees assured him. "It happens all the time. If the agents have long-term field assignments like you do, we usually ask the agents to put off the wedding day until after their terms are up. After that, they are assigned desk jobs or analyst functions to keep them out of harm's way."

Ori frowned. He had not considered that angle. He did not want to give up his opportunity to be an aide to a future prime minister, but he did not want to put off marriage for a decade either.

"Is there some way we could…"

Ortees anticipated the question and interrupted. "You see, the Service does not like long engagements. We have had some incidents in the past, where agents have hidden their love and a child was born in their mission field. When the agents finally have to leave, we end up with young adults being taken up in spacecraft that are unaccustomed to any mode of transportation faster than a horse and who cannot speak a word of Grellish. Their adjustment is very difficult when they find out who they really are."

"They never mentioned this at the Academy."

"It is rare, but it happens. In fact, it happened once right here on Earth 48."

"On Earth 48?" Svavapass echoed.

"It was about three or four hundred years ago, involving two agents who were working on the Italian peninsula. Our agent had a strategic relationship with members of a powerful family who controlled a republic. A female agent was sent to pose as a peasant, to whom he fed the information he gained. They fell in love and had a child together. They were afraid their team leader might terminate their fruitful field service, so they kept the existence of the baby a secret. They kept volunteering to extend their deployment, but, finally, they were recalled. They refused to show up at the meeting points and just went rogue, joining the natives."

"Didn't the Service send agents in after them?" Svavapass wondered.

"No, they just let them be," Ortees continued. "At the time, we had no knowledge that there was a child involved. But later, other agents working in Italy began to hear of a certain genius. At first our agents thought nothing of it. The wealthy family had been patrons to many talented people. But one of our agents began to become suspicious when he saw the depth of this man's talent. He was inventing bridges, flying machines, mapping human anatomy, and making advances in every field you could imagine. Then one of our agents noticed the man was left-handed. Our agent scratched the genius with a sampler. A DNA test showed that he was not of that planet."

"Then Leonardo da Vinci was one of us!" Ori exclaimed with a prideful grin.

Ortees leaped out of his chair in shock. "How did you hear of Leonardo? That is highly classified information!"

"Not on this planet, it isn't," Ori retorted. "Everyone here has heard of Leonardo da Vinci."

"Not everyone, not in my experience. Then again, I suppose things in England might be different than in Spain or its colonies," Ortees surmised. He sat back in his chair. "But *never* mention this name to anyone who is not from Earth 48."

"Right," Ori recalled. "But why didn't the Confederation suppress Leonardo's discoveries? We are sent to watch but not affect, right?"

"We were going to, but the prevailing religious institution in Italy did our work for us. Most of Leonardo's inventions were never published or built in his lifetime, in part because he was afraid of their Inquisition."

"A fascinating story, but I suppose that still leaves me having to choose between the woman I love and the mission I love."

Ortees paused for a moment. "Of course, we could have Jenny Carter become Mrs. Weatherby as well. But, Ori, do you have a backup plan?"

"A backup plan?"

"How will you handle the emotional blow if Unni rejects your proposal?"

Ori answered without thought. "I doubt that would happen. But in the off chance that Unni did not want to proceed, I suppose I would...go on as I have been for the last several years."

"I will be back in seven days," Ortees closed the discussion. "Plan on further discussions then."

Ori had a real spring in his step as he left the field where the transport vehicle had landed. He skipped with joy into the night back to his quarters.

Three days later, Ori went to see Unni at her desk at the close of the workday. Instead of lingering to talk, he led her out right away. He said he wanted to show her something. It was a beautiful late afternoon, as one sometimes observes in May.

Ori was walking Unni in the direction of her dwelling when they passed a place that he had selected for the occasion, a small park with a garden flowing with lavender flowers. There was a bench under a short shade tree facing the flower garden.

Ori led Unni to sit on the bench and he stood and faced her with an earnest look on his face.

"Unni Vlaytork, would you marry me?"

Unni paused for a moment. Ori thought she was deciding whether to accept. Actually, she was deciding whether to point out that it was the custom in England for a man to get on one knee when he asked such a question.

Unni decided that formality was unnecessary. She simply answered his question. She firmly and politely declined.

"Might you want to think about it?" Ori asked her, gripped with pain and disbelief.

"No, Ori. For the past several months I have feared this might happen, and I have already decided. I admire your dedication and skill as a fellow agent, but I do not want to marry you."

Ori stood dumbfounded as Unni got up and walked away toward her rented room.

He turned and walked toward his residence in the faculty dormitory. He was emotionally wounded.

Ori grieved for days. He recalled that he had said that if Unni had declined his proposal he would "go on as I have been for the last several years."

But that was far more difficult than he had imagined. Two days later, Ori went to a social gathering in London. All of the usual persons of note were present. Ori was like an empty shell.

"What is the matter, old chap?" Lt. Col. Keaton asked. "You don't appear to be your usual self."

Alice asked him if he was ill. Others noted that Major Weatherby was "unusually silent."

The main topic of discussion that evening was that Princess Charlotte, second in line to the throne, was expecting a baby. If the baby was a boy, he would be the future king. There was much concern for Charlotte's wellbeing. Her first pregnancy had ended in a miscarriage the previous August. The chatter was energetic, but Ori was barely able to go through the motions of a social evening.

On Saturday evening, Ori met with his team leader. Ortees quickly detected Ori's dejection. The older agent showed his human side, consoling his younger charge.

Ortees advised Ori to give himself to his work. That would help him get his mind off of it. In particular, Ori was to change his main emphasis from Wellington to Princess Charlotte and find out everything he could about her. "Find two more women like Alice and pump the three of them for every bit of gossip you can obtain!"

Whenever Ori succeeded in concentrating on his work, he was somewhat better, but an hour later, the pain would return. Things were slower during the summer at the Royal Military College. But Ori managed to put up a convincing façade at the social events, and in so doing, he was able to escape his feeling of loss, at least until he left the gathering.

Ori stopped going to the administration building unless absolutely necessary. When he did go, he did not stop to talk with Unni. This meant Unni had to come to him. Their meetings were brief and to the point.

In early June, Ori did go to the administration building to pick up some papers. It could not escape Ori's notice that Katy Keaton was seated at her new desk. Katy went out of her way to make sure Major Weatherby saw her.

Over the next several weeks, Agent Vlaytork did not visit Ori at all. Ori Svavapass had a lot of information to convey, and he felt it was unprofessional for Agent Vlaytork to let her personal feelings interfere with the mission.

What Ori did not know was that Jenny Carter had been told by Katy Keaton that she should no longer handle Major Weatherby's clerical work. She was forbidden to visit his office.

On the other hand, Katy Keaton would drop in to Weatherby's office and stay for a half hour at a time, engaging Ori in small talk.

"You are spending a lot of time here, Katy" Ori observed. "Won't you get into trouble with your superiors?"

"Not at all," she laughed. "My father encourages it, and the colonel turns a blind eye. My parents want me to spend time with you."

"Really?"

"Certainly. You see, Major, they want to get us together. They want us to marry."

Ori was shocked at Katy's frankness, and her foolish lack of discretion.

She went on. "Oh, I know that would probably never happen, but my parents are determined. When Mother is determined, nothing can stop her."

Ori tried not to react. But he was very uncomfortable with Katy's frequent advances.

Agent Vlaytork was even more uncomfortable. She no longer had a mission at Sandhurst. She was barred from visiting Agent Svavapass. Even if she could see him, it would be awkward after his proposal.

Lt. Col. Keaton was satisfied that Jenny Carter had been neutralized as a rival to Katy for Weatherby's attention. But Mrs. Keaton was not. She simply could not believe that her daughter was failing to win the young major. After two weeks without any positive report by her daughter in her pursuit of Weatherby, she told her husband that he needed to sack Jenny.

Keaton did not want to do that. He considered it to be unfair. Instead, he met with Jenny privately and told her that he would give her an excellent reference if she would voluntarily resign her position.

Agent Vlaytork agreed to resign without consulting Ortees because she saw no profit for the Confederation coming from remaining at Sandhurst.

One week later, Ori felt a buzzing from his transponder, signaling a rendezvous with Ortees.

Besides the team leader and the military crew, there was another agent in attendance. Svavapass recognized the young agent from the Academy, but he had forgotten his name.

It was then that Ori found why he was no longer being visited by Jenny Carter.

"Jenny Carter has already turned in her notice," Ortees informed Ori. "She will be moving to Surrey. We have arranged for her to be hired as a nanny to take care of Princess Charlotte's child, which should be born in late October."

"Agent Vlaytork will be able to bond with the child and perhaps even influence him (or her)," the team leader explained.

"This is an excellent arrangement," Ori agreed mechanically. "But this landing site is a very long walk and I have a lot to do, with both my teaching and my social engagements."

Ortees handed Ori a large number of shillings.

"Do you expect me to hire a carriage to drive me out of town through a farm to the transport vehicle?" Ori asked in disbelief.

"Don't be silly, Ori," Ortees chided his agent. "You squeeze the coin on the edges. It will record your voice. You can talk for up to an hour, conveying all of the intelligence that you gather. Once every week, Agent Mlai will meet you by your townhouse and you will pass him the coin with your recorded voice."

Agent Mlai approached Ori with a rusty cup and said in lower-class English, "Beg yer pardon, Guvna. Might you 'elp a poor man in need?"

"You've learned the native language?" Ori asked Mlai in English.

"Please kind, sir," Mlai replied. "I've come on 'ard times. I can't piy me rent."

Ortees smiled. "No, Mlai can't speak much English. He only knows a few phrases. But he can do the leg work to and from the landing site."

"Please, Guvna," Mlai went on. "I've got little ones to feed."

"He sounds authentic," Svavapass admitted.

"I was rated by computer analysis to be 97.6 percent authentic," Mlai boasted, breaking into Grellish.

"Now we can move Vlaytork to a better use of her skills," Ortees declared.

Ori nodded, but inwardly he was still hurting.

Several days later, Ori had to go to the administration building to take care of a practical matter. As he passed through the open area where the secretarial staff worked, he could not help but cast his eye on the empty seat once occupied by Unni Vlaytork.

Ori drifted toward Unni's former work bench. The young woman who sat to the right of that spot looked up from her work. "You won't find Jenny here anymore, Major. She is gone. She turned in her notice two weeks ago."

The woman to the left was somewhat older. She said, "And I am glad for that! Nothing but trouble, that Jenny."

"Come now, Debbie," the woman to the right countered. "Jenny was a good worker and was rather nice."

"Jenny was left-'anded, she was," Debbie argued. "She was always bumping me elbow when I was trying to write."

"I am sure she didn't mean anything by it," Ori tried to assure Debbie.

"Stay away from me, Major," Debbie shot back. "I want nothing to do with the likes of you!"

3

"I beg your pardon," Ori replied.

"I know your kind," Debbie went on. "You take advantage of a girl below your station. After you've 'ad yer pleasure, you refuse to marry the girl, and she is left to crawl away in shame!"

"This is complete rubbish!" Ori protested.

"Oh, go on!" the secretary exclaimed.

"Not so loud, Debbie," the other secretary exhorted her fellow worker. "The Lt. Colonel might hear you, and you'll be sacked!"

"His daughter is 'ere now. Someone needs to tell 'im before it's too late!"

"Please ignore her, Major," the other secretary implored.

"That I shall." Ori turned and left.

The next Saturday, Ori hired a two-horse carriage and had the driver take him out of the city to the camp where his former regiment was stationed. Ori had not seen his old partner, Agent Sraymlat, in a long time and he badly needed someone to talk to, someone who understood.

When he got to the camp, he sought out the officers he had served with. He found some of them, but Sraymlat was not among them.

After some jovial chatter, Ori inquired about Lt. Greenhill.

"He is doing well," one of his old comrades replied. "Bill is Captain Greenhill now. He has cut back on his drinking. But he was transferred a few weeks ago."

"Transferred?" Ori was surprised.

"Yes, to Surrey. Captain Greenhill is heading up the Coburg's security detail at Claremont House."

Ori knew at once what that meant. Princess Charlotte's husband was Prince Leopold Saxe-Coburg-Saalfeld. The couple was known as the Coburgs. Parliament had voted a large sum of money for the Coburgs to purchase a large house in Surrey known as Claremont house. No doubt, the Interplanetary Intelligence Service had "arranged" (as they do) for Agents Sraymlat and Vlaytork to operate in close proximity.

The officers implored Ori to spend the night, but when he heard that Sraymlat was no longer there, he cut his visit short and returned to Sandhurst. The driver of the carriage was somewhat talkative, but Ori was not in the mood for conversation. He felt unsettled. Ori found it odd that Sraymlat and Vlaytork were going to be working together, but he would be almost alone, save for brief encounters with Agent Mlai who was posing as a street beggar.

Agents were trained to work alone, but right now, Ori badly needed a friend.

6.

Calamity in Surrey

Agent Svavapass tried to forget Agent Vlaytork and immerse himself in his work. He spent the rest of the summer preparing the notes for a course on calculus for the cadets the following fall. He continued to attend social events as Wellington raised his profile for a reentry into politics. The main subject of the small talk at the social events was the speculation as to the gender of Princess Charlotte's child. Everything Ori learned was dutifully passed on to the Interplanetary Intelligence Service via Agent Mlai's wretched tin cup.

Ori really did not enjoy the balls and banquettes. He saw them as work. His only recreation was the time he spent at the Keatons' residence. He especially enjoyed his time outdoors fox hunting and bird shooting. He really did not care for either sport, but he loved being in the English countryside. Ori knew that these times with the Keatons would end because he was not going to marry Katy. Even Katy's shameless passes at Major Weatherby were becoming more halfhearted.

Late in the summer, the Coburgs began to ready the nursery for their new arrival. Jenny Carter, the nanny, was sent to London with one of the maids to pick up items the Coburgs had ordered for the baby's room. When the carriage arrived back at Surrey, the two women began to carry the items into Claremont House and up the stairs to the nursery. Normally, a footman would assist with the heavy lifting, but Claremont House was short-staffed. Prince Leopold was not very wealthy. Even with the generous allowance from Parliament that the Coburgs received, they still were not that well off.

The head of the security detail, Captain Greenhill, saw Jenny Carter laden with boxes heading for the staircase. "May I help you with these?"

Unni grinned at the irony. "Yes, thank you, Captain."

Urelt Sraymlat took most of the weight from Unni and carried the items up the long staircase.

Over the next few weeks, Urelt never lost an opportunity to assist the nanny with any chores that involved lifting.

Sometimes Urelt and Unni would meet in the foyer and have short conversations. "I am worried that the princess is not getting enough exercise," the captain said once. "She is overeating, and she spends much of her day sitting for that portrait."

Sir Thomas Lawrence was painting a portrait of Princess Charlotte.

Later, when the doctors became concerned about her weight, they began to restrict her eating and began to bleed her. Unni was aghast. She dared not to express her opinion, except to Agent Sraymlat. "All they are doing is weakening her. I think the princess would do better without her doctors," she told him.

"Doctors?" Urelt raised an eyebrow. "Sir Richard Croft is no doctor. He is a…I do not know the English word. May I whisper the Grellish word in your ear?"

"He is an accoucheur," Unni informed him. "They are quite in fashion with the upper class these days."

"May I whisper in your ear anyway?" he asked.

Unni blushed and said, "Now, Captain!"

Unni did not want to become an item of conversation again, but she was drawn to Urelt. Unlike Agent Svavapass the previous year, Urelt was much less stiff, even somewhat playful.

Unni had hoped to have some contact with the princess, but it was impossible. The lower orders were quite restricted from having any contact with the aristocracy. Even most commands came from servants of higher rank. And if that were not enough of a barrier, the princess was being shielded from the rest of the world by her overprotective inner circle.

By October, Ori was running low on "shillings." He had not had an encounter with Ortees for months. He supposed that Ortees was waiting until the birth of the royal heir to convene a meeting. It would matter whether the baby was a boy or a girl, and at Level 8 technology, there was no way for anyone to know the baby's gender until birth.

October ended, and the baby had still not been born. At last on November 3, Princess Charlotte's contractions began. There was a flurry of activity at Claremont House. Captain Greenhill and his men were receiving officials into the house who would attest to the royal birth.

The following morning there was still no birth. At one point, Unni saw Urelt and said, "This is not going well. She is having difficulty delivering the baby, and her doctors are not up to the task of providing real help. I am very worried."

Later in the evening, Unni passed Urelt and groaned in frustration. "Their inaction is going to kill the baby! If it were not for the Noninterference Protocol, I would burst in there and push natal technology on this planet ahead two centuries!"

Unni was helping the servants bring things to the room where the Princess was. She never got to go inside. She was always met at the door. She hoped against hope to hear the cry of a newborn baby.

By the morning of the fifth, Unni was in great fear. What if the baby did not survive? What would become of this operation? And she knew enough from what she learned in school that this entire delivery was being mishandled. Why was there no obstetrician?

Much to his relief, Captain Greenhill received the command to send for John Sims, an obstetrician. He commanded his men to move with all haste. Would Sims be in time?

Indeed, Sims was on time, but now Sir Richard Croft would not allow him to see the princess. Unni was almost in a panic. It was hard enough to watch a tragedy unfold, but it was sheer torture to watch this play out knowing what could be done and not being able to say anything.

Shortly after nine in the evening, Unni's worst fears were confirmed. The child was stillborn. As grief took hold of the staff, she received a double portion, the grief of Jenny Carter, the household servant, and Unni Vlaytork, the Agent from the Interplanetary Intelligence Service. Both had lost their job, one as a nanny having lost a baby to care for, and the other, the agent having lost a mission to carry out.

Unni wanted to find Urelt to cry on his shoulder, but he was occupied, seeing doctors and officials alike out of the house.

Things got worse. Shortly after midnight, Jenny heard some commotion upstairs. She ran to offer the other servants her help. She found out that the princess was vomiting, having trouble breathing, and was bleeding.

Within minutes, the household got the horrible news that Princess Charlotte was dead.

No one was paying any attention to a nanny that would not be needed. Unni went down the stairs and ran toward Urelt. She embraced him and wept. As Urelt was quite a bit taller than Unni, she was not weeping on his shoulder but into it. The two agents felt very hollow, almost as if they had lost their own child.

On that awful Thursday morning, November 6, 1817, Ori was in his classroom teaching when Debbie, a member of the administrative staff, entered his classroom. She told the instructor that he and all of the cadets were to immediately assemble in the courtyard.

"We will continue this discussion on the Chain Rule tomorrow," Ori announced. "We are to gather at once in the courtyard for an announcement. Since this gathering is no doubt related to the birth in the royal family, there will be no assignment of homework today."

The cadets immediately rose and headed for the door with some measure of joy. Ori was concerned because Debbie's face was red, as if she were grieving. As the cadets assembled themselves, Ori prepared himself for the worst.

General Sir Alexander Hope, the Governor of the Royal Military College was seated on a platform, flanked by Colonel James Butler, the Lt. Governor, and Lt. Colonel Keaton, who were standing. The three were somber. General Hope addressed the cadets from his seat, as he was lame from wounds sustained in battle.

Everyone gasped as they heard that Princess Charlotte's baby had been stillborn. They were further grieved to find out that it had been a boy, "and a handsome one at that."

"But that is not the worst of it," the General went on. He paused for a moment to compose himself. "Divine Providence has seen fit to take from us Princess Charlotte as well. The late Princess departed from this world shortly past midnight."

Ori was shaken by the news. Of the three agents with long-term assignments in England, two were assigned to Surrey. He recognized at once that this would totally alter the mission and approach of the Interplanetary Intelligence Service for the British Empire and perhaps for Earth 48 as a whole.

After the gathering, Ori spoke briefly with Lt. Col. Keaton. Keaton was in shock and worry. Ori realized that he had best withdraw from the Keatons during this time of tragedy.

Indeed, Ori was shaken, but England was devastated. The whole country went into deep mourning. Shops were closed, as were the law courts and schools. At Sandhurst, classes were cancelled for the rest of the week "and beyond." There was black ribbon everywhere. Even the poor wore black armbands.

Later that day, Ori felt a buzzing in his shoulder. He was to report Saturday night to the designated spot to meet with the atmospheric entry vehicle.

With classes cancelled, Ori went to London and tried to gauge the public mood. All social events were cancelled, so he took to the streets to learn what he could. Ori was aware of the fact that King George III had fifteen children, of whom twelve were living; but he had no living legitimate grandchildren, and only one of the king's sons was presently married and not estranged from his wife. Unless something changed, the line of succession to the British throne would be broken within twenty years.

The trek to the transport was a long one. The military did not like landing space vehicles close to populated areas. Ori saw the red glow of the underside of the vehicle and climbed aboard. Agent Tekalta was there to greet him on the lower deck. Ori was not surprised that Ortees was not present. He surmised that the recent events called for a wider conference.

Ori climbed the ladder to the upper deck. Major Hortu was at the controls. The "Prussians" Metchavork and Svortomit were present, as were the "French" Lorbank and Duvass.

"Where are the others, Svavapass?" Hortu asked.

"I have not seen them in months," Ori replied. "Agents Sraymlat and Vlaytork are working together in a different location from me."

"Maybe Sraymlat has had one too many," Svortomit jested. "He would be rather heavy for poor Unni to carry."

"I heard Sraymlat has stopped drinking," Ori pointed out.

"Unni probably knocked him in line," Svortomit quipped.

Ori informed his fellow agents of the dreadful news. Lorbank then asked, "What is the mood of the people in England?"

Before Ori could answer, Agents Vlaytork and Sraymlat emerged and strapped in. Hortu was eager to leave. Not too many seconds went by between the click of Tekalta's seatbelt and the lift off.

The transport was heading west at high speed. Svavapass was not surprised to be heading to North America.

"Why are we flying this far north?" Metchavork asked. "Louisiana is to the south."

Hortu did not answer. He did not like backseat drivers. Squeem gave the answer. "We have a pickup in Noaork...Neeaerk...I can't pronounce these weird alien names."

"New York?" Vlaytork asked.

The copilot flashed the name to Vlaytork's armrest screen. "Yes, that is New York."

"So Ortees got his way," Duvass observed.

Before long, the transport touched down in a wooded area in central Manhattan, and Agent Vlevlan Qlat stepped aboard dressed in the fancy native clothing of a New York gentleman. He had removed his black top hat, which he placed on his lap, and he strapped in. Svavapass did not know Qlat very well. He soon found out that his alias was Stephen Galt, a banker. Hortu promptly took the transport to New Orleans to pick up his last passenger, Huha Srot.

Qlat and Srot were shocked to hear about the deaths of Princess Charlotte and her baby. The subject dominated the discussion all the way to Station 48-3.

"Perhaps Britain will have to become a republic when the royals die out," Srot speculated.

"One could only hope they could achieve a republic without a bloody revolution," Lorbank agreed.

"I doubt that would ever happen," Vlaytork said. "From my vantage point, it appears that monarchy is an entrenched tradition in Great Britain."

"It is programmed into their genes," Sraymlat quipped.

"I agree," Metchavork added. "When the royal family dies out, their parliament will seek a prince from the continent. Since he will necessarily be a Protestant, one can be reasonably certain that the British Empire will be ruled by a German. And when Germany unifies behind the King of Prussia, the new Reich will include Great Britain and all of its colonies."

Vlaytork rolled her eyes.

"And a century later, Berlin will be the leading city on Earth 48," Sraymlat said in a sarcastic tone of voice.

But Metchavork took his assessment seriously. "You have come to agree with me, then. It is the destiny of the German people to become the leaders of Europe and this entire planet."

"It was a joke, Metchavork, a joke," Ori said. Everyone laughed except Metchavork and Svortomit.

When the transport reached the space station, the agents went through the same routine as two years before: decontamination, a good meal, a time to submit a written report, and several hours of sleep. The next morning, the agents were assembled in the conference room with two analysts, Agent Grugar Tekalta and a woman Svavapass did not recognize, Agent Gutsatal Leka.

After breakfast, the team leader, Special Agent Ortees entered the room. He called the meeting to order.

"I wanted to meet with all of you several weeks ago to discuss some recent developments in the galaxy, but I put off the meeting until after the birth of the British royal heir so we could also assess the situation on Planet 48," Ortees began.

"Of course, I had no idea at the time that such a tragic calamity would befall the British people. As I read the reports this morning, I was totally surprised by the turn of events. But first, we must come to more important matters."

The other agents wondered what could be more important than the double loss of Princess Charlotte and her baby.

Just then, Tekalta announced that the Subdirector was ready.

"Put her on," Ortees commanded.

A hologram appeared at the head of the conference table.

"Good day," Ustipas Keepetta greeted the agents from her seat in Tlat Mlang. The Subdirector's face was drawn, and there was sadness in her eyes.

"What you are about to hear is highly classified," she began. "You are not to discuss this with anyone outside of this room."

A three-dimensional map appeared in the middle of the conference table. The suns of the 51 Earths were illuminated. The 27 members of the Confederation were gold, including Earths 1 to 7, 16, 18 to 20, 22, 25, 26, 28, 30, 32 to 37, 40, and 42 to 44. The twenty-two planets that were under surveillance were silver, including Earths 8 to 10, 12 to 15, 17, 21, 23, 29, 31, 38, 39, 41, and 45 to 51. Earths 11 and 27 were bronze. Earth 11 declined to join the Confederation but maintained diplomatic relations. Earth 27 was a partial member, as the leading nations there were divided on the subject of entry into the Confederation.

All of the agents in the room were familiar with this map.

"Ten years ago, one of our starships picked up signals indicative of intelligent life. They followed that signal and discovered Earth 52."

Suddenly, a blue point appeared on the side of the map where the cluster of Earths 45 to 51 was located. The new planet was distant, however. It was as far from Earth 50 as Earth 50 was from Earths 1 and 2.

"From orbit, our starship intercepted signals of an advanced race, Technology Level 12, but when we landed transports on the surface, we made a horrifying discovery. Earth 52 is actually at Technology Level 7, and is occupied by military forces from another starfaring race.

"Earth 52 has been colonized and enslaved. Its resources are being robbed and exported to another planet. Since that time, we have discovered another twenty enslaved worlds."

Another twenty blue illuminated points appeared. The new points were added beyond Earth 52 on the side of the original map where Earths 45 to 51 were located.

"We also located their leading planet," the Subdirector continued.

A star lit up in bright red inside the cluster of blue points.

"In effect, we have discovered a belligerent interstellar empire," Keepetta announced.

The field agents gasped.

"Have they discovered us?" Svortomit asked.

"We do not believe so," Keepetta replied.

"We have placed clandestine satellites around some of the planets and are learning their language. On their home planet, a totalitarian dictatorship prevailed during their ideological wars. Since they developed interstellar flight, this empire has embarked on an expansionist policy of deceit and conquest."

The agents were silent.

"We now know the Empire is expanding in this direction," Keepetta concluded.

A red arrow appeared. It ran through Earth 52 toward the cluster of Earths 45 to 51.

"I only learned of this when I was promoted to team leader a year and a half ago," Ortees interjected.

"What is the High Commission going to do about it?" Lorbank asked, gesturing with both hands.

"Are we going to contact them?" Qlat asked.

"Are we building warships? Armies to stop them?" Metchavork asked, waving his fist.

"I am not at liberty to answer those questions," Keepetta replied. "But decisions have been made concerning the missions of agents operating on the planets closest to the Empire."

The Subdirector did not give details of those decisions. The meeting moved on to a report from the field agents.

Metchavork and Svortomit maintained that Prussia would one day lead a united Germany and that the German empire would become the preeminent power in Europe and the whole planet.

Lorbank and Duvass reported that France was continuing to recover from defeat and would one day be an important power again.

Svavapass, Sraymlat, and Vlaytork were undeterred by the recent tragedy and maintained that the British Empire was the leading power on the planet. They believed that the postwar economic difficulties and the public unrest that resulted were temporary.

Qlat and Srot reported that the United States of America was continuing to grow as a nation and was likely to continue its westward expansion. Qlat said that the new president, James Monroe, was an able administrator and a man of conciliation and compromise.

The Subdirector interrupted the presentation. "New president? What happened to Deaymes Madasohn? Did I pronounce it correctly?"

"Close enough," Lorbank replied.

Qlat fielded the question. "President Madison's term of office expired on 37528.10.18."

"We generally use the local calendar in these meetings," Ortees interjected.

"That would be March 4, 1817. Monroe had been elected the previous fall as his successor."

"And the former president is still living?" The Subdirector raised an eyebrow with interest.

"Yes, he is, at his home in the State of Virginia."

"Are you saying that there was an orderly transfer of power?" The Subdirector was intrigued.

"Yes, Madam Subdirector."

"Amazing!" Keepetta remarked.

"This has happened before," Qlat added. "This is the fourth consecutive orderly transfer of such kind in the United States of America."

"Special Agent Ortees, you should write a memorandum to the Exploration Commission," the Subdirector ordered. "Perhaps we need to upgrade Earth 48 to Cultural Level 7. Continue Agent Qlat."

"President Monroe is also seeking a compromise on sectional disputes."

"What seems to be the issue?" the Subdirector asked.

"The northern states seek to abolish slavery. The southern states are resisting such efforts."

"Slavery? Did you say slavery?" The Subdirector was displeased. "Special Agent Ortees, please disregard my last order."

Moments later, the Subdirector's holograph vanished. Ortees went over a few practical matters.

"This conference has been rather somber, but we do have one joyful piece of news," the team leader announced. "Agent Sraymlat, maybe you want to make the announcement."

Urelt and Unni both stood. The heaviness in the room seemed to lift because everyone knew the custom of the Confederation and what it meant when two people stood.

Ori smiled on the outside along with everyone in the room, but inwardly his heart sank.

Unni looked up adoringly at Urelt as he declared, "Unni and I are engaged to be married!"

Vlaytork pulled the stone of her engagement necklace above the neckline of her uniform for all to see.

"Congratulations Urelt and Unni!" came the replies of everyone in the room.

There were various lighthearted comments and congratulatory expressions.

"Special Agent Ortees, do you plan to send any female agents to work in Paris?" Duvass asked in jest.

As the agents all enjoyed the moment, Ori was inwardly reeling in shock.

The teams took turns visiting the ship's surgeon, watching classified videos about the Empire and meeting privately with the team leader.

The three agents assigned to England had their audience with Ortees last. This was the team whose mission was to be the most altered.

"Obviously, Unni's mission to be the nanny of a future monarch is terminated," Ortees began. "And Urelt's mission to guard two future monarchs is also over. But I liked the idea you put forth in your report..."

"It was Unni's idea really..." Urelt interjected.

"Especially now with the discovery of this empire," Ortees continued. "Ori, what Unni and Urelt are considering is to stay on Earth 48 and become Mr. and Mrs. Greenhill. They would have a son, and Unni would tutor him and prepare him for a political career, and he would use his office to accelerate the technical and cultural development of the British Empire and of the whole planet."

"Where do I fit into this plan?" Ori asked.

"In two roles," Ortees explained. Both involve your relationship with the Duke of Wellington. There is the obvious benefit of influencing public policy to start the reform process early. But the second role is more important. You could form relationships among the Tories that we can use to cut a path for the younger Greenhill, to increase the probability of his rise to high position."

"Is this legal?" Ori asked. "This appears to be outside of the guidelines of the maxim 'Sent to Watch.' Has the Subdirector sanctioned this?"

Ortees smiled. "No, not really. But it will be years before any real influence has occurred. By that time, the Interplanetary Intelligence Service may change its mind about noninterference, and we will already have saved them a decade or more in getting the operation in place."

"And why might the Commission change a centuries-old policy in the near future?" Ori asked.

"Ori, look where Earth 48 is located with respect to the Empire's vector of advance!" Vlaytork exclaimed.

"It will be next to impossible for the Confederation to defend these primitive worlds from attack and not reveal itself," Urelt interjected. "But what if one of the planets were already at a point in their development where they are ready for admission to the Confederation?"

"I ran a simulation last night," Unni said. "In essence, Earth 48 has only about one to two hundred years before it is attacked, and it is about 275 years away from being ready for admission to the Confederation. Their rate of development needs to double."

"I plan to make this program palatable to the Commission by making this a very indirect form of interference," Ortees continued. "Urelt's son won't know he is an alien to this planet. The British won't know. No one will know. He will simply be schooled in such a way that he makes the best decisions."

"Your son would never know his real surname is Sraymlat, would he?" Ori asked his two fellow agents.

"That is correct. In fact, he would never even know a word of Grellish," Vlaytork added.

Ori paused. "This is a lot to take in. I suppose we could never discuss this with other agents."

"It may be years before this plan is sanctioned," Ortees observed. "But who knows? By then our agents may have to engage in sabotage and assassinations and counter-espionage against the Empire. If this plan is accepted, it could become the model for Earths 46, 47, and 49. Just leave the internal politics to me. But for now, the four of us need to devise the details as to how to execute this plan."

An hour later, the other agents were shuttled back to their stations on the surface of Earth 48. Agents Svavapass, Sraymlat, and Vlaytork stayed behind on Station 48-3 with Ortees. With all of England shut down for mourning, they would have some time to lay the strategic groundwork for their plan.

7.
The Accusation

Agent Svavapass was to stay at Sandhurst and bide his time until Wellesley's anticipated rise to power. Agent Sraymlat was to enter the diplomatic service and begin building relationships with other officials to become politically connected. Agent Vlaytork would take a secretarial position in the Foreign Office to stage a courtship believable to the natives.

Captain Greenhill was transferred back to his old regiment after Princess Charlotte's funeral on November 19. The regiment was stationed twenty miles south of the city and at least as far east of Sandhurst. From there, he had to wait to hear from Ortees when a job had been "arranged" with the Foreign Office.

For her part, Jenny Carter needed no help getting a secretarial job in the Foreign Office. She still had the letter of reference that Lt. Col. Keaton had written when she left Sandhurst. She was hired right after her interview. Within days, Unni found a young widow named Gwen with whom she could share the rent in a small flat.

The flat consisted of one room above a store. On one side were two beds. On the other side was a sofa and a table with two chairs. Between was a fireplace that included a range for the women to cook. There was also a cupboard and an icebox. For water, they had to go outside and draw from a public well. By the time Unni moved in, it was well into November, when the days were short; the flat always seemed dark.

Unni found Gwen a lot more agreeable than her roommates in Sandhurst. As they performed their house chores, Gwen liked to talk. Most women would tire of Gwen's constant chatter, but Unni welcomed it, as it helped her to learn more about Earth 48.

Gwen had had more than her share of tragedy in her life. She had grown up on a farm, the oldest daughter of the owner. But when her father died, she could not inherit because she was a woman, and the land went to her younger brother. A year later, he got married, and his new wife persuaded him to make Gwen leave. At that time, the young man from the next farm whom she loved was conscripted into the Army and died the next year in the Peninsular War. She moved to London and married, but she lost her only child to infant mortality. Her husband died shortly thereafter in an industrial accident.

Unni was moved by the story, especially after her bad experience in Surrey just weeks before. Unni never told Gwen she was present when that national tragedy took place. In fact, she feared that Gwen would ask her to tell her story. However, that unwelcome event never materialized; Gwen was too much of a chatterbox to give Unni a serious chance to say that much about herself.

One evening, Unni had just gotten in when there was a knock at the door. Unni let Gwen answer it. After all, she did not know anyone in London yet.

"It's your Uncle Sebastian," Gwen announced.

"My Uncle Seb...? Oh, yes," Unni caught herself as she recognized Ortees's face. "Uncle Sebastian! It is so good to see you."

Ortees was dressed in a long overcoat, with a top hat and a walking stick. Jenny and her "uncle" embraced. Uncle Sebastian kissed Jenny.

"I am so glad I was able to locate you," Ortees said. Of course, it helps if your "niece" has a transponder in her left shoulder. "Perhaps we could go out together for dinner."

Ortees had an accent that was part Spanish and part Grellish. He was hoping not to sound too unusual to the native roommate.

He turned to Gwen. "I would love to invite you as well, but we have family matters to discuss. So take this and go out and enjoy a good meal in town." He handed her three shillings.

"Oh, I couldn't take this..."

"And perhaps next time we could all go out together," Ortees interrupted her.

Unni donned her coat and left with her "uncle" as he was showered with words of gratitude from Gwen.

Ortees led Unni to a rather nice restaurant. He was greeted at the door. "Ah, Mr. De Leon, your table is ready for you."

Ortees and his "niece" made their way to a table near the corner. After they were seated and placed their order, they were able to speak.

"Uncle Sebastian, I never knew your English was so fluent," Unni said.

"You flatter me. Actually, it is not. I was just becoming conversant when I had to leave New Orleans."

"Why then are we here and not on the…in a place where we could use a language with which you are more comfortable?"

"It is complicated," he began. "I could not risk being overheard by Major Horton."

"Yes, I see," Unni replied. She perceived that Ortees might be somehow out of step with the policies of higher-ranking agents.

The waiter came to their table and poured some tea.

"There seems to be some sort of misunderstanding between me and Sral Vlaris," he went on.

"Mr. Harris, did you say?" Jenny corrected him. "What kind of misunderstanding?"

Ortees took a small sip of tea. Finding it to be too hot, he continued.

"He still takes an interest in his former venue of work. The reports written by you and William and Robert were uploaded to the central data bank, and he decided to read them out of curiosity. From those reports, Mr. Harris began to get concerned that I was leading my team beyond the limits of our Noninterference Protocol. He showed the reports to the Subdirector. I am told she became quite angry. I fear she may have me removed from my post—or worse."

"I only reported what I saw," Unni said. "I talked about the death of the princess and her son. Should I not have also mentioned my suggestion of going to work as a secretary at the Foreign Office?"

"Nothing you wrote caused a problem," her uncle assured her. "At least not by itself. Robert wrote about Wellington and the current debt crisis the government faces. He predicted that Wellington might become prime minister and he might be close to him. But he was careful not to suggest any attempt to influence the Duke.

"The problem is what William wrote, about marrying and becoming the father of a future prime minister who could accelerate Britain's technical development and…"

"No! He didn't!" Unni interrupted.

"Ah, but he did," Ortees said grimly.

"But couldn't you say that was just his opinion or suggestion, subject to your approval?"

"I can try," he replied. "But you have to remember that Vlaris—uh, Harris—had already heard this kind of talk two years ago. If you put William's report together with yours and Robert's, a picture emerges."

"I see," Uni nodded slowly.

"And it did not help matters when he read that part of Stephen Galt's report about wanting to assist a political campaign to prevent that wild man Andrew Jackson from becoming president of the United States. Don't you see? It gives the appearance that my team is out of control."

"What can we do?" Unni asked. "Shall we write something in your defense? Shall we write that you asked us for ideas, and these things were only raw suggestions?"

"No, Unni. I am afraid that won't help. The ship sails in two days for Tlat Mlang. I intend to go there in person and talk to Mr. Harris and the Subdirector. I will present a defense. I will tell them I was setting up a situation that would save time should it become necessary in the future to influence the development of this world."

Ortees paused as the waiter set the first course of their dinner before them.

"But I want you to know that I may not ever be back," he continued. "There is a chance they will remove me."

There were tears in Unni's eyes. "And William—will he get into trouble?"

"It is possible, but not likely. It is my leadership that will be blamed. And I accept the responsibility."

Ortees wanted to enjoy his dinner, and he wanted Unni to enjoy hers as well. He changed the subject to the cuisine in different counties, such as Spain, Italy, and New Spain. He also dished up some of his characteristic humor. Unni admitted that over the year and a half she had spent in England, this was the best dinner she'd had.

After dinner, they walked in a cool drizzle back to the door of the building where Unni's flat was.

Ortees then said goodbye to Unni. "I hope we meet again, but if not, I want you to know that I have considered it a great privilege to be your team leader. You can tell everyone on the team. You are all fine agents, and I enjoyed working with you these past two years."

Before Unni could reply, Ortees turned and walked away into the mist of the night.

Due to the nature of their mission, Ori, Urelt, and Unni could not meet often. In addition to the distances, Urelt and Ori did not want any gossip at this stage, and the person of Jenny Carter had to be kept absolutely free from even a hint of scandal to protect the image of their future son or sons. Similarly, Captain Greenhill was not supposed to be acquainted with Jenny Carter yet.

But Urelt did not let that get in the way of spending at least a little time with Unni. Whenever he had the opportunity to leave his regiment, he would go to London. Being a well-trained spy, he soon found where Unni lived. Every several weeks, they met in secret.

Unni told Urelt about her meeting with Ortees. She told him that Ortees had had to go away to straighten out a misunderstanding within the leadership of the Service concerning his handling of his team. She even told him the concern was about the Noninterference Protocol. She did not mention that it was his report that precipitated the crisis or that she knew what he had written.

Urelt surmised that with Ortees gone from his position in orbit above the planet, there might be a delay in his getting a job in the Foreign Office. This presented a problem. The longer the delay in getting a job in the Foreign Office, the longer their courtship and wedding would be delayed. That in turn would delay the birth of the future Prime Minister Greenhill, and thus delay their plan to accelerate Britain's development.

The delay presented another problem for Urelt. While he waited for his opportunity to join the foreign office, he had to stay in the army. France was to be occupied for five years by the victorious Coalition Powers. At any time, his regiment could be sent across the channel to France, to say nothing of India, Canada or the Caribbean. If that occurred, his usefulness to the Service would be greatly reduced.

After his November 1817 appearance as Uncle Sebastian, Ortees never made contact with any of his agents. Agent Mlai went from rare to absent altogether.

The three agents were mystified as the weeks turned into months. The agents felt isolated. Ori was the most isolated of all, and he was uninformed as to the political trouble Ortees was in. Agents were trained to perform their duty for months or years without contact, but to be isolated at a time when the mission was in transition was unexpected to say the least.

Unni and Urelt were aware of Ori's isolation. Urelt was thinking of sacrificing one of his opportunities to see Unni and visiting Ori's townhouse one weekend, but he never followed through.

In March, he received a written invitation from Major Weatherby to come visit. Ori had a backlog of information to pass on to Ortees, not the least of which was the news of engagements of two of King George's sons.

The two men met on a cold Saturday evening at the townhouse. On account of the presence of the cook and the butler Ori had hired, Urelt was forced to discuss the events in a metaphorical way. Ori immediately recognized Uncle Sebastian as Ortees because this alias was well known to the other agents on the team.

"That explains a lot," Ori said. "For a while I was beginning to think that the Empire had attacked and forced our people to retreat from this sector. I was wondering if I would have to have my "shrapnel" removed so that I could not be found by the enemy."

Soon after Special Agent Ortees had visited Earth 48 to confer with Unni, the starship left Earth 48 orbit and took him to Earth 32 from which he found a vessel bound for Earth 1.

When Ortees got to Tlat Mlang, he wasted no time reporting to the headquarters of the Interplanetary Intelligence Service. Special Agent Ortees was a bit of a celebrity among the younger agents, but that morning he received a very cool reception.

Ortees was led to an empty office. When he logged into the computer, there were instructions that he should write a full report about Earth 48 and the specific missions of each of the nine long-term undercover agents. He had access to the agents' reports filed on 37529.6.39 (November 8, 1817, by the natives' calendar).

After an hour and a half (about 108 minutes by Earth 48 time, as the Confederation clock has twenty hours), Ortees was interrupted and summoned to the Subdirector's office.

Subdirector Keepetta was there, as was Special Agent Vlaris. Keepetta looked grieved, but Vlaris was glaring at Ortees with thinly veiled anger.

They informed Ortees that he was under investigation for violating the Noninterference Protocol, for carrying on a non-sanctioned mission, and for willful deception of his superior agents. There was to be a hearing in five days to determine if any or all of the charges merited referral to an internal Service Court, in which case he would be placed on trial. If convicted, he was looking at a penalty ranging from demotion to prison time, depending on the findings of the court.

Ortees was told he had a day to write his account of what had occurred. The next day he would meet with an attorney from within the Interplanetary Intelligence Service who was assigned to defend him at the preliminary hearing.

Ortees tried to explain what had occurred, but he was interrupted by Vlaris. "Save it for the hearing, Ortees."

Keepetta promptly dismissed Ortees from her office.

Ortees worked on the report for the rest of the morning, reading reports and writing his side of the story. In the middle of the day, Ortees went to the dining hall. No one would talk to him, and old friends ignored him. He ate at the end of a half-empty table alone.

Ortees stayed into the evening working on his report.

The next morning, he went to his office to reread what he had written. In the middle of the morning, he received a buzz at the door. A short, stocky man stepped in, with balding brown hair, a prominent nose and deep blue eyes.

"Good morning, Special Agent Ortees," he began. "My name is Utrat Smapront. I am an attorney, and I have been assigned to your case."

"Saibert Ortees," the agent replied and gestured to the attorney to sit down.

"Actually, I was not assigned," Smapront corrected himself. "I asked for this case. You see, I am from Earth 19, and when I heard you were from my home planet, and even the same continent..."

"I see," Ortees cut him short. He was eager to get beyond the introduction and get down to business.

"I read the reports of your agents, and I read your report this morning," Smapront began. "I think I can cut a deal and get the charges reduced to third degree running a non-sanctioned mission, and limit the penalty to demotion by one paygrade and termination with benefits."

Ortees frowned. "I am not interested in any kind of plea bargain. I am innocent, and I intend to fight the charges and clear my name."

"If that is your decision, I must abide by it," the attorney replied. "But I read Agent Sraymlat's report and he clearly said…"

"I know what he said," Ortees interrupted. "I am innocent. If you do not believe me, then I will request a different defense attorney."

"I want to be your attorney. I want to believe that you are innocent. So convince me. If you can convince me, I can convince the court."

Ortees conceded that his plan had a component of influence, of affecting the course of history of a faction on Earth 48 known as the British Empire. But he strenuously contended that no such influence had taken place yet. He was simply positioning his agents so that the Confederation would be prepared to influence the British Empire in the future should the need arise. Having such a contingency in place would save the Service forty years should the policy change.

"Yes, yes, I read that," Smapront replied. "But the court will find the notion lame. We would have to demonstrate that a policy that has been in place for millennia is about to change in a few decades."

Ortees slapped the table.

"The Confederation just discovered an aggressive empire! Isn't that reason enough to change policy? And they will reach that sector in about a century or two. Left to itself, Earth 48 is projected to be fit for admission to the Confederation in 275 years. Those forty years my plan saves will be crucial if Earth 48 has any hope of avoiding a horrible fate."

"I like that, Ortees. I can work with that. But if this is such a good idea, why did you have to hide it from the Subdirector?"

"Why should I have to tell them, Mr. Smapront? It was within my purview to gather information as I saw fit, because I had no intention of influencing the development of Earth 48 before discussing it with them before the Service began to lay out its plans for dealing with the Empire."

"That is reasonable Mr. Ortees, but…"

"You can call me Saibert," Ortees interjected.

"Very well, Saibert. You can call me Utrat. But, as I was saying, this kind of defense would require corroborating testimony from the field agents. It may be good enough to acquit, but I do not think it would be strong enough to avoid an indictment."

The preliminary hearing was a mixture of positive and negative developments for Ortees. Vlaris was very adversarial, painting the deeds of Ortees in the darkest hues. At the same time, his accusatory account came off as shrill and extreme. Keepetta was more objective. While her testimony indicated doubts on her part that Ortees's actions were within the Noninterference Protocol, she admitted on cross-examination that it was possible Ortees's actions never actually crossed the line of interfering with the natural development of Earth 48.

Smapront showed skill in his questioning. He was always probing, trying to get the witnesses to bring out both sides and create doubt in the minds of the three-judge panel that Ortees broke any laws.

Orcha Lyba, the prosecutor, was a middle-aged woman from Earth 7. She was experienced and "by-the-book."

Ortees testified in his own defense. He was cool under pressure and was in command of the facts.

One point that seemed to be troublesome for Ortees on cross-examination was the timeline. Agent Sraymlat wrote his report about the plan for his future son to be a prime minister *before* the strategy meeting for the agents in England, and Agent Qlat wrote about working against Andrew Jackson before the agents in the United States had their meeting. While it was difficult to prove Ortees gave orders on 37529.7.2 that violated Confederation policy, there appeared to be a pattern in place prior to that time of looseness with regard to the Noninterference Protocol.

The following morning, the judges rendered their verdict. They dropped the charge of violating the Noninterference Protocol. In the first degree, that charge could have carried the death penalty, although the prosecutor had never indicated that Ortees had committed First Degree Interference. They also said there was insufficient evidence that Ortees had been carrying on a non-sanctioned mission. However, they upgraded the charge of willful deception of his superior agents to conspiracy to violate the Noninterference Protocol.

The judges ruled that Ortees be suspended with pay from his role in the Interplanetary Intelligence Service pending trial. He was also forbidden to leave Earth 1.

After the hearing, Smapront cautioned his client that it could be months before a trial could take place. The field agents on Earth 48 would need to be deposed, and the logistics of setting up depositions with agents on long-term assignments was not easy.

During his suspension, Ortees was allowed to come into the office, but there was nothing for him to do. He spent a lot of time reading, but his security clearance was lowered. He wanted to read about the Empire, but the more interesting material was not available to him.

Smapront had submitted a motion to bar Keepetta from replacing Ortees as Team Leader for Earth 48 until after the trial, and the motion was granted. From a personal standpoint, this was good for Ortees, but not for his agents in England, particularly with regard to getting Sraymlat into the Foreign Office.

Station 48-3 had no team leader on board, and there had not been anyone directing surface operations there for a long time. Ortees could imagine what it was like for his agents in England. All three of them were young. Only Svavapass had more than five years of field experience.

Ortees was concerned for them. And his concerns were not unfounded.

8.

Trial in Orbit

Urelt's heart sank as he heard the news that his regiment was being sent to Upper Canada. In a sense, he was not surprised. It was inevitable that his unit would be sent someplace. With the wars against Napoleon being over, he did not see the value to the Interplanetary Intelligence Service for him to be sitting in the woods on a sparsely populated continent. While Ortees was absent, Urelt doubted he would ever get a job in the Foreign Office.

It was likely that the Interplanetary Intelligence Service would retire his alias of Captain Greenhill and assign him to some other role, and he would be away from his fiancé, who was well placed to gain good intelligence. His five-year deployment on Earth 48 had less than a year to go.

On what was likely to be his last weekend leave before his regiment was sent out, Urelt made his way to London to meet with Unni.

"What can we do?" he asked. "We won't be able to see each other."

Urelt reached out and took Unni's hand.

"This delay in getting you a position in government is very bad in every way," Unni agreed. "Even if you opt to 'come in' at the end of your five-year deployment, I would still have two years to go. We would have to wait three years to marry."

"And this is no longer about delaying the birth of Prime Minister Greenhill," Urelt rued. "Prime Minister Greenhill simply will never occur. The Service couldn't give me a new alias. It would be too risky. What if someone Greenhill knew were to recognize my new alias?"

"This whole plan to accelerate Britain's technical progress is over," Unni conceded. "It was a brilliant idea because it could have been in motion for decades without violating the Noninterference Protocol. The Service would have had an option to save this planet from attack or even occupation."

"It could have worked," Urelt agreed. "Too bad old Ortees had to go and get himself in political trouble. I always knew he was a bit of a maverick."

Unni was taken aback. She withdrew her hand from Urelt's suddenly. Then she let it out.

"Urelt, do you know why Ortees got into political trouble?"

"Something to do with the Noninterference Protocol, I think."

"Right, but do you know what got this conflict going?"

"Do you?" Urelt asked nervously.

"Yes. Ortees told me."

Unni explained how Vlaris had become alarmed at Urelt's report, and how Vlaris went to Keepetta and got Ortees in hot water.

"That report was for Ortees. How was I to know anyone else would ever read it?"

"Anything you upload goes into the project file, Urelt. I am afraid your looseness is the cause of this entire firestorm we are in."

"My report could not possibly have ignited a firestorm. What I wrote was just an idea. I did not chronicle any violation of protocol. Surely this has to be something Ori wrote, maybe something about his relationship with the Duke of Wellington. You know how doctrinaire he can be sometimes."

"No, Urelt. Ori did not write anything of that nature."

"I wouldn't be so sure."

"Ortees read all of the reports, and he told me what was in them. It was not Ori's report."

Urelt was stunned. He gazed beyond Unni at the wall. For a moment, he saw the implications of his momentary lapse in discretion.

"How do we fix this, Unni?" he asked after a long pause.

"I don't know. It is out of our hands."

"I have been the link holding this team together," Urelt declared. "You can't just go visit with Svavapass. How will we go on?"

"The two of us will have to work independently, Ori with his social contacts, and I with the documents that I will be exposed to. We will just continue to watch and report what we see."

A starship entered orbit around Earth 48 on 37529.10.38 (April 8, 1818, by the natives' calendar). The passengers included Sral Vlaris, Saibert Ortees, Orcha Lyba, and Utrat Smapront, Ortees's defense attorney.

Vlaris sent a request to Station 48-3 to give him the positions of the agents on the surface of the planet. Grugar Tekalta soon located all nine field agents by their transponders and began to send them messages. They were going to be summoned to testify. Tekalta immediately noticed that Agent Sraymlat was at sea. This was going to present a problem in obtaining his testimony.

Three days later, a transport landed outside of Potsdam in Prussia and picked up Agent Svortomit. He was scheduled to testify first. As was the usual procedure, the encounter took place on a Saturday night. Metchavork was also picked up that night in case they could work in two witnesses in the same night. He was in Magdeburg. The two agents were taken to the starship.

Svortomit sat in the witness stand, with the three judges behind him to his right. In front of him was the prosecutor's bench. Vlaris was seated with Lyba, the prosecutor, occasionally whispering comments to her. To her left was the bench, where Smapront was seated, and further to the left was the defendant's docket, where Ortees was seated.

Svortomit's testimony helped the defense. He was asked if he had ever been directed by Team Leader Ortees to do anything to influence the course of development on Earth 48 in general or in Prussia specifically. Svortomit emphatically answered no. Svortomit denied ever hearing anything from Ortees to himself or any other agent that violated the Noninterference Protocol.

Similarly, Metchavork was asked the same things, many times in many ways by the prosecutor, and he denied that Ortees had ever directed him or any other agent to influence the course of development on Earth 48. When Metchavork was asked about the British Empire specifically, Metchavork admitted that he had no way of knowing what may have been said or directed in private discussions with the agents assigned there. But he knew of no such directive from Ortees and strongly doubted such a directive was ever given.

On cross-examination, Smapront asked Metchavork how he could be so sure no such directive had been given to Svavapass, Vlaytork or Sraymlat. Lyba objected to the question, claiming that it called for speculation on the part of the witness. But the judges overruled the objection on the grounds that this was a conspiracy trial, and the opinion of one of the defendant's subordinates was relevant.

Metchavork answered, "Ortees is of the questionable opinion that the faction that will prevail on Earth 48 is the United States of America. As unlikely as that is, I doubt that anyone who held that opinion would try to accelerate the development of the planet by influencing the British Empire. Would he not rather try to influence the trajectory of the United States? Ortees may hold unusual opinions, but he is still a logical man. That is why I strongly doubt the allegations that Ortees is trying to influence the British Empire."

The following weekend, the transport picked up Agents Lorbank and Duvass from a spot just outside Paris. The two agents also denied having heard any talk about violating the Noninterference Protocol. The agents also stressed that Ortees, having been a field agent himself for many years, was a supportive and effective team leader.

Lorbank said he did recall some talk about influencing Wellington, but that comment was made by Agents Svavapass and Sraymlat while Vlaris was still the team leader. And since Wellington was not in any important political office at the time, the talk was only hypothetical.

The judges decided that the next agents to testify should be those in the United States of America. In particular, they wanted to hear from Qlat, who had written about wanting to help prevent a certain popular general Andrew Jackson from being elected to that nation's highest office.

The following weekend, Qlat and Srot gave testimonies that corroborated the other agents' testimonies, that Ortees did not ever ask them to violate the Noninterference Protocol. Srot had worked in the field with Ortees and testified that there was no hint of his wanting to influence Spain or its colonies.

Qlat was asked about his plans to assist a political campaign to prevent Andrew Jackson from becoming president of the United States.

"You know that a Jackson presidency would be inconvenient for Ortees's plans to accelerate the development of Earth 48," the prosecutor reminded him. "This is why Ortees wanted you to campaign against Jackson, right?"

"No, I wanted to campaign against Jackson because his views on banking were inconvenient for native bankers," Qlat retorted. "My alias is a banker from New York, the largest native settlement in the United States of America. For a New York banker *not* to oppose Jackson given his views on banks would seem odd and out of place. Our orders are to blend in with the natives."

After Qlat's testimony, Smapront moved that the charges be dropped. "This trial has gone on for a long time. The testimony of the field agents has contradicted the charges and has provided no evidence of any wrongdoing. We are disrupting the missions of undercover field agents. It is time to stop this fruitless endeavor."

But Lyba argued that her most important witnesses were the agents working in the British Empire. They had not been heard from yet.

The judges retreated to a private room. After two hours of debate, they denied the motion to dismiss the charges. The next weekend, Svavapass and Vlaytork would be deposed.

Because neither agent wanted to be late, they both ended up at the rendezvous point, a freshly planted field, before sunset and had to wait more than an hour for the spacecraft to land. They had not seen each other in months, and the meeting was very awkward. They talked about their respective missions.

Unni told Ori that some of the communications she had seen indicated that the government was in a financial straight and was trying to cut back spending anywhere it could. Ori told Unni about the upcoming wedding of the Duke of Kent and Strathearn with Princess Victoria. The wedding was to take place in Coburg, a German state. One thing they did not talk about very much was Special Agent Ortees.

Unni Vlaytork's presence was hard for Ori Svavapass to fathom without his feelings rising up. He still had not fully gotten over her, and he had to exercise his self-control to keep his conversation on the highest plain of professionalism. After all, she was spoken for.

The sun set. At long last, they could see the spacecraft appear, a small spot of light in the night sky at first, and eventually a disk. When the vehicle landed, the two wasted no time climbing aboard. As soon as they were seated, Major Hortu lifted off.

The agents filed their reports on all the intelligence they had gathered and retired to bed. After several hours, they were given a wakeup call. Agent Vlaytork was called to testify first. Agent Svavapass was not allowed to be present during her deposition.

The prosecutor probed the matter of Ortees's intentions in having Vlaytork serve as a nanny to the expected child of Princess Charlotte. Unni said that she saw her function to be to bond with the child. She admitted that she would be an influence to the child, had it been born alive.

"Don't all nannies influence the children they serve?" she testified.

Lyba suddenly smiled and took a step toward the witness stand. "Do I understand correctly that you are engaged to be married?"

Smapront jumped out of his seat. "Objection; irrelevant."

"Overruled," one of the judges responded. He turned to Unni. "Answer the question."

"Yes, I am engaged," Unni replied, unconsciously stroking the part of her uniform that concealed her engagement necklace.

"To whom?"

"Objection," Smapront interrupted from his seat.

The same judge quickly overruled the defense attorney.

"To Agent Urelt Sraymlat," Unni answered.

"Do you and Agent Sraymlat plan to have children in your field of assignment?" Lyba probed.

Smapront rose from his seat, but the judge motioned for him to sit down before he could object. "Mr. Smapront, this question is very relevant to this case."

"According to the reports on file, you view your upcoming marriage as an opportunity to bring forth 'a future British prime minister.' Am I right?"

Unni moved forward in her chair. "We plan to have children, but it is a huge leap to say…"

"Am I right?"

The judge seated in the center of the three banged his cylindrical silver gavel. "Allow the witness to answer the question."

"This was a consideration," Unni admitted, "but we did not plan to do anything to influence the development of Earth 48 without the go-ahead from the Interplanetary Intelligence Service."

Lyba smiled incredulously. "Agent Vlaytork, is it your testimony that you plan to have one or more children and then ask permission to waive a Confederation policy that has been in place for centuries?"

Unni calmly looked at the panel of judges. "Indeed, the Noninterference Protocol has been in place for a long time, and we were aware that any change in policy would be long in coming. But any prospective future cabinet member or prime minister would not attain office for forty to fifty years. It is not unreasonable to expect that the Confederation might change its policy over that timeframe, given the recent discovery of an aggressive star empire. Certain kinds of intervention might become sanctioned as we come to better understand the threat we face. The Service would have a fifty-year head start, should such a plan be needed."

Lyba had a sarcastic grin. "You were assigned to be a nanny to an expected heir to the throne of a major faction on Earth 48, Agent Vlaytork. Would you have the court believe that you were going to wait fifty years to influence this prince?"

"Objection!"

"Sustained."

"I withdraw the question. Your witness." Lyba motioned to Smapront.

On cross examination from Smapront, Unni clarified that the influence she intended to exert on the offspring of Princess Charlotte was to be a moral influence, nothing more. She also emphasized that the idea of raising future government officials was a voluntary proposal by Sraymlat and herself, and not at all a directive from Ortees.

When Lyba accused Unni on redirect of taking advantage of an "atmosphere of looseness" bred by the defendant with regard to noninterference, Unni responded, "You mistake our team's proactive approach to the unique situation on Earth 48 for looseness. I question the morality of your rigid interpretation of the Noninterference Protocol with regard to a planet whose people are in danger of invasion by the Empire with all the suffering that will entail."

Unni looked down from the witness stand to the docket where Ortees was seated. He looked back at her with a faint but distinct smile of approval.

After a few questions from Smapront, Unni was allowed to step down. Having already testified, she was allowed to remain in the room when Agent Svavapass was called to the stand.

After some initial questions about Ori's role in the Interplanetary Intelligence Service, Lyba began to ask about the agent's relationships with native politicians and with the Duke of Wellington. Ori sat in an upright and rigid position in the witness stand, answering the prosecutor's questions with almost no gestures or movement.

"We may summarize your testimony that you used your relationships with powerful people to learn about public policy in the British Empire," Lyba concluded.

"That would be a fair assessment," Ori agreed.

"And to pass everything you learned to Special Agent Ortees?"

"Correct."

"And to influence these high-ranking officials so as to hasten the technical and cultural development of the Empire."

"Objection!"

Before Smapront could state his grounds for his objection, one of the judges waved her silver gavel in a gesture understood by Confederation attorneys to mean that they were to cease speaking. "Overruled. This question touches a central matter of this case."

Ori turned his head toward Smapront and curled his lips to express his annoyance. "Could you repeat the question please?"

"Did your duties include influencing high-ranking officials in the British Empire so as to hasten its technical and cultural development?"

Ori stiffened in his chair. "No, they did not."

"Did Special Agent Ortees ask you to influence these high-ranking officials…?"

"No."

"Or imply that you were to do so?"

Smapront leaped from his seat. "Objection! Asked and answered!"

The same judge rapidly overruled the objection.

Ori scowled at the prosecutor. "Special Agent Ortees *never* explicitly or implicitly commanded me to influence any government official to change the course of the development of the British Empire."

"So it was *your* idea to try to influence policy in that native faction?"

"Objection!"

"Sustained."

Lyba turned to the three-judge panel. "May it please the court to consider the sworn testimony of Special Agent Sral Vlaris that this witness discussed with him on 37527.7.6 a plan to use his friendship with the Duke of Wellington to influence policy."

The judge seated in the center shook his head in reluctant acquiescence. "Proceed, but cautiously."

Ori did not wait for Lyba to repeat the question. "It is true that Sraymlat and I originated the idea to help steer the natives in the right direction, but we sought the approval of our team leader on the date to which you referred, 37527.7.6. Vlaris was still the team leader at that time, and we put our idea before him to obtain his approval before acting."

"You know and understand the Noninterference Protocol," the prosecutor reminded the witness, "so why might you think it was permissible to influence the Duke or any native official at all?"

At this point, Ori began to loosen up, even sometimes gesturing with his left hand.

"That protocol forbids agents of the Confederation from imparting knowledge or technology or any aid to another planet before that planet has joined the Confederation," Ori explained. "But I see nothing wrong with pointing natives in the right direction so that they might advance under their own power. That is different from giving them a technology."

"And what gives you the right to make that kind of decision, Agent Sva-vapass?" the prosecutor asked sternly.

"Every move I make is with the knowledge and consent of my superiors," Ori maintained.

"So Special Agent Ortees put you up to this then?"

"No, Ma'am," Ori replied. "Ortees is the kind of team leader that interacts with his agents, a conduit through which information and action is passed up and down the chain of command. He is an excellent team leader, and all the agents know he has our back."

"And you obviously have his," she countered. "It appears to me that you are influencing a government official of a native planet that is not yet in the Confederation."

"The Duke of Wellington is not yet in office. If he reaches office, and an opportunity arises for me to give him advice, I would check with my superiors before I acted. And I might add that the Duke of Wellington is an independent thinker and not easily influenced."

No longer the statue he had been earlier in his testimony, Ori was now leaning forward in this seat looking Lyba straight in the eyes and tapping the rail to emphasize the main words he was speaking.

"Ortees did *not* put me up to *anything*, and if my behavior was wrong in *any* way, I would bear the responsibility.

He added, "I believe the Confederation needs to review its Noninterference Protocol. Its purpose is to spare the Confederation from the debacle of Earth 5 centuries ago. But what if a planet is facing the tragic fate of conquest and enslavement by an aggressive empire? Don't we have an *obligation* to protect them or at least prepare them?"

Unni was taken by surprise by the flexibility and boldness of the usually doctrinaire Svavapass. She had never seen that side of him before. She nodded with approval as he made that statement. Ori in turn was encouraged by the look of approval from Unni. He did not notice Ortees's smile.

"I have a good mind to throw you into the docket with Ortees and with Agent Vlaytork as well!" Lyba shot back. "Know for a certainty that if you or Vlaytork or Sraymlat deviate so much as one degree from the Noninterference Protocol, I will…"

One of the judges slammed his silver gavel onto the table. "This witness is not on trial. I must admonish you to refrain from such tirades in this court!"

After the hearing, Ori and Unni were directed to the docking port where their transport was. But Unni did not want to return to Earth 48. She wanted to stay aloft so that she would see Urelt when he came aboard. Without a team leader, she did not know whom to ask, so she approached her former team leader, Vlaris.

"Don't you have a position in the natives' Foreign Office?" Vlaris asked.

"I was given leave," she replied. "They believe I am visiting my mother in the country."

"They have not yet devised paid leave on this planet," Vlaris observed. "How will Jenny Carter afford this leave?"

Unni had not considered that. Her alias, like many women in England, lived from hand to mouth. But she was desperate to see Urelt and was ready to make sacrifices.

Ori overheard her request. "I can take care of that," he assured her.

Vlaris raised an eyebrow and granted her request.

Ori went to the storage area just before the portal that led out of the artificial gravity area toward the docking stations. He quickly dressed into his British Army uniform and made his way to Unni with several British coins. "Weatherby is wealthy and can afford to give you these, Jenny," he told her with an ironic grin.

"Thank you, kind sir," she replied in English.

The two shared a brief chuckle. Then Ori made his way back to the docking station where a transport was waiting. It was then that he suddenly became conscious of the spectacle that he was, walking in Technology Level 8 native clothing among uniformed starship personnel.

Unni made her way to her assigned cabin. She happened to pass the Subdirector, who was walking alone. The Subdirector stopped and turned around.

"Agent Vlaytork, I am beginning to see that Ortees is innocent of these charges. I regret that I let them go this far. But I would be careful if I were you. They may acquit Ortees and come after the three of you."

Unni understood that Keepetta was referring to Ori and Urelt. She was going to reply, but Keepetta continued. "It is Vlaris who persuaded me to charge Ortees. He is overly sensitive, even uptight concerning noninterference. And I cannot fathom why."

By that time, Vlaris had reached his quarters. He had closed his door and sat down in his comfortable chair. He activated an audio file on his computer and closed his eyes. It was a recording he had secretly made years before in a concert hall in Vienna of the fortieth symphony of his favorite native composer.

It was not a perfect recording, as one could hear some coughing and rustling from the audience. And if one knew what to listen for, one could also hear the faint sobs of young Vlaris. And even now, twenty-six years after the fact, Vlaris was still mourning the death of Wolfgang Amadeus Mozart.

9.
Time to Think Things Over

Unni's request to ride the transport down to Upper Canada was denied. She had wanted to get some extra time with Urelt, but the court did not want her mingling with him until after he had testified. The court had been in recess for days since Ori had concluded his testimony.

The prosecutor wasted little time cutting to the heart of the controversy: she asked Urelt what he had meant when he wrote about marrying and becoming the father of a future prime minister who could accelerate Britain's technical development.

"That was the plan to have Earth 48 ready to join the Confederation before the Empire got here," Urelt explained. "It had been estimated that Earth 48 has only about one to two hundred years before it is attacked, and it is about 275 years away from being ready for admission to the Confederation. Obviously, the rate of development would need to double.

"Our job was to have a son on Earth 48 and school him well. He was not to know he was not of Earth 48 and would never hear a word of Grellish. While he grew, Svavapass and I were to strengthen our political contacts to prepare the boy for a rise to high position."

The prosecutor could barely hide her delight. "Did Ortees have a role in this plan?"

"He was with Svavapass and Unni and me when we planned it. He said his role was to 'make this program palatable to the Commission by making this a very indirect form of interference.' He told us it might be years before this plan is sanctioned, but he figured that by then our agents would be fighting the Empire, even engaging in sabotage and assassinations and counterespionage. I distinctly remember him saying this plan would become the model for Earths 46, 47, and 49."

"Did it not concern you that this sort of operation was in contradiction of the Noninterference Protocol?"

"Of course it did," Urelt admitted. "But Ortees assured us not to worry about that. He told us to leave the internal politics to him. So what is a young agent to do? Follow orders and not worry. He was older and wiser. We naturally assumed it must be permissible to carry out this operation if our superior officer said so. We were to leave the policy implications to our team leader and follow orders."

"So then, Agent Sraymlat, you were ordered to interfere in the course of the development of Earth 48, right?"

"Well, I would not go so far as to say we were ordered, but…"

"In fact, you already said the word 'orders' twice…"

"What I meant was…"

Smapront rose to his feet. "Objection! The prosecution is twisting the witness's words."

"Overruled," the chief judge immediately responded. "Continue."

"I have no further questions," Lyba concluded. "Your witness."

Smapront tried to undo the damage on cross examination. He got Urelt to say that he misspoke, and that 'orders' was too strong a word. But when questioned about the plan to have sons and usher them into higher office, Urelt only reaffirmed that he was only doing what he felt Ortees wanted him to do.

Urelt was clearly trying to protect himself, struggling to avoid appearance of wrongdoing on his own part. This made it difficult for Smapront to set the record straight during cross examination. As he fended off questions from Smapront, Urelt never noticed Unni's fallen countenance.

After Urelt's testimony, the court went into recess. The judges set a time the following day for closing arguments.

After the recess, Urelt approached Unni. They walked together into the dining hall and ate together at a small table. As they ate, Urelt related the story of his voyage across the Atlantic Ocean on a ship powered only by sails. Unni said little.

After dinner, the two retreated to Urelt's quarters. They needed to talk about their future and how to handle the fact that their aliases were assigned to roles thousands of miles apart.

"I have been doing some thinking," Urelt began. "Captain Greenhill could be sent anywhere on this planet, but Jenny Carter will always be in London. At first I thought I could ask our new team leader's permission if I could leave the army and pursue a career of some kind in London…"

"What makes you think we would have a new team leader, Urelt?" Unni interrupted him.

"Ortees or whoever replaces him—anyway, then I got to thinking. Why don't we leave the Interplanetary Intelligence Service when our contracts expire? I have a few months to go and you have just two years. We could go back to Earth 19. With our knowledge of Grellish and our service records, we could each get a job with some interplanetary corporation and live comfortably and raise a family."

Unni did not say anything.

"You've been very quiet tonight," Urelt observed. "I would like to know what you are thinking."

"First, I would like to know what *you* were thinking when you were testifying today," Unni responded. "That Ortees put you up to everything you did? I suppose he put you up to marrying me too?"

"Unni, don't be that way! It is simply that the direction of the questions was beginning to look as if the prosecutor was interested in indicting you or me. That is why I spun the story that way. I did it for us."

"For us? You would sacrifice another agent's career and reputation for us?"

"You see, what I meant was…"

"I am wondering if there should be an 'us,'" Unni declared.

"Unni…"

"I was all alone on my first mission and there were only two men who really knew me and one of them was too serious and rigid, too mission-focused for my liking, so I fell for the other. But I think I acted too quickly. I made a mistake."

Unni took off her engagement necklace and handed it back to Urelt.

"Unni, please reconsider," Urelt pleaded.

"I need time to think things over," Unni replied. "I just need time."

"I suppose we would not be able to see each other much for the next two years anyway. But please keep this necklace while you think this through. You are very special to me."

Urelt held out the necklace, but Unni did not take it.

"I need time to think things over," she repeated. Then she turned and left the room.

Unni went to her cabin and wept.

Several hours later, Urelt was placed on board a transport and sent back to Canada. Unni declined to return to Earth 48. She wanted to stay aloft until the trial was over.

The next day, the two attorneys gave their closing arguments. They were predictable. Lyba reiterated every shred of evidence that suggested Ortees had an agenda to accelerate the development of Earth 48 generally and the British Empire specifically. She quoted Urelt's testimony. "If this isn't evidence of a conspiracy to ignore the Noninterference Protocol, I do not know what is. You heard it for yourselves."

Smapront recapped all of the testimony by agents that they never knew Ortees to want to interfere with the development of Earth 48. He emphasized that Ortees had a plan merely to put the Interplanetary Intelligence Service and the Confederation into position where they would have options years from now to strengthen their strategic position against an expanding aggressive empire. "There is no evidence that Ortees would have crossed the line and acted to interfere without the consent of the Service. I ask you to find this defendant not guilty."

After the closing arguments, the judges retreated to a private chamber to deliberate.

Hours went by. Ortees spent the time with his defense attorney. Unni spent the time alone in her quarters, trying to fathom what had just occurred in her life and what she was going to do in the future. From her vantage point in the Foreign Office, she did learn a few things about British foreign policy that could help the Service understand global politics on Earth 48. But the main reason she had been sent there was as a stepping stone for a marriage that was now in doubt.

Unni found Urelt's lack of integrity to be troubling. Was that not an undesirable character flaw? Or was it perhaps an asset that would be needed in the dirty world of politics to get her son into high office? Did that even matter? The Subdirector and everyone else knew that if she were on Earth 48 married to Urelt there would be children, and they would always suspect the children would be ministers-in-training.

At mealtime, Unni went to the dining hall. She got her food and was about to sit when she saw Ortees waving, beckoning her to join him. She picked up her tray and went to the table where Ortees and Smapront were seated.

Ortees noticed her fallen countenance and her red face. "Please don't be so glum," he said. "You worry too much for your Uncle Sebastian."

"That it is taking this long to deliberate is a good sign," Smapront added. "It means we planted a lot of doubt in the judges' minds. If they were weighing Sraymlat's testimony heavily, they would have finished by now."

When Smapront mentioned Urelt's name, a tear formed in Unni's eye.

"What is the matter, Unni?" Ortees asked. But he knew the answer before she spoke.

Unni told Ortees exactly what had occurred between Urelt and her. "I need time to think things over." How many times had she said that to others and herself in the past day?

Ortees spent the next hour comforting the young agent, as if his own life and career were not at stake. Soon the three of them were alone in the empty dining hall.

Then Smapront received a beep in his communicator. "We need to return to court. A verdict has been reached."

Only then did Ortees show any sign of anxiety. The three made their way to the makeshift courtroom. Ortees and Smapront took their places at the defense bench and docket. Unni sat in the gallery.

When the judges were seated, they asked Ortees to rise.

The chief of the panel then stated, "Special Agent Saibert Ortees, with regard to the charge of conspiracy to violate the Noninterference Protocol, this court finds you...Not Guilty."

Ortees was visibly relieved. Smapront's face lit up with delight. Unni smiled for the first time in a day. Lyba did not react at all. Subdirector Keepetta seemed unsurprised. Vlaris scowled.

"However," the judge continued, "I would exhort you in the future to put forth a better effort to communicate with your superior officers in the Service. This verdict in no way protects your position as Team Leader for Earth 48; your role is at the discretion of the Subdirector. This case is dismissed."

Several agents including Unni huddled around Ortees to congratulate him. The Subdirector came forward and tapped Ortees. "Meet me in my office in one hour," she commanded.

As Ortees walked to her office, he was under no illusion that things would go back to the way they had been before. He expected the Subdirector to remove him as Team Leader for Earth 48. He only wanted to know what his new role would be. Perhaps it would be a desk job in Tlat Mlang.

Subdirector Keepetta courteously asked him to sit down. She apologized for the ordeal he had been put through in the past few months. And she did indeed inform him that he was no longer assigned to Earth 48 as its team leader or in any other capacity.

"While you were suspended, there have been sweeping changes in this agency," she explained. "These changes are in response to the threat the Empire poses to our peace and freedom. We have had to open a whole new branch of the Service, the Bureau of Protective Action. The Noninterference Protocol does not apply to that office. It only applies to the Bureau of Exploratory Surveillance, which has jurisdiction over Earth 48.

"And since you seem so fond of taking action, you have been assigned to the new office. You have been appointed Team Leader for Earth 55, an occupied planet inside the Empire."

Keepetta explained that experienced agents were badly needed by the new Bureau of Protective Action. As a result, every team needed to give up some personnel for the formation of the new teams in the occupied territory.

"What is my mission exactly?" Ortees asked.

"You are to learn the languages of the occupied peoples, and find out as much as you can about the enemy, their capabilities, and how to stop them. You will have access to documents with all we know about the Empire and its primary language. You will be in an orbital space station with shuttles, and spies will be blending in among the occupied people to learn what they can."

"Does the Empire know the Confederation exists?"

"The short answer is no, but we are not fully certain."

"The Empire is technically sophisticated. How will we hide our orbital spacecraft?" Ortees asked.

"Using the same technologies we perfected for making our spacecraft undetectable to Technology Level 11 planets. We had developed the next generation of stealth but never needed it until now."

Ortees was given a list of agents to select from in building his team. The list included analysts, field agents, and long-term undercover agents from planets under surveillance by the older arm of the agency. The list was already picked over, as Ortees was late getting into the game. There were a few names from the Earth 48 team, including Huha Srot and Urelt Sraymlat. He was told that there should be more names, but the new team leader had not yet completed his designation as to who was shielded from the draft.

"Has a new team leader been selected for Earth 48?" Ortees was interested to know.

"Yes. Vlaris is down on the surface informing the agent of his promotion. It has not been announced yet, but I suppose he knows, so I can tell you: it is Agent Sreedro Metchavork."

"Metchavork? I am not sure if he is the right choice," Ortees opined. "He is a good agent but…"

"Metchavork is the senior agent on Earth 48. He has the experience and the knowledge of the team."

"He is also drunk with German nationalism. He will probably focus all of his resources on German-speaking states."

"I am aware of this matter," Keepetta acknowledged. "In Tlat Mlang some senior officials in the Service call him 'von Metchavork.'"

The two had a momentary chuckle, their first in months.

"But the only other option was to find someone from outside the team," Keepetta continued. "Right now, with the reorganization, that would be next to impossible. And who knows? Perhaps he will not be so drunk when we remove him from the saloon."

"Well said," Ortees agreed.

After the meeting, Ortees found Unni and told her the news of his appointment as Team Leader for Earth 55.

Unni immediately asked Ortees if she could come with him.

"That would be very easy to arrange," Ortees said. "Team leaders are being pressed by the leadership to donate trained agents to the new branch of the Service. And I would be glad to have you, but…"

"But what?"

"Unni, you don't look like the people on Earth 55. They are darker-skinned and have black hair and brown eyes. They look more like the people from the eastern part of Continent 1 on Earth 48. You would never be able to blend in there."

"I could be an analyst again," she offered. "You know that I am a linguist, and you will need help figuring out the native languages there."

"You speak English like a native. I doubt Metchavork would let you go."

Vlaytork was stunned. "Metchavork? Is that our new team leader? What use would he have for me?"

"I heard your German is pretty good…"

"Please, Uncle Sebastian, please consider my request."

When Unni called him Uncle Sebastian, Ortees was touched. "I will consider it. Are you really sure you don't want to proceed with marrying Urelt?"

"I need time to think. A lot of time," she replied. "Getting away from this planet would help me clear my mind."

"I will consider your request," Ortees promised her. "But you see, a lot has happened today. I need time to think too."

10.

Reorganization of the Team

Urelt felt the pulses from the transponder in his shoulder. He was being summoned to the landing point to meet with a transport.

"Again?" he thought to himself. "I was just up there." He began to worry that Ortees had been acquitted and was calling him to reprimand him for his testimony. Or maybe Ortees was convicted and now they were going to indict the agents under him. He left the stockade that functioned as a base for his regiment. He told the sentry he needed to catch up with a patrol. It was the early evening and the sun was setting.

Urelt needed to cross a wooded area about one mile across to reach the meadow where the transport would be waiting. The woods would be the most dangerous part, and Urelt was still getting used to Canada.

He was almost out of the woods when he was accosted by two Indians. The British had a treaty with the Iroquois, but these looked like Hurons.

Before he knew what had happened, the Indians had taken his musket and his sword. One of his assailants pointed a spear at him. The other stripped him, throwing his uniform to the ground. Urelt was terrified.

Then the Indians hauled him into the clearing. It was dusk, but Urelt could see a red glow off to the east. He knew that was the transport. If only someone on board noticed his plight!

It seemed the Indians were hauling him in the direction of the ship. Maybe someone would come out with a stun gun and rescue him. If he could just get close enough to the vehicle.

Urelt pretended to trip, and broke the grip one of the Indians had on his upper left arm. He struck the other with his left arm, causing him also to lose his grip. Now free, Urelt began to run half-naked toward the spacecraft.

The Indians gave chase. They were laughing. That made Urelt angry. Then he heard the spear whiz by to his right. They had missed! He had a chance.

His feet were in pain, running on the ground without his boots, but he maintained a lead.

As he approached the vehicle, he hoped that the Indians would become frightened and run away, but they did not. He hoped someone inside the vehicle would come out and help him, but no one emerged.

Urelt reached the ladder and climbed, barefooted as quickly as he could. As his head broke the plane of the floor, he noticed that no one was on the lower deck. By the time he reached the hatch controls, one of the Indians was already partly above the plane of the floor. Now a safety device would prevent the hatch from closing.

"Would someone please help me!" He cried in Grellish. No one came. The first Indian was now on board, and the second was almost up the ladder. Urelt started up the second ladder to the upper deck, but the first Indian grabbed his ankle and prevented his ascent. The other went to the cabinet and pulled out a silver flight suit.

In clear Grellish, the Indian said, "Don't you think you ought to put this on before you go up there?"

Urelt was too shocked to answer.

"I am Agent Lorku," he said. "I am new to the Earth 48 team."

"And I am Agent Mlai," the other said. "Didn't you recognize me?"

Urelt stared at him, drawing a blank. "The beggar outside of Svavapass's townhouse?"

Mlai grinned and said in English, "Beg yer pardon, Guvna. Might you 'elp a poor man in need?"

"I guess we were never formally introduced," Mlai concluded.

Agents Lorku and Mlai had a belly laugh.

"Very funny, fellas," Urelt said with annoyance. "I could have gotten hurt out there."

"Will you spies stop fooling around and get up here so we can leave?" the humorless pilot barked.

The two "Indians" climbed up to the upper deck while Urelt quickly got dressed.

"I suppose the William Greenhill alias has been retired," Urelt observed as the spacecraft lifted off.

"They will find your uniform and the spear and assume the worst," Mlai affirmed.

"Wait, wait!" Urelt called out. "We have to go back. My medical packet was in my inside pocket!"

"You mean this?" Lorku asked as he tossed Urelt his emergency medical kit.

"Come on, Sraymlat, we're professionals," Mlai chided.

Urelt groaned.

Metchavork rode one hundred miles by horse-driven carriage from Berlin to Magdeburg to see Agent Svortomit. It was early May and still cool in Prussia, especially at night.

Lt. Dieter Dehrmann was now stationed at a military base in Magdeburg, near Prussia's western frontier. Oberst Friedrich von Mecklenburg arrived at the base in the early evening. Soon after his arrival he asked to meet with Dehrmann. The two men met in the administrative building, which was mostly vacant at that hour.

When the two were seated and the door was shut, Metchavork announced to Svortomit that he had been promoted.

"You are now a general?" Svortomit asked with excitement.

"Dummkopf!" Metchavork replied in jest. "I am now Team Leader for Earth 48."

"Very interesting!" Svortomit replied. "This has its possibilities."

"We can now put our plan in place!" Metchavork exclaimed with a gleam in his eye. He explained to Svortomit the changes in the organization of the Interplanetary Intelligence Service.

"Ortees is taking Vlaytork with him to Earth 55," Metchavork explained. "Srot has also joined the Bureau of Protective Action. I had the alias of Wilhelm Greenhill retired. Sraymlat is on his way back to Tlat Mlang to brush up on his German. After that I am bringing him here under a new alias."

Svortomit was elated that he would be working with his old buddy from the Academy.

"He will be a university professor in the University of Tübingen, Herr Professor Doktor Gerd Wolkenhein. I've almost gotten his appointment worked out. We will be getting four new agents in the next five months. I will place one in Vienna, one in Munich, one in Hannover, and other will work with you in Berlin, where you will soon find yourself transferred."

"Let's see, that leaves Qlat in the United States of America, Lorbank and Duvass in France, and Svavapass all by himself in England. Shouldn't there be a second agent in the British Empire?"

"No, Svavapass can handle it himself. Besides, the British Empire is about to fall."

"It doesn't look that way to me," Svortomit countered. "They are at their zenith."

"For the moment, Dieter, for the moment. Recall what happened the last time the British defeated France in 1763. They raised taxes throughout the empire to pay for the war. And in so doing, they lost thirteen colonies in North America."

"Surely they learned from their mistake..."

"Not quite, Dieter. I am team leader now, and I read Svavapass's last report. The British government discontinued the wartime income tax, but they passed very unpopular "Corn Laws" and now Lord Liverpool is considering a return to the gold standard! Svavapass reports discontent everywhere. I predict their colonies will rebel all over the planet. They are borrowing heavily and cannot afford to put down these uprisings. They are about to lose Canada. I read Sraymlat's last report about the trouble there. They will lose India. In fact, I would not be surprised to see them lose Ireland and Scotland as well.

"And the best is this: King George III has no living legitimate grandchildren," Metchavork declared with glee. "When the last of his children die off, they will have to turn to Germany for an heir to their throne."

"And when the German people unify..." Svortomit began.

"Yes," Metchavork smiled. "England and Wales will be a part of the Reich."

"So, *mein Oberst*, what do we do?"

"You will stay in the military, but all of the new agents will be placed in leading universities to fill all of the brightest young Germans with thoughts of unification. They will have the resources from me to influence other academics as well. Once this movement is turned over to the students, we won't need to do a thing. The natives will do our work for us. In the center of the most advanced continent, there will be a mighty and unified German Reich, where arts and sciences will flourish. War will be mostly absent, as no one would dare attack Germany. Within 150 years, our commissioners will be in Berlin to sign the documents to make Earth 48 a member of the Confederation of Civilized Planets."

"And you don't think you will be caught and put on trial like Ortees?" Svortomit asked cautiously.

"Certainly not! I happen to know from reliable sources that Vlaris got taken to the woodshed over his false accusations against Ortees. His bottom is very warm right now, figuratively speaking. If anyone has any interest in checking our team out with regard to the Noninterference Protocol, they will be looking at Svavapass, not me. By the time anyone thought to look at Germany, we will all be retired and the natives will be carrying on our work with an unstoppable momentum."

"If only we could talk Unni into marrying Ori!" Svortomit joked. "That would really keep the spotlight on England."

"Wouldn't that be convenient," Metchavork agreed. "Too bad Ori is so dull and unlovable."

Mr. and Mrs. Vlaytork stood just outside the door of their home in Yoilafa. It was always hard to say goodbye. Zeri Vlaytork gave her daughter one last hug. "Now Unni, don't let another year go by without visiting!"

The ten days Unni had spent with her parents went by too quickly. Undercover agents often have a lot of unused vacation time, and Unni took the chance to visit her family. Unni's friends and relatives believed that Unni worked for a major interplanetary corporation as a marketing director. Only her father knew the truth.

Unni took a jet to Omtvumx. From there, she caught a spaceship to an orbital spaceport. Commercial surface-to-orbit transports were built for comfort, unlike the transports Unni had been riding to and from Earth 48, which were built for stealth and evasive maneuvers. Earth 19 had two orbital spaceports. Unni preferred the smaller one because it was less congested, but today she was to fly out of the larger one. They were running a special on lower fares. After a few hours, she boarded a commercial starship bound for Tlat Mlang, the capital city of both Earth 1 and the Confederation of Civilized Planets.

Three days later, Unni arrived at Earth 1 for a special training course and briefing for her new duties in the Bureau of Protective Action. She noticed that most of the students were racially similar to the people in the Empire. Many of them came from Earths 4, 18, and 25.

On the first day, the trainer said, "The new motto of the Interplanetary Intelligence Service is 'The eyes and ears of the Confederation.' The old motto, 'Sent to watch but not to affect' pertains only to the Bureau of Exploratory Surveillance. But our bureau does not have any motto. We only have a maxim: to do whatever it takes. All of you transferring in from the other bureau need a paradigm shift. We must learn what our enemy is up to, defeat the enemy, make the galaxy safe for the peace- and freedom-loving planets, and protect our way of life."

The trainees learned enough about the Empire to realize the need for vigilance—and for action. They learned about how the enemy conquered planets, enslaved the natives, and took their natural resources. They learned about the genocide and torture used by the Empire to achieve their means. Apparently, their mother planet, Earth 89, had been taken over by a totalitarian nation that eventually eliminated the people who were racially different from themselves. On every planet they conquered, the Empire spared the people of the race that most resembled themselves and eliminated everyone else.

Agent Vlaytork spent time on the shooting range learning to fire a handheld laser weapon. She had to run obstacle courses. She also had to practice walking in an encapsulated suit with self-contained breathing apparatus. Apparently, they might have to explore ruined cities on the occupied planets that were still radioactive. Toward the end of the course, the class went to Earth 1's largest moon to practice working and exploring in a hostile environment.

After three forty-day months, Agent Vlaytork completed her training. She got permission to take another vacation on Earth 19. Then she was transported by starship to join her team at Earth 55.

Earth 55 had six moons. To avoid detection, the starship came no closer than a half million miles from the planet. The orbital space station, named Station 55-1, was located at a stable point in the same orbit as the largest moon, ahead of the moon in its orbit. Like the moon, the space station circled Earth 55 every nineteen days. The trip to Station 55-1 took about five hours in a transport vehicle accelerating and decelerating at approximately 1g, or 32 feet per second squared. This made for a comfortable ride for the passengers.

Station 55-1 consisted of two large parallel wheels with an axial hub. One wheel contained the work stations and living quarters of the crew. The other wheel was agricultural and provided the feedstock for the food synthesizer. The spinning of the wheels gave much of the space station artificial gravity from centrifugal force. Station 55-1, like its counterparts circling other occupied planets, was designed to avoid detection. It was covered with solar panels and was black, absorbing nearly all of the light it received.

The space station had several defense mechanisms for protection against attack, including six force fields, laser cannons, and nuclear torpedo tubes. The space station also had a propulsion system, but it was mostly used to maintain its orbit. The orbit was theoretically stable, but in fact it was not perfectly so, due to secular perturbations caused by the other moons.

The space station ran by nuclear power and needed to be refueled every two years. However, if the nuclear power core was not refueled, it could also run on solar power. In that mode, the weapons, force fields and the propulsion system would not work, but the life support systems and other essential systems were theoretically sustainable.

Station 55-1 had a capacity for 154 crew members. When Unni and three others arrived, they brought the number of crew members to 73. The crew included analysts, field agents, and military personnel who ran and maintained the station. The field agents were mostly from Earth 18 and Earth 25, people who most resembled the inhabitants and invaders of Earth 55.

There were two leaders on Station 55-1. Captain Oind Burxa of Earth 3 was technically in command as she led the military personnel that ran the station. But since the station was there to serve the Interplanetary Intelligence Service, Special Agent Saibert Ortees, the team leader, was the de facto leader. Ortees was respected and well-liked by everyone on Station 55-1. Despite the difficult conditions associated with the need to avoid detection, morale was high.

Most of the analysts were working on a project assigned by headquarters to determine the population of the planet. This was being done using high resolution imaging of the surface from space. There were no windows on Station 55-1 in the plane of the planet's equator. This was necessary to limit the visibility of the station. To view the planet, one had to look at images captured by external cameras.

Uni often brought up the live images of the planet on her computer screen. Only half of the planet was illuminated at their present position in orbit, but it looked like the other Earths, blue with land forms and white swirls of clouds. The serenity of the view belied the terror that reigned below.

Unni immersed herself in her work, trying to decipher the languages on Earth 55. The analysts were trying to piece together what Earth 55 was like at the time it was overrun.

It still had not been determined what the planet's level of technical development had been. The night side of the planet was almost completely dark, devoid of the bright illuminated spots on other Earths where cities were located. There was one exception, no doubt the invaders' headquarters or capital. The otherwise lack of illumination could mean that electricity had not been invented yet by the time of the invasion or that it had been confiscated and banned.

Three blemishes on the planet's surface were positively identified as locations where hydrogen bombs had been detonated. Roads leading to these spots confirmed that they had been cities and not test sites. At first, some thought that this was evidence of nuclear capability suggesting Technology Level 10. But the nuclides detected from orbital instruments indicated that the blasts occurred about sixty years earlier, right at the time of the invasion. This suggested that the bombs had been dropped by the invaders, not the natives.

A key piece of evidence that Earth 55 had not attained to Technology Level 10 was the absence of space junk in lower orbits. This meant the natives had not yet developed satellites or space flight by the time of the invasion. Spectrographic scans detected low levels of air contamination, indicating either a Level 8 technological development or that the invaders were conducting industrial activity. Instruments detected an occasional flight, no doubt by the invaders. Railroad tracks were also observed in one part of the planet near the equator, but it was unclear who had built them, the natives or the invaders. The invaders did not have an orbital space station, but every fifty to one hundred days, the planet was visited by one of their starships.

Due to the lack of radio transmission from the surface, the strategy for learning the native languages was tiered. First, remote surveillance was used to determine what the natives looked like, including their clothing. Then the clothing was synthesized and agents of racial similarity to the natives would be clandestinely inserted into the populated areas with recording devices on their clothes with both audio and visual capability. These recordings could then be used by analysts to try to decipher their spoken language.

Visitation was tricky because the initial agents could only remain on the surface for a short time to avoid detection. That meant the distance from the drop-off point had to be attainable by foot. On the other hand, the transport could not land too close to the populated areas or it might be sighted.

Ortees chose a more cautious approach. He had been sending his agents among the ruins of cities in the less populated regions. Some of the ruins pre-dated the invasion by centuries. The search teams wanted to find something representative of the civilization at the time they were overrun.

A group of towns was spotted in the southern part of the northern temperate zone that was on a plain near a river. The climate there was semi-arid. There was no evidence in the imaging of any human activity, and the roads between the towns were deserted. The buildings were made mostly of wood. The project team felt that those ghost towns were likely to be recent. After four more days of surveillance and no observed activity, Ortees sent a team of six agents to the surface at that location. All of the agents selected for the mission were racially similar to the natives.

The team spent almost the entire day there and found a number of interesting artifacts. The main street of the town had a number of shops. In front of the shops were hitching posts for horses. They also found a blacksmith shop. Some of the shops had signs in front written in an unknown alphabet. All of these items were photographed and some artifacts were bagged for recovery.

Ominously, there were some round burn marks in the walls of some of the wooden buildings, apparent evidence of laser fire. Some of the affected wood was analyzed using the field kit, and the hypothesis was confirmed.

The greatest find of the day was a mechanical clock. It had ten numbers, indicating that the natives had a twenty-hour day, just like the Confederation. The clock was carefully bagged for study on the space station.

This was the first of a series of expeditions to the surface. Later trips would yield paper books, family portraits, farming tools, eating utensils, dishes, pots, and other artifacts. In almost every town, the burn marks in the wood were also evident. There was no evidence of electrical devices or of internal combustion engines. It was now clear that Earth 55 had been at Technology Level 8 at the time it was plundered—the same level as Earth 48.

The artifacts gave the analysts a window into the natives of the planet below. When they got the clock to run, it kept time fairly commensurately with the rotation of the planet. But the clock ran in the opposite direction from those on most of the planets of the Confederation, just like the clocks in England. The placement of the doorknobs and the shapes of the tools also suggested that the natives were mostly righthanded, another anomaly Earth 55 shared with Earth 48.

Unni began to study the alphabet and the wording on the signs and the books. She sought for some key piece of evidence to crack the code of the natives' written language. She knew that would have to wait until she got a recording of natives speaking. Further, it would require that the natives spoke the same language as was used in the towns that these books had come from.

As Unni studied the artifacts, her heart became heavy. These people were at the same level of development as the English whom she had come to know. She thought of the horror of the invasion. She thought of the friends and acquaintances she had made in England—Gwen, Debbie, the maids in Claremont, the secretaries in the Foreign Office in London, and even the maladroit Katy Keaton. She pictured them panicking, fleeing, suffering, and dying as the world they had built up and had lived in was torn from them.

"This must *never* happen to Earth 48," she said to herself. But what could be done about it?

The captain of the Starship *Mrastlot* entered the bridge. The first officer yielded the conn.

"Report, Commander," the captain ordered.

"All systems are functioning normally, sir," he replied. "The ship is on course. There are no problems to report except for, well, never mind. It's not important."

"I'll be the judge of that, Commander," the captain replied. "Except for what?"

"There have been some complaints by various crew members about the seven spies we are transporting to Earth 48."

"Complaints? What kind of complaints?"

"It seems those seven are a bit unruly, sir," the commander replied uncomfortably. He felt the whole matter was trivial and regretted that he had brought it up. "They are a close-knit group. They sit together at the same table in the dining hall and talk to one another in a native language and behave like the natives."

"I see nothing wrong with that," the captain replied. "They have to get into their roles and act the part. They have to *become* natives. Their lives will depend on it."

"That's what I told the crew," the commander explained. "But today they have been singing native songs."

"Singing native songs? On my ship?"

"Yes, sir. They said that today is the most important holiday on Earth 48. They called it Vinockten or something."

The captain grunted with displeasure. "Oh, just let them sing. We will reach Earth 48 in a day and a half and this will be all over with. Spies! What a bunch of spoiled prima donnas."

Urelt was in the dining hall with his six buddies. Four of them were assigned aliases as college professors in Berlin, Hanover, Munich, and Vienna. The other two would be analysts and performing "arrangements" for Metchavork. Having completed training in Tlat Mlang on Earth 1, they were now very fluent in German and spoke it all of the time.

The seven were very close, and to the chagrin of the other trainees on Earth 1, they had formed a clique. That day, they were celebrating *Weihnachten*, also known on Earth 48 as Christmas.

They annoyed the staff in the dining hall by their lingering, and on that day, they had been overeating and singing boisterously. They had placed a frond of an evergreen tree that they had picked up on a stopover on Earth 32 on the table and had covered it with gaudy trinkets. The frond was dropping needles, and the staff were loath to clean up the mess after the men left.

Just then, Urelt led them in another chorus:

> *O Tannenbaum, o Tannenbaum,*
> *Wie treu sind deine Blätter!*

Ori was in the dining room of his townhouse all alone reading a calculus book he had purchased. He had given his cook and his butler several days off to be with their families for their native holidays. He was alternating between resting and preparing himself for the coming semester at Sandhurst.

Suddenly, there was a knock at the door. He peered out the window and saw a coach parked in front of his door. He got up to answer it. He recognized this visitor as a footman from Apsley House, where the Duke of Wellington lived. He was told that the duke wanted to see him.

When "Major Weatherby" reached Apsley House, he was informed by a visiting Tory member of Parliament that the duke had been appointed two days before to be Master General of the Ordnance. This meant that Wellington was now in the government of the Second Earl of Liverpool, the prime minister. The Master General of the Ordnance was responsible for all fortifications, artillery, military engineers, military supplies, and other such areas important to the army. Wellington had specifically requested that Weatherby come to work for the Board of Ordnance.

Ori accepted the offer at once. A half-hour later, Wellington came downstairs to briefly meet with him. It was then that Ori realized that Wellington's aloofness was going to make his job more difficult. Wellington barely spoke four sentences and returned back upstairs.

Ori was to report to work on Monday, January 4 at the Tower of London. He was to work in the Ordnance Survey, the department responsible for the quality of war materiel purchased by the government.

Ori made haste to see Lt. Col. Keaton to inform him that he was leaving his position at Sandhurst. Keaton was sorry to lose Ori, but he recognized the opportunity. During his visit, Ori did not see Katy. She stayed in her room. He had not seen her in months, not since her carriage accident.

Ori was pleased that Wellington was in the government and that he was to serve under him. He wanted to report this to the team leader, but he had not seen Metchavork in months. Instead, he recorded his new role on a shilling which he passed a few days later to his street-beggar colleague, Agent Mlai.

11.

Ryla

It was midmorning in that cluster of ghost towns that was being investigated on Earth 55. Six agents were exploring the ruins and gathering evidence. One of the agents, Allot Moynon, stepped out of a barn and called her fellow agents, "Look at this!"

The others immediately began to come to the barn. "What is it? What have you found?"

The agent had discovered a wooden bucket full of nuts. The nuts appeared recent.

They broke one of the nuts open and analyzed it. "This nut is fresh. And it is edible."

The leader of the expedition, Urt Fonxu, cautioned the team. "We have to assume there are living people nearby. There is no way these nuts could have been preserved for sixty or more years."

Allot walked to a burlap sack. "I wonder what is in here?"

Before anyone answered she opened it up. It was filled with fruit. The fruit was not fresh, but it had not spoiled either. The team began to check out all of the sacks and found some tubers, similar to potatoes.

Agent Fonxu alerted the two men on the transport. "Run a scan for us. We have evidence that there might be survivors nearby."

"What makes you so sure they aren't invaders, Urt?" another agent asked.

"I am not sure of anything," he replied. "But why would the invaders leave a bucket of nuts and a few sacks of tubers and fruit in a barn?"

"We have company!" an agent near the barn door suddenly announced. The other agents instinctively moved toward the door.

A woman in wretched burnt orange garments walked toward the barn with a bucket in her hand. She had black, disheveled hair and a light brown complexion similar to the appearance of the invading race. The native looked undernourished. When she was about twenty-five yards from the barn door, she noticed the agent near the door in a silver suit. She dropped her bucket and ran.

The agents pursued. The native was swift, but she quickly tired and was overtaken by two agents. The agents grabbed her so that she could not get away. Fonxu called the transport to inform them what had occurred. The transport relayed the message to Ortees and Captain Burxa for instructions as to how to proceed.

Unni was working in her quarters with the native books and signs, trying to decipher one of the languages of Earth 55 when she received an urgent message to proceed to the conference room. Ortees was already there along with several analysts when Unni arrived.

"We have had an incident on the surface," he began. He related what had occurred. As he was speaking, the captain entered the room.

"Whatever you do, you must decide quickly," the captain exhorted the team leader. "There may be more of them."

"If we let her go, she may tell others," Ortees pointed out.

"Even if she is not one of the invaders, the news may spread that there are other extraterrestrials on the surface," Unni cautioned.

"But the Interplanetary Intelligence Service is not in the business of taking prisoners, either," Ortees said.

"What is the protocol for this situation?" an analyst asked.

"The Bureau of Protective Action is still writing its protocols," Ortees replied. "The foremost order I was given was not to be detected by the Empire. I see no option but to detain her and bring her back to the space station."

"Very well," Captain Burxa replied. "These matters are your call. I will have a security detail waiting at the docking station when our guest arrives."

Agent Fonxu called off the rest of the exploration for the day. The native was cuffed to Agent Moynon and escorted to the transport. She resisted all of the way and needed two others to control her.

She cried out loudly as she was brought aboard the spacecraft. She was strapped into a seat and the straps were locked so she could not get up. She screamed when the transport lifted off and she wept loudly during the entire two-hour trip to Station 55-1.

When the transport docked, the crew became weightless. The native cried out. Moving her to the tube that led to the spinning part of the space station was difficult. The weightless woman was terrified, flailing about. All six agents worked to get her to the hatch while the pilot and copilot assisted with opening and closing the hatches.

She cried out in terror as she tumbled into artificial gravity. The agents stripped her and put her into the decontamination chamber. She screamed as the cleaning jets fired the decontaminants, and she accidentally ingested some of the fluids. When she was given a uniform to put on, she calmed down, and was able to dress herself. But she had to be dragged to the brig, where she was placed for security reasons.

After an hour, she calmed down. Unni volunteered to go into the brig to bring the captive her dinner. But Ortees preferred to send Agent Moynon because her physical appearance was closer to that of the native.

Ortees and Unni observed by camera as Moynon entered the brig with dinner. But the native got violent and attacked Moynon, who immediately fled. One hour later, a covered plate of food was delivered into the brig through a small opening designed for the purpose. Ortees and Unni watched in disappointment as the native only stared at the plate and refused to eat.

Captain Burxa was concerned that the native was thin and needed to eat soon. She decided to send in Mr. Beeku, a military man and a security officer, to force-feed the captive.

Ortees was opposed to the idea. "This is totally wrong. Any use of force will just make her more frightened and will close her up further. Besides, Mr. Beeku is black. He is the wrong gender and the wrong race. She will probably not accept someone who does not look like her. She might even be frightened by his brawn."

"I am not sure bringing an alien on board this station was the correct decision," the captain replied. "And I will not take responsibility if she dies in captivity. I am the captain, and I am ordering Mr. Beeku to enter the brig and force-feed the alien."

Although the captain usually allowed Ortees to make decisions in matters that did not involve the station itself, she did outrank him, and it was within her authority to order that the captive be force-fed. Ortees knew it, and grudgingly agreed to her decision.

Mr. Beeku entered the brig with a covered plate of food as Unni, Ortees, Burxa, and others watched with apprehension. But when Beeku entered the room, the native did not react.

He placed the food in front of her, uncovered the dish, and motioned to her to eat it. He did not force her because she appeared to be contemplating eating voluntarily. Beeku took the other plate, which was now cold, and set it on the small table and began to eat. The native watched for a moment. Then she cautiously took her first bite.

She paused and took a second bite. Then, in the next two minutes, she wolfed down everything on the plate.

He smiled approvingly and she smiled back. Soon they were talking to each other, although neither understood a word of what the other was saying.

Beeku turned to the camera above the door. "I think this lady wants seconds," he said.

When another plate arrived, he stepped out, got it and brought it in. The native ate everything she was given.

Afterward, the other crew began to joke about Beeku's charm with women.

After dinner, Mr. Beeku left the brig. The lights were dimmed, and the bed was mechanically lowered from the wall. The native got into bed and slept as a guard watched by camera.

Eight hours later, Unni went to Ortees and asked if she could take the native her breakfast. Ortees was reluctant. "You are not very tall. If she turns violent, you could be injured."

"But she won't get violent," Unni assured him. "Everything I have read about the Empire indicates that they exterminate the races that differ from them. My theory is that she trusted Beeku because he is black. She will likewise trust me because I am white. The native must think we are okay because we belong to races that the invaders have been killing. If I am correct, she will accept me."

"And if you are wrong, she may injure you," Ortees replied.

"I did not join the Interplanetary Intelligence Service out of concern for my safety."

Ortees checked with Captain Burxa, and she agreed to let Vlaytork bring the native her breakfast.

When the native had gotten out of bed, Unni entered the brig with two plates of breakfast. The native received her. Vlaytork set the two plates down on the table, one for the native and the other for her.

The native perceived that Unni was friendly, and the two began to connect with each other. Vlaytork pointed to herself and said, "Unni."

"Unni?" the native asked. Then she pointed to herself and said, "Ryla."

Ortees and Burxa were watching from the conference room view screen. Both of them were elated.

Unni displayed her knowledge in linguistics as she began to communicate with Ryla. Unni was picking up words in the native language, and Ryla was picking up rudimentary Grellish. Unni spent hours with Ryla.

When she came out, Ortees told her that she was being taken off all of her other projects. She was assigned to Ryla full time. After two days, Agent Moynon came into the brig with Unni. Moynon introduced herself as Allot. Unni was able to convey to Ryla that Moynon was a friend. Ryla rapidly realized that everyone on Station 55-1 was a friend.

Ryla was removed from the brig and given her own quarters later that day. After forty days, Ryla was conversant in Grellish. She also gained some weight and began to look healthy. Unni wanted to learn everything she could about Ryla, her family, and her planet.

Ryla told Unni that her maternal grandfather had been a shopkeeper. He lived in a city just south of the equator. Ryla showed Unni where the city was on a holographic globe of Earth 55. One day, terror appeared from the air. Hundreds of silvery spaceships descended all over the world, and their occupants, the Vittmians took control. People were forcibly relocated, and many were killed. Her family was moved to a collective farm.

Conditions on the farm were harsh. There were quotas of food production, and if these quotas were not met, every eighth person was executed. Similarly, in the mines and factories, if quotas were not met, there would be executions of every eighth person, selected at random.

All the while, the Vittmians were exterminating the white race and the black race, and only keeping the "proper" race alive. Ryla's parents met on a farm. She hardly knew her father due to the hours he had to work. He died when she was only nine. Children were given only four years of education, just enough to learn to read and write and add and subtract.

Ryla got married when she was only seventeen. Her husband's name was Folf. The following year, he was relocated to the mines hundreds of miles to the north. The miners worked very long hours and were forced to work even when they were sick. The women had to do all other work as the men were totally given to the mining.

Ryla had a baby daughter two years later. In the night, a secret society, a resistance movement, would meet. Folf had become a member. He told Ryla that if he were ever arrested, she should flee because he would be interrogated and forced to reveal the names of other members. The Vittmians often interrogated people by arresting their relatives and torturing them in front of the person who was not cooperating with the questioning.

The inevitable day came when Folf was arrested. Ryla never saw him again. She took her daughter and fled north across the border into another country. It had been inhabited by a black race, and its citizens had already been taken away to their doom. Ryla tried to survive by eating fruit, nuts, and vegetables from any volunteer plants that still lived in the fallow lands by the river.

Then Ryla came to the part of her story that she could barely utter: the following year, her daughter fell ill and died. Nearly three years later, she was found by "the friends," that is, the agents from Station 55-1.

Ryla taught Unni and Allot her native language and how to read and write in it. As it turned out, it was a different language than the one spoken in the ghost towns.

Allot and Unni told Ryla about the Confederation, their homes on other worlds, and their personal stories. Ryla was particularly fascinated by Unni's two-year experience on Earth 48 because England seemed to match her mental image of her own world before the invasion based on the stories her mother would tell.

As time passed, Ryla mingled with other agents and crew members. Her life was not all work. She began to participate in the limited recreational opportunities on Station 55-1. She told her new friends that she was happy for the first time in her life.

But that evening, Ryla admitted to Unni that she had been happy once before. When she was married to Folf and had her little girl, she was sometimes able to forget the suffering of life under the Vittmians.

Unni dared to ask her about Folf, how they met and courted, and what it was like being married.

Ryla said she had known Folf since they were children. He was two years older than she. She knew him to be diligent and a man of character. For that reason, when he asked her to marry him, Ryla immediately accepted. The got married twenty days later.

"Did you love him?" Unni asked with interest.

"Not really," Ryla candidly replied. "I did it out of duty to my people. I wanted to have children to keep our numbers up. I knew Folf to be a decent man, a man I could respect, so I married him."

"You are saying you married out of duty and not out of love?"

"Yes," Ryla admitted. "But Folf was someone I could admire and look up to. I eventually did begin to love him, and when I lost him…"

Ryla choked up and Unni did not want to press her any further. Unni put her arm around Ryla and thanked her for sharing. "What you said means a lot to me," Unni assured her friend.

Three months later, Ortees approached Unni about a message he had received from Headquarters in Tlat Mlang. They wanted to hire Ryla as an agent of the Bureau of Protective Action. She would have to go to Earth 1 and be trained. Many senior analysts wanted to meet her and learn from her about the Vittmians and their cruel methods. After two years, she would be sent back to Station 55-1. Vlaytork would accompany her on the voyage and come back to Earth 55 on the next starship.

Ortees wanted to know if Unni thought Ryla would be interested in the job and if she was ready for the trip. Unni said she would discuss the matter with Ryla. The next starship was due in three weeks, so she had some time to make up her mind.

Two days later, the opportunity arose for Unni to pose the question. Ryla's eyes became wide and she said, "Yes, yes! I would love to become an agent just like you. I want nothing more than to help my people."

Then after a pause, Ryla added, "And I want to get those [not translatable]'s that stole my world and killed my husband and daughter!"

Several hours later, Unni entered Ortees's office to tell him that Ryla agreed to go to Earth 1. Ortees was very glad to hear. "Ryla will render invaluable help to the planners at Headquarters. She will come back here in two years trained and ready to make a great contribution to our mission."

Unni agreed.

"Of course," the team leader continued, "we will certainly miss the two of you in the meantime. At least I will have one of you back in just a month or two."

Unni swallowed hard. She admired Ortees as a leader and a friend and she did not want to hurt his feelings by what she was about to ask. "Sir, I have very much enjoyed working with you and all of my colleagues on Station 55-1, but I feel I need to ask to be transferred back to Earth 48."

"That can be arranged," he replied hesitantly. "Many of the agents from the Bureau of Exploratory Surveillance are transferring back to their old assignments, where they know that language and culture…But why, Unni?"

"I have had time to think…"

"About marrying?"

"Yes. I feel I need to do it."

Ortees was disappointed. He liked Unni a lot, but he had lost all respect for Agent Sraymlat. Ortees was as concerned for her happiness as he would be if she were his own daughter. "I know you have had time to think, but if you allow me, I feel you are making a big mistake. You would never be the mother of a head of government. Are you not aware of the fact that Sraymlat is in Germany somewhere?"

"Yes, but…"

"Even if Metchavork is right about Germany emerging as the dominant power on that planet, it would be as an absolute monarchy. You would never be the mother of a future head of government there."

"I know a united German Empire would be a…"

"Most importantly, I do not think that Sraymlat matches you."

Unni was a little irritated at being interrupted twice. She blurted, "I am not talking about Urelt Sraymlat. I want to marry Orishackt Svavapass!"

"Ori?" Ortees's entire countenance changed. "I didn't think you loved him. You said you found him to be cold and rigid."

"I am not sure if I love him even now," Unni admitted. "But I admire him. And when it comes to integrity and commitment, rigidity is a virtue."

"You make a compelling point," Ortees agreed.

"On the day it was invaded, Earth 55 was just as Earth 48 is today. Ryla has told me enough," Unni declared with emotion. "That must *never* happen to Earth 48. I want to…I need to have a son in England. I am willing to sacrifice my life for this mission. I know I can count on Ori to commit to the mission and carry it to completion."

"And you are willing to marry a man you have called narrow and doctrinaire?"

"I would gladly marry a man who is resolute and genuine!"

Unni paused and lowered her voice. "Do you think he would still want me?"

Ortees smiled. "I suppose there is only one way to find out. I will sign your transfer application, effective when you feel Ryla has adequately settled in at Headquarters."

"Thank you so much!" Unni leaned over the desk and kissed her boss.

Ortees shook his head. "I wish you and Ori the best on this mission of yours. But you know, I still think the future of that planet is with the United States of America. It will be at least sixty years before Weatherby Junior is old enough for high office, probably about 37595 or so. What is that, sometime in the 1880s with their calendar?"

Unni did a quick mental calculation. "That's about right."

Ortees continued, "By that time, every analyst in the Service will see the trajectories of the British Empire and the American republic and agree with me. I suppose a Prime Minister of the British Empire would be an asset, but our real need will be a president of the United States."

12.

An Act of Duty and Sacrifice

It was lively that summer evening in the crowded beerhall. The beer was flowing and the men were drinking. The room was noisy and well-lit, and there was a six-piece German band playing local favorites.

At a small corner table sat a recently retired military officer, Oberst Friedrich von Mecklenburg. He came almost every week and waited for his close friend Leutnant Dieter Dehrmann, who was still active in the Prussian Army.

The old oberst ordered steins of beer for himself and his friend, and he never took a sip before Dehrmann arrived.

At last Dehrmann entered the beer hall and immediately took his seat across from von Mecklenburg. The two agents felt they could speak freely in that noisy place with little fear of being overheard.

"I have heard some unsettling news, Dieter," Metchavork began. "An agent has returned from the occupied zone and has reported to me all of the worst horrors that I suspected: genocide, torture, enslavement...."

"That bad?" Svortomit asked almost mechanically.

"I was told stories that came from the mouth of a native that were deeply moving. It was far worse than anything that Napoleon ever did here. The invaders make the natives work long hours in mines and farms, and if a production quota is missed, they kill every eighth worker. We have to get this world ready for admission to the Confederation before the Empire can reach here."

"We cannot let the invaders capture this place," Svortomit affirmed. "Our mission must succeed."

"Which is why I was not happy to hear who the new Subdirector will be when Keepetta retires in two months. It will be Sral Vlaris."

"No, it can't be," Svortomit reacted with surprise. "Didn't you tell me last year that he was in disfavor?"

"Yes, but all the alternate candidates for the job have joined Protective Action," Metchavork explained. "Vlaris is just about the only one left in Exploratory Surveillance with any seniority."

"This is terrible! That conservative old man will be watching the Earth 48 team like a hawk. We will have a difficult time covering our tracks."

"All of this is the bad news," Metchavork said with a sly grin.

"And I take it you have some good news?"

"For one thing, the name of the agent I spoke to…"

"Unni Vlaytork?"

"You are correct. She has transferred back to our team."

Svortomit's eyes got big. "And you think you might be able to persuade her to marry Orishackt Svavapass?"

"Let me put it this way," Metchavork beamed. "She asked my *permission* to marry him."

"What did you say?"

"I told her we could discuss this matter on a transport flight to the surface," Metchavork jested. "We dropped her off outside London a little over an hour ago."

"And you think Ori will agree to this?"

"Without a doubt," Metchavork assured his friend. "He has been like a wounded dog ever since she refused him two years ago. He would leap at the chance."

"Isn't Jenny Carter supposed to be dead? How can you assign an agent a second alias in the same zone of operation? She would certainly be recognized."

"But Jenny Carter is not dead," the team leader said with a grin. "Unni had the forethought to resign her job at the British Foreign Office, saying she needed to go home to her sick mother in the countryside."

"So we have the perfect lightning rod," Svortomit grinned.

"Oh, yes! Old Vlaris is no fool. Imagine what he must be thinking!" Metchavork went on with glee. "Unni spends half a year with Ortees and then decides to return to England to marry a man whom she previously rejected."

"Vlaris will be watching for the slightest hint that they are trying to bring forth Prime Minister da Vinci…"

"Right, while we do the real work here in Germany right under his nose. I will be writing reports as to how concerned I am that they might be trying something outside of the limits of the Noninterference Protocol, and what steps I am taking to be sure no rules are broken…"

"While we have a free hand over here on the continent," Svortomit concluded. "Of course, Sraymlat will be very angry."

"Oh, he mustn't hear a word about this courtship until it is too late."

Both men were smiling deviously. They lifted up their beer steins to a toast. "To Robert and Jenny!"

Just then, the band began to play a lively song and Dehrmann rose up to dance. Any observer in the beer hall, might have thought Dehrmann was drunk, but his joy was very sober.

Ori sat down at the dinner table. Mr. Shelby, the butler, set his dinner down before him. "Your dinner, Major."

Everyone still called Robert Weatherby "Major" even though he had resigned his commission to take a civilian job with the Board of Ordnance. Now that Weatherby was no longer in the Army, he grew a beard. It covered up the scar on his face and spared him the tedious job of shaving around the scar with Technology Level 8 shaving tools.

"Thank you, Mr. Shelby," Ori replied. He sat at a vast empty dining table, where he dined alone quietly most evenings.

"Oh, Major, I almost forgot." Mr. Shelby handed Ori an envelope made of fine stationery. "A young lady came to the door and asked me to hand this note to you."

On the envelope was written, "To Major Robert Weatherby" in elegant handwriting. The script was tilted slightly to the left, betraying that it was written by a left-handed person.

Ori thought he recognized the handwriting, and he began to tremble with excitement. He carefully tore the envelope open.

There was a card, and it said, "Dear Major Weatherby, After some deliberation, I have reconsidered your invitation to meet me for a picnic in Green Park on Saturday at one o'clock. I do hope your invitation is still open. I will be there. Respectfully yours, Jenny Carter."

His excitement turned into elation. Ori tried to caution himself against getting his hopes up too high, but he could not help himself.

After he had finished dining, Mr. Shelby picked up the plates and brought them to the cook, Mrs. Anders.

"I think you are right, Mrs. Anders," the butler said. "I have not seen him this happy in two years."

The older Mrs. Anders smiled. "Of course I was right. Why else would a young lady write to a dashing young man like Major Weatherby?"

The following afternoon, Ori was walking down the avenue when he spotted a jewelry shop. He ended up staying for over an hour and left with a diamond ring.

The two days until Saturday passed quickly, as Svavapass composed in his mind what he would say to Unni Vlaytork. Ori left his townhouse early and walked to Green Park. It was foggy and humid. Ori was dressed with a stylish ruffled white shirt and a light overcoat. He kept putting his left hand in his pocket to handle the small box that housed the diamond ring.

Ori arrived at the park forty-five minutes early. A summer breeze dissipated the fog, and the sun was beginning to shine through.

Ori spotted Unni at a distance; she also was early. He walked toward her with a swift gait, unable to conceal his excitement, occasionally fingering the little box in his pocket.

Unni was wearing a light blue dress like a well-to-do lady, a very different image from her poor country girl look in the past. No doubt, Metchavork had given her some money.

The two converged near a park bench, where they soon seated themselves.

"You grew a beard, Robert," Unni began.

Ori told Unni how Wellington had been appointed to head up the Board of Ordnance, the second largest department in the government. Ori had resigned his commission to take the civilian political post offered by Wellington, and now he could grow a beard.

Ori listened with great interest as Unni described what it had been like working on a space station at an occupied planet. Unni told him about the people she had been working with and the things they did. She described the evidence of genocide and oppression. She talked about the ghost towns and what they found there.

But it was when Unni began to tell the story of Ryla that Ori became truly captivated and deeply moved. Ori looked around him at the natural beauty of the park and at the children playing and an older couple walking at a distance.

"Those butchers cannot be allowed to do that to this planet," Ori declared with conviction. "I don't care what it takes, and I am not interested in any protocols. Earth 48 must not become like Earth 55!"

The bells from a clock at a nearby church struck two. Ori and Unni realized that they had not yet eaten the lunch Mrs. Anders had prepared. They had lost all track of time.

They got up from the bench and moved toward a large tree. Unni handed Ori the blanket and he spread it out while Unni got out the sandwiches. The sun went in, and it was beginning to get cloudy as they began to eat.

"I have been gone for over a year, so tell me what has been going on in England," Unni inquired.

Ori was becoming eager to discuss more substantive topics, such as why Unni had returned to Earth 48. He began to finger the little box in his pocket with building anxiety and summed up the events of the past year with brevity.

"There is popular discontent over taxes and the Corn Laws. Last summer, Prince William and Prince Edward contracted legal marriages, and Prince Edward now has a daughter, Alexandrina Victoria, born in May. There is now a proper heiress to the throne."

"I am very glad to hear that," Unni said.

"Now I don't suppose that you came thirty-two light years to seek employment as Alexandrina's nanny, have you?" Ori suddenly asked.

"Now I don't suppose the object you have been handling in your pocket is a shilling for Agent Mlai, is it?" Unni countered.

"It is obvious that we understand one another, so I will get right to the point," Ori declared.

He dropped to one knee and produced the diamond ring.

"Unni Vlaytork, will you marry me?"

"I believe you would get a more desirable answer if you called me Jenny," Unni answered.

Ori's heart was pounding now. "Jennifer Carter, will you marry me?"

"Indeed I will, Robert Weatherby," Unni replied in a resolute tone. "And the sooner, the better."

Ori immediately embraced his fiancé and kissed her with passion. He was in total ecstasy.

Unni had prepared herself mentally for this moment for two months. But the energy of the embrace and the kiss brought the entire concept of marrying

Orishackt Svavapass from a mission plan to reality. When Ori had completed his burst of affection, Unni took the ring and put it on.

The gravity of what she had just allowed to occur was still sinking in. Jenny Carter loved Robert Weatherly, but Unni Vlaytork did not love Ori Svavapass. Rather, Unni was determined to carry out her self-chosen mission to get Earth 48 into the Confederation before the invaders got here. This meant she needed to bear a son, educate him, and prepare him for high government office to accelerate the development of the greatest nation on the planet.

For this, Unni needed an agent for a husband. And not just any agent, but someone who shared her vision, someone whom she could trust to remain true to the cause. She had no doubt that Svavapass was that man. Unni was prepared to sacrifice her life for the success of her mission, and if it meant marrying a dull and mechanical agent, so be it.

And could it be that bad? Ori was clearly devoted to her, having carried the torch for two years without any outward signs to encourage him. And Unni was still fathoming the intensity of that embrace and that kiss—his reaction to her acceptance of the proposal—was anything but dull and mechanical.

13.
Two Weddings

The light from the window of the train woke Ori. Although it was cloudy, the snow cover made the light much brighter. He looked across at Unni. She was already awake. He tapped his wrist computer. The train was still more than an hour out from Yoilafa, Unni's hometown.

Unni's arms were crossed and her lips were tight. Ori asked what was troubling her.

"I don't think your stepfather approves of me," she replied.

"You have company. My stepfather doesn't approve of me either," Ori stated dryly.

The train was plodding along at only 180 miles per hour. Svavapass wondered why after all these years the continent of Zarfixu could not have the high-speed trains that Svartolk had, to say nothing of Earth 1. It was a ten-hour ride from his home country of Olistoss to Unni's country, Botvrayt.

Ori had taken time off from his job in London to introduce his fiancé to his family and to be introduced to hers. His colleagues at work believed he was in the English countryside. Most of the time off was spent on commercial starships traveling to and from Earth 19. To save time, Ori decided to take the night train.

"Your mother seemed nice, but your stepfather seems rather selfish, and he has her completely under his thumb."

The first part of their whirlwind trip to Earth 19 was marred by the fact that Ori's stepfather still had not forgiven Ori from missing the wedding to his mother. Ori was used to the chill of his stepfather, but Unni was uncomfortable during the entire visit.

"Maybe if we had had more time, you could have gotten to know my mother better," Ori said.

It suddenly occurred to Ori that they were speaking to one another in English and not in Grellish or Omtvumxian, the international language of Earth 19. She had also preferred English on the starship as well. Ori was unaware of the fact that Unni had not yet fully adjusted to the thought of marrying Ori Svavapass. Unni desperately did not want to hurt Ori's feelings, so she played the role of Jenny Carter at all times; it was Jenny who loved Robert Weatherby.

In a matter of minutes, Unni would be in the home where she grew up and would not be able to be Jenny. She was grappling with how she would conduct herself in front of her parents with Ori present.

When the train arrived at Yoilafa Station, the Vlaytorks were at the forefront of the platform, eager to meet their future son-in-law. Unni embraced her mother. Her father stepped forward and greeted Ori.

"Huhane Vlaytork," he greeted his future son-in-law.

"Orishackt Svavapass," Ori returned the greeting.

Mr. Vlaytork grinned. "Orishackt Svavapass. Now there's a typical Olistossian name."

As they made their way to the waiting vehicle, Huhane showed off all of the phrases he knew in Olistossian as if to impress Ori. Unni rolled her eyes, and Ori did not react at all to the gross mispronunciations. "I learned that in the hotel," he explained. "I have worked in hotels for years, and I have met a number of guests from Olistoss."

Unni's brother Maykot was waiting in the vehicle. Although Maykot had already entered the coordinates of his parents' home, he did not get out to help with the baggage.

The Vlaytorks lived in a modest home, but the atmosphere was pleasant. Ori was directed to Maykot's former room where he set his bags, and Unni carried her own bags to the bedroom she had as a girl. Then the family sat down at the table, where a special dinner was ready. Ori could tell that Unni's mother Zeri had put a lot of effort into it. Ori and Unni were very hungry because they had skipped breakfast.

Ori did not speak Botvraytish, and Maykot did not know very much Grellish, so the discussion was in Omtvumxian. "Tell us how you met, how you got together," Unni's mother requested.

The couple had rehearsed this answer and were well prepared. Unni said that they met through work. Unni was a marketing director in the same territory where Ori was in sales.

"We have Earths 40, 42, 43, and 44," Ori explained.

"We have known each other for years, really," Unni said. "But one day Ori came back from landing us a huge contract on Earth 43, and our whole sales team was celebrating, and that was when I noticed Ori for the first time."

"It was mutual," Ori added. "It was the way she looked at me."

"Then I was sent out of the territory to help with a startup line of sales," Unni went on. "While we were apart, I realized how much I missed Ori. More than missing him, I realized I *needed* him."

Although her mother asked the question, the couple seemed to direct the answer to Mr. Vlaytork, who knew the truth about Unni's real profession and was able translate the story in his head into something much closer to the truth.

Huhane Vlaytork nodded as they couple continued. Then the discussion turned to wedding plans.

Throughout the conversation, Maykot was silent and aloof. After two hours, Maykot left the house to "take care of some things." Once he was gone, the conversation switched to Grellish, which Unni's parents knew well form their hotel work.

They began to discuss the details of the wedding, including the venue, the date, and the invitation list. The Vlaytorks took Ori on a tour of the city, showing him Unni's schools, the hotel, and other sites of which they were proud. They met two sets of Unni's uncles and aunts, as well as her grandmother.

Unni's parents embarrassed her when they began showing holographs of Unni's childhood.

"She was beautiful even back then," Ori said. Unni thought he was trying to ease her out of an embarrassing situation, but Ori was sincere. He was too much in awe of the images to have considered such a thing.

Zeri was unrelenting in continuing the display of three-dimensional images. One image depicted Unni's recital when she was fourteen. It prompted her father to say, "Unni, you must play for us!"

"I am very much out of practice," she protested. But minutes later, her parents prevailed and Unni was before a traditional Zarfixuan keyboard instrument. Perhaps she was a little rusty, but Ori was spellbound by her music. His rapture was not lost on Mrs. Vlaytork.

At one point, Zeri caught Ori alone and she unveiled her real feelings. "We are so happy to meet you. We are getting on in years, and Huhane and I still do not have any grandchildren. Maykot is nearing forty. He is unmarried and has no prospects that we can see. So, when the arrangement with that other fellow Urelt fell through, we began to lose hope."

Ori did not know what to say. He wanted to assure her that he would make her a grandmother very soon, as much as it was up to him. But he held his tongue and only smiled.

While Unni and her mother sat at the table working on the wedding invitation list, Unni noticed how comfortable Ori was with her father, and how well the two were bonding. The outgoing Ori in her living room seemed so different from the stiff and guarded Ori she knew on Earth 48. Another facet of Ori's personality was showing forth. And she liked it.

Three days later, in the final hours before the couple left the Vlaytork house, Zeri had a quiet moment with her daughter. "I really like that young man, Unni. And your father is very pleased. I can see he truly loves you. Everything seems just perfect. It is just that...maybe I should not say it..."

"Just that what, Mom?" Unni was uncomfortable because she knew her mother was very perceptive.

"You don't seem to be like a young woman in love," her mother observed. "You appear to be holding back."

"I have made up my mind," Unni countered. "I am marrying this man."

"And your father and I are well pleased. And Ori is head-over-heels in love with you. But you are not like you were last year when you brought Urelt here..."

"And look how that ended up. And, Mom, don't mention that name again. Ever."

"I am sorry. What I mean is, you are not acting like a young woman carried away with joy and love."

"Looks can be deceiving. I wish to spend the rest of my life with Robert, uh, Ori."

"Robert? Is there another?"

"Robert is a funny affectionate name that I call him."

"Is this true? And what does he call you?"

"He calls me Jenny. It's an inside thing. We have affectionate names for one another. It is a really private thing we have."

Zeri raised an eyebrow. But her curiosity was piqued. She quietly sneaked into Maykot's former bedroom where Ori had spent the last two nights and crept up behind him as he packed his bags.

"Robert," she called softly.

"Just a moment, Jenny," he replied in English. "I'll be ready in just a moment."

He turned and saw Mrs. Vlaytork. He blushed so red one could almost see it through his beard.

"How do you know that name? Only Unni calls me that," he said in Grellish.

"And what do you call her?"

"It's our little secret. But surely if she told you she called me Robert, then you must know I call her Jenny."

Zeri Vlaytork nodded and smiled. "Please excuse me if I do not tell you what Huhane used to call me when we were newlyweds."

Zeri Vlaytork left the room satisfied. Perhaps her daughter's affection for Ori was more private than with her last fiancé. Perhaps this wedding will go all the way to fruition, she thought.

At last the wedding day came. November 13, 1819 was a foggy, cloudy day. At first, the couple thought the best venue would be in the English countryside, in Unni's supposed hometown of Wallingford. That way, the lack of relatives on either side of the family would not have to be explained. But they realized that the wedding had to be in London for image's sake. This wedding was really for their future children's sake.

But then who would present the bride? The official story was that Jenny's father was no longer living and her mother was too weak to travel. They considered having Metchavork do it, but his English was accented. Metchavork said he would "arrange" it.

And that he did. He arranged for "Uncle Sebastian" to be flown in all the way from Earth 55. Ortees was aware of the tradition of the father or uncle presenting a bride in an Earth 48 wedding, and he was more than pleased to have the honor of performing that duty.

The wedding took place late in the afternoon in a small chapel under the auspices of the Church of England. A number of officers from Weatherby's regiment showed up for the wedding, as well as several coworkers from the Board of Ordnance. Lt. Col. Keaton was there, as well as Mr. Shelby and Mrs.

Anders. The Duke of Wellington and his wife had been invited, but they did not come.

On the bride's side of the aisle were Uncle Sebastian, Gwen, and three former coworkers from the Foreign Office.

Although the gathering was small, Weatherby paid for the organist to be playing. The white-haired pastor, Matthew T. Higgins, officiated the wedding in a very traditional way.

Unni was very interested in native religions. Pastor Higgins did not disappoint. In his perfect diction and elegant elocution, he read from 1 Corinthians 13 about the virtue of love. But then he added, "God's intention in this universe involves man. St. Peter tells us in his first Epistle that we who have obeyed the gospel of our Lord Jesus Christ are elect according to the foreknowledge of God the Father. Since we the chosen ones were foreordained, it follows that our natural birth was foreknown. Our birth required the marriage of our parents. That being the case, marriage is under the holy government of God. Therefore, what God has joined together let no man put asunder."

Pastor Higgins's joyful message turned ominous. "If you part for *any* reason other than death, *you shall answer to God!*"

The tone of that last phrase sent a chill down Unni's spine. She realized why divorce was so rare in England.

Robert and Jennifer exchanged their vows in an unwavering and strong voice. When the old pastor pronounced them man and wife, their kiss was very convincing. Ori expressed his true feelings, and Unni put on an excellent performance of Jenny, the grateful country girl being rescued from her low estate by a dashing upper-middle-class gentleman.

After a brief reception, the bride and groom left in a horse-drawn carriage, supposedly for a honeymoon in the countryside. The driver of the carriage, Agent Mlai, let the couple off on a deserted stretch of road just west of London. Fortunately, it was dark as Robert and Jennifer Weatherby, still dressed in wedding clothes, made their way into a field to the awaiting transport.

When they reached the spaceship, Robert looked up the ten-foot ladder and said, "I hope you are not expecting me to 'carry you over the threshold.'" Unni laughed for a moment, but now she had the awkward task of climbing a ladder in an English wedding dress. Ori was behind her, and Ortees reached down from the deck and helped her up.

Ortees spent some time with the couple on the starship to Earth 40. From the orbital spaceport there, Ortees was to catch a military vessel bound for Earth 55, while the Ori and Unni were to go on to Earth 19 for their second wedding.

Ortees was his old self, full of puns and good humor. The puns cannot be repeated in this treatise, as they are only funny in Grellish.

During the discussion, Unni noticed another side to Ori, relaxed, personable, and outgoing. Could it be that the real Ori Svavapass was a man of good cheer, and that it was Robert Weatherby who was guarded and dull? Could it be that Orishackt Svavapass the student and the field agent on duty in the field was totally different from Ori off duty? She would know soon enough.

Her former team leader caught Unni up with the latest developments from their work on Station 55-1. Ryla was still not back from her training. From what they had learned from Ryla, two agents became proficient in her language and were now on the planet's surface infiltrating the oppressed natives. More field agents would follow.

Unni had a separate cabin from Ori during the passage to Earth 19. "I may be Mrs. Weatherby in the eyes of the Church of England, but I am not yet Mrs. Svavapass to the Confederation," she maintained.

Ori did not like the arrangement, but he went along. "Just a few more days," he said to himself.

The wedding in Yoilafa went according to plans. A sizable number of Unni's relatives showed up. But for Ori, only his mother and one cousin showed up. Ori's mother said his stepfather "was not well." The surprise of the day was the appearance of Metchavork and Svortomit. Svortomit claimed to be a college buddy of Svavapass, which was true. Metchavork told the guests that he was the regional vice president where the couple worked. Of course, Ori's mother and Huhane Vlaytork knew better.

Metchavork told Zeri Vlaytork during the reception that Unni was one of his best marketing directors, and that Orishackt was "born to sell."

"And if your daughter and son-in-law don't visit enough, you can blame me," Metchavork said slyly. "I will be keeping them busy on a high-profile project. Earth 45 might join the confederation soon, and when it does, we are positioning ourselves to beat the competition into that market."

After the reception, the new Mr. and Mrs. Svavapass took a train to the south coast of the continent of Zarfixu. Then they took an automated taxi to a rented cottage on the south shore for their week-long honeymoon. It was springtime in the Southern Hemisphere of Earth 19. It was sunny, windy, and cool. The meadow around the cottage was filled with wildflowers. South of the cottage was a sharp cliff and below that was the rocky coast and the turbulent ocean. The roar of the waves, the west-to-east wind, and the seagulls made for a noisy backdrop to the picturesque scenery.

To the north was a village where the couple could find shops and places to eat. To the west was a fishing village. There were walking paths through the woods. There was a steep wooden stairway to the ocean one mile to the west, where there was a short stretch of beach.

Ori and Unni walked through the meadow, down the paths, and down to the beach, and up a sand dune to the north, talking, planning, laughing, and enjoying. One of the days, a severe rainstorm came in from the sea. The couple had to spend the entire day in the cottage with nothing to eat but crackers and some canned soup and a few leftovers. They did not seem to mind one bit.

Unni had never seen Ori so relaxed and warm, not even at her parents' house.

As the days of the honeymoon passed, the couple began to discover little things about each other, things that only a spouse could notice. Unni continued to explore the other side of Ori, and a love began to blossom. Unni was all alone with Ori, with nothing to shield her from the tide of affection that emanated from him. In that intense furnace of his love, her heart began to soften, to melt, and eventually, to match and reflect Ori's.

On the final day, Ori and Unni made their way down the cliff on the old wooden staircase to the seashore. They walked barefoot along the water for the full length of the beach several times, which was bounded on both ends by boulders.

Ori stooped and bent down. He wrote with his finger in the wet sand, "I love Unni" in Grellish capital letters. Unni then stooped down and wrote under it, "I love Ori."

A wave came in unexpectedly and knocked both of them down, Unni falling on Ori. They laughed. The wave smoothed the sand and the words were erased. In their place, a large pink seashell had washed ashore, perfectly formed, the size of a hand. Unni picked it up and showed it to Ori. She said, "I want to keep this as a memory of this time and a token of the bond between us."

Ori had a large pocket, and the shell fit snugly.

The sun was beginning to lower in the horizon, so Ori and Unni began to return to their cottage. They put their sandals back on and made their way to the old wooden stairs up the cliff face. Unni was in front with Ori a few steps behind.

When they were three-quarters of the way to the top, one of the wooden steps failed. As Unni's right leg fell through, she fell forward, striking and breaking the handrail on the right side, and tumbling to the right. Ori lunged and grabbed Unni's left leg.

The step that held Ori was beginning to falter under the weight of two persons. Ori briefly glanced at the rocks and waves ninety feet below.

Ori was not sure what his next move would be. He only knew he needed to move quickly.

"Let me go, Ori," Unni cried. "Why should we both die?"

With uncertain footing, Ori swung Unni leftward with all of his might. She caught hold of the steps above and pulled herself up. But the force of Ori's swing caused the step he was on to crack. He lunged forward so that the step below would catch him. But several more steps failed in a chain reaction. As his thigh hit the failing wooden structure in front of him, he felt the pain of the sea shell digging into him through his pocket. When Ori came to rest, he and Uni were more than ten feet apart.

Ori knew he had no option but to climb to the bottom. But after that, how would he get off the beach? Between him and the fishing docks were about one hundred yards of rocky shoreline. It would be a difficult trek even if the sun were not setting.

Unni shouted down that she would get help. Ori safely made it to the bottom and looked up to see if Unni had reached the top. Unni would not leave until she was sure Ori had made it to the bottom safely. They waved to each other with large arm motions. They were both relieved that the other was safe.

Ori sat on the beach and watched the sun set. As he thought of what had almost just happened, he began to tremble.

The wind began to blow on his wet clothing. He sat in the dark shivering for an hour and a half that seemed much longer. Then a rowboat appeared. Two men came up to him.

"Ori?" one asked.

Ori responded in the affirmative, but he soon discovered that the fishermen only spoke their own local language. Their knowledge of Omtvumxian was limited to "yes" and "no."

They rowed hard against the waves and reached the dock. Unni was there waiting for Ori's arrival.

Ori tried to reward the fishermen, but they would not accept his money.

Ori and Unni walked into the village to find a place to eat.

"What a chance you took!" Unni declared. "You saved my life!"

Ori looked into Unni's eyes and said, "Your life is more precious to me than my own because without you I would not have any real life to live."

Unni was deeply moved. It was as if Ori's words had been engraved into her heart.

They found a small, dimly lit restaurant and had a fish dinner. When they were seated, Ori noticed Unni's bruises on her face. He took some napkins and dipped them in water and tried to wash her wounds.

She asked Ori if he was okay. He had numerous splinters in his hands from the fall. He told her he was sure there would be cuts in this upper thigh from the broken seashell.

Ori reached into his pocket to extract the pieces. To his utter surprise, the shell was intact! He placed it on the table.

"This is a symbol that this bond between us is unbreakable," Unni concluded.

Early the next morning Ori and Unni left for Yoilafa. They were to make a brief visit to the Vlaytorks before their departure for Earth 48.

The young couple sat on the couch. Unni lay with her head on Ori's shoulder has he told Unni's parents of their accident on the old wooden staircase. Huhane was shaken by the near loss. Zeri was chilled by the story as well. But looking at the way her daughter was leaning on her new husband, Zeri was comforted with the knowledge that her daughter would have a happy marriage.

Whether she was Unni or Jenny, her love for Ori was no longer the performance of an alias.

14.
An Angry Enemy

Ori and Unni arrived by starship at Station 48-3 just hours ahead of the transport with the other field agents for their biannual meeting. Each went to their assigned cabins to write their reports.

When Ori logged in, he was presented with a nomenclature form. Whenever an agent got married, this form allowed the agent to change his or her name. The Confederation was sensitive to the cultures of the various planets with their continents and nations of which they were comprised. In some cultures, the wife took her husband's surname, but there were cultures where the opposite was practiced, as well as cultures where a new name was composed, or that had no surnames at all. Ori responded that his name was unchanged.

Then he filed his report. It covered matters such as the deteriorating health of King George III, the popular discontent of the people over taxes and the Corn Laws, and the violent suppression of protest in August 1819 known as the Peterloo Massacre. He also wrote of Wellington's appointment as the head of the second largest department of the government and his own appointment to a post in that organization.

Unni had little to report, as she had only recently returned to Earth 48. As for the nomenclature form, Unni's situation was a bit complicated. According to Botvrayti tradition and law, women took the surnames of their husbands. Of course, the same was true under English law; her alias had become Jennifer Weatherby. But from the beginning of the engagement, Unni had expressed her desire to keep her maiden name in the interplanetary context, specifically of the Interplanetary Intelligence Service. Ori went along with it.

But that evening, Unni entered her name on the form as "Agent Unni Svavapass." The events of the past days caused her to identify as the other half of one person whom she loved. She stared at the completed form. After a while, she pressed the equivalent of "Enter." She picked up her things and took them into Ori's cabin.

There was only one bed and it was not large. Ori offered to sleep on the floor.

"And so will I," she declared. She went to her cabin to collect the cushion and covers.

The next morning eleven agents, two analysts, and the team leader were scheduled to meet for breakfast in the conference room. Besides Svortomit, the field agents had not been told that Unni and Ori had gotten engaged, much less married.

When the two Agents Svavapass entered the room, Tekalta offered his congratulations to the new couple, followed by Leka. The other agents in the room, Lorbank, Duvass, and Qlat immediately joined the analysts in expressing their best wishes.

While this well-wishing was in progress, Metchavork was meeting separately in the hall outside his quarters with the six agents covering the German speaking world. The discussion was in German.

"Remember, now," he exhorted them, "when you discuss the Burschenschaft, you must simply state what is going on. Do not say anything to suggest that you are orchestrating or even participating in it."

"*Mein Gruppenführer*, I am afraid I may have written something like that in my report last night," one agent admitted.

"Don't worry, *Herr Professor Doktor*," Metchavork replied with a smile. "That's why I had you handwrite your reports and send them directly to me and to no one else. I told the Subdirector that since there were so many agents in Germany, I would compile it all into one report. I only wrote what the Subdirector needs to know."

"Writing by hand is tedious," Svortomit complained. "I had to use both hands just to get everything down in the time you allotted."

Metchavork and his agents all entered the conference room together. By that time, the discussion had shifted to other things. The agents were poking fun at Agent Qlat, who was having trouble staying awake. Station 48-3 ran on European time, and Qlat's body clock was on New York time.

Svortomit and Metchavork felt no need to congratulate Ori and Unni, as they had already done so in Yoilafa at the wedding.

Sraymlat was seated on the end of the row of "Germans" next to his former partner, Ori Svavapass.

The meeting agenda appeared in the center of the table. It listed the names of all present, including "Agent Unni Svavapass."

Sraymlat turned to Ori. Pointing, he said, "This has got to be a mistake!"

"It is," Svavapass replied. Ori did not know that Sraymlat was unaware of his wedding. He thought he was commenting on Unni's name change. Ori did not know that Unni had officially taken his name in the Interplanetary Intelligence Service.

Before long, the connection was made with Earth 1 and the holographs of Subdirector Keepetta and Sral Vlaris appeared.

Keepetta announced that she was retiring in twelve days and that Vlaris would be taking her place.

"Of course, Sral Vlaris needs no introduction to most of you, as he used to serve with you on the Earth 48 team," she observed.

"I see some new faces in the room," Vlaris said, "but I am quite familiar with the situation on that planet, having lived for twenty years on the surface and having been team leader there for another twenty."

The agents gave their reports. Lorbank went first. In France, the foreign occupation had ended two years early. At least for the short term, the Bourbon Dynasty was in power, and France was picking up the pieces from its ruinous wars.

In the United States, there was an unprecedented food shortage caused by unusually cool weather that summer. President Monroe was popular and likely to be reelected to another four-year term in the coming year.

Agent Svavapass pointed out that Wellington was now in the government of Prime Minister Liverpool. Ori had resigned his commission and was appointed to a position in the Board of Ordnance, a perch from which he was able to know a lot about the goings-on in the British Empire. Ori also reported that the royal succession was less uncertain with the birth of a legitimate granddaughter to the King, Princess Alexandrina Victoria.

Then it was the Germans' turn. Svortomit reported that a student movement had arisen on the university campuses throughout the German states called the Burschenschaft. This movement advocated German unification. With the German youth becoming more patriotic and committed to unification, it was inevitable that a united Germany would come into being within a generation.

The analysts then gave the results of the newest simulations. "Based on the reports from the agents, it appears that all of the natives who speak the German language are unifying rapidly. A united Germany would stretch from the north coast to the south coast of the western part of Continent 1 called Europe. With its vast population and developing technical prowess and well-organized military, it now appears that Germany will be the dominant nation on Earth 48. As Britain swoons under its load of public debt and France recovers from its defeat, Germany is on the rise."

Unni looked at Ori with a puzzled expression. Duvass whispered something to Lorbank. Qlat was struggling to appear awake.

Keepetta shook her head. "I put little trust in these simulations. The last several times we have met, you analysts have given me totally different views as to which culture was gaining dominance. First it was that Napoleon Binnaypart. Did I pronounce it correctly?"

"Close enough," Lorbank offered.

"Then it was the British Empire, and now it is that faction in the center of the continent, Durchlan. I am saying it correctly, am I not?"

"No, but we understand," Metchavork assured her. Then he impulsively said, "It is Deutschland."

"Well, in any case, it seems the situation on Earth 48 is very fluid, so you agents have your work cut out for you. You need to carefully observe the situation and come to some consensus as to what is actually developing on that planet. The Vittmian Empire is expanding in that direction, and if that trend continues, all of the non-member planets in that sector will be taken over with the exception of Earth 45."

Then Vlaris spoke. "That said, I would like to remind you agents that you serve the Bureau of Exploratory Surveillance, and our mission is still that we are sent to watch, not to affect. Do I make myself clear?"

There was a mumbled affirmative from the agents.

"I will be watching you especially, Unni Svavapass," he went on. "I will personally see to it that no children you bear in England will rise to any public office, not even court clerk!"

Sraymlat was beginning to realize what had occurred. He was visibly shaken.

The moment the holographs of Keepetta and Vlaris disappeared, he blurted, "Unni, how could you do this without telling me? You said you needed to think about it."

Everyone in the room fell silent.

"I returned the necklace," she replied. "Need I have said more?"

Ori stood up from his seat.

Sraymlat stood also, fuming with anger. "Ori, I thought you were my friend. How could you do this behind my back?"

Svavapass started to say something, but Sraymlat turned and left the room. Svortomit ran out after him.

"Obviously, this team has some issues with unity," Metchavork observed. "Let's have the agents covering England and France report to the docking stations for an immediate return to the surface. The agents assigned to Germany will stay here to sort a few things out."

"And what about the United States?" Qlat asked.

"And the agent assigned to the United States can report to sickbay for a medical examination."

"But I am not sick, just time-lagged," Qlat protested.

"And that is an order," Metchavork added.

Ori and Unni searched for Sraymlat and Svortomit, but they had to give up after a few minutes because they knew the transport was waiting. By the time they got to the hatch leading out to the docking area, Lorbank and Duvass had already transformed themselves into Louis LeBlanc and Jean-Pierre DuBois.

"What took you so long?" Lorbank asked.

"We were trying to find Sraymlat," Ori explained.

"To clear the air," Unni completed the thought.

"I understand," Lorbank replied. "But somehow I don't think Metchavork cares if the air is cleared."

To save time, Ori and Unni went into the dressing room together.

"I don't see what either of us could have done to inform Urelt," Unni maintained. "What was I supposed to do? Ask Metchavork to fly me to Germany?"

"You had clearly broken it off," Ori assured her. "You did what you could. If he has a problem with that, it is not your problem."

141

They placed their uniforms into the cleaning bin and got their English clothing from the designated cabinet.

Unni suddenly remembered something she needed to tell Ori. "While we are on the subject of things I did not say, my name on the agenda was not a mistake. I changed it on the nomenclature form last night. I just never had the chance to mention it last night, given the reception you gave me when I returned with the bedding."

"But I thought you said you wanted…"

"I suppose I did say that," Unni went on. "But I changed my mind. I made the decision back in South Zarfixu."

"Because I saved your life?"

"Because you *are* my life."

Ori suddenly found it necessary to lock the latch on the dressing room door.

Several minutes later, Duvass pounded on the door. "Hurry up in there! Hortu is getting impatient."

"Just a moment!" Ori responded.

"We're almost ready," Unni added.

Sraymlat and Svortomit were in the small room where the life support system was regulated for a quarter of Station 48-3.

"Don't you see, Urelt?" Svortomit pleaded. "This is part of the mission. Metchavork had to do it that way. With Vlaris taking over as Subdirector, we needed a smoke screen."

"Part of the mission? Part of the mission! Listen to yourself, Huha. What about me?"

"What about you? It was over between you and Unni. Nothing was going to change that. But this arrangement…"

"I suppose you knew about this all along," Sraymlat surmised. "Am I right, Huha?"

"Metchavork needs to confide in me in order to coordinate the work…"

"Am I right, Huha? Answer me!"

"I suppose I…"

"Suppose nothing! Tell me plainly. Did you or did you not know that Ori and Unni were getting married?"

"Did you expect me to get on a horse and ride four hundred miles from Berlin all the way to Tübingen to inform you?"

"I take that as a yes," Sraymlat fumed. "You are a traitor, just like that serpent Metchavork. He has poisoned you. But I will get even with that viper. I will get even with Ori. I will get even with all of you!"

"Come with me back to the conference room, Urelt," Svortomit exhorted his friend. "You will get over this one day. Just don't do anything you will regret. You are a good agent and we need you. Earth 48 needs you. Germany needs you."

Sraymlat huffed and grudgingly followed Svortomit back to the conference room.

Agent Mlai drove Ori and Unni to the townhouse. It was late in November and winter had already set in. Shelby helped the couple with their bags. Unni was as unaccustomed to having servants as Jenny would be; she carried some of her own bags to her new bedroom. Unni placed the large seashell on her dresser in a prominent place.

The whole house was filled with the aroma of the dinner Mrs. Anders had prepared. They had been expecting the newlyweds, and Robert and Jenny showed up just as expected.

As the couple walked down the hall, Jenny said to her husband, "You are right. We should just forget about William Greenhill and enjoy what we have and carry out our mission."

"Indeed," Robert agreed. "Only this: I fear that we have made an enemy."

15.
A New Generation

Ori and Unni settled into their new routine. In the day, Ori went to work at the Board of Ordnance and Unni went throughout London pursuing British culture. She visited museums, libraries, and book stores, learning as much as she could. In the evening, the couple went out often to social events, the concert hall, and the theatre. They recorded all of their observations on the "shillings" and "donated" them to Agent Mlai every ten to twenty days.

Unni was not afraid to venture into the city alone. She not only saw the palace, the opulence, and the symbols of the British Empire; she also saw the slums, the poverty, and the vast gulf between the rich and the poor.

Once, Unni was attacked by a thief who attempted to snatch her purse. Although Unni was not a large woman, she was a trained agent in excellent health. As an experienced spy, Unni caught the thief's motion in the corner of her eye and used the momentum of the attempted snatch to flip her assailant to the hard pavement. A policeman ran to her aid. When the policeman tried to arrest the thief, Unni told him she did not intend to press charges. "This man does not need a flogging," she reasoned. "I believe he has learned his lesson."

Ori and Unni attended church on Sunday with regularity. They did it largely for appearance and for the image it would later foster for the son they hoped to have. On Sunday morning, January 30, 1820, Ori and Unni bundled up to brave the cold and walk to church. There was a lot of commotion in the streets.

"Did someone say the King has died?" Unni asked her husband.

"Certainly, they are referring to Prince Edward, the Duke of Kent and Strathearn, who died last week," Ori replied. "Perhaps the funeral is to take place today."

But they eventually realized that King George III had indeed died the night before. Although he had been infirm for nearly a decade, the king was popular and the country went into mourning. The funeral was held February 16.

Given Ori's political connections, he and his wife definitely planned to attend. But that morning, Unni woke up sick and nauseous. Ori was concerned and suggested that she stay home. He did not believe that she should go out in the cold under the circumstances. But Unni was determined to go. She took some medication from her medical kit.

It did not seem to help. Unni was weak, and the couple had to leave the ceremony before it was over. The following morning, she got worse. Now Ori was very worried. He sent for a doctor.

The doctor spent some time to examine Unni and asked her a lot of questions. Ori was puzzled, because when the doctor emerged from the bedroom, he was smiling.

"Major Weatherby, your wife is not sick; she is pregnant," the doctor announced. "My congratulations."

Ori went from fear and worry to elation. As soon as the doctor left the house, he went into the bedroom. "Jenny! This is wonderful!"

"Yes," she agreed from her bed. "He will be fifty by the latter part of 1870."

"And the planet will be at Technology Level 10 within a century," Ori declared. "Picture being able to take an airplane to Berlin to meet with Dieter Dehrmann."

"At this point, I'd settle for a train ride to Wallingford," Unni replied.

"You know, they have already invented the steam locomotive. That Stephenson chap has a working model. I saw it once. I think commercial rail transport is only a decade away."

"Are you telling me that the English invented something before the Germans?"

"England is first in steam locomotives," Ori affirmed.

"Because I am still puzzled at the analysis Tekalta prepared the last time we were aloft," Unni said. "I know how those simulations are built, and the assessment of German progress seemed to be far ahead of where we were projecting them back when I was an analyst."

146

"You don't think Metch…von Mecklenburg is stretching the truth in official reports, do you?"

"I honestly don't know."

"Well, I only hope he is right," Ori said. "I frankly don't care how disaster is averted for this planet, whether through the English or the Prussians."

"Or the Americans?"

Ori chuckled. "Even those backward Americans. Just so long as it is not the French."

Unni agreed with a laugh.

For the next two months, Unni had morning sickness, but she was still able to leave the house and explore the city and its libraries. The agents informed their team leader through the "shillings" that Unni was expecting a baby.

One day in early April, Ori was in his office when he felt a series of pulses in his shoulder. They were coordinates of a location. The location was within the city. It could not possibly be a rendezvous with a transport, he reasoned. A spacecraft would never be landed within a major city.

On his way home from work he walked to the spot. It was less than a mile from his townhouse. He found himself on a street with buildings on both sides. There were shops on the lower level and dwellings on the upper floors.

Why did the Interplanetary Intelligence Service want him here? Was he to meet with someone?

He looked around and he saw the shingle on the other side of the street of a certain Dr. John Stanton. Ori crossed the street and tried to open the door. Just then, he received a pulse in the affirmative. The door was locked and the sign indicated that he had arrived after hours. But Ori was clear that his colleagues aloft on Station 48-3 had found him a competent doctor.

Unni went to visit the doctor the following day. Dr. Stanton was about forty years of age with some premature gray hair and was balding. He was a soft-spoken man with small eyeglasses and modest clothing. Dr. Stanton was not an obstetrician, but he demonstrated common sense. Unni noted that he washed his hands before and after touching a patient.

Dr. Stanton projected that the baby would be born in late October or early November at the latest.

Unni's bad experience in Surrey with Princess Charlotte had taught her that many of the high-priced doctors that the wealthy were using were not competent even by the standards of Technology Level 8. Unni told her husband that Dr. Stanton was the best one could hope for among the native physicians.

Ori wondered how much effort Tekalta and Leka must have exerted to find Dr. Stanton.

Although Ori and Unni came to respect Dr. Stanton, Unni began to get anxious. Even the activity of furnishing and decorating the baby's room was not enough to distract her from her worries. Her due date in late October was the same as Princess Charlotte's had been just three years before. Unni could not get the bad memory of that unsuccessful delivery out of her mind. Unni was doubly anxious: concerned about her baby and concerned about her mission.

Ori felt the same way. Unni was very dear to him. Her misgivings about having a baby on a primitive planet began to weigh on him until he finally stated them on one of his "shillings."

It was in late August that he passed the shilling to Agent Mlai. The response was almost immediate. Ori received a summons to an open field outside of London the following day for a meeting two days hence.

Ori saw the glow of the underside of the spacecraft on that dark night and immediately boarded it. To his surprise, he was greeted on the lower deck by Agent Lorbank, who was dressed in a silver suit rather than his French native clothing.

"Good evening, Agent Svavapass," he greeted his colleague in a formal tone.

"Good evening, Agent Lorbank, or is that Special Agent Lorbank?"

"Always perceptive, Ori," Lorbank replied. "There have been changes to the makeup of this team. Where do I even begin?"

"What happened to Metchavork?" Ori asked.

"Sreedro Metchavork is no longer a member of the Interplanetary Intelligence Service," Lorbank stated. "He resigned two months ago and returned to Botvrayt on Earth 19. Last I heard, he had gotten a position as an administrator in the public school system in a small town outside of Yoilafa."

"What?" Ori was shocked. It seemed like Metchavork had long-term plans for the Earth 48 team. "I take it this was not voluntary."

"The official version is that Metchavork decided to take early retirement on 37532.1.36. Of the six agents assigned to the German speaking world, two resigned to 'pursue other career opportunities,' and the other three put in for a transfer to the Bureau of Protective Action. Only Sraymlat is left."

"Sraymlat. I get the picture. Was Svortomit one of the ones fired?"

"No, he is on Earth 1 being trained for Protective Action. I was promoted to team leader a few days later. I lead a team with just five fulltime field agents: Qlat in New York, Duvass in Paris, you and Unni in London, and just one agent in the German-speaking world, and he is not in Berlin or Vienna."

"Are you getting new recruits?"

"Yes, but not for at least another year. Learning the languages takes time."

"Perhaps you could spend half of your time in Paris while you wait for more agents."

"A lot of my job involves coordinating what goes on in the labs and assimilating data," Lorbank explained. "I am needed up there on Station 48-3. Besides, I cannot return to Paris. Louis LeBlanc is dead."

"You killed off your own alias?"

"No, Vlaris did. I was eating lunch at a café in Paris when an agent slipped something into my wine without my knowledge. I was walking back to my office with two colleagues when I began to feel chest pains. I thought I was having a heart attack. My friends sat me on a bench and called for a doctor. I passed out. I woke up in sickbay on Station 48-3. When I was able to sit up, Vlaris came in to see me and told me that I was the new team leader and that LeBlanc had died of a heart attack. The next day, he fully briefed me about Metchavork's misdeeds."

"So, we are down to five field agents," Ori said.

"And for the next few months, really only four. I am placing Unni on maternity leave. I have gotten authorization to move her to her home city. A starship is arriving in three days to take her to Earth 19 to have her baby in Yoilafa in a proper hospital."

"I could tell our friends I am taking her to the countryside to have the baby there," Ori offered.

"That's the plan. Here is a letter from your mother-in-law inviting her to Wallingford."

"My mother-in-law?"

Ori looked at the letter. It was addressed to Mrs. Jennifer Weatherby and from Mrs. Abigail Carter.

"Oh, yes, that mother-in-law."

"We need to move her right away. Soon she will be too large to travel comfortably. Agent Mlai will be arriving at your home with a carriage in three days, so be ready."

"We will be ready," Ori assured him. "Thanks for taking care of this. Unni will be relieved to hear."

"Oh, one last thing, Ori. Watch out for Sraymlat. I am not sure he is done taking out his revenge."

Unni was indeed relieved when she heard about having her baby in a proper hospital on Earth 19. She was disappointed but not surprised when she heard about Metchavork. "Something odd was going on in Germany. Whatever it was, Urelt must have blown the whistle."

"Whatever it was, you can bet Huha Svortomit was involved," Ori conjectured. "He and Metchavork were really tight. The thing I can't figure out is how Huha avoided getting fired."

Unni and Ori packed their things in trunks as if they were going into the country. Agent Mlai came to their townhouse three days later as scheduled and loaded their things onto the horse-drawn carriage. They rode out to a field west of London. It was dusk when the transport landed. Ori and Unni walked to the vehicle, and Mlai left with the carriage.

When Ori and Unni reached the vehicle, a harness was dropped so that Unni would not have to climb the ladder. But Unni refused it and climbed the ladder anyway, as awkward as that was for her.

The flight to the orbiting starship took longer than usual as Major Hortu avoided any major accelerations, trying his best to give Unni the smoothest possible ride. The transport went straight to the starship without stopping off at Station 48-3 so that Unni would not have to pass through a transport hangar more than once. The transfer was unpleasant, as it is very uncomfortable to be both weightless and pregnant.

Unni was taken to sickbay for an examination and some overdue prenatal care. Ori was with her during the examination.

The ship's surgeon was pleased with what he saw. "Mother and baby are in very good shape," he declared. Would you like to see the baby?"

A three-dimensional holograph appeared over Unni as she lay on the examination table. The surgeon rotated the image so that both parents could see the baby from every angle. Ori was awestruck. "That is *our* baby."

"Indeed it is," the surgeon replied, feeling some of the joy of the new parents. "And as you can plainly see, your baby is a girl."

The surgeon left the room. "I never thought we might be having a girl," Unni said. "I haven't considered any girls' names."

"Neither have I," Ori admitted. "We'll have to work that out when I arrive at Earth 19 two months from now."

"What happens if I have the baby early, before you get there?"

"I trust your judgment," he replied. "If I am late, you name her. But I do not plan to be late."

An officer entered sickbay. "Agent Orishackt Svavapass, you need to proceed to the transport hangar at once. We will be departing shortly."

Ori and Unni managed a quick kiss, and Ori was on his way. He changed into his native clothing and made his way out of the gravity zone, swimming in zero gravity to the transport. Ori hated being weightless while dressed as an English gentleman.

He entered the transport and closed the hatch behind him. He found Squeem all alone on the flight deck strapped into the pilot's seat. "It's just going to be you and me this time, Svavapass" Squeem announced. "If you like, you can sit up here."

Ori took him up on his offer and strapped himself into the copilot's seat. As Squeem undocked the transport, Ori noticed the insignia on Squeem's collar. He had been promoted to captain.

Squeem punched in a course and the vehicle began its long descent to the surface of Earth 48.

"So Hortu isn't coming with us?" Ori surmised.

"No, he is leaving us on the starship, bound for Earth 46. That planet is technology Level 10, and Station 46-4 was hearing too many radio transmissions from the natives on the surface about sightings of unidentified flying objects. And they were happening at times and places where we knew we were conducting operations. The military wanted a more skillful pilot, one who was better at avoiding detection."

Ori was hoping to use the trip to think about girl's names for his baby, but Squeem was being chatty.

"Do you know what the natives on Earth 46 call our Atmospheric Entry Vehicles?" Squeem asked. "They call them flying saucers. Isn't that a laugh? The natives on Earth 13 and Earth 21 also call them flying saucers. Once, we transport pilots were shown a movie intercepted from television transmissions from the surface of Earth 21 and translated into Grellish. It was a science fiction film about flying saucers. We were laughing so hard! Why, even Hortu broke a grin! Let me tell you about this film…"

Squeem spared Ori no detail. He chattered nonstop, even through the "flip" maneuver.

"Now old Hortu, he doesn't perform the flip that way," Squeem chattered on. "He does it more slowly, drawing it out. But I get it over with for my passengers in one quick jolt."

Ori was thankful Squeem wasn't driving when his expectant wife was on board. "Would you even do it that way if there were a woman on board with child?"

"It's funny you should ask. Hortu was supposed to be transferred last month, you know, but Lorbank held him over just for picking up your wife. Her being pregnant and all, the Interplanetary Intelligence Service wanted her to have the smoothest possible ride. My pride's not too wounded, even though I know I was up to giving your wife a comfortable trip, but with your wife being a celebrity within the Service and all…"

"A celebrity?" Ori asked.

"I heard the talk in the halls. Your wife was the handler of a native of one of the occupied planets and helped recruit her into the Service. She cracked their language as well. That native woman helped our side enormously."

"You know all of that is confidential and classified," Ori reminded the pilot.

"Classified? Are you serious? There are no secrets on a small space station packed with 120 people. Now you take that whole affair with that corrupt team leader, Sreedro Metchavork. Everyone on the whole space station knows he didn't really retire. Vlaris did not want to turn him over for trial after that Ortees debacle. And Metchavork didn't want to go to prison, so they cut a deal."

"What rules did he break?" Ori asked, even though he had already guessed.

"The Noninterference Protocol, for openers. He had all of his agents in the parts of Continent 1 that spoke a certain language…Doish I think they call it…"

"Deutsch, German…"

"Right. He had those six agents stirring up the young natives to join a fraternity dedicated to unifying all of those countries into one Empire. That's interference big time, wouldn't you say?"

"Yes, that would…"

"So anyway, one day, one of the agents, your old friend Sraymlat got really angry. It was about your wife Unni. He was angry at Metchavork for hiding

from him her engagement to you until after you were married. He threatened
to blow the whistle on Metchavork's whole scheme. The next two times the
team for that language was summoned to Station 48-3, Sraymlat was not at
the pickup point. Hortu waited as long as he could, but Sraymlat was a no-
show. Eventually, Svortomit rode four hundred miles on a horse to check in
on his old buddy. Come to find out, Sraymlat never received any summons.
Metchavork deliberately had the communications officer type the wrong code
to his transponder. He didn't want Sraymlat coming on board the space station
and sending a message to Subdirector Vlaris."

"What was Metchavork going to do, strand him down there forever?" Ori
asked.

"I don't know, but Svortomit ultimately called Vlaris. Vlaris came all the
way out here in person. I remember flying him down to Terb… whatever that
place is where Sraymlat lives."

"Tübingen?"

"Yes, that's the place. And within hours, Metchavork retired."

"Now I see how Svortomit survived the massacre."

"Vlaris still felt Svortomit needed to leave the Bureau of Exploratory Surveillance. He said something about wanting to go to Earth 55 to be with his
old leader Ortees."

"That would make sense," Ori nodded. "But what about Unni and me?
Do you get the impression Sraymlat is looking to make trouble for us?"

"He already has. Sraymlat told Vlaris you two are trying have a baby and
groom him to be a political leader in the native faction you are living in. The
only reason Vlaris hasn't acted is that Unni is too hot to handle right now. She
is too much of a hero. So Vlaris is biding his time. But the scuttlebutt I hear
is that Vlaris thinks you will violate the Noninterference Protocol at some
time in the future. He is just waiting for the hard evidence. So, if I were you,
I would watch my step."

Two months later, Ori felt the pulses in his shoulder telling him it was time to
go to Earth 19 for the birth of his daughter. Shelby knew that Major Weatherby would be going to the countryside to be with his wife when she gave birth.
He helped his employer pack for the journey. Agent Mlai showed up with the
coach and drove him to the pickup point. Squeem and his new copilot shuttled

Ori to an orbiting starship. Several days later, he was on Earth 19 in Yoilafa with his wife.

Unni was very happy to see Ori. They had never been apart this long since their engagement. Unni's parents were also glad to see Ori.

Unni complained that she was tired of being so large and awkward. She wanted the baby right now. When the due date came and went, Unni began to become anxious.

"Don't worry," Ori said. "I have heard that the first one is always a few days late."

"Well, I have heard that walking can help the baby come sooner," Unni replied.

Ori took the hint. He suggested they go to for a walk. It was early springtime in Yoilafa and still quite cool. They came to a nearby park and found a trail. There were a few flowers along the trail, the first of the spring.

"I have been thinking about a name for our baby girl," Unni said. "I think she should have an English name. That way she would not have to deal with having two identities like we professional spies do."

"I had been thinking the same thing myself," Ori agreed.

"What English names do you like?" Unni asked.

"Well, my favorite one is Jenny, but it is already taken."

Unni laughed. Then she told Ori what was on her mind. "I was considering naming her Charlotte. It is a name of influence. England has had a queen by that name until late and several princesses. Also, she is likely to be born near the third anniversary of the parting of the Princess Charlotte by whom I was briefly employed."

"Charlotte Weatherby has a nice sound to it," Ori observed.

"How about Charlotte Svavapass? Do you think my parents will find it strange?"

"Does it matter? I think any English name would seem strange to our families."

"Then Charlotte it is," Unni concluded.

They walked for hours. "All of this walking has not initiated labor," Unni said. "All I have succeeded in doing is tiring myself out."

Three days later, Unni's obstetrician instructed her to report to the hospital the next morning so that he could induce her. He was concerned about the relative size of the baby to her slight mother. But that evening, Unni felt her labor coming on. Huhane Vlaytork drove Ori and Unni to the hospital. Three hours later, after a relatively uneventful labor, Charlotte Svavapass came into the world.

Mother and baby were in good health. The date was 37532.5.30 by the interplanetary calendar. Ori noted that it was November 5, 1820 in England, the third anniversary of Princess Charlotte's ill-fated delivery in Surrey. But this delivery in Yoilafa was quite the opposite. It had transpired with near perfection.

16.

Detected

Robert and Jenny Weatherby arrived home from the coronation of King George IV to the great relief of their baby sitter. Charlotte was teething and was either fussy or crying the entire time. Ori had hired a maid, Lizzy, but he never hired a fulltime nanny. Unni wanted the role of raising her children, for reasons that were not obvious to those outside the immediate family.

It was now July and Charlotte was eight months old. Despite the noise of a crying baby, all of the household servants seemed to enjoy the Weatherby home due to the harmony between the major and his wife. Many of their acquaintances working as maids or butlers suffered the tensions of serving in a home headed by a couple that was unhappily married. Robert and Jenny Weatherby appeared to be two halves of one coordinated entity. And indeed they were.

Unni went upstairs to comfort little Charlotte. Soon, dinner was served. Ori and Unni had been out all day, first watching the royal procession, followed by the coronation service at Westminster Abbey. They were tired.

After dinner, Shelby brought them the mail. Unni was curious to open a letter addressed to her from her supposed mother, Mrs. Abigail Carter in Wallingford. The address on the envelope was written in the flowing and elegant script that her non-existent English mother had. She opened the letter. Although Jenny knew the letter was from the Interplanetary Intelligence Service, Jenny was surprised to see that the letter was completely in Grellish. It was highly unusual for even written Grellish to be seen in the field on a planet under surveillance.

Unni read the first part of it and realized that she needed to show this to Ori right away. She hid the letter in its envelope and seized Ori by his left wrist and towed him to their bedroom. The servants had grown accustomed to this sort of thing from Unni. They would always wait until the couple's door closed before they exchanged wry grins.

"Robert, look at this," Unni said in a soft voice. The letter was two pages long printed on both sides in the Grellish alphabet. They read it silently, following the protocol against speaking any languages on a planet under surveillance that were not native to that planet.

The letter was full of new rules. It said that field agents should no longer communicate with their orbital support or team leaders using disguised recording devices (in their case shillings) but in hand writing, addressed to pseudo-persons with dummy mailboxes established by the Interplanetary Intelligence Service. That would be Jenny Weatherby's "mother" in their case. Agents were to expect written correspondence more often and were required to reply within two days of receiving a letter. Letters from the Interplanetary Intelligence Service were to be memorized and burned.

Robert stopped after just one page. "What brought this on? The rules have been the same for centuries."

The letter went on and on with changes. Trips between the surface of planets and orbital stations by field agents were to be restricted and left to non-permanent agents. All orbital space stations were to be armed, and their hulls refitted with black solar panels to provide stealth, even if the space station was not in occupied territory. All communication between space stations and Service headquarters was to be in code. Codes would change every thirty-eight days…

"Look at this Robert," Unni said. "Agents' tours of duty will henceforth be ten years instead of five. And our transponders have to be replaced with a new model…"

"I haven't gotten that far, Jenny."

"We are going to be issued suicide pills in our medical kits?" Unni could not believe what she was reading.

"Has Vlaris gone crazy?" Ori asked in dismay.

But Unni remembered some of these measures being in place for agents serving in the Bureau of Protective Action when she was on Station 55-1. "I think I know what this is about. This has something to do with the Vittmian Empire. I am sure of it."

"Could they have spies or satellites all the way out here?" Ori wondered. "I don't know, but I am afraid we will find out soon enough."

Several days later, another letter came from Wallingford in a similar envelope with the same handwriting. This time, the contents were in English. It was a note from Dr. Stanton, "reminding" Robert and Jennifer that Charlotte was going to be nine months old, and therefore needed a specific kind of checkup. The letter exhorted both parents to show up. The cost of the examination was to be fourteen shillings, and it said they needed to bring "exact change."

Robert went to his dresser and counted his recording shillings. There were exactly fourteen. It was clear that the letter was a message from the Interplanetary Intelligence Service to come to meet at Dr. Stanton's office.

On the day and time of the appointment, Robert and Jenny took Charlotte and proceeded to the street where the doctor's office was located. They stood in front of the office for nearly fifteen minutes waiting for an agent to show up, but no one appeared.

At last, Dr. Stanton stepped out and urged them to come in. "Are you going to stand there all afternoon?" he asked.

Jenny was afraid that if they stepped in, they might miss the agent or agents that sent the letter, but somehow, Dr. Stanton was expecting them.

They entered his waiting area. It was completely empty. Even his receptionist was not present. The doctor let them into the treatment room. His nurse was not to be seen. As they entered the treatment room, the doctor said, "The real reason I summoned you here was to replace your transponders."

Robert and Jenny were both shocked and mortified. Was Dr. John Stanton an agent? If so, for whom? Was he going to perform the surgery using methods of Technology Level 8?

The couple heard a sound behind them and they turned to see three men standing against the wall, out of view as one entered the room. The three were Special Agent Lorch Lorbank, Agent Mlai, and the surgeon from Station 48-3, all dressed in native clothing. Ori and Unni were relieved to see familiar faces.

"Let me introduce you to my guests," the doctor continued. "This is my longtime friend Dr. Albert Meyer from Hanover." Agent Mlai nodded. "Dr. Meyer and I were classmates in medical school. He attended an international medical convention last week at Oxford, and when it ended, Dr. Meyer came to London to look me up. He brought two French doctors with him, as they are traveling together back to the continent. This is Dr. Louis LeBlanc and Dr. Jacques Dubocq."

The men extended their hands to greet Robert. Lorbank said, "*Bonjour.*"

"Albert and I have been doing a little catching up," the doctor went on. "It is a pity that I do not speak a word of French."

"But I do," Jenny said. "*Je parle français.*"

The two purported Frenchmen nodded in approval.

"No need to worry," Lorbank said in French. "Dr. Dubocq will perform the surgery. He brought his medical kit from the station."

Ori proceeded to Dr. Stanton's operating table and the surgeon immediately anesthetized his shoulder.

"I am sure you are wondering what is going on here," Lorbank began in his excellent French. "But first, are you familiar with hypnotic mind wipes?"

"I remember hearing about them at the Academy," Unni replied. "We used to call them…how would you say it in French?... 'hypno-wipes.'"

"You had better get familiar with them. Hypno-wipes are now standard in everyone's medical packet. There are directions how to use them on the wrapper. Needless to say, Dr. Stanton here is under the influence of a such a substance. He sincerely believes that Agent Mlai is an old friend. And when he emerges from the trance, he will remember only what we want him to remember.

"To the point, several weeks ago, agents of the Bureau of Protective Action were on the surface of Earth 62, when they were found by Vittmians."

"Vittmians?" Unni immediately perceived the direction of this discussion.

"When our agents knew they had been detected, they fled to their transport but one agent was shot dead. We believe the Vittmians did some DNA testing and realized he was not a native of Earth 62. In any case, they traced the course of the transport back to the vicinity of Station 62-1.

"Hours after reporting to Tlat Mlang what had occurred, Station 62-1 came under attack by three Vittmian warships. The station was destroyed and all personnel were lost. Since that time two other stations were destroyed. In short, the Empire now knows we exist, and the High Commission has notified the populations of all planets in the Confederation that we are at war."

"What is he saying, Jenny?" Ori asked. "I know a little French. Did he say *guerre*? Are we at war?"

"I will explain later," she answered quickly.

160

The anesthetic had taken effect, and Dr. Dubocq began his work on Ori's shoulder.

"Saibert Ortees—is he all right?"

"I cannot answer that," Lorbank replied. "That sort of information is released on a need-to-know basis."

"Need-to-know basis!" Unni echoed with frustration.

"Now that we are at war, all of the procedures are changing," Lorbank went on. "Except, of course, our Bureau is maintaining the Noninterference Protocol. One of the changes we are making is that henceforth, most if not all of our long-term field agents will be married. Agents are being assigned in pairs."

"I suppose Ori and I are ahead of the rest of our fellow agents," Unni surmised.

"I don't think there are more than five married couples deployed on the twenty-two planets our Bureau has under surveillance," Lorbank conjectured. "There are schools on Earth 2 for the children of the agents to acclimate them to their parents' fields of work."

"Of course, Charlotte won't need that kind of training," Unni said. "She is starting her life here in England."

"You are correct for the most part," Lorbank replied. "But I am afraid Charlotte will be required to go to Earth 2 to attend school. We will come for her when she turns five."

"That is totally unnecessary," Unni protested. "Ori and I will appeal to the Subdirector!"

"That will do no good," Lorbank explained. "The order originated from Vlaris."

"But why?" Unni was clearly annoyed.

"Vlaris considers your situation here in England perfect, but he cannot trust you not to try to groom a future government official and break the Noninterference Protocol. You know, Sraymlat told him exactly what you and Ori have planned. Vlaris wants to be able to trust you. To do so, he needs to have his teachers train your children."

"What is this about Vlaris?" Ori asked Unni as he got up from the table.

But Unni was becoming exasperated at Lorbank. "You won't tell me if my former team leader on two different planets is alive, and now you want to take my daughter hostage. This is no way to build team loyalty!"

The surgeon administered the anesthetic to Unni's left shoulder.

"Very well, if you must know," Lorbank conceded, "Special Agent Ortees is alive, as is Huha Svortomit. But Huha Srot is missing and presumed dead. And this goes no further than Ori. Are you happy now?"

As Ori dressed, Agent Mlai engaged him in a discussion in English. Mlai's grammar and vocabulary had improved greatly in the past two years, but his pronunciation was insufficient to land him a permanent job on the surface of Earth 48 with an alias. Like many people, terrestrial and extra-terrestrial, Mlai could not properly pronounce the letter w or the "th" consonant blend. He spoke with an accent that did not even sound like an authentic German accent.

Mlai, as Dr. Meyer, told Ori humorous stories of his exploits in medical school with his friend Dr. John Stanton. Ori clearly perceived that the stories were really for Dr. Stanton's consumption.

When Unni's procedure was complete, the surgeon began to place his equipment back in his medical bag. Unni picked up her baby, who had been uncharacteristically patient throughout the entire visit. Mlai asked Ori for the fourteen shillings.

"They are in my purse," Unni said. "Robert, could you hold Charlotte for me?"

Unni fumbled for a moment, apparently from the numbness, and produced the shillings and handed them directly to Agent Mlai.

Mlai put the shillings into his pocket and produced a piece of orange synthetic cloth. He placed it on Dr. Stanton's face.

"Dr. Stanton, you remember nothing about transponders."

"I remember nothing about transponders," he compliantly responded.

"You never saw any surgery performed on Mr. or Mrs. Weatherby."

"I never saw any surgery performed on Mr. or Mrs. Weatherby."

"And when Mr. Weatherby says 'Good day" you will forget this whole trance."

Mlai removed the cloth and the three agents made for the door. As he exited, Lorbank said, "*Au revoir pour le moment.*"

Unni wondered how long it would be before Mlai or Lorbank noticed that she had only given them thirteen shillings.

When Ori heard the front door close, he said, "Good day."

"And good day to you too," Dr. Stanton greeted him. "You are here for your baby's nine-month examination, am I correct?"

"Yes, we are," Unni replied.

Dr. Stanton took Charlotte from Robert and placed her on the table. "I am dreadfully sorry none of my staff were here to let you in. I sent them home early today. A colleague of mine from the continent came to visit, actually my classmate from medical school. So, I cleared my schedule."

Unni waited until they were home to tell Ori what Lorbank had said. The couple went to the nursery with Charlotte and closed the door.

"Well, Robert, you don't seem very concerned."

"No, Jenny, I am not very worried at all," Ori replied. "Charlotte will not be five years old for more than another four years. By that time, who knows what the policy will be or if Sral Vlaris will still be Subdirector. Ever since that Empire was discovered, senior leaders and protocols have been changing on a regular basis."

"Except one," Unni reminded him.

"Which one is that?" Ori asked.

"Sent to watch but not to affect."

17.
Touching the Subdirector's Heart

Ori and Unni wanted another baby. The sooner the baby was born, the sooner the child could reach high office and start the British Empire on a program of technical advance. But the ban on agents' space travel indicated that the baby would be born on the surface of a technically primitive planet with a native doctor. This gave Ori and Unni pause.

Unni asked her husband if she could have a piano. She wanted to learn to play a native instrument. Ori acquired one for his wife. At first Unni was mystified by the instrument. The keys ascended in pitch from left to right. This meant that the treble notes would be played by the right hand instead of the left. This was totally backward from instruments on her native Earth 19.

Ori hired a certain Karl Kurzler to teach her to play the piano. Kurzler was an older man who had come to London from Vienna with Josef Haydn in 1794 but had stayed. After the first weekly lesson, Unni was assigned Lesson One in a music book that she had purchased. Kurzler told Unni she could go on to Lesson Two if she felt she had adequately mastered Lesson One. She was also to learn to play the C scale and its arpeggio.

Jenny practiced ninety minutes each day, thirty minutes before each meal. After two days, she had fully mastered both lessons and decided to take on the next three. Additionally, Jenny figured out the pattern of sharps and flats from the book and learned all twelve major and minor scales, as well as the chromatic scale. By the time Kurzler came back the following week, she was playing all of the scales and arpeggios flawlessly at high speed.

Kurzler was angry at first. He thought Unni was an experienced pianist who had merely hired him as a joke. But when he saw her incorrect finger positions, he realized that she was not a rich young lady playing a trick. He surmised that she was a musical prodigy. From then on, Kurzler helped Unni with her hand positions and gave her challenging assignments. Within months, Unni was playing such works as the *Well-Tempered Clavier* by Johann Sebastian Bach. Charlotte was over a year old, and she would sit on her rocking horse and rock to her mother's music.

Kurzler was mystified as to why his star pupil would not appear in a public recital. But Unni had a motive for learning the piano. For more than two years, Unni had worked as an analyst on Station 48-3 under then Team Leader Sral Vlaris. She had often entered his quarters and heard the native music he was listening to. She had memorized some of the tunes.

One day, as Kurzler was getting ready to leave at the end of a lesson, Unni said she had a request. "There is a certain composer that I had heard of years ago, and I was wondering if you could help me identify him. I believe he was in Vienna."

"Tell me about this man. Maybe I can help you," Kurzler offered.

"I know he was in Vienna in the 1780s, and I know he died young."

"That could be several composers. Mozart comes to mind."

"What is this?" She played a melody on the piano.

"That is *Eine Kleine Nachtmusik*, by Mozart."

"And this?"

Unni played a longer excerpt.

"The overture to *Cosi Fan Tutte*, an opera by Mozart."

"And this?"

"My dear young lady, that is the first melody of the first movement of Mozart's Fortieth Symphony. The man you are seeking is undoubtedly Wolfgang Amadeus Mozart."

"Did Mozart write anything for piano?"

Kurzler burst out laughing. "What planet do you come from?"

Unni paused for a moment, not realizing Kurzler was using an idiom. Before Unni could inquire as to how Kurzler knew of her extraterrestrial origin, he informed her that Mozart wrote 27 concerti and nineteen sonatas for piano.

"I would like to learn some of these," she stated.

"I will bring you the scores to several of them free of charge, but under one condition: you must agree to perform in a recital."

"I must ask my husband's permission," she replied. Unni ran into the study and related the matter to Ori.

"I thought you said you were learning for the children," Ori reminded her. "We are spies on a mission, not performers. A public performance would attract too much attention."

"This is part of the mission," Unni replied. "Let me agree to perform and after Mr. Kurzler leaves, I will explain."

Ori had grown to trust his wife to such an extent that he acquiesced. After Shelby had shown Karl Kurzler out of the townhouse, Unni went into the bedroom and beckoned Ori to follow her. She reached into her dresser drawer and produced a shiny shilling.

"What is this? Ori asked. "This looks like…"

"It is," Unni said. "When we 'paid' for Charlotte's exam last summer, I held one back. It has a recording capacity of one Mraznian hour of seventy-two minutes. I intend to record three pieces of piano music by that composer Vlaris loved and send it to him in one of our 'letters' as a gift."

"You mean a bribe?"

"You can read my mind," Unni said with smile.

"As you can read mine," Ori replied. Ori wrapped his arms around his wife and kissed her passionately. A minute later, he fell onto the bed taking her with him.

"Ori, be careful!" she cautioned. "It is the wrong day…"

It seemed as if all of the agents on Earth 48 were gathered to Station 48-3 for a conference every two years in the autumn of an odd-numbered year. At least that had been the pattern since Waterloo. But it was already March 1822 and a conference had not been called. Ori and Unni had no idea how their teammates were progressing in Germany, France or America. All they knew was what they were told in "letters" from Jenny's "mother" in Wallingford.

The Duke of Wellington was as aloof as ever. Ori rarely saw him, although Wellington had had him promoted to a higher position on the Board of Ordnance in 1821.

Wellington was fifty-two years old and his influence in the government was increasing, but the prime minister, Lord Liverpool, showed every sign of continuing in office. Liverpool was approaching his tenth anniversary as prime minister, despite the Corn Laws and the Six Acts suppressing dissent, which made him unpopular with the people. His position was secure because he was in favor with the king and with most of the three percent of the population who had the right to vote.

"Do you think Charlotte could ever be a prime minister?" Ori wondered. "She will reach the right age sometime in the late 1870s."

"I doubt women will have the right to vote by then, much less hold office," Unni replied. "At the rate of social progress in this country, it will likely be the late *1970s* before the British have a female prime minister!"

But Ori and Unni were still reluctant to have another baby.

In the summer of 1822, there was a two-page note in the letter they received from "Abigail Carter" in addition to the report from the Bureau of Exploratory Surveillance. The note was not written by hand, but a printout, and it was not in Grellish, but in Urgstish, a language from Earth 19 that Unni understood. The note was from Special Agent Ortees.

Unni immediately showed it to Ori. It started, "If you are reading this letter, then it made it through to you. Do not ask how I was able to slip this letter into your envelope.

"Due to the help rendered by Ryla and the excellent work by Unni, the Bureau of Protective Action was able to plant five agents on the surface of Earth 55 by the beginning of the year 37533. Suddenly, on 37533.2.13, a Confederation starship appeared unannounced and told us that the entire crew of Station 55-1 was being extracted. Two space stations in the occupied territories had been located, attacked and destroyed by the Vittmians, and all of the others were being evacuated. We had three hours to get out.

"I was forced to abandon the five agents on the surface. I barely had time to send them a Code 98."

Ori and Unni knew what Code 98 meant. It was the transponder message that every field agent dreaded. It meant that they were on their own. Ortees went on to explain how Station 55-1 was powered down and towed to an orbit around a distant gas giant planet for later retrieval.

"Twice since the evacuation, Earth 55 has been briefly visited by a starship. The agents got a few pulses, and all five transponders are still showing activity. But there has been no communication from the agents. Whatever intelligence they have received remains with them."

Ortees said that the Bureau was working on plans to get agents onto some of the other occupied planets and to get data out without being detected. He said he was active in that effort.

One of the most disturbing things that Ortees reported was that he knew "as a fact" that none of the other four couples with children born on surveillance planets were being made to send their children to the Adaptation School on Earth 2. He confirmed what Ori and Unni had suspected: that they were being singled out by Vlaris.

Ori and Unni were angry and disappointed. But what could they do?

Unni increased her practice time on the piano to nearly three hours each day. She was becoming quite proficient at Mozart's Piano Concerto #21 in C Major, even learning the skill of being expressive in the slow movement. Perhaps they could get Vlaris to listen to reason. He would certainly listen to Mozart.

In the fall, Kurzler arranged for a recital for "Jennifer Weatherby." She performed a prelude and fugue by Bach from the *Well-Tempered Clavier* and Mozart's Piano Concerto #21. An orchestra comprised of music students accompanied her. Ori recorded the dress rehearsal so as to avoid the rustling noises of a live audience. In January, Unni gave a second recital that included another prelude and fugue and Mozart's Piano Concerto #20. Again, Ori made a recording.

The "shilling" now had two Mozart concerti and ten minutes of empty recording time. Unni recorded some of Mozart's variations on *Twinkle, Twinkle Little Star*. With the final minute of recording time, she had Charlotte, now two years old, sing that song with her mother accompanying her on the piano.

Charlotte sang very sweetly. Certainly, this recording should touch Vlaris's heart, Unni thought. Ori considered that ending the perfect argument as to why Charlotte should not be required to go to Earth 2 for schooling. Unni wrote a note to Vlaris and enclosed it with the shilling in an envelope addressed to Mrs. Abigail Carter in Wallingford.

Two months later, Unni received a note from Vlaris. He cordially thanked her for the gift and said he would always treasure it. But he made no mention of reversing his decision regarding Charlotte's compulsory education. In fact, he never acknowledged the matter of Charlotte's impending separation from her parents at all.

Ori and Unni were becoming desperate. They did not want to be separated from their daughter. They knew Vlaris was only seventy-two, a long way from the retirement age of eighty-five. He could be in his position indefinitely. They did not know what to do.

169

18.

Second Try

Ori and Unni still wanted another baby. At the beginning of 1824, when Charlotte was three years old, Unni approached Ori privately in the study and told him of an idea she had. It would not help Charlotte, but it could save their mission.

"What if we simply had another baby, and let him be born here in London? How would Vlaris ever find out? There is next to no physical contact between the Service and field agents these days. They only know what we write to them."

"Do you realize what you are suggesting?" Ori cautioned his wife. "That would mean Technology Level 8 prenatal care."

"Having a baby on Earth 48 is not impossible," Unni protested. "There are one billion people on this planet. They all got here somehow."

"Not impossible, but very risky," Ori replied. "And painful."

"They say the first baby is the most difficult. My last delivery entailed only three hours of labor. It shouldn't be too hard. And while Vlaris has our little girl, we would have our future prime minister right here out of his grasp."

"There are too many variables," Ori countered. "How could we prevent Charlotte from talking about her baby brother when she gets to Earth 2? How can we locate a doctor who washes his hands and follows common sense like Stanton?"

"What's wrong with Dr. Stanton?"

"Jenny, for all we know, Mlai has programmed him to write to Mrs. Carter if you ever had another baby. Have you thought about that?"

"You could go down to Dr. Stanton's surgery and find out," Unni suggested.

"What are you saying? Shall I subdue Dr. Stanton with a hypno-wipe and ask him?"

"You are a trained spy, Robert. Break in, find his address book and his patient registry, and make sure there is no one listed named Abigail Carter."

"Oh, that's all? I simply break in and take a look at his papers? Jenny, it is too risky. But I would gladly do that were it not for the real risk: I cannot afford losing you."

"If I were risk-averse, I never would have volunteered to become a field agent," Unni countered. "Besides, it's my body. I'm the one volunteering to suffer."

Ori was silent.

"Ori, don't you remember when we first got engaged? You promised me that you would be committed to the mission of saving this planet from invasion. Everyone in the whole Interplanetary Intelligence Service is thinking about so many things, but who realizes the suffering that is about to befall the people on this planet?"

"I am very uncomfortable with this whole idea," Ori maintained.

Unni turned and hurried out of the study to the bedroom in tears.

"Jenny! Jenny! Come back here! Please!"

"The things a man would do for the woman he loves," Ori said to himself.

He was standing in the dark and bitter cold on a January night waiting for Dr. Stanton's assistant to blow out her candles and leave the office. The doctor himself had left only half an hour before. There was a breeze and a light snow was falling.

At long last, the assistant left the medical office and locked the door behind her. When she was out of view, Ori went up to the door. How easy these locks were to pick at Technology Level 8! Soon Ori was inside. The fireplace had gone out, but it was much warmer than it was outside, especially without the breeze.

Ori lit a candle he had taken with him. He went to the patient files to look for anyone named Carter. It was difficult to do by candlelight. Ori thought how much easier this would be at Technology Level 11. He could simply hack into Dr. Stanton's computer. At this point, Ori would have settled for a Technology Level 9 electric flashlight with an incandescent lightbulb!

The files contained records of several patients with the surname Carter, but none who had a Wallingford address. This was a good sign, but to be fully satisfied, Ori needed to see Dr. Stanton's private address book. Where would he keep that?

Just then, Ori heard a sound at the door. It was opening and someone was coming in! Ori quickly extinguished his candle. He wanted to duck into another room, but he knew from his training that would be self-defeating because of the sound it would make.

Ori backed to the wall and stood still.

"My word," said a female voice. "I could swear I locked that door."

She lit a candle. It was the assistant who was responsible for the doctor's appointments, among other things. She was searching at the desk in the waiting area.

"Ah, yes, right where I left it," she said. She picked up an object, possibly a glove, and left the office and carefully locked the door.

This would pose a problem for Ori. He could surely unlock the door when he left, but it would not be easy to lock it again after he was outside. Self-locking doors were not in widespread use by the natives. The assistant was very careful to lock the door the second time, and would know something was amiss if she or anyone else found it unlocked the next morning.

But that was a problem for later. For now, Ori needed to find the address book. He lit his candle and made his way into Dr. Stanton's office. He searched all of the drawers, looking for an address book, being careful to memorize where every object was stored so as to leave everything in its original place. It was a slow process. He could not find any address book.

Ori began returning the last contents into the bottom drawer. His hand kept bumping a smooth wooden object on the desk. Out of curiosity, he shined the light on it. It was a card file. Ori began to look through the cards. There were no references to anyone named Carter or Weatherby. He even looked under Svavapass. The cards only had addresses to his personal friends, colleagues, and family.

Ori was satisfied that Dr. Stanton did not have the address to the mailbox in Wallingford. Of course, there is a difference between not finding something and proving it did not exist. Then again, the Interplanetary Intelligence Service was in trouble if it had to spy on its own members at a time when their resources were stretched so thin.

Ori extinguished his candle. He went to the door, unlocked it and left. Then he began to consider whether it was prudent to leave the door unlocked. He had been so careful to leave no sign that he had been there. Nothing was taken; nothing was out of place. He had left fingerprints, but the native police did not yet realize the value of looking for them.

Ori turned around and went back and began to try to lock the door the same way he had unlocked it. He tried the knob. It opened, indicating that he had not succeeded. He tried again, but with no success. The third time, he felt he was beginning to move the main tumbler. He tried the knob. The door opened. Just then, he heard a whistle.

"Stop! Police!"

Ori took off down the street. London was one of the few cities on Earth 48 with gas lighting, but the lights were not very strong. This made running treacherous. But the policeman had the same problem.

Ori built a significant lead and ducked into an alley. The policeman ran past him. After a minute, Ori stepped back onto the street and walked home. The police would record the incident as a foiled break-in.

Several nights later, Ori was in his study writing his report to Lorbank concerning the things he had learned from his position in the government. He was alone, when Unni entered the room.

"Robert, I believe it is time for bed," she informed him.

"But, Jenny, this letter has to be mailed tomorrow. You know the rules. We must respond within two days…"

"Yes, I remember. I will wait for you. Try not to be too long."

"I suppose I will just have to work twice as quickly." Ori took out a second piece of paper and a second pen and began to write with both of his hands. Within a few minutes he was done, and he placed the letter into an envelope.

"There," he said. "That did not take too long."

"That is the third time you've done that this winter, Robert," Jenny said with a small grin. "How will you give an account for yourself if a native saw you writing with both hands?"

"You are worth the risk, Jenny," he replied. "Every bit worth the risk."

"One of these days, you are going to get caught."

"Maybe so, but you are the one getting caught tonight!"

Ori got up from his seat to seize her. Unni ran toward the bedroom, and Ori playfully chased her. The couple ran across the townhouse laughing all of the way.

Dr. Stanton smiled pleasantly and said, "Mrs. Weatherby, I am pleased to inform you that you are expecting a baby."

"Oh, that's wonderful! I can hardly wait to tell Robert."

"I would recommend that you come in regularly for the next several months so that I can monitor your progress."

Unni walked out of the doctor's office into the early spring sunshine very pleased with the news, although she fully expected such a diagnosis.

Unni wanted to learn more about the British system of government. After the next baby came, her opportunity to go to the library would be more limited. She had spent a lot of her time on Mozart the past two years, and now it was time to study the things she would need to pass on to the future prime minister she would soon be tutoring.

Throughout the year 1824, it seemed to Ori and Unni that their entire universe held onto a tenuous status quo with British politics, British diplomacy, the Confederation of Civilized Planets, and their family.

The political situation continued as it had been. Lord Liverpool, who had been prime minister for twelve years, held his factious party together against debate over Catholic emancipation. This kept the Tories in power and kept the Duke of Wellington in high position.

Ori and Unni wanted to see relations between the British Empire and the United States continue to improve. President Monroe was stepping down after two terms in office. It was feared that relations would sour if the popular Andrew Jackson were elected president. But John Quincy Adams, a diplomat and voice of reason, was emerging as a potential successor to Monroe. A Jackson victory seemed less inevitable.

The war between the Confederation and the Vittmian Empire had consisted of a series of attacks on each other's convoys. But two Vittmian warships entered the solar system of Earth 40. It was unknown if they were going to attack the planet, disrupt shipping or plant spies on the surface. In any case, a

Confederation force intercepted the Vittmian vessels and destroyed them. This victory raised morale in the Confederation and shattered the myth that the Vittmians were unstoppable.

As for their family, it still appeared that Charlotte would be separated from her parents to go to school on Earth 2. Vlaris was still Subdirector and his policies were unchanged. There was no indication that anyone from the Interplanetary Intelligence Service knew Unni was expecting a baby.

It was against this backdrop that Unni prepared to give birth. Dr. Stanton was pleased with Unni's progress and gave positive reports after every examination. He believed Unni would be due sometime in early November.

On a partly cloudy Sunday in September, the family went to the park. Ori sat on a park bench with his wife, who was already quite large. Charlotte was playing with some other small children.

"Robert, I believe we need to select a name for our baby," Jenny said.

"I suppose you have been giving it thought," Ori surmised.

"Yes, and I have a few possibilities. Have you been thinking of names?"

"As a matter of fact, I have," he affirmed. "Even from the last pregnancy, I have been considering the name Leonard."

"Leonard? Why Leonard?" she wondered.

"I wanted to name him after Leonardo da Vinci."

"Ah, yes," Jenny agreed. "A man ahead of his time, an inventor and innovator."

"And a man with whom our son will have something in common."

Jenny gasped. "Leonardo da Vinci was an agent?"

"No, Jenny, but his parents were. He lived his whole life never knowing he was an extraterrestrial."

"How come I never heard about that?"

Ori blushed. "Because it's classified. Ortees told me. And I thought you knew already because you laughed at Svortomit's private joke to us on our wedding day in Yoilafa. Remember? He said something about Prime Minister Leonardo?"

Unni thought for a moment. "Oh, yes, I remember now."

"And I just divulged classified information," Ori lamented.

"Seriously, Robert. If even Svortomit knew about it, the secret cannot be too sensitive."

"It was somewhat embarrassing to the Service."

Unni quickly changed the subject back to the matter at hand. "I like that name. It is full of meaning. And it has a nice cadence. Leonard Weatherby. The Right Honourable Leonard Weatherby."

"And what names were you thinking of, my dear?" Ori inquired.

"Never mind. That is not relevant. Leonard would be perfect."

Ori and Unni planned a birthday celebration for Charlotte. Her birthday, November 5, fell on a Friday, which was convenient for the purpose. Ori invited several of his friends from his social circle. They also invited the Duke and Duchess of Wellington. The Wellingtons declined to come but sent a gift. That evening, the townhouse had thirty-six guests, as full as it ever had been. Ori hired two cooks for the week to help Mrs. Anders with the main meal and two footmen to assist Shelby.

The highlight of the evening was when Unni went to the piano and played while young Charlotte sang. Unni was so large, that she could barely reach the keyboard from the piano bench.

But the time had come for Leonard to arrive. As the days went by, Unni began to worry. Had the baby become too large?

As the sun rose on the morning of November 11, Unni's labor began. Ori had Shelby send for Dr. Stanton. Labor had taken three hours last time. Ori was confident that he would be looking at Leonard's face by lunchtime.

Lunchtime came and the baby was not yet born. Ori tried to remember if those three hours were Earth 48 hours or Earth 19 hours. Perhaps they were Mraznian hours of seventy-two minutes. If so, maybe the baby would arrive in another half-hour or so.

Ori had some food brought in, but Unni ate very little. Every time Ori went into the bedroom to check on Unni, he would become anxious. She was clearly uncomfortable and no progress seemed to be made. He would hold her hand and talk to her, sometimes spending an hour with her.

By the late afternoon, the contractions were five minutes apart, and Unni was dilating, but the baby was still not coming.

At dinnertime, Ori had no appetite. Dr. Stanton was tiring. He suggested they send for an obstetrician. Ori was worried that the obstetrician might use forceps and that they might convey an infection. Dr. Stanton stayed until nearly midnight and left exhausted. But he had sent for a nurse who was also a midwife.

Unni labored through the night. The nurse saw how tired Ori was and suggested he nap, but he would not. He sat in an upholstered chair at her bedside. He dozed a few times, but he stayed with her all night. Unni's pushing was to no avail. Unni was in pain, and Ori was being consumed with anxiety.

At one point in the night, when the nurse stepped out, Unni turned to Ori with tears in her eyes. "I don't know if I can bear too much more. But if the worst is to occur, I want you to know that I love you. For all eternity, Ori, I love you."

"The worst will not occur," Ori replied. "It cannot occur. I could not live without you."

Dr. Stanton returned shortly after sunrise. He examined Unni and did not like what he saw. He strongly recommended to Ori that he be allowed to call for a colleague, Dr. Zanes, an obstetrician.

Ori was still reluctant. Dr. Stanton told Ori that in the last seven years, since the time of Princess Charlotte, his profession was increasingly favoring the use of forceps in long, protracted labor. Ori frankly told the doctor about his concern about infection.

The doctor acknowledged Ori's concern. "But I know of a way that this risk can be reduced. I will call Dr. Zanes. While I am gone, have one of your servants prepare a pot of boiling water."

Ori went to the kitchen and told Mrs. Anders to boil water. Ori surmised that Dr. Stanton was going to have the forceps sterilized using the boiling water. Ori doubted Dr. Stanton knew why this process was a good course of action; the natives on Earth 48 did not yet know about microbial organisms. Nonetheless, washing the forceps was the best move.

But with what would the hot and wet instruments be dried? Towels were notorious habitats for bacteria. Suddenly, Ori remembered that he had an antiseptic in his medical pack in the suit he was issued on Station 48-3. He could disinfect the instruments after they were dried. He went to his wardrobe and discreetly got his medical pack.

After what seemed like an eternity, Dr. Stanton returned with a thin, bespectacled gentleman carrying a large leather bag of equipment. This was no doubt Dr. Zanes. The two doctors were engaged in a lively discussion as Shelby admitted them to the townhouse.

"Very well, then, John," Dr. Zanes acquiesced. "Boil my forceps in water."

"Shelby, show these doctors to the bedroom," Ori directed the butler. "I will bring them the forceps myself."

Ori thoroughly washed his hands. Then he took the pot, poured out most of the water and took hold of the forceps with a clean towel. Just before he entered the room, he applied the antiseptic to the forceps. Then he entered the room, carefully handing the instrument to Dr. Zanes.

Poor Unni was exhausted and distressed. Dr. Zanes guided the instruments and delivered the baby.

The baby immediately began to cry. Dr. Stanton was relieved to see the baby breathing after the delayed delivery. Dr. Zanes passed the newborn to the nurse to have the baby cleaned up.

"Congratulations, Mr. and Mrs. Weatherby," he announced. "It's a girl."

19.
Military Reverse

Unni was totally exhausted but relieved to hear that the baby was healthy. The nurse let Unni hold the baby briefly and took her to the nursery to let the mother rest. Dr. Stanton examined Unni again and gave the opinion that she was doing well. He said he would be back in several hours and left with Dr. Zanes.

The baby girl was brought to Unni several times that day for feeding. In the evening, Ori and Unni had some time alone with their newborn. Ori was much relieved that the delivery was over and that mother and daughter were fine.

"We never considered what the name of the child would be if it were a girl," Ori observed.

"After all of this, what I have just endured, I have begun to appreciate my mother," Unni replied. "I would like to name our daughter after my mother."

"I also appreciate your mother," Ori agreed. "But Zeri is not a proper English name. People will think her name is strange."

"What name would you give to her?" Jenny asked.

"I have always liked the name Elizabeth or Eliza," Ori said. "There is a princess by that name and there was once a great queen. It is a respected English name, and I like the sound of it."

"Is there an English name like Zeri?"

"Let me think," Ori paused. "There is Mary. And there is Sherry."

"I like Sherry," Unni said. "Sherry Weatherby has a nice sound to it. Elizabeth Weatherby sounds a bit pretentious. My mother thought the name Charlotte was alien and strange. But she would like Sherry."

Ori was not so sure about naming his daughter Sherry, but Unni was very tired and not fully herself. He was going to suggest that they put off the naming until the next day, but Unni appeared to have fallen asleep. He quietly made his way to the door, not to wake his wife.

But before he could reach the door, Unni called to him. "Robert, I want you to know that I never want to try this again. If you want another baby, you will need to find a way to get me home to Yoilafa, or to a space station or even a starship. But I never want to have a baby on a primitive planet again. NEVER!"

In Tlat Mlang, the High Commission of the Confederation of Civilized Planets was faced with many decisions with regard to the conduct of the war with the Vittmians. The government had vastly increased the size of the army and was building new warships at an unprecedented pace.

A bill was proposed that the Confederation reveal itself to all of the planets under surveillance that faced the Vittmian Empire, Earth 45 through Earth 49, with a view to rapidly admitting them to the Confederation. Earth 45 was already at Technology Level 12, but they were only at Cultural Level 7. Their admission had been debated by the Exploration Commission for the past several years. The other planets were still too primitive. Earth 46 was only at Technology Level 10 and preparing to launch their first manned space vehicles. Earth 48 was just developing the steam engine. Earth 47 and Earth 49 were no further than the bronze age.

It was argued that these planets simply were not ready. But the bill's proponents argued that it was a time of war, and the usual rules should not apply. Further, Earth 46 would make an excellent base of operations for an offensive campaign against the Vittmians.

During the hearings, several senior members of the Interplanetary Intelligence Service were called to testify, including Subdirector Vlaris, the highest-ranking member of the Bureau of Exploratory Surveillance. Vlaris cautioned the High Commission against the bill.

Eventually, the bill was voted down.

The new Commissioner of Defense, Bonfel Grusett of Earth 5, unveiled his strategy to take the offensive in the war. It was a phased approach to capturing one of the occupied solar systems.

Sent to Watch

Commissioner Grusett pointed out that there were two occupied planets with active agents of the Confederation present, Earth 55 and Earth 64. Phase 1 of the plan was to send a large fleet into one of those solar systems and clear it of all Vittmian warships. Phase 2 was to visit the spies to collect all of the intelligence they had on Vittmian troop strength. Phase 3 was to send in a huge fleet of troop transports and invade the planet with hundreds of thousands of troops, capturing the most populated continent, and waging global war in Phase 4 to capture the rest of the planet. Phase 5 was to build bases and conscript the natives.

The plan was based on three assumptions. First, it would take time for the Vittmians to send in a second fleet for a counterattack. Second, the Vittmian garrisons were only equipped for controlling civilians. Third, the natives were hungry for revenge and would gladly join the Confederation side.

The High Commission was pleased with the plan and endorsed it. Grusett assured the High Commission that the military was prepared and ready to launch the first phase very soon.

Ori held Sherry in order to free Unni's hands so she could play the piano for Charlotte. Every night, Unni would play as Charlotte sang. After three songs, Unni said, "Now it's off to bed with you, Charlotte."

"Oh, mother, can't we sing just one more song?"

"It is past your bedtime," Unni told her daughter.

"Oh, please?" Charlotte begged.

"Listen to your mother," Ori exhorted his daughter. "To bed with you."

"Would you tuck me in, Daddy?"

Charlotte knew her father was a soft touch. He immediately complied. Unni took Sherry from her father's arms. Her eyelids were heavy. Unni carefully walked Sherry to the nursery and placed her in the crib.

Unni went straight to the bedroom. She was eager to get some sleep. Sherry was four months old and was still not sleeping through the night. But Ori wanted to tell his wife the news he had read in a letter from "Wallingford." Unni was already in bed when he reached the bedroom. She had left one gas lamp burning for Ori.

"Jenny, I just read that a large fleet of Confederation warships won a victory against a Vittmian fleet in the solar system of Earth 55," Ori announced, waving the letter he had pulled from his pocket.

Unni sat up in the bed. "Did you say 'Earth 55?'"

"Yes, Earth 55. The surviving Vittmian vessels fled, leaving the entire system in Confederation control."

Unni smiled and returned her head to the pillow. "I wish I could have seen the look on Ryla's face when she heard this! Earth 55 of all places."

"With that solar system clear of Vittmian vessels, I believe an invasion of Earth 55 by Confederation troops is imminent," Ori opined.

"That would be wonderful," Unni replied softly.

"Perhaps the transports will be able to resume taking agents to and from the surface of this planet," Ori said hopefully. "And when we can travel again, we can try again for a son."

Unni tuned out the last phrase about another baby; she was very happy to hear that Ryla's home planet was on the threshold of liberation. She fell into a satisfied slumber—until about 2 a.m. when she heard Sherry cry.

Among the warships in the victorious fleet was a small frigate, the *Sessetta*, with a crew of thirty-four, as well as six agents of the Bureau of Protective Action. This ship was commanded by Captain Oind Burxa, the former captain of Station 55-1, and half of her crew was from that station. The agents on board included Saibert Ortees, former Team Leader for Earth 55, and three members of his old team.

Ryla wanted to come on this mission more than anything; however, the senior agents in the Bureau of Protective Action did not want to risk losing her. Over the past several years, Ryla had trained over thirty agents in the language and culture of her people, including the five agents on the surface and two of the agents on the *Sessetta*. Only one of four agents who were trained were sent into the field; only the best were selected.

Ortees was to meet with the agents on the surface and learn as much as he could from them as to enemy troop strength and location. He also planned to drop off the two new agents. At his discretion, he was authorized to extract one agent to be brought back to Earth 1 to further the Confederation's knowledge of Earth 55 and to assist in the training of other agents.

When the battle ended, the *Sessetta* broke for Earth 55. When they came near, they sent pulses to the embedded agents to let them know they were there.

Ortees was pleased to find out that all five transponders were visible. The Vittmians' favorite method of execution was vaporization, so the detection of five transponders was a sign that all five agents were alive.

The agents were instructed to go to their rendezvous points. Ortees boarded a transport with the other agents and went to meet with the agents on the surface. Agent Irsid was the first one to get away and reach his pickup point. He was visited first.

The transport landed in the dark, and Irsid was ready. He climbed the ladder and met with his fellow agents. Irsid was somewhat short, and he was thinner than Ortees remembered him being.

Irsid said that the news had leaked to the general population that there was another empire besides the Vittmians and that they were at war. This gave the people hope. There were more acts of sabotage, as if to weaken the war effort. The Vittmians told the natives that the other empire would exterminate them if they captured Earth 55, but the natives did not believe it.

Irsid's assessment of the soldiers confirmed the beliefs of the Confederation generals and admirals: the Vittmian garrison was only fit for fighting civilians.

But one thing Irsid said was going to cause a change in plans. The Vittmians had injected an identification chip into all of the natives. Anyone without one was to be executed. Until the Confederation knew how to duplicate those chips, they would not be able to plant more agents on the surface.

Ortees made a decision on the spot. Two of the agents would be swapped out. They would be brought back to the *Sessetta* to have their chip transferred to the two other agents. While the chips were out, they would be photographed in three dimensions in minute detail so that the chips could be reproduced for sending in more agents later, perhaps even on other occupied planets.

Ortees met with three more agents that night. All four agents he spoke to corroborated Irsid's story. The fifth agent never made it to his rendezvous point.

The transport returned to the *Sessetta* with two veteran field agents selected for the return to Earth 1. All the way up to the *Sessetta*, and all the way back down to the surface, the field agents talked at length, as the agents briefed their replacements on details of what they would need to know to take their places. They even talked in sickbay during the chip transplantation procedures.

The following evening (local time), the fresh agents were placed on the surface in their respective positions. Shortly after docking with the transport, Captain Burxa wanted to leave. But as they were preparing to leave orbit, the fifth agent's transponder indicated that she was in position. Ortees convinced the captain to let him return to the surface to interview her.

Only Agent Moynon went with Ortees, in addition to the pilot and the copilot. Just as the transport entered the atmosphere, the pilot announced to Ortees that they had company. Three Vittmian fighters were flying on a course to intercept the transport.

The pilot aborted the landing and tried to evade the Vittmian fighters, dodging missiles and laser fire all the way. The copilot sent a message to the *Sessetta* as the transport exited the atmosphere. At that point, the Vittmians began to fire surface-to-space missiles. One of them narrowly missed the transport.

Captain Burxa made the risky move of closing in on the transport to shorten the time and distance until they could dock. The move succeeded in retrieving the transport, but it also gave away the position of the *Sessetta*. Immediately after the docking, the frigate left orbit and began to speed away from Earth 55. But Ortees and the other three persons in the transport were unable to get out of their seats to exit the docking bay due to the violent evasive maneuvers the frigate had to make.

"We should be out of range by now," Ortees shouted to the pilot.

"We are," the pilot said. "But look at that."

The transport was docked by its lower deck, so the upper deck was facing outward. From the forward window, Ortees could see an enemy warship pursuing the *Sessetta*.

"A battleship?" Ortees asked.

"No, a heavy cruiser," the pilot replied.

"We are outgunned all the same," Moynon fretted.

The *Sessetta* was somewhat faster than the Vittmian cruiser and definitely more maneuverable. But it would only take one salvo to finish the Confederation vessel off.

The enemy fired, and the *Sessetta* took a sharp turn southward, out of the plane of the ecliptic. The volley missed. To the surprise of the four men in the transport, the enemy cruiser did not turn to pursue but continued its course to the outer solar system.

The *Sessetta* had stopped lurching, so Ortees and his companions ventured into the transport bay and into the part of the vessel with artificial gravity.

On his way to his quarters, Ortees saw Mr. Beeku, a member of the ship's crew.

"A large enemy fleet has entered the system. A huge battle is shaping up out there, and the admiral has ordered us out of here."

Indeed, the *Sessetta* had a precious cargo of intelligence. The frigate was out of harm's way, speeding out of the system.

But over the next few hours, the grim reports began to reach the bridge as they confirmed the destruction of one Confederation ship after another. Ortees soon realized that the Confederation fleet had been defeated. Before long, Ortees was told by Captain Burxa that the fleet had not just been defeated, but routed. Very few ships had escaped, and those that had were badly damaged. The admiral was dead, and more than ninety percent of the personnel were lost.

It was late in the evening. Charlotte was in bed, and Unni had just put Sherry into her crib. Ori and Unni were in the study together when Shelby entered the room.

"Major Weatherby, there is a visitor at the door, a Frenchman, Louis Le-Blanc, who said he urgently needs to speak with you. Shall I have him return tomorrow?"

Ori was surprised. "No, Shelby. Send him in," he replied.

"Perhaps after the victory at Earth 55 the Service has resumed direct contact with its agents," Ori guessed.

"I hope he isn't here to take Charlotte off to school," Unni said. "It is barely April. She will not be five years old for another seven months."

"I won't let him," Ori assured his wife.

Just then, Shelby reappeared with the visitor. Lorbank looked tired and drawn, and there was worry in his eyes.

"My English is not sufficient to convey this message so urgent," he began. "Please excuse me, Robert, if I bear you the bad news in French."

Speaking through Unni as an interpreter, Lorbank informed them about the major Vittmian victory over the Confederation fleet near Earth 55. The army bound for Earth 55 had been turned around, Confederation forces were in full retreat, and the Commissioner of Defense, Bonfel Grusett, had resigned. All forces were being withdrawn from this sector due to its proximity to the Vittmian Empire. The Director of the Interplanetary Intelligence Service had ordered the extraction of all of its agents working on or around Earths

45 to 49. All Space Station personnel were being evacuated. The military had requisitioned a commercial starship for the purpose, and it would arrive at Earth 48 in three days.

Lorbank said the situation was so bad, that he had felt compelled to inform all of the field agents personally.

The Svavapass family had to prepare to leave Earth 48. They were to meet the transport at a specific location in three nights.

Ori and Unni were totally stunned. "I read that we had won the battle," Ori replied.

"The first battle," Lorbank corrected him. "The Vittmians counterattacked. Our fleet has been destroyed."

"But we cannot leave," Ori protested. "I am politically well-placed. I paid for this opportunity dearly at Waterloo."

Ori pointed to his scar. He continued, "If the Weatherby alias was removed, it would be a huge loss to the Service. It could take years for another opportunity like this to arise."

"Don't be a fool, Robert," Lorbank admonished his agent. "Get out while you can."

"My wife and I would like to discuss this alone."

Ori called for Shelby and asked that their guest be taken to the dining room and be given tea and biscuits. Lorbank was short of time. He had been to Germany and France that evening to inform the agents there, and he still had to go to New York to inform Agent Qlat. But he agreed to leave his hosts if that might allow them to make a better decision.

Ori got up and closed the door behind Lorbank.

The moment the door was shut, Unni immediately said, "I don't want to leave. We have no reason to go. If we stay on Earth 48, the family would not have to be broken up. Charlotte won't be compelled to go to school on Earth 2."

Ori agreed. "One reason for leaving might be our safety, but I don't believe Earth 48 would be the first planet taken. Strategically, Earth 45, the most advanced, is the biggest prize. On the other hand, if the Vittmians prioritized the planets by proximity, then Earth 47 would be first to fall."

Ori walked to the window and stared at the stars.

"And I remember Ryla's description of the invasion of Earth 55," Unni continued Ori's reasoning. "She indicated that the Vittmians would take the planets one at a time and would need about twenty years to assimilate each one. If Earth 48 was not invaded first, there would be time for the Confederation to turn the war around."

Ori turned from the window to face his wife. "Of course, that is predicated on the assumption that the Empire's procedures have not been altered by the discovery of the Confederation."

"Or by the war."

"In any case, our best course of action is clear," Ori concluded, gazing into Unni's eyes.

When Lorbank came back to the study, Ori let him in and seated himself beside his wife. Unni informed Lorbank of their decision, speaking in French.

"You are taking a great risk," Lorbank pointed out. "All of the agents I have spoken to so far are leaving, you know. We are closing Station 48-3. You would be alone."

Ori took his wife's hand. "We have made up our minds. We are going to stay."

Lorbank turned his eyes toward the ceiling before Unni could translate.

"I thought you would say that," Lorbank replied in resignation. "So I brought you these. You might need them."

He handed them a plastic package. Ori and Unni both recognized the contents: extra medical supplies.

Lorbank felt frustrated. "May we meet again," he said as he turned to leave.

Shelby showed him out the door.

Three nights later, Ori and Unni were awakened from their sleep by a series of sharp pulses.

"Code 98," Unni observed.

"We are alone now," Ori said. "It's just you and me."

"And Charlotte and Sherry," Unni added. "We are alone, but together."

20.

The Nudge

From the spring of 1825, the Svavapass family was actively pursuing the course of their mission. Ori was busily courting the political favor of powerful people in the government while Unni was spending all of her energy on the children, practicing her educational skills for her efforts to groom a future son for high office.

Charlotte and Sherry were totally unaware of their extraterrestrial identities and did not know a word of Grellish. Before she was five, Charlotte could add and subtract and had memorized the multiplication table up to 12 x 12. She could also read children's books and write simple sentences. Unni also was giving Charlotte piano lessons. By the end of the summer, Sherry was crawling.

By 1825, the Duke of Wellington's power and prestige were substantial in the government. Wellington could choose who was nominated to run for Parliament as a Tory in a growing number of boroughs. Prime Minister Liverpool's righthand man was George Canning. But Wellington and Sir Robert Peel were very influential.

In June, there was a banquet at Apsley House to mark the tenth anniversary of Wellington's victory at Waterloo. Ori and Unni were invited. A former staff officer gave a lengthy speech in Wellington's honor that included a detailed account of the events in the battle. When the account got to the part when the center of the line almost broke under cannister fire from French horse artillery and from heavy cavalry charges, Wellington looked down at Ori from his seat of honor. He seemed to gaze at Ori for more than a solid minute until the mention of Blücher's arrival.

Beginning from that time, Ori was invited to Apsley House regularly for private consultation. But the meetings were short, and the Duke of Wellington did most of the talking. Most of the discussion was concerning the Board of Ordnance.

Beginning from 1823, a burning issue in British politics was Catholic emancipation. Robert Peel was totally opposed to the idea, as was Liverpool. Wellington's view on the subject was more complex. He had definite sympathy for the Irish Catholics, but he was reluctant to go so far as favoring granting Catholics full civil rights. Sometimes he appeared interested in the concept only to prevent civil strife.

Of course, Ori and Unni strongly favored Catholic emancipation. The experience of centuries of history on Earth 19 and the other worlds of the Confederation had taught them that technical progress was hampered when parts of the population were disenfranchised. Great minds are kept in the obscurity of menial occupations when a race or segment of the population is marginalized.

In the army, Wellington actually disapproved of cheering by his men because it was "too nearly an expression of opinion." Ori was well aware of this, and he knew he would have to tread carefully. He wanted to do what he could to help Wellington into a position that was more strongly in line with the emancipation of Catholics. At the same time, he did not want to dispute with Wellington. Ori needed to time his speaking on the subject perfectly.

The Catholic Relief Bill of 1825 passed the House of Commons but was voted down by the House of Lords, with Wellington leading the effort to defeat the bill. Had it passed, the Bill would have required Royal Assent, and King George IV was strongly opposed to the idea. Ori began to wonder if he would ever have any influence at all.

The years 1825 to 1827 were somewhat frustrating for Ori and Unni. Ori was using his decade of knowledge of the persons and situations to build strong political relationships. But for all of his friends and connections, he was unable to influence policy in the least. Unni was spending all of her energy tutoring Charlotte and Sherry. They were progressing well, but there was no progress on the important matter of bringing forth a son who could be a future cabinet member or prime minister.

However, those years were a golden time for the Svavapass family. They were spending a lot of time together. The atmosphere of love and joy in their townhouse was the envy of all who knew them.

In November 1825, Charlotte's fifth birthday came and went without her being taken away for schooling on Earth 2. At that time in England, a working man never got any paid time off, except perhaps on Christmas Day. But the Weatherby family, being of wealth and privilege, was able to take a holiday together several times per year, often longer than a week in length.

In the beginning of 1827, the Duke of Wellington attained two more high honors. On January 22, he was appointed Commander-in-Chief of the British Army. Two weeks later, he was appointed Constable of the Tower of London. Just twelve days after that, on February 17, 1827, Prime Minister Liverpool suffered a stroke. On April 9, he resigned from office.

Wellington had hoped to succeed Liverpool, but King George IV chose George Canning instead. The king did not like Wellington or Sir Robert Peel. Ori was disappointed. Wellington was about to turn fifty-eight, and Ori was concerned that his patron might never attain to the office of prime minister.

To make matters worse, Wellington and Peel refused to serve in Canning's government due to their opposition to Catholic emancipation and free trade. This meant that Wellington was no longer the Master General of the Ordnance, and his political power was diminished. Due to the refusal of other Tories to support the new Prime Minster, Canning was forced to cobble a coalition that included some Whigs.

As Major Weatherby, Ori was known in political circles to be tied to Wellington. With Wellington's departure as Master General of the Ordnance, Ori's potential for advancement was weakened.

But Canning's health was already in steep decline by the time he took office. He died on August 8, 1827, having had the shortest tenure of any Prime Minster of the United Kingdom to date. The King was angry at Wellington and Peel for their refusal to join Canning's government, so he bypassed Wellington and appointed Frederick Robinson, the Viscount Goderich, to be the next prime minister.

Wellington was quite displeased when he heard he had again been passed over for appointment as prime minister. The following day, Ori happened to meet up with Wellington at the Tower of London. Wellington wanted to vent his frustration, and seeing a familiar and friendly face, he bade Ori to step into his office.

Wellington had a reputation for concise speech, but on that day, he had somewhat more to say. The Duke was concerned that Goderich was young and the Tories had a huge majority in the House of Commons. If Goderich could heal the fractures in the party, he might last for ten to fifteen years. By that time, Wellington would be too old to be prime minister.

Wellington was also irked at the contradictions in the King's decision. The King was upset at Wellington for refusing to join Canning's government, but Prime Minister Canning favored reforms to which the King himself was strongly opposed.

Eventually, Wellington stopped speaking, as if he expected some comfort or comment from Ori. Ori knew this was his one chance. It was now or never; it might be the only chance he would ever have to speak his views to his benefactor.

Ori Svavapass seized the opportunity. He spoke loudly because Wellington was deaf in one ear. At the same time, he spoke respectfully, choosing his words with care.

"Sir, you have dedicated your entire life to your King and to the British Empire," he began. "Your dedication to duty has nearly cost you your life on several occasions. To one of those occasions I was an eyewitness.

"And so, you must ask yourself two questions: first, what course of action best serves the Empire to which you have devoted your life? Is it that of maintaining the present social order that preserves the position of the Protestants or in changing it to one that offers opportunity and a stake in that empire by a large, disenfranchised minority?

"And the second question is, what is the greater danger to the Empire? Is it a popish plot, perhaps to assassinate some important official or to impose the Romish Church on England? Or is it a restive minority dispossessed by the present order with nothing to lose?

"I believe that when you have answered these two questions to your satisfaction, you will see the most prudent course of action for yourself and for those who loyally follow you."

When Ori had finished speaking, Wellington sat as if posing for a portrait. After a moment of silence, he bade Ori "Good day," and motioned for him to leave the room.

Ori was not sure if he had persuaded the great Field Marshall or if he had offended him. There was no sign in Wellington's demeanor to indicate either. The Duke was no longer Master General of the Ordnance, so he could not fire Ori. The major would have to wait until the next social event at Apsley House to see if he was disinvited.

That evening when he got home, he told Unni everything that had transpired in great detail. Unni was pleased and even relieved when she heard. It helped address her concern that their mission was not making any progress.

In the ensuing months, it became evident that Goderich was not up to the task of holding together the fragile coalition Canning had formed. Neither did he prove himself able to balance the demands of the King and of his Whig allies. At one point, the King even called Goderich a "sniveling, blubbering blockhead."

While Prime Minister Goderich was floundering, the Duke of Wellington was distancing himself from the ultra-Tory wing of his party. Ori began to believe that his words had had some effect on his war hero patron.

Then on January 22, 1828, the King summoned the prime minister to Windsor and dismissed him. The King sent for Wellington to form a government.

His actions as prime minister left no doubt that the Duke of Wellington planned to address the issue of Catholic rights. On February 26, just weeks into his government, a bill was introduced to repeal the Test Acts. These seventeenth-century laws imposed civil disabilities on Catholics and on "nonconformists," Protestants who did not go along with the Church of England.

Amazingly, Sir Robert Peel took the lead for the government in the effort to repeal the Test Acts. Unni believed that Peel may have been influenced by Wellington, that Ori's work had affected both conservative leaders. The repeal effort went through smoothly, and by March, the bill was already at the House of Lords. Several weeks later, the repeal was approved and sent to the King, who gave it Royal Assent on May 9.

That evening, the Svavapass family sat in the center of their long dining table in their usual way with Ori on the long side with his back to the kitchen and his wife facing him on the opposite long side, with Charlotte and Sherry seated beside her.

Ori and Unni were delighted with themselves. They knew they had violated protocol, but they felt justified in their actions. "They would never be able to prove in a court of law that I played a role in this," Ori assured his wife."

"Quite honestly, I am more afraid of the Vittmians than of Vlaris," Unni added.

Unni raised her wine glass in a lighthearted toast, "To Prime Minister Wellington, the reformer."

Ori echoed her toast, "To Wellington the reformer."

As they sipped their wine, Sherry, now three years old, asked, "Mommy, what does 'reformer' mean?"

21.

Compulsory Education

Wellington the reformer was not done. Weeks later, a Catholic Emancipation bill passed the House of Commons. The bill gave Catholics almost all of the same civil rights as their Protestant peers, including the right to serve in Parliament. But the bill faced stiff opposition in the House of Lords. Beginning from June 10, Wellington began to make speeches in that chamber in favor of the bill.

The situation came to a head in July, when Daniel O'Connell, an Irish Catholic political leader who championed the cause of Catholic emancipation, won a by-election for a seat in Parliament. Without a change in the law, O'Connell was required to take an Oath of Supremacy to take his seat. That oath contained wording that was incompatible with his Catholic religion.

O'Connell refused to take the oath and was thus barred from taking his seat. Wellington and Peel feared that unless O'Connell was allowed to be seated in the House of Commons, there would be an uprising in Ireland.

With much difficulty, Wellington persuaded the King to allow the bill to be introduced in the House of Lords. From February to April, Wellington gave twenty-three speeches in the House of Lords in favor of Catholic Emancipation.

The King's anti-Catholic brother, the Duke of Cumberland, persuaded the King to withdraw his support for the bill. The entire cabinet resigned in protest on March 4. The next day, under intense political pressure, the King was forced to reluctantly agree to the bill. On March 31, the bill passed its first reading in the House of Lords. Finally, on April 10, 1829, the bill passed its third reading and was sent to King George IV for his approval.

Wellington threatened to resign if the King did not give his assent to the bill. But on April 13, King George IV gave Royal Assent and the bill became law.

Several days later, Ori passed Wellington walking on the grounds of the Tower of London. As they passed, Wellington looked at Ori and nodded as if to acknowledge the role the major had played in changing his position on the Catholic question.

Naturally, Ori and Unni were pleased with the outcome. They no longer felt as if their time in England was wasted. Even their two daughters sensed the rise in their parents' morale.

Charlotte was eight years old and Sherry was four. By that time, Charlotte was learning trigonometry, having mastered the basic principles of algebra, and Sherry was almost done with her memorization of the multiplication table.

But the joy in the Svavapass household was short-lived. One evening in early May, after Unni had put the girls to bed, there was a knock at the door.

Shelby came into the study and announced that an American wanted to speak with them.

"An American?" Unni asked in surprise. "At this hour?"

"I asked that he return tomorrow at an earlier hour, but he said it was urgent," Shelby explained. "He said his name was Stephen Galt."

Ori and Unni immediately recognized that name as the alias of Agent Vlevlan Qlat. Unni's heart sank. Ori fumbled for words for a moment and instructed the butler to show him in.

Ori motioned to Shelby to close the door as he left the study. He offered Agent Qlat a seat.

"I dare say I was not expecting to see you this evening," Ori began.

Unni sat in silence as Qlat related the nature of the visit. All she could think about was the prospect of Charlotte being taken away to a school on Earth 2.

Qlat told Ori and Unni that the war with the Vittmian Empire had ended in a ceasefire. Formal negotiations were in progress to craft a full peace accord.

"Why would the Vittmians agree to stop the war?" Ori wondered. "Last I heard, our fleet was destroyed."

"Right after that, the Vittmians invaded Earth 43," Qlat explained. "I suppose we never figured they would invade a planet that was a member of the Confederation. They landed more than a million soldiers. With our fleet in ruins, the Confederation had no way to reinforce the army on Earth 43, and we were very limited in what supplies we could send.

"But Earth 43 raised an army of many millions. For the next three years, it was Vittmian superior arms and tactics against Earth 43's superior numbers, not to mention their bravery and determination. The Vittmians were advancing almost the whole time, but at a greater cost than they could afford. They began to conscript people from the occupied planets, but those units fought poorly and some even changed sides.

"Eventually, they agreed to a ceasefire. We estimate that they lost upward of 600,000 troops. We lost nearly ten million, but Earth 43 never fell. As of the last few days, the Vittmians completed their troop withdrawal. Earth 43 is free."

"I suppose you are the new team leader?" Ori asked.

"Not at all," Qlat admitted. "I am just a messenger for Vlaris. There is no team for this planet, except for the two of you. Lorbank is on Earth 2 teaching French, and the other agents have taken up various roles elsewhere."

"Teaching French? To whom?"

"To about twenty agents," Qlat replied. "You know the new way at the Bureau. They are sending families now to work in the field. Now that we have competition, they feel it is less conspicuous for a family to be performing surveillance. Each major faction on each planet under surveillance at Technology Level 9 or lower will have two to three families living there. They are training four families for every one that will be selected."

"So, there will eventually be families of agents in England, France, and Germany," Ori inferred.

"Yes, and in America," Qlat added. "I got married three years ago, and I have a baby boy. We named him Daniel."

"Congratulations, Vlevlan. What are your plans?"

"Orsti and I, we plan to return to New York in a few months. In the evacuation, I told my friends I was going west to St. Louis. Now 'Stephen Galt' is moving back. Orsti just needs to pass her English exam. You know the rules, no accents allowed. Her alias is Christine, but she will go by Christy."

"Christy Galt has a nice sound to it," Ori agreed.

"You've been asking all of the questions, and now it is my turn," Qlat said. "Did Jackson get elected president in 1824?"

"No, he lost to John Quincy Adams," Ori replied.

"Thank goodness!" Qlat exclaimed in relief. "Adams is a good man. By contrast, that populist rabble-rouser Jackson would have made a disastrous president."

"But four years later, Jackson ran again and defeated Adams," Ori continued. "The Americans just inaugurated him two months ago."

"Jackson is in the White House? That's terrible! Why, that wild man will ruin the country! How could Adams lose? A one-termer; like father, like son. Tell me, did Wellington ever become prime minister?"

"Indeed, he has. He has been in office for over a year now."

"He doesn't hold a grudge against Jackson for killing his brother-in-law, does he?"

"Wellington never mentions it. I believe he understands the fortunes of war too well to hold Jackson personally responsible," Ori replied. "Well, Vlevlan, it was good to see you. I suppose it is late, and you need to be going..."

"I am not in any hurry to leave, Ori," Qlat interrupted his host. "You see, Vlaris sent me here to collect Charlotte and take her to school on Earth 2."

"I thought so!" Unni shot back with anger in her voice. "And you are going to just haul her away like a criminal under arrest? She doesn't know she is extraterrestrial. She can't speak a word of Grellish. How can you be so cruel?"

"Calm down, Unni," Qlat tried to assure her. "Vlaris is not so heartless. We are coming back in three days so you have some time to prepare her. There was another family that did not evacuate, the Krajorts on Earth 47. They have a son on Earth 2 that they have not seen in four years, and a daughter who is six who needs to go. We went there three days ago to tell them that the war is over, and they are all going together to Earth 2 to deliver their daughter and see their son.

"The starship is going to Earth 47 to pick them up, and in three days, we will come for your children. And you and Ori are invited to accompany them on the voyage, maybe teach them a little Grellish..."

"Did you say children, plural?" Ori asked.

"We know you have more than one," Qlat replied. "Four years ago, Lorbank was sent to the kitchen for biscuits and tea while you conferred. He heard the crying of another child that could not have been Charlotte. He said it sounded like an infant. Vlaris wants that one too."

"Sherry is not five yet…" Unni began.

"Vlaris gave orders that your second child is to come too."

"Rubbish! This is totally unnecessary!" Unni retorted. "I have been teaching my children all along. They know everything a young English girl needs to know and then some. They can read and write. Their math skills are up-to-date for their age according to the curriculum I had on Earth 19; multiplication for Sherry, and trigonometry for Charlotte. They are learning world history for Earth 48, and in science, Charlotte knows the laws of motion and half the periodic table."

"Case in point," Qlat declared. "A lot of parents make that mistake when they home-school on another planet."

"What mistake?" Unni demanded to know.

"You mentioned the periodic table. Does Charlotte know what a proton is? Does she know what electrons and neutrons are?"

"Of course, she does!" Unni replied indignantly.

"Mrs. Svavapass, the natives on this planet have not yet discovered or even postulated any of these particles, and they have not yet devised the periodic table. Your eight-year-old knows more chemistry and atomic particles than any scientist in any university on Earth 48."

"Is that true, Ori?" Unni asked sheepishly.

"I'm afraid so," Ori admitted. "And the other day I heard Charlotte say that the eighth planet in this solar system circles its sun every 165 years. But the natives haven't even discovered that planet."

"Didn't you say that a German immigrant named Herschel discovered Planet #8?" Unni asked her husband.

"That was the seventh planet, dear. The natives still don't know there is an eighth."

Unni huffed.

"Do you see why at least some of the education should be left to professional teachers?" Qlat asked.

"That is irrelevant," Unni retorted. "You are talking about taking two little girls away from their parents. There needs to be an exception for agents who are already deployed."

"You make a good point, Unni," Qlat admitted. "But I have my orders…"

"And I must have my children!" Unni bolted from the room.

After a few minutes of discussing logistics with Qlat, Ori had Shelby lead him out.

When Ori entered the bedroom, he found his wife face down on the bed in tears.

When he tried to comfort her, she proposed that they flee with their children.

"We could go to Scotland," she suggested. "Better yet, we could go to America."

"We cannot flee, Unni. Not with transponders in our left shoulders."

"What do we do then, Ori?" Unni sobbed.

"We have no choice but to send Charlotte and Sherry to Earth 2. You should go with them and stay with them until they settle in. After that, you need to go to Earth 1 to reason with Vlaris. Hopefully he will agree to some limit to the time our children have to spend in that school, like one year. But I have to stay here, at least as long as Wellington is prime minister."

Unni realized that Ori was right, but she was still very unhappy.

"Unni, remember the day I proposed to you? I mean the second time."

"Yes," Unni answered weakly.

"Do you remember the context? You wanted me to be committed to the mission. The mission is to accelerate the technical progress of Earth 48 so that they will be eligible for membership in the Confederation before the Vittmians get here."

Unni looked up.

Ori continued, "We have to give up our children to a school so that millions of other parents on this planet won't have to give up their children to the mines, collective farms, and extermination camps in about a century or two. Tomorrow is Friday. I will take off from work right before lunch and help you prepare our children for the next three days."

Unni nodded silently. Her vision of her mission was refreshed. But she was still unhappy.

The following day, Ori returned home to find his daughters giggling in the dining room.

"What is so funny?" Ori asked.

"Mommy said that you and she are from one of the stars," Charlotte replied.

"And that we are going to fly off in two nights in a flying carriage into the sky," Sherry said.

"Mommy says we have a real grandma and grandpa on a star we cannot see," Charlotte continued.

"Because it is in the southern hemmy-spear," Sherry finished the thought.

"Hemisphere," Charlotte corrected her sister.

"That's what I said," Sherry maintained. "Hemmy-spear."

"Daddy, do you have funny stories for us too?"

Mrs. Anders was washing the dishes as Shelby brought them to her from the dining room. It was Sunday night, and the Weatherby family had just eaten their last dinner together for the foreseeable future.

"I simply do not understand it," Mrs. Anders said to the butler. "Why are the Weatherbys sending their daughters off to a private school in Scotland?"

"I could not say," Shelby replied.

"In all my years of service, I have never seen a happier family," Mrs. Anders went on. "Why would they want this to end? And why do these girls need a private school? I have never seen a better teacher than Mrs. Weatherby."

"I don't understand it either," the butler agreed.

"They are leaving so early tomorrow morning, even before the sun rises."

"Scotland is a long journey," Shelby said.

"I offered to come in early to make them a nice breakfast for the journey, but Major Weatherby did not agree to it," the cook went on.

Shelby shrugged. "I have never tried to understand my employers. I only serve them."

Ori hid his emotions as he kissed his wife and children goodbye the next morning. He had driven them in his own coach to the spot Qlat had instructed him. It was a lonely road near farmland. The sky was just beginning to show signs of a coming dawn. Ori could see the space vehicle in the distance.

Qlat and two others came to the roadside to help carry the trunks. Usually, agents would leave their native clothes and implements behind when they traveled into space, but this time they had been instructed to bring them.

"I hope to be back in a few weeks," Unni assured Ori.

"Take as long as the girls need," he replied.

Unni gave a moment's thought to the fact that she would have to leave her children to return to her husband. She gave her husband one last kiss.

"And send my greeting to Subdirector Vlaris," Ori added, masking his sarcasm.

Ori stayed with the horses as his family departed toward the transport vehicle. He did not leave until the vehicle lifted off toward the rising sun twenty minutes later.

22.

School Days

Unni was very concerned as to how her children would react to space travel, having never ridden in any vehicle not propelled by an animal. The girls were awestruck by the metallic vehicle and all of the tiny lights twinkling on and off on the controls.

The small monitors at the seats were showing the underside of the vehicle. Unni tried to explain to the girls what it would be like when the transport lifted off, but they could not relate to what she was saying.

Shortly, the vehicle did lift off. The monitors showed an aerial view of London in the early light of dawn, becoming smaller and vanishing to the rear. Charlotte was visibly apprehensive, but Sherry began to giggle. Soon, Sherry had her older sister laughing as well.

After about ten minutes, the girls were used to spaceflight, and the pilot was careful to maintain an acceleration of 1.0 gravity. At the halfway point, the pilot told Unni that the children should expect the lurch as the vehicle flipped around to start its deceleration. Unni had to act as interpreter because the children knew no Grellish at all.

As the vehicle flipped around, Unni was inwardly thankful that Captain Squeem wasn't driving. The girls actually enjoyed it. When they finally stopped laughing, they asked, "Mommy, could we do that again?"

The starship had a docking port on the "top" of its rotating fuselage. Unni was thankful of that because it meant that Charlotte and Sherry would not have to move from the transport to the main decks of the ship under weightless conditions. During the approach, the passengers and crew were weightless momentarily, and the children became queasy. Ori had been wise not to arrange for one of Mrs. Anders' fine English breakfasts before this maneuver!

Once on board the starship, the children had to remove their clothes and pass through the disinfection chamber. Unni went in with them. Again, the children were more amused than terrified.

Soon after they boarded the vessel, it left orbit bound for Earth 34. There, they would change to another vessel bound for Earth 2.

Unni lost no time uploading images of Ori's handwritten reports. In the past three days, Ori desperately wanted to spend as much time as possible with his daughters, but he knew he had to make his reports. He wrote about all of the political news of the past four years, including what he had read in *The Times*. Thus, he was also able to report on Prussia, France, Spain and the United States. The knowledge he had acquired on the inner workings of the British government was voluminous, and he wrote frantically with both hands to report it all and leave some time for the children. As Unni uploaded page after page, she was impressed with just how much Ori had to say.

During the trip, Unni befriended the Krajorts. They were from Earth 3, but had lived on Earth 47 for more than ten years. They were the only other agents to stay behind four years earlier when the sector was evacuated. The Krajorts had two children. Their son was on Earth 2 attending school. They had not seen him since the evacuation. Their daughter was six and was quickly befriended by Charlotte and Sherry, even though they did not know each other's languages.

"Did your daughter know she is extraterrestrial?" Unni asked.

"After the adjustment our son had to go through, we were tempted to tell her," Mrs. Krajort explained.

"But the society on Earth 47 is only Cultural Level 5, and we were not sure how the superstitious natives would react if she leaked it out," Mr. Krajort finished the thought. The Krajorts talked about the bronze age empire they were living in, and Unni spoke of life in England.

Unni discovered that the Krajorts had not been compelled to send their children to school on Earth 2, but were sending them voluntarily. This corroborated what Ortees had told Ori and her in his letter several years ago. She could not fathom why the Krajorts would agree to send their children away voluntarily.

Unni tried to teach her girls some basic Grellish. Charlotte and Sherry were very fortunate to have such a gifted teacher for a mother. Unni also told them stories, such as how she and their father met, and about their grandparents on Earth 19.

After six days of space travel, Unni and her daughters arrived on Earth 2. Their transport touched down in the great city of Dufa Da. Unni had never been in Grelland before, and the city of Dufa Da was awesome, far more beautiful than the practical city of Tlat Mlang on Earth 1. She wanted to tour the city, but the school was on a different continent, and after just two hours, she was on a suborbital flight.

The Adaptation School was part of a huge complex in a rural area. It was a subsidiary of the Bureau of Exploratory Surveillance training center that abutted it. The training center existed for training married agents in the language and culture of the specific planet and nation to which they were to be assigned. Families lived with their children in one-story quadplex apartments.

The Adaptation School had two sections. One was designated Regular Education Hall in a modern building where students learned Confederation history, science, mathematics, and Grellish. The other section, called the Adaptation Hall, consisted of schools and school houses that resembled conditions on the planets and cultures to which the children had to adapt. Some weeks, the students spent their mornings in Adaptation Hall and their afternoons in the modern building. Other weeks the program was reversed. The week was ten days long, with three days off and seven days of school.

In Adaptation Hall, they learned the language and history of the nation to which their parents hoped to be assigned. In addition, they had special math and science education. They were taught what items of their regular education they are not supposed to know and how to avoid giving away that one knew about such things. For example, Charlotte had to hide her knowledge of subatomic particles and the Krajorts had to hide their knowledge that Earth 47 was a sphere and revolved around its sun.

Sherry was not supposed to know the multiplication table until she was eight, and Charlotte was not supposed to know trigonometry at all (although she would know it in her secondary school years if she had been an English boy and not a girl). One other rule they learned: *never* write with both hands at once on an alien planet.

Physical education for Earth 48 students did not involve sports. Rather it was about planting and harvesting crops. The students were also taught how to ride a horse, milk a cow, build a fire, raise livestock, and other such skills, using ancient tools commensurate with the technical level of development of the planet for which they were being trained. Girls had to know how to spin and weave, how to cook on an iron stove and how to sew. They needed to know how to make bread from scratch (grains) and how to cook meat beginning from skinning the animal.

Children learning to be Americans had a rigorous curriculum that not only included agricultural skills, but also safety training. All of the boys over nine were required to learn how to stop a bear or a wolf from attacking their home. The final exam involved the real thing, tended by armed agents to protect any student not up to the test.

Some of the teachers were human, but some were life-like androids. In particular, classroom teachers in Adaptation Hall were often robots because of the difficulty finding agents who were qualified to teach the languages of some of the factions their parents were assigned. The best language teachers, like Special Agent Lorch Lorbank, were usually assigned to teaching adults. Some androids had multiple roles. By changing programs on the remote control, the same android could "become" a different person with a different language or curriculum.

Because adaptation was the goal, students in Adaptation Hall were required to speak to one another in the language of the alien planet to which their parents might be sent and not their mother tongue. They were forbidden to address one another by their real names and had to always use their aliases.

Unni Svavapass was not a student or an instructor in the Exploratory Surveillance training school but did volunteer some of her time teaching English during the day when the girls were gone at school. Her first order of business was to write a lengthy letter of protest to Subdirector Vlaris. In the letter, she laid out all of the reasons her girls should not be required to go to Adaptation School and should be allowed to return to England. In her letter, she also asked for an appointment to meet Vlaris to discuss the matter.

The first two weeks were difficult. Charlotte and Sherry were not relating well to the other students because they could not speak Grellish very well.

They did not always respond when a teacher called them "Miss Svavapass." Rather, they identified with the name Weatherby. They would sometimes be admonished for using their aliases in Regular Education Hall. Not all the teachers knew that their first names were not aliases, but their legal names.

The girls were also having to adjust to simple, everyday conveniences like light switches, computers, processed foods, and holograms. They did not like their tight-fitting synthetic clothing. Charlotte said her clothes were uncomfortable, and Sherry complained that they made her itch.

Everything was different. The trees were different; the weather was different. There were two small moons in the sky at night instead of one large one.

Whenever they went to Adaptation Hall, students were required to wear native costumes. But Sherry and Charlotte were relieved to get back into the clothing they were accustomed to. The girls had authentic English clothing that their mother had purchased for them in London.

In one of her letters to Ori, Unni joked that Adaptation Hall was really Adapted Hall for the girls. The real adaptation for Charlotte and Sherry was in Regular Education Hall, which was not designed to help anyone adapt.

After two more weeks, the girls were beginning to accept their new surroundings, and Unni was contemplating going back to Earth 48. It was then that she finally received a reply from Subdirector Vlaris. He apologized for being slow to respond and excused himself with being so busy.

Vlaris said he was going on vacation to Earth 19 in a few days to visit with some of his relatives. He offered to meet Unni in Yoilafa on a certain date. Unni thought Vlaris' conscience might have been bothering him because he offered to give Charlotte and Sherry a vacation from school to come along and meet their grandparents. He even agreed to pay their roundtrip fare on a commercial starship with Bureau funds.

When the time came for the trip, Unni asked her daughters a small favor. In the Botvraytish language, there is no "sh" sound. She asked the girls if they would go by the names Zarlotte and Zerry while they were with their grandparents. Of course, Unni's mom's name was Zeri, and she would think Sherry was named after her. In a sense she was.

The Vlaytorks were thrilled to see their grandchildren after so many years. They had not seen Charlotte since she was an infant, and they had never met

Sherry. The Vlaytorks had been told that Ori and Unni had been working on Earth 44 and were stranded there when Earth 43 was invaded by the Vittmians. There was little communication in that part of the Confederation during the war for security reasons.

Sherry and Charlotte were coming along in their Grellish, but they still needed their mother to interpret sometimes. Like all good grandparents, the Vlaytorks showered the girls with gifts including toys. Unni secretly had to take the girls aside to show them how to play with them.

"Mommy, why does Grandma call you Unni?" Charlotte asked. "Isn't your name Jenny?" That question afforded Unni an opportunity to fill in more gaps in the girls' knowledge about their extraterrestrial parents.

Toward the end of the week, Unni took leave of her family to meet with the Subdirector. The Vlaytorks were all too happy to have a private time with their granddaughters.

Vlaris was dressed informally when he appeared in a park at the designated location. But even in the most casual clothes, Vlaris appeared as rigid as when he was on duty.

The discussion began informally. They recalled their two years together on Space Station 48-3. Vlaris thanked Unni once again for the recordings of Mozart's piano concerti.

"Those recordings were clean, with no background noise of an audience. What did you do, go to a rehearsal or something?"

"Ori recorded them, actually," Unni explained. "I was the pianist."

Vlaris was surprised. "That was you? You can play an Earth 48 piano?"

"It took a little getting used to. Like everything else on Earth 48, the keyboard is backward."

Vlaris appeared to be somewhat softened when he realized that Unni had played the concerti just for him.

Then Vlaris got down to business. "I read what you wrote about how your daughters have no need for acclimation and how you would rather they returned with you to England. You raised some valid points.

"But I also know what you and Ori plan to do. You want to have a baby boy and raise him to be a high-ranking office holder in the British Empire and use his position to accelerate the technical progress of the planet. You want Earth 48 to be ready to join the Confederation before the Vittmians invade.

"That is what I like about you two," the Subdirector went on. "You genuinely care about others. But, Unni, you need to drop that misguided mission. It cannot work. Aside from the fact that it is against protocol, it is just not workable."

"What do you mean, not workable?" Unni asked.

"Do you know how many parents in England would love to see their son be the prime minister some day? Do you realize the probability against him reaching that office? What if he makes it to party leader? How do you know he won't spend a decade or two as leader of the opposition? Even if he became prime minister, how do you know he would be able to enact his policies?"

"We do not know," Unni admitted. "But one thing we do know. The Vittmians are ruthless and aggressive, and Earth 48 is in the way of their expansion. They are coming, and when they take over, they are cruel tyrants."

"Let me rephrase my question," Vlaris said. "Let us say, hypothetically, that you had the power to enact policy in the British Empire. Let us say that the Noninterference Protocol were of none effect, and you had full permission. Your son is prime minister, and he checks with his mother every time he acts. Tell me, Grandma Weatherby, what policies would you enact to achieve your goal?"

"There are certain reforms that are needed," Unni replied. "Firstly…"

Vlaris interrupted her. "You may not correctly understand the history of Earth 5, but you surely know from the history of our native planet, Earth 19, that socialism actually hindered social progress. Socialism failed on every planet it was tried. As Subdirector, I regularly read the surveillance reports from Earth 39. That planet is almost completely socialist. If you like, I can give you some redacted copies and you can see firsthand what a hopeless mess that planet is in."

"Who said anything about socialism?" Unni countered. "Quite the opposite, I would promote economic and political freedom. In a free market, the creative energies of the British people can be unleashed. New inventions and ideas need to be able to reach the free marketplace without all of the barriers put in place by the privileged few. The entrepreneurs and the innovators must be free to pursue their ideas and dreams.

"We need to push away the veils of ignorance by making education more available and by identifying the most gifted and talented young people in science, engineering, medicine and the arts, and opening the doors of higher education to them. I could go on."

"Please do," Vlaris said. "I am enjoying this."

"Racial and ethnic discrimination can be ended. How many great scientists, engineers, and artists are lost to menial occupations when a segment of the population is marginalized? Due to its geographic spread, the British Empire is uniquely situated to influence the whole planet in breaking this shackle."

"At Cultural Level 6?" Vlaris scoffed.

"And there are diplomatic steps that can be taken early to avoid the destructive world wars that convulsed nearly all of the members of the Confederation when they were at Technology Levels 9 and 10."

"Oh, come now, Unni!" Vlaris beckoned condescendingly. "Don't you remember your history? How many great innovations came about during the world wars? War brings about invention."

"Not necessarily, Vlaris. Both earths that avoided their world wars developed more rapidly."

Vlaris sighed.

"In short," Unni concluded, "I would, in your hypothetical situation, promote freedom."

"That already exists on Earth 48," Vlaris countered. "It is called the United States of America."

"Even if they could miraculously preserve their union from their present sectional disputes, the Americans are technologically behind the Europeans. Britain has the enormous advantage of a better starting point in terms of the present infrastructure and institutions. If the British Empire could adopt American freedom, they would afford their planet the fastest pathway to development."

"So that is why Ori 'nudged' Prime Minister Wellington into emancipating the Catholics in Britain?"

"That was the work of Wellington and Peel. You cannot prove Ori had any hand in that."

"Indeed, I cannot, which is why you two are not on trial like your beloved 'Uncle Sebastian.' And if Ori really did play a role in that reform, I do not want to know about it. He is a good agent and so are you."

"Thank you," Unni replied, part in sarcasm.

"Coming back to the point," Vlaris continued, "those goals you laid out are far-reaching and could not possibly be achieved by a single prime minister. Frankly, Metchavork's plan to unify Germany made more sense."

"You have no proof that Ori and I are doing anything other than gathering information," Unni maintained.

"You have well said that I have no proof," Vlaris agreed. "But I do have the power of the office of Subdirector. I have more than a dozen ways I could put an end to this silly scheme of yours."

Unni's lips tightened.

"Some of them are quite positive. For example, I could promote Ori to Team Leader for Earth 48," Vlaris pointed out with a sly grin. "After all, he will be the most senior agent on the planet when the new agents arrive."

"What if Ori doesn't accept the promotion?" Unni countered.

"Are you aware of the circumstances by which Lorbank was promoted?"

"Yes, Lorbank told Ori."

"I was there when Lorbank was revived in sickbay on the space station," Vlaris said. "Even Lorbank thought the heart attack was real."

"If you are so sure that our alleged scheme won't work, why don't you give me my daughters and let me return to Earth 48?" Unni demanded.

"Because I need you. The Confederation needs you," Vlaris said. "I want to make a deal with you and Ori. We have thousands of men on Earth 43 from the occupied planets who were conscripted by the Vittmians and who defected to the Confederation during the war. We need people like you who can learn their languages and train agents to infiltrate their planets. Think of it, Unni, thousands of people just like Ryla."

"I want to be with Ori and my daughters!"

"Oh, of course, Unni, of course. You could work remotely from the space station in orbit of Earth 48. Ori would be promoted to team leader, and you would be promoted to special analyst. I know Station 48-3 is a bit cramped; it is over three hundred years old. I have money in my budget for a brand new space station. Station 48-4 will be equipped with two wheels just like Station 55-1 was. I will have a park installed in the agricultural wheel so that Charlotte and her sister can play outdoors.

"What do you think, Unni? Is it a deal?"

"How will you justify to the Director removing Ori from his post so close to the prime minister of the greatest empire on the planet?"

"It will be a year or more before Space Station 48-4 is built and the new agents arrive. While we wait, Ori could lead his two-person team from the Tower of London. By then, Wellington will likely be out of office anyway."

"Even if I agreed with you, there is no way I could accept your offer," Unni replied. "You see, Ori and I always do everything together. I would need to discuss it with him."

"Very well then," Vlaris agreed. "I am in no hurry, not without the completion of the agents' training. Go back to Earth 48 and talk to Ori."

23.
Team Leader

Unni's absence was not a pleasant time for Ori. He missed his wife very much. To his view, May, June and July were as cold and drab as November, December, and January without her warmth and presence. Starships came by infrequently, and her letters were sporadic. Sometimes, three letters would arrive on the same day and after that none at all for a month.

Ori focused on his mission as he always did when he was lonely. The Wellington government had another legislative accomplishment, the Metropolitan Police Act, which organized policing in the thirty-two boroughs of greater London and greatly reduced crime. The bill was the product of a committee formed the previous year by Wellington's political ally Robert Peel and included principles for the proper conduct of the police. Ori was very pleased with this development because consistent law enforcement could only enhance the technical and cultural development of Britain. And in this case, progress had occurred without any "nudge" being necessary.

Other aspects of Wellington's government were not so favorable to Ori's desire to accelerate progress in the British Empire. Following Catholic Emancipation, the next reform that was needed was to increase the size of the electorate. But Wellington and Peel were opposed to further reform.

At that time, one had to live in a dwelling worth at least ten pounds to be eligible to vote. Thus, only a small portion of the male population could vote. Members of Parliament represented boroughs. The number of eligible voters in a borough varied from about a dozen to twelve thousand. This meant that a handful of voters could elect a member of Parliament in some boroughs. These small boroughs were often controlled by a wealthy patron and were thus called "rotten boroughs."

A reform bill was proposed to greatly reduce the property requirements for voters and eliminate the rotten boroughs. Wellington's opposition to this reform led to his unpopularity with the people. The press began to call him "the Iron Duke," a reference to his strong will in opposing the reform bill.

Wellington's opposition to this reform put Ori in an awkward position. Under these circumstances, Ori felt that the only good he could do was to attend social gatherings and enhance his political connections. But even these banquets were unpleasant in Unni's absence. Ori did not feel comfortable talking to women without his wife being present. True to what he had learned in his training at the Academy, Ori observed that many of the natives did not honor the bond of marriage in the same way as the peoples of the advanced worlds.

The men would retreat into private rooms to smoke and play cards. Ori entered those private rooms, but could not enjoy his time there as the others could. Unlike the natives, Ori was painfully aware of the dangers posed by exposure to tobacco smoke. Furthermore, he recognized the probabilistic odds that were against him in the card games. As a consequence, the natives could enjoy their time in ways that Ori could not.

It was against this backdrop that Ori received Unni's letter concerning her meeting with Vlaris. The offer Vlaris made to Ori and Unni would make it more difficult to carry out the one aspect of their mission that was still viable, that of raising a future British leader.

It was late in the month of August when Unni showed up at the door of the townhouse. It was already night, and she looked quite tired from the carriage ride.

When he saw her face, he felt as though his heart had passed from winter to springtime. From the look in her eyes, Ori knew she was feeling the same thing. Ori's embrace reminded Unni of their very first when they were engaged. After a brief meal, Ori took his wife to their room.

Ori and Unni spent the next three days doing nothing but spending time together. They went to the seashore and talked about their daughters, about Unni's parents, about how much they missed each other, about every subject imaginable, except Vlaris and his offer.

It was only on the third evening, as they returned from the seashore, that they addressed it. Ori told Unni all that had happened with regard to their mission, including the declining popularity of Wellington. Unni explained the offer Vlaris had made in detail.

Then the two talked of all of the aspects of the offer and the obstacles Vlaris had created. In the course of the discussion, Unni admitted she was interested in the possibility of working with the Vittmian conscripts on Earth 43 who had switched sides.

At last, Ori came up with a plan that would let them go on with their mission and satisfy Vlaris at the same time. They could accept his proposal. Ori, the team leader, would be able to determine the missions of the agents on the team. As such, he could assign himself to spend half of his time on the surface of the planet in England. Vlaris would never have to know just how much time he spent in England. When the children returned, they could live in London. Unni could be a part-time consultant to the agents who worked on the Vittmian project.

Of course, he would have to resign his job at the Board of Ordnance, but not before he arranged for another agent to be hired there. In this way, he could continue oiling his political connections for his future son. The girls would be getting a lot more fresh air in England than in the agricultural wheel of Station 48-4!

Unni loved the idea. She had just one concern. "They are certain to summon me often to Earth 2 or Earth 43 for consultation."

"They would have to settle for remote holographic communication," Ori replied.

"I doubt they would settle for that," Unni said. "And these consultations could keep me away for several weeks."

"But what if you were pregnant?" Ori asked with a sly grin.

"And after that, I would be the mother of an infant," Unni added with a glow in her eye.

As a token of good faith, Unni offered to go to Earth 2 immediately to work with the former Vittmian soldiers and train other agents how to learn their languages and cultures. During the time Ori waited for the new space station and for trained agents to arrive, Charlotte and Sherry would be able to live with their mother.

One Mraznian month later, Ori and Unni arrived on Earth 2. Charlotte and Sherry were elated to see their parents. They were glad to be out of the dormitory and back in a quadplex. They also knew they would be receiving visits from their father from time to time.

Vlaris was pleased when he heard that Ori and Unni had agreed with his proposal, and he was even happier yet that Unni agreed not to wait to begin the project to work with the Vittmian defectors. Vlaris sent a message to his counterpart in the Bureau of Protective Action and arranged for Ryla to join Unni for a week to help out with the project.

During his week on Earth 2, Ori spent the evenings with his family, but during the day, he went to the training school to have a look at the agents training to serve on Earth 48. Many of the instructors and staff were eager to meet the new team leader, especially the agents who were candidates for long-term assignments.

He started by visiting the agents training to serve in England. There were now twenty-four agents, all of them married couples. They had a firm command of the English language, and all were nearly accent-free.

He watched them performing basic social functions. He observed the way they ate, the way they wore their English clothing, usage of idioms, and their subtle mannerisms. Ori took note of four agents who were particularly good. Two of them were married to one another, Clayton and Emily Anderson. Ori found out their real names, Sraytel and Mlee Erdisek. Since both the spouses were excelling, this couple was Ori's first choice to be assigned long-term roles in England.

As team leader, one of Ori's responsibilities was to call Vlaris weekly (every ten days). Vlaris believed he had won the two agents Svavapass over to his side and was quite cordial toward Ori.

Ori's first call as team leader was made from a room within the training school. "Good day, Subdirector Vlaris," Ori began.

"You can call me Sral," Vlaris said with a smile. "And the other agents need to start calling you Special Agent Svavapass. You know that comes with your new role."

"Thank you, Sub... uh, Sral."

"So, I see you are on Earth 2 at the training school. Excellent. What I need you to do, Ori, is get acquainted with the candidates and start building your team. The instructors have ranked them, but I want you to rank them also, at least the ones you find most promising. Then you need to pick where you would like to deploy them. I have made Lorbank's last few reports available to you. You may want to talk to Lorbank directly. He will be a good resource for building your French team."

"I have already begun by observing the candidates for the English team," Ori said.

"That's what I like about you Ori, you are proactive. Then you need to return to Earth 2 every so often to see how the candidates are progressing and perhaps revise your ranking."

"I plan on it," Ori assured his boss.

"You know, Ori, your task of selecting agents is a lot more difficult than mine was back in 37525 when I picked you. Back then, I had to select single agents. But you have to pick couples. If one spouse is great and the other is weak, you can't use them. But I have my full confidence you will make good choices."

Later that day, Ori met with Agent Ovackt Alkass, who headed up the program for agents training for England. Agent Alkass was from Olistoss, the same country Ori was from on Earth 19.

Ori told Alkass that he was very interested in the Erdisek family.

Alkass rolled his eyes in dismay. "Ah, the Erdiseks."

"What is the matter?" Ori asked. "I have lived in England for the past sixteen years, and I think they are perfect."

"That is just the problem," Alkass said. "They *are* perfect. But their rebellious son Beempu is resisting his instruction. He is spoiling everything! Unless he comes around, there will be no way to send the Erdiseks into the field."

"Is Beempu a teenager?" Ori asked.

"He is still ten," Alkass replied.

"Then perhaps there is still a way to reach him," Ori opined.

"The principal of Adaptation Hall has tried almost everything."

"Well, keep trying," Ori exhorted the instructor. "Oh, one other thing. Agent Ipskist is mispronouncing the 'th' sound. The English words 'the' and 'thought' are subtly different. She needs to work on this or she will not make the team."

"I'll make note of that," Alkass assured the team leader. "Unless, of course, you would like to speak to the language teacher yourself."

"I would like to meet him," Ori said.

"That would be Agent Urelt Sraymlat in Building 24, third floor."

Ori went immediately to Building 24. He needed to speak with Sraymlat to find out if he still held a grudge, and if so, to determine if that was going to undermine the efforts of the team. Sraymlat was returning to his office from having just taught a class.

"Urelt Sraymlat, it has been a long time," Ori greeted his former partner. "I did not know you were on Earth 2."

Sraymlat did not seem very happy to see Ori. He gave a cool reply. "I suppose it has been a long time. I just transferred here from Tlat Mlang. All things related to Earths 46 to 51 are now in this facility. So, I heard Vlaris made you team leader."

"That's right. I am building a new team from scratch. Besides Unni and me, all the other agents from the old team scattered to other roles during the war."

"I heard you and Unni stayed behind in the evacuation," Sraymlat said without looking up from his desk. "You took quite a chance with your lives."

"We felt someone needed to stay," Ori replied casually, trying to warm up his cold former teammate.

"Or, more accurately, you have never given up your plot to change the course of Earth 48's development," Sraymlat accused his former friend.

"Please be careful, Urelt. That kind of remark will not build up a professional relationship."

"Don't skirt the issue, Svavapass. I know what you are up to. Vlaris is crazy to trust you. If you were sincere in working with Vlaris, you would shave that native beard, go to a surgeon, and get that scar fixed. But you can't do that because you still want to live in London and be Robert Weatherby. Vlaris has to be blind not to see that."

"I am keeping the alias because London is as good a place as any to run a two-person team. They are building a new space station. It just doesn't pay to reactivate old Station 48-3 after it has been sitting for four years. Just the cost of getting life support back up and running would be…"

"Spare me the details."

"And Weatherby is uniquely placed to gather crucial intelligence. The Duke of Wellington is prime minister now."

"It figures. You know, Wellington is no different from Bonaparte. The only difference is that Bonaparte had the opportunity to make himself an emperor, and Wellington did not, at least not yet."

"What are you talking about, Urelt?"

"You remember what a harsh disciplinarian he was. I have no doubt that reactionary will soon have England in rebellion. George IV and his elderly brothers will soon be so dependent on their generals that Wellington will be running the place in no time. When that tottering monarchy falls, Wellington will arise to become First Consul, just like his secret idol, Bonaparte."

Ori began to get angry. "That is not the Wellington I know…"

"When he promotes you from major to major general, you will not be able to say no. Wellington is no different than Bonaparte or even Arjus Ferrute. And when Wellington embarks on his campaign for world conquest, you'll be sent to Canada to invade America. Knowing you, you'd probably succeed in taking Albany, but you will die trying to take New York. Andrew Jackson will kill you just like he killed Ned Pakenham."

Ori bristled. But Sraymlat kept on his rant.

"And when you are decomposing in American soil, I will come and rescue Unni from the drudgery of primitive Britain, and give her the life you never would…"

"That's enough, Sraymlat! I demand a message of apology by tomorrow morning or you're fired."

"You can't fire me. My boss is Ovackt Alkass."

"And his boss is the Team Leader for Earth 48! Start writing, Sraymlat."

"You *would* fire me, wouldn't you? First you take my fiancé, and now you want my job."

"I did not take your fiancé. She came to me, and that was after she dropped you. But as for your job, you're fired!"

"And who will you find to teach English here?"

"There are plenty of agents who may have been rejected for field work, who nonetheless speak better English than you do. Now get packing!"

Ori turned to leave the office. Behind him, he could hear Sraymlat's threatening. "I'll get you, Svavapass! You haven't heard the last of me."

That evening, Ori told Unni of his encounter with Sraymlat and of his insulting remarks. Unni suggested that he fire him.

"I already have. You and I always did think alike."

The night before Ori had to depart to return to Earth 48, Ryla arrived. Ryla embraced Unni with tears. Ori told Ryla he had always wanted to meet her, that he had heard so much about her.

"I also have always wanted to meet you too. Unni has written to me about you."

"I feel I owe you a great debt, Ryla," Ori admitted. "I believe it was your influence on Unni that has brought me the joy of my life."

Ryla turned to Unni. "Now I have met your Folf. Enjoy every day that you have together."

The Svavapass family went out to eat that evening with their guest.

The England that Ori returned to was very different from the one he had left. It was October and the leaves and flowers were gone. Wellington's unpopularity had progressed to the point that one could feel the tension while walking the streets.

Mrs. Anders was forced to retire due to an illness of advancing age. She had moved to the countryside to live with her sister, who could care for her. Ori sent her twenty pounds as a retirement gift. He hired a new cook, Mrs. Morris, who was a widow.

Vlaris sent Ori a holographic communication device with which he could stay in touch with his team on Earth 2 and with Vlaris on Earth 1. Two members of the starship crew boarded the dormant Station 48-3 and reactivated part of the communications station so that Ori's messages could be relayed. It was a rare thing for an agent to have any devices of advanced technology on the surface of a planet under surveillance. It was the size of a soup bowl, and Ori took precautions to keep it hidden.

Ori was now team leader. Vlaris was pacified. Sraymlat was neutralized. All Ori had to do now was make it through the year alone. At least he got to see his wife and children for about twelve days every two to three months. And the mission was back on course.

24.
Miss West

Unni was very busy working on instructing agents from the Bureau of Protective Action on how to learn the languages and cultures of the planets that were enslaved by the Vittmians. Most of the soldiers from the occupied Vittmian planets wanted to simply start a new life on Earth 43. But there were a number of soldiers who were willing to work for the Confederation, even as spies.

The big prize was General Rorsh, a native of Earth 89, a defector from the Vittmians' home planet. Unni worked with Rorsh's handlers, and even got to talk with Rorsh on more than one occasion. In the time since his defection, Rorsh had learned Grellish. The general was a gold mine of intelligence.

Unni asked him why he defected. Rorsh explained that the cities he had conquered on Earth 43 were filled with things that gave him a window to see what freedom and justice were. His reasons for defecting were simple. "I wanted to be free. I wanted to live on a world where justice reigned."

Charlotte and Sherry were beginning to make friends with the other children of the agents who wanted to work in England. The more they made new friends, the better they adjusted to their new situation.

In Regular Education Hall, the children were grouped by age. The classrooms held a mixture of children whose parents were trying out for positions in different factions and even different planets. One morning, Sherry conjured up the boldness to go to the front of the classroom when the teacher asked for volunteers to each speak for two minutes. Up to this point,

Sherry had never tried it. Her Grellish was weak, and she was the youngest child in the class.

She told the class that it was her birthday and that she was five.

The teacher, Mr. Movel, was puzzled. His holographic class book always prompted him whenever a student had a birthday. He quickly looked Sherry Svavapass up in his roster. It confirmed his suspicion. "But, Sherry, today is the eighteenth day of the second month. Your birthday is the sixteenth of month four."

"That is the confederation calendar," she pointed out. "But on my planet, today is the twelfth of November. My birthday is November 12."

"What is November?" the teacher asked in bewilderment. "I am unfamiliar with the calendar on Earth 19 and I have never heard of this term 'November.' Can someone confirm Sherry's assertion?"

Roha Veelot, a blond-haired six-year old from Earth 19, stood. "It is not from the calendar of Earth 19, but of Earth 48, where my family hopes to serve. November is the eleventh month on their calendar."

"Well then, happy birthday, Sherry," the teacher conceded. "Do you know your birthday on your home planet, Earth 19?"

"I don't know," Sherry replied. "I've only been to Earth 19 once. I could ask my mother."

The class began to rumble with chatter. How could this girl only have visited her home planet once?

"Sherry was born on Earth 48 during the war," Roha explained. "She told me she had lived almost her whole life there. I talk to her a lot about that. One day, my family will move to a city there called Berlin, and my name will be Rolf Wertz."

"That is, *if* your family is selected," Mr. Movel cautioned.

From that day forward, Sherry considered Roha to be her best friend. But she always called him Rolf.

Several days later Charlotte sat with Beempu Erdisek in the lunchroom.

She greeted him in English, "Hello, Billy. My name is Charlotte."

"My name is not Billy, it's Beempu," he responded gruffly in Grellish. "And don't address me in that primitive language when we are not in Adaptation Hall. I want to speak that language as little as possible!"

"What have you got against English?" Charlotte asked.

"Because it is spoken on Earth 48. Now leave me alone!" Beempu demanded.

"I want to be your friend," Charlotte said. "Tell me, what is wrong with Earth 48?"

"I don't know," Beempu replied with annoyance. "Maybe there is nothing wrong with that planet, except that my parents want to move there and I don't want to."

"Why not? I have lived there for most of my life. It is not a bad place at all."

"Oh, yes, it is," Beempu argued. "They don't have electricity there, so I will not be able to play my holographic games. I'll be bored out of my head."

"Before a few months ago, I did not know there was such a thing as electricity," Charlotte replied. "I was perfectly happy without it, and I wish I could go back. I find this world with its electricity and holograms and flying carriages confusing. If my family said we were going back to England tomorrow, I would leap for joy."

"Well, isn't that funny?" Beempu remarked. "I dread going to Earth 48, and wish I could stay here. You don't like it here, and wish you were on Earth 48. What opposites we are!"

"Or maybe we are just the same, following our parents to places we would rather not be," Charlotte observed.

"But we are not the same," Beempu countered. "You are being a good little girl, and you are not doing anything about your situation. But I am a boy of iron, and I intend to resist, to make it impossible for our family to be chosen for their mission. You'll see."

"I feel sorry for you, Billy," Charlotte replied as she picked up her things and walked away.

"My name is not Billy! It's Beempu!" he shouted after her.

That afternoon in Adaptation Hall, Beempu was especially misbehaved in class. Miss Ellington, the android teacher, was trying to prepare the class for a history test on William the Conqueror. Unlike the Regular Education Hall, the students in her classroom were of mixed ages, similar to some school houses on Earth 48. The students ranged in age from six to twelve, except for Sherry, who was not quite five by the official calendar.

"In what year did the Battle of Hastings take place?" the teacher asked.

Charlotte quickly put up her hand and was recognized. "On October 14, 1066."

225

"Very good, Charlotte," the teacher responded with a smile.

"I've been to Hastings once with my mother and father," Charlotte went on.

"I'll bet you have," Beempu called out.

"Perhaps at another time you could tell us about that," the teacher replied, trying to ignore Beempu's heckling. "Who was the losing general at Hastings?"

Charlotte raised her hand again, "I know, I know."

"Let's see if someone else besides Charlotte Weatherby knows," Miss Ellington said.

"Let's see if anyone else in this room could give a brass farthing!" Beempu remarked.

"Billy Anderson!" Miss Ellington shouted crossly. "If you want to say something raise your hand! I will not tolerate any more of your disruptive behavior!"

A boy named Jonathan raised his hand and was called upon. "It was King Harold Godwinson," he replied. "He was an Anglo-Saxon."

"Very good," the teacher replied.

"No, it wasn't," Beempu called out. "It was Arjus Ferrute of Earth 5."

Most of the children laughed.

Miss Ellingson was not amused. "Billy Anderson! I have *had* it with your uncooperative behavior! Come up here to the front of the classroom."

Beempu casually strolled to the front with no fear or deference to the teacher's authority. The android pulled him between her desk and the chalkboard. She reached into the right drawer of the desk and produced a black leather paddle. "Drop your trousers and bend over the chair, young man!"

Beempu did not comply. Miss Ellington made a move toward him, when suddenly she froze. Her jaw dropped and a mechanical female voice, not her usual voice, said in Grellish, "Corporal punishment sequence disabled."

A moment later, the android came back to life and said, "I hope you have learned your lesson, young man! The next time will be much worse!"

Beempu triumphantly strode back to his desk.

The following afternoon, Beempu misbehaved again. As in the day before, he was summoned to the front. Miss Ellington took out the paddle and commanded Beempu to bend over on the chair. Once again, the android froze, and the mechanical voice said in Grellish, "Corporal punishment sequence disabled."

About ten minutes later, Mr. Toezh the principal entered the classroom.

He had a metallic remote-control device in his hand. He pressed a button and Miss Ellington froze in place.

Mr. Toezh addressed the class in Grellish. "I have become concerned with the poor behavior of this class. There have been no less than eleven incidents this term in which the corporal punishment sequence was invoked by our android teacher, and two such incidents in the last two days. Every time that happens, I get an automatic message in my office.

"I cannot impress you students enough with the seriousness of this matter. Some of you will find yourselves in a real classroom on an alien planet. If you misbehave, the teacher really will punish you, and you could be seriously injured. Earth 48 is at Cultural Level 6. Under those conditions, teachers are not regulated and they can mete out any punishment they wish. There is no standard, and they can be quite subjective. Neither the Interplanetary Intelligence Service nor your parents will have any way to save you, nor will they have any legal recourse.

"I charge you to mend your ways, and learn to behave in this kind of classroom setting while the corporal punishment sequence is inactive."

A student named Alyork raised his hand. "Mr. Toezh, it might be helpful for you to know that all eleven of these incidents involved the same student. The rest of us are interested to learn about that alien world and about the faction called England."

"Oh, thanks a lot, Alyork," Beempu blurted sarcastically.

"Are you the one triggering the punishment sequence, Beempu?" the principal asked.

"Of course, I am the one," Beempu answered with a touch of insolent pride.

"I should have guessed," Mr. Toezh said. "Very well then, class. Carry on. But you Beempu, you are coming with me."

"Are you going to spank me?" Beempu asked with sarcasm.

"Don't give me any ideas," the principal replied grimly.

After Beempu left the classroom, things became orderly. Charlotte and Sherry were relieved, as were many of the other students.

The following day, Miss Ellington was just beginning her math lesson when she suddenly froze. She then said, "*Bon matin, classe. Mon nom est Mademoiselle Duvall.*"

"What is she saying?" the students were asking.

"She is speaking French," Charlotte told the class.

Beempu was holding a small metallic device in his hand. "I stole the remote control for this android from the principal's office yesterday," the boy of iron declared with pride. "Watch this."

Beempu turned a knob on the remote control. The teacher froze again. Then she began to speak.

"*Guten Morgen, Klasse. Ich heisse Fraülein Ingrid Meyer, eure neue Lehrerin.*"

"That is German," Alyork said. "My friend Orlyap has her for Adaptation Hall. His family is supposed to serve in a place called Preussen."

Beempu turned the nob again.

"*Grüss Gott, Klasse. Ich heisse Fraülein Theresa Bechtold.*"

"Why are there two Germans?" one girl asked.

"I have no idea," Beempu replied. "Let's see what this is."

He turned the knob again. "Good morning, class. My name is Miss Jane West, and I am your new teacher."

"She is speaking English, but she sounds different, one boy pointed out."

"I like her better than the others," Beempu said. "We'll stick with Miss West."

"Pardon me, young man?" the teacher inquired of Beempu.

Alyork decided to cover for Beempu. "He was just pointing out that you said 'good morning,' but it is the afternoon."

"Well, I reckon it is the afternoon," she said. "Today we will memorize the capitals of all twenty-four states. Let us begin from the very north. Can someone please tell me the capital of New Hampshire?"

Several weeks later, Unni entered the quadplex in the afternoon after working with defectors and their handlers. The girls were doing their homework.

"Mom, could you help me with my homework, please?" Charlotte asked.

"I would be happy to, but I only have a moment," Unni replied. "We need to clean house. Daddy is coming tomorrow."

Charlotte handed her mother a page with a paragraph in her own handwriting. "I am supposed to memorize this. I need you to read along while I recite."

"Very well," Unni agreed as she took the page.

Charlotte began her recitation, "We hold these truths to be self-evident, that all men are created equal, that they are endowed by their Creator with certain unalienable Rights, that among these are Life, Liberty, and the pursuit of Happiness—That to secure these rights, Governments are instituted among Men deriving their just powers from the consent of the governed,— That whenever any Form of Government becomes destructive of these ends, it is the Right of the People to abolish it, and to institute new Government, laying its foundation on such principles and organizing its powers in such form, as to them seem most likely to effect their Safety and Happiness."

"Very good, Charlotte," her mother praised her. "You have memorized it perfectly."

Unni knew she had read these words somewhere when she was an analyst on Station 48-3, but she could not be sure where. She liked the theme because people with this mindset would certainly progress. Unni was glad this sort of thing was being taught to the children of agents and began to wonder if her vision of the Bureau of Exploratory Surveillance was beginning to take root.

"Charlotte is done with her homework," Unni declared. "Sherry, are you ready?"

"Almost, Mommy."

"Very good, because I will need two little helpers to assist me to get this house ready for when Daddy comes."

For the next hour, Unni, Charlotte, and Sherry worked together to clean the house. As the girls set their room in order, they were singing in English. Unni was proud of them.

Charlotte and Sherry were very happy to see their father walk through the door. The family had a pleasant dinner together. Ori was glad to see his wife and children. He was also happy to be out of the harsh London winter weather.

Unni told Ori about her work with the defectors. Ori told Unni of his heavy workload. He had to evaluate so many agents. But he could only stay on Earth 2 for a week because of all the things he had to do on Earth 48, finding housing and jobs for two families in England, two families in France, three in the German-speaking world, and one in America.

"I am having to restart the team from scratch," Ori declared. "And if that is not enough, there is the recommissioning of old Space Station 48-3."

"But, Ori, I thought we were getting a new one," Unni said.

"We are, but there is some kind of holdup in the funding," Ori replied. "The military is tired of having to keep a starship parked in orbit, and I need a place to put my agents and analysts. I have six agents shuttling back and forth to the surface preparing the way for the families to come."

"How is your friend the prime minister coming along?" Unni asked.

"Very poorly, I'm afraid," Ori said. "His party is fractured and his popularity has slipped to new lows. Fortunately, the next election is still three years away."

"Ori, Charlotte has been memorizing excerpts from great works of literature. Charlotte, can you recite today's portion?"

She ran and got a sheet of paper and handed it to her mother. Then she began to recite.

"But when a long train of abuses and usurpations, pursuing invariably the same Object evinces a design to reduce them under absolute Despotism, it is their right, it is their duty, to throw off such Government, and to provide new Guards for their future security."

At first, Ori was smiling with pride at his daughter's excellent recitation. But as she continued to speak, his smile faded and turned to concern.

Charlotte continued, "Such has been the patient sufferance of these Colonies; and such is now the necessity that constrains them to alter their former Systems of Government. The history of the present King of Great Britain is a history of repeated injuries and usurpations, all having in direct object the establishment of an absolute Tyranny over these States. To prove this, let Facts be submitted to a candid world."

"Very good, Charlotte," Unni said.

"Isn't that from the Declaration of Independence by the United States of America?" Ori asked.

"Why, yes," Unni replied. "That is where I have heard this before."

"Can I sing you a song from school, Daddy?" Sherry asked.

Ori smiled. "Of course." He was looking forward to the sweet little voice of his youngest daughter.

"You know this song, too," Sherry said to her sister. "Would you sing with me?" Charlotte agreed. The two of them sang:

"That seat of science Athens,
And earth's proud mistress, Rome,
Where now are all thy glories
We scarce can find a tomb.
Then guard your rights Americans,

Nor stoop to lawless sway,
Oppose, oppose, oppose, oppose
For North America."

The girls sang all six verses of this American Revolutionary song with a hearty voice. Ori and Unni were both taken aback at the defiant anti-British tone of their singing.

"You see, Ori," their mother explained, "it would seem that their teacher, Miss West, is teaching her students a unit about the United States."

"I can see that," Ori agreed. "But it would also seem this Miss West has lost sight of the fact that this is a school for the children of agents, for them to adapt and learn to blend in. This sort of rebellious song—and for heaven's sake the Declaration of Independence—is not at all profitable for our mission."

"Ori, you *will* go down to the Adaptation Hall and have a word with the principal, won't you?" Unni requested.

"Indeed, I shall," Ori promised. "That's one more thing that I have to take care of! And is that an American accent I hear? Are my daughters picking up American accents?"

The girls were crestfallen. They did not understand why they had made their father unhappy. Ori realized that and gave both of his daughters a big hug and called for dessert.

But it was not until Ori was on the starship part way back to Earth 48 that he remembered that he was supposed to talk to Mr. Toezh, the principal. Ori had been going over the progress reports of all of the candidate agents. His first choice for England was the Erdisek family. His one concern was that one of the children of Sraytel and Mlee Erdisek, their son Beempu was questionable. Beempu had not had any bad reports for the past two months, and Ori wanted to talk to the principal to confirm this improvement. It was then that he remembered he was also supposed to talk about the curriculum in the English section of the Adaptation Hall.

Over the next several weeks, Beempu continued to relish the disruption Miss West was causing. He seemed to understand the profound political differences between the United States and Great Britain, and secretly enjoyed watching his classmates converted into "American patriots."

The "boy of iron" played his part well, going out of his way to cooperate with the android teacher. He would ask cleverly devised questions in class that would provide the opportunity for Miss West to expound patriotic American themes. Miss West was programmed to make her students blend in well in the United States, and, given the opportunity, she would gladly underscore the glories of the Republic and the "foul corruption" of the British monarchy and its tyrannical rulers.

Miss West was programmed to initiate field trips and often took the children to the farms that were a part of the Adaptation School. It was there that Charlotte learned to defeather a chicken and to milk a cow. The boys chopped down a tree and spent three different sessions removing its stump. While they heaved at the recalcitrant stump, Beempu would get his classmates to sing.

> "Let tyrants clank their iron rod,
> And Slav'ry clank her galling chains,
> We fear them not, we trust in God,
> New England's God forever reigns."

Miss West called "William Anderson" a budding American patriot and was programmed to favor students who espoused the ideals of Americanism. The robot would give reports on students' progress into a data base, and Beempu's file began to fill with high grades and glowingly positive reports.

But the boy of iron's clever plot to disrupt the education of the children studying to live in the United Kingdom was due to come to an abrupt end.

25.
The Fall of the Iron Duke

It was four months after Beempu had switched the program on the android from Miss Ellington to Miss West that the children were asked to memorize a poem by Francis Scott Key, *The Star-Bangled Banner.*

That afternoon, Sherry went to Roha's (Rolf's) house to play and Unni was alone with her older daughter in the girls' bedroom. Charlotte recited a stanza of the poem.

As Charlotte recited about the "Land of the free and the home of the brave," Unni's eyes darted around the room. The picture frames on the wall of King George IV and Prime Minister Wellington had been reprogrammed to George Washington and President Andrew Jackson. There was a twenty-four-star cloth American flag over Sherry's bed. Charlotte had pinned a paper map of the state of Virginia to the wall.

This supposed "unit about America" had been going on for four thirty-eight-day months and was growing in its intensity. Unni was now certain that something was wrong.

Unni proposed to Charlotte that they take a walk in the late afternoon sunshine. As they walked through the florid paths of the residential section of the complex, Unni began to ask her daughter questions. Charlotte told her mother that Beempu did not want to move to Earth 48. He did not want to give up his holographic video games. She told her mother how Beempu had stolen the remote control to the android teacher from the principal's office and had turned the teacher into an American.

"This is not such a bad thing, Mommy," Charlotte said. "Before, Beempu would never cooperate in class, and he was very disruptive, and he made school miserable for all of us. Now he is a model student, and Miss West really likes him. The whole class is relieved that he is no longer causing trouble."

Unni quickly deduced exactly what that naughty boy had done, and why he had done it. She wanted to laugh at the cleverness of his plot, but she remembered her mission to prevent a Vittmian takeover of Earth 48. Unni explained the entire ploy to her daughter.

"What are you going to do about it, Mommy?" Charlotte asked.

"I plan to go down to see Mr. Toezh first thing tomorrow morning. Oh, no. I have meetings all day with agents from the Bureau of Protective Action. The day after that is bad, too. I have to meet with several agents recruited from the defectors. I won't get to it until the day following. But I *will* go to the principal and have him put a stop to this."

"What should I do?" Charlotte asked.

"Just go along with it for two more days," her mother instructed. "So long as you are clear that the things you hear about your King are just the American point of view, designed for extraterrestrial children like you, who are to blend in with the American children."

"Okay, Mommy. I mean, very well, Mommy," Charlotte corrected herself.

They walked in the sunshine back toward their dwelling. Suddenly, Charlotte asked, "Mommy, do you think I would ever be able to visit America some day?"

The next day during lunch period, Charlotte sought Beempu out. "Hi, Billy," she greeted him.

"My name is Beempu, remember?"

"Beempu, I know what you are trying to do. I know you using Miss West to fill our heads with American liberty in a clever plot to make us misfits when we get to England."

Beempu smiled broadly. "Living for eight years on a primitive planet does not seem to have dulled your perception," he said smugly. "You know, I am actually getting to like you."

"Beempu, listen to me," Charlotte implored. "You have to switch the android teacher back to Miss Ellington. My mother is going to tell the principal in two days. Your game is over. You need to grow up and accept the fact that the world…that is, the galaxy does not revolve around you."

Beempu scoffed and said, "I am the boy of iron! Nothing can stop me." Charlotte was already getting up from the table before Beempu finished speaking.

Moments later, in Adaptation Hall, Beempu stood from his seat in the back of the class and said in Grellish, "I have an announcement. I am not going to be allowed to make Miss West our teacher anymore because Charlotte told her parents on me and her Daddy is Orishackt Svavapass, the big boss."

"William, what are you saying?" Miss West said in bewilderment. "What is this nonsensical language you are speaking?"

"I am sorry, Miss West," Beempu said in English. "I am going to miss you." Beempu held up the remote control.

"What in creation are you…" Miss West froze as Beempu turned the knob.

In a moment, the android came back to life. Charlotte was relieved. For a brief moment, it appeared that the boy of iron was taking a more reasonable course of action.

But that was not to be the case.

"*Grüss Gott, Klasse. Ich heisse Fraülein Theresa Bechtold.*"

"If I am not allowed to have Miss West, then we will have this Fraulein Bechtold."

"But we don't speak German," Alyork complained.

Beempu defiantly said, "I hold the remote. I make the decisions."

Beempu placed the remote in a hidden place under his desk and sat down.

"*Was sagt euch? Was für eine Sprache ist das?*" the teacher demanded.

Everyone was silent.

"*Heute studieren wir die Belagerung Wiens durch das Osmanische Reich,*" the teacher began.

No one in the class had the slightest idea that she was giving them a history lesson on the Turkish siege of Vienna. The class quickly grew anxious and restless as the teacher lectured them in a language they did not know about a city they were unfamiliar with in a war they had never heard of.

The exception was Beempu. He thought the whole thing was very funny and could not hide his glee.

"*Wilhelm Anderson! Was ist dein Problem?*" Fraülein Bechtold demanded.

Beempu did not answer her. She glared at him crossly. Then she continued.

"*Im Jahre 1683 marschierten die Türkischen nach Österreich.*"

Beempu suddenly broke out laughing.

"*Herr Anderson! Kommen Sie sofort zur Vorderseite der Klasse!*" the teacher commanded him.

Although Beempu knew no German, he was clear that he had been summoned to the front of the classroom. He merrily strode to the front of the room, pleased with himself at the chaos he was creating.

"Anything you say, Bechtold," he said in English in a defiant tone of voice.

The teacher was not amused. There was anger in her face.

"*Ach, was müss man oft von bösen Kinder hören oder sehen!*"

The teacher fumbled in the top drawer of the desk, looking for something.

"*Wo ist meine Peitsche? Wo ist meine Peitsche?*"

Not able to locate a whip, she settled for the paddle. With her other hand, she grabbed Beempu by the ear and hauled him outside of the classroom as the other students looked on helplessly.

"Ouch! That hurts!" Beempu cried out. He said in Grellish, "Corporal punishment sequence disabled!"

But she did not stop. As the door closed, the students heard Beempu shout in desperation, "Corporal punishment sequence: abort!"

"Hey, what are you doing to me?" You can't do that!" he yelled. "Abort sequence!"

Beempu's classmates heard the solid smack of the paddle against bare flesh.

"Youch! That really hurt!"

Immediately, they heard a whole series of smacks, one after the other. Beempu was screaming.

"Please stop! Stop it, please! I promise to behave! Stop!"

The class was frozen, not knowing what to do. On the one hand, they felt Beempu deserved it, but on the other hand, they were worried as to what might come of this.

After a few minutes of unrelenting blows, Beempu was roaring, "Help me! Somebody, help me please!"

Charlotte and Alyork got up and ran out into the hall. With one hand, the robot held Beempu's wrists in a tight grip. With the other, she wielded the paddle.

The teachers in the other classrooms were also robots. One came out in the hall and said in American English, "Please do not make so much noise. You are disrupting my class."

Charlotte thought quickly. She ran to the principal's office. Alyork followed. They burst into the office. "Quick! Help us! A robot is attacking a student!"

Mr. Toezh came out of his office into the administrative area where the children were.

Charlotte quickly explained what was going on. "You have to come quickly!"

Mr. Toezh quickly went into his desk. "English class, right?"

"Yes, quickly."

"That is android 20367-48-5. I can't find the remote control for that machine!"

"Beempu stole it," Alyork declared.

He turned to his administrative assistants. "Call Security!"

The two children ran back to the scene with Mr. Toezh trailing behind.

Beempu was screaming in agony.

Mr. Toezh tried to pull the android off, but the machine was stronger than he and was totally undeterred.

Charlotte ran into the classroom. Several students were swarming Beempu's desk trying to find where he hid the remote.

Eventually, one of them produced it. "Give it to me!" Charlotte cried out.

Charlotte ran out the door and handed the remote control to the principal. He held down a button and turned the knob. The robot released Beempu, stood at attention, and shut down.

Beempu was still roaring in pain.

Just then, two security guards showed up, running down the corridor.

"This boy is badly bruised," Mr. Toezh told one the security guards. "Take him to the infirmary at once."

The principal handed the other guard the remote control and told him to escort the android to the Maintenance Department for a thorough inspection. The security guard set the android into compatibility mode and walked her to the shop.

The principal entered the classroom and began to ask the class what had occurred. They told him everything, about how Beempu stole the remote control and changed the teacher into an American for nearly four months. Then they related how Beempu had changed her into a German.

"I still do not see how this happened," Mr. Toezh pondered. "The corporal punishment sequence was disabled for all five programs: German, French, English, Spanish, and American. This should not have occurred."

"What about the other German?" Alyork asked.

"What other German?" Mr. Toezh. "There is only one, Miss Ingrid Meyer."

"What about Miss Theresa Bechtold?" Charlotte asked.

"There is no…" Mr. Toezh stopped himself. "The Theresa Bechtold program is for Austria. But we haven't been deploying agents there for years, at least none with children. That program was taken off all of our robots long ago.

"It sure wasn't taken off this robot," a student remarked.

"The IT department must have missed one. Android 20367-48-5 is one of our older models. And when the upgrades came out, the programs all went back to default settings. The default settings are Cultural Accuracy. When the toggles were set, the technicians must not have adjusted the Bechtold program. We need to review our procedures."

"What will happen to Beempu?" Charlotte asked.

"He will be absent for a few days while he recovers," Mr. Toezh replied. "It will be a while before he can sit in a chair again. I hope you students all learned a lesson from this. Corporal punishment in a Cultural Level 6 society is to be avoided at all costs. This class is being dismissed early."

"Oh, Mr. Toezh? Will we have class tomorrow?"

"Yes," he replied. "I will find a spare android, set her on the Miss Ellington program and program her to pick up where the last Miss Ellington left off."

"That would be the Norman Invasion," Alyork said.

"I'll find the place from the records," the principal assured the class.

It was four days before Beempu returned to school. Charlotte saw him in the lunch room and sat across from him.

"Hi, Billy," she greeted.

"I prefer to be called…"

"I know," she interposed.

"Will. I prefer to be called Will."

Charlotte nodded. "Will? Very well then. It shall be Will. How are you feeling, Will?"

"Still sore," Beempu admitted. There was a humility in his voice that Charlotte had never heard before. "Thanks for trying to help me."

"What else could I do? You know there was a programming error with the android."

"Yes, I was told. Really, thanks for helping me."

Beempu Erdisek never misbehaved in class again.

Ori made another trip to Earth 2. He visited all of the candidate families. Ori finalized his list of the nine families selected to move to Earth 48 in the first wave. Now he could begin the task of obtaining the reference letters that would make it possible for agents to be hired in key positions to provide good intelligence of the progress of the planet.

Among the selected families were the Erdiseks. Agent Sraytel Erdisek would be posing as Clayton Anderson, an engineer building steam engines for England's fledgling railroad industry. Ori was relieved that their son Beempu's behavior was no longer an issue. Charlotte filled her father in on the details as to how Beempu had a change in heart.

Ori completely deferred to Lorbank's recommendations for the two families to settle in Paris. Lorbank also had some advice for Ori on managing field agents.

"Oh, yes, Ori, one more thing," Lorbank added. "I heard that Sraymlat got a job as an officer on a vessel in the Planet Patrol. He sought to become a starship officer in the fleet, but his application was turned down when the admiral read your report on his firing."

"Sraymlat is in the Planet Patrol?" Ori repeated. "I suppose he will do well there."

The Planet Patrol consisted of small, lightly-armed warships whose mission was to assist private and commercial vessels in trouble and to intercept smugglers and contraband. They were a branch of the military tasked with the enforcement of interplanetary law and security matters. The vessels in the Planet Patrol were able to enter interstellar space but usually stayed in the specific solar system they were assigned.

When Ori returned to Earth 48, he stopped off at Station 48-3, which was once again operational. He gave his agents their instructions for arranging jobs and housing for the families that were to arrive in a few months. He also issued the agents with several boxes of hypno-wipes each, as Ori now understood how a team leader "arranged" jobs for the permanent field agents.

With all of his agents and staff in motion, Ori could now devote his attention to British politics. By the native calendar it was now May 1830, which meant that Ori had three years to remedy Wellington's plummeting political fortunes. In addition to deep personal unpopularity, Wellington's Tory Party was now split into three factions. Worse yet, the populace was becoming increasingly restive.

But on June 26, 1830, before Ori could reach out to Wellington, King George IV died. The King's death could not have occurred at a worse time. It was a constitutional tradition that the death of the King triggered the dissolution of Parliament and an immediate election.

The results of the election were as bad as Ori feared they would be. Wellington lost 178 seats. Although he still had a plurality, his position was now extremely unstable. Rioting began to break out.

King George IV had no living legitimate heirs, so the throne passed to his brother William. King William IV earnestly tried to take up a conciliatory tone. But the rioting continued.

On September 15, 1830, the prime minister went to attend the opening of the Liverpool and Manchester Railway, a railroad that connected Manchester, a major industrial city, with Liverpool, a major seaport. Wellington rode the train from Liverpool to Manchester, but when he arrived at Manchester, he was met by a hostile crowd. The crowd waved banners with anti-Wellington slogans and pelted him with vegetables. Wellington refused to get off the train and rode it back to Liverpool.

Ori remembered Sraymlat's rant about rioting and a tottering monarchy of the elderly brothers of King George IV. He began to worry that there might be some truth in it.

In early November, Wellington announced in Parliament that the constitution needed no improvement and that he would resist any measure of parliamentary reform as long as he was in office. This stance caused a number of members of his own party to fear a new wave of public unrest. On November 15, Wellington lost a vote of confidence. He resigned the next day. The Iron Duke's government had lasted just under three years.

Ori resigned his position in the Board of Ordnance several days after that. His alias, Robert Weatherby, was independently wealthy; Ori did not need the job. Now he could devote himself to his other two jobs: team leader and increasing his political connections to serve another prime minister, his yet unborn son.

26.

Return to London

"Daddy's home!" Sherry announced. The two girls ran and hugged their father while Unni waited her turn. When Ori put his bags down, he announced that he had some good news.

"I just got word from Vlaris. We can all go back to England at the end of the month."

"Really, Ori?" Unni was ecstatic.

"Yes, Vlaris said we are done here."

"Even Sherry and me?" Charlotte asked.

"Especially Sherry and you," their father replied.

"First we will stop off on Earth 19 to visit Grandpa and Grandma, and then it will be London," her father assured them.

The girls began to dance and sing in the middle of the living room.

It was just after New Year's Day 1831 when the Svavapass family returned to London. After more than a year and a half, the household was returning to normal. Ori no longer had a formal job, but he did have a busy schedule of social engagements. He was trying to get better acquainted with Sir Robert Peel. He also had increased responsibilities as agents began to arrive and get situated on Earth 48.

Unni resumed her role as tutor for the girls. Charlotte and Sherry were glad to be back in a world to which they were accustomed, eating real food, wearing clothing made of real material and being able to speak their mother tongue, English.

Shelby marveled at how much the children had grown. Charlotte was now ten years old, and Sherry was six. He was also uplifted by the atmosphere in the house. Since May 1830, there had been no children, and when Ori was gone to "Scotland," there was no one to serve at all, a difficult prospect for a butler. The new cook, Mrs. Morris, had never met the children before because they were away when she took over from Mrs. Anders.

The weather was cold and windy, but the atmosphere in the Weatherby home was warm and happy. Ori and Unni were confident that their mission was going forward, to accelerate Earth 48's development so that the planet would be a member of the Confederation before the Vittmians could arrive. Charlotte and Sherry felt secure in a home sheltered from a galaxy and a nation that were anything but secure.

In late March, amid signs of spring, Dr. Stanton made a house call. He examined the entire family, giving everyone a clean bill of health, corroborating the assessment of the medical team on Earth 2 just months before. He also informed Unni that she was expecting another child.

The Erdiseks arrived in Britain in April. They moved to Reading, where Sraytel had a job with a railroad company. Beempu wanted to see Charlotte. He was disappointed to find out that the Andersons were not supposed to know the Weatherbys and that it would be impossible for him to meet his friend without compromising both families' covers.

By the middle of April, it was obvious to the new prime minister, the Earl Grey, that his electoral reform bill was not going to pass. Wellington and the Tory opposition proved too effective in blocking it. On April 22, King William IV went to Parliament and personally dissolved it calling for a new election. On April 27, an angry mob targeted Apsley house, Wellington's home, smashing windows.

The election was a landslide victory for the Whigs; they gained 174 seats in the House of Commons and now had a clear majority. Ori and Unni hoped this reform could occur while their Tory friends were out of power.

Every ten to twelve days, Ori would go aloft to Station 48-3 to meet with his analysts and coordinate the arrival of more agents and their families. At first, Vlaris was impatient with Ori for not ending the Weatherby alias and moving to the space station. When Ori told the Subdirector that Unni was expecting a baby, the Subdirector became more understanding of Ori's decision to remain in London.

Every month, Unni accompanied Ori to the space station, hiring a nanny to watch the children for a few days. This allowed Unni to receive prenatal care from the station surgeon and to do some analyst work, assisting the team working with the defectors. Within a year, the Interplanetary Intelligence Service would be moving agents onto planets occupied by the Vittmians.

On her first such trip in May, Unni was elated to find out that the baby was a boy. At long last, Ori and Unni were expecting a child they could groom to be a cabinet member and, hopefully, a prime minister!

By August, Unni was becoming quite large. Ori and she had decided from the beginning Unni would have the baby in Yoilafa on Earth 19. But King William IV was to be coronated on September 8. Ori felt they needed to attend the event and be seen doing so. For that reason, Unni delayed her departure to her mother's home "in Wallingford" until the day after the coronation.

King William's coronation was much less elaborate than the one Ori and Unni had witnessed ten years earlier for King George IV. This lower-budget ceremony was consistent with the new King's desire to relate to his subjects. William never expected to reach the throne and had lived a life that was more in touch with ordinary people. He had served in the Royal Navy, starting as a midshipman and working his way up to Lord High Admiral. William was not unaccustomed to hard work and was conscientious in all he did.

Ori and Unni had high hopes for his reign. Unfortunately, King William was sixty-four years old when he reached the throne, the oldest person ever to begin to reign in English history.

Unni became tired during the coronation ceremony. It was hot in Westminster Abbey, and she was uncomfortable.

The following morning, the entire family rose before sunrise to go to "Wallingford." Agent Mlai drove their carriage to the rendezvous point, and the family was aloft before sunrise.

Unni was not pleased to see Captain Squeem at the controls. She was weak and tired. She asked her husband in English why he had taken on Squeem as a member of the team. He told her that Squeem was available and was more familiar with this solar system and with Earth 48's geography.

"You should be more familiar with his style of driving," she retorted. "And as for his availability, I can only imagine…"

"Don't worry, Unni. I had a word with him about being more careful in trips with you on board."

Squeem turned to Ori. "What is all this chatter in a native language? I am very sensitive to that, you know, ever since I accidentally brought a native couple to Station 41-4. I got dropped from the team for that."

At least Charlotte and Sherry enjoyed the ride.

Three days later, Ori convened a meeting of all of the agents serving long-term on the surface of Earth 48. Since all of the agents were married with children, and given the social norms on the surface, Ori only summoned the men. By that time, Unni was refreshed and able to participate. There were two agents from England besides Ori and Unni, including Agent Erdisek. There were two agents from France, two from Prussia, and two from the United States, including Agent Qlat.

Ori began the meeting with reminders of protocol. No spoken Grellish was allowed on the surface; all communication was to be in handwriting, in Grellish, and to addresses of "relatives" in Wallingford, Potsdam, Vichy, and Trenton. Ori reminded the agents of the Noninterference Protocol, and especially admonished the two agents working as engineers not to accidentally "invent" anything.

"We have to be able to document to the Subdirector that all inventions were independently devised by the natives," Ori explained.

He also exhorted the agents to subscribe to a major newspaper in their venue.

Ori had the agents go around the room and talk about their families' adjustment to life on another planet.

They were almost done with that part of the discussion when Subdirector Vlaris called in. The agents gave their reports. There was political unrest in England, France, and Prussia. It was worst in France, where King Charles X had just been forced to abdicate, ending the Bourbon monarchy. The new King was Louis Philippe I, who appeared to be more reform-minded and likely to restore order.

Ori let Agent Erdisek give the report for the United Kingdom. He underplayed the political crisis over electoral reform and instead talked about the progress the British were making in building railroads.

The United States was in relatively good order, but the slavery issue was still simmering under the surface. Jackson was working on increasing foreign trade, even with the United Kingdom. All of the major powers seemed to be seeking peaceful relations with one another.

When asked by Vlaris which nation the agents expected to emerge as dominant on the planet, the agents said they were not sure. Agent Leka, the analyst, was still projecting the British Empire, but her analysis was full of caveats. She was concerned about the stability of the monarchy in the British Empire, with so few legitimate grandchildren of King George III. The United States was gaining economic strength all of the time, but sectional problems between the north and the south were dark clouds.

After the meeting ended, the agents returned to the surface. The Svava-pass family stayed aloft and boarded a starship two days later bound for Earth 19. The Vlaytorks were very happy to hear that another grandchild was due. Unni and the two girls were to stay with them for a few months until after the birth. The Vlaytorks relished the opportunity to entertain their granddaughters. Ori did not stay long. After three days, he went back to Earth 48.

During the next two months, Ori spent more time on the space station than on the ground. He also made his rounds, visiting Prussia, France, and New York State to confer privately with agents. The two families in England were more easily contacted by horse and buggy.

In early November, Ori went aloft to Station 48-3 to stay until the baby would be born. From there, he could call Unni every day and wait to catch the first starship that passed through. The only ship in the area was bound for Earth 36. When he got to the orbital spaceport, he discovered that there were no commercial ships going to Earth 19 in time to ensure he would be there before the baby arrived.

Ori did find some flights that might work, but they involved multiple stops, and he would be cutting it too close to Unni's due date. Then he got an idea: he rented a spaceship. The rates were reasonable, and one could return the ship at any major commercial spaceport.

The rental vehicle was not too unlike the Atmospheric Entry Vehicles that were used as transports. They were bowl-shaped and had two decks, but the rentals were somewhat larger than the transports. The upper deck consisted of a single round room with a large window in the front and the ship's helm and controls. There were two seats at the controls and five seats toward the rear. The lower deck had two private cabins and an open area that included a dining table and food synthesizer. The engines and life support systems were also on the lower deck, making it somewhat cramped.

The rental ships were a little slower than commercial liners, but they could operate automatically so that Ori could sleep during parts of the four-day journey. The main downside was that artificial gravity was dependent on accelerations and decelerations. While in interstellar mode, gravity was not consistent or comfortable. Although the accommodations were less comfortable than a commercial starship, the rented spaceship afforded Ori more certainty of not being late for the birth of his son.

Ori had not flown a spacecraft in twenty years since his days at the Academy, and the controls on this ship were different from what he was used to. He often needed help from the Advice Module on the ship's computer. Over the four-day trip, he got better at operating the vehicle, but he was glad Unni was not there, or she would have subjected him to uncomplimentary comparisons to Captain Squeem. By the time he docked at the spaceport at Earth 19, Ori decided never to criticize Squeem again.

Ori reached the home of Unni's parents four days before the due date. It was apparent that his daughters were enjoying their vacation. Unni was very large, and it was hard for her to get comfortable. She was eager to get this pregnancy over with.

The due date came and went with no result. Three days later, the obstetrician examined Unni. "This baby is getting to be too large. If nothing happens tonight, you are to report to the hospital tomorrow morning for induction."

The next morning, Huhane Vlaytork drove his daughter and son-in-law to the hospital. Ten hours later, Leonard Weatherby Svavapass came into the world. He was an amazing ten pounds, zero ounces using Earth 48 units and was quite red in appearance. Both mother and father were glad he was born in a hospital on Earth 19 rather than in their townhouse on Earth 48.

Unni held the baby adoringly, looking into his little blue eyes. "What is today's date?" she asked Ori.

"Today is the thirty-third, 37543.1.33. His birthday is the thirty-third of Month 1."

"But what day is it today in England?" Unni wanted to know. "We need to correctly record the date when we get back."

Ori switched to English. "Let me see…November 19, 1831. So, our children all have November birthdays: November fifth, twelfth, and nineteenth. And our anniversary is November thirteenth.

Unni repeated the date with some deliberation, "November 19, 1831."

"That makes Leonard the prime minister sometime in the late 1880s," Ori observed. "With good health, Alexandrina Victoria will still be Queen."

The grandparents soon arrived at the hospital. Once again, Zeri Vlaytork was perplexed at the name her daughter and son-in-law had chosen for their child. "Why do you always give your children strange names from other planets? Why can't you give them names from Zarfixu? Leonard is so unusual, and I cannot even pronounce that middle name."

The W sound is not in the Botvraytish language.

"What about our second child, Zeri?" Unni pointed out.

Mrs. Vlaytork nodded and agreed that at least one child had a normal-sounding name.

The grandparents began to carefully study the appearance of the child. "He is definitely a Vlaytork," Huhane beamed. "Look at that forehead. And that chin. There is no doubt about it. He is a Vlaytork."

Zeri said, "I can see some of my side of the family in him. Look at his fingers."

The grandfather and grandmother were attributing so many features of baby Leonard to one side or other of their family that they completely left the Svavapass component out of the picture.

Never one to offend, Ori did not say anything. It was an exhausted Unni that spoke up. "But he certainly has the Svavapass size. He is huge!"

While they were reveling over the birth of the baby boy, there was a commotion in the corridor. Ori stepped out to find out what was going on. Someone told him that a peace treaty had been finalized in the negotiations with the Vittmians. The ceasefire was to become a real peace. Normally, Ori would have been interested in the details of the treaty, but that evening, he was only interested in one thing: he had a son at last.

Two days later, Ori went for a bite to eat in the hospital dining hall. Unni and Leonard were to be released within hours. He heard the chair across from him scrape the floor. He looked up and saw an old familiar face, Sreedro Metchavork.

"Ori, I read that you and Unni had a baby, so I came out to congratulate the two of you," Metchavork greeted his old teammate.

"How kind of you to come, Sreedro" Ori replied. "How have you been?"

"Very well. I work as an administrator in a small-town school district. I am married now with two wonderful children, Friedrich and Ursula. And you know, my dear wife Mlemi makes the most excellent bratwurst."

"Do you miss the Service?"

Metchavork evaded Ori's question. "So, I hear you are Team Leader for Earth 48 now."

"That's right. I am team leader now."

"And I heard your new baby is a boy, and that you named him *Leonard* of all things," Metchavork said with a sly grin. "You never gave up on your little scheme to have a son and raise him to be prime minister. And you know, Ori, with your tenacity and dedication, you and Unni might have pulled it off. It is such an awful twist of fate that the whole plan should derail on the very day you finally had a son."

"Scheme? Derail? Sreedro, what are you talking about?"

"Haven't you heard? The Confederation diplomats reached a deal with the Vittmian Empire to formally end the war. The two parties will normalize relations, exchange ambassadors, and set up embassies. The two parties even worked out a trade agreement."

"That sounds good," Ori replied. "You make it sound like there is something wrong with that."

"I suppose you have been so absorbed with the new addition to your family that you haven't been paying attention to the news," Metchavork surmised. "Everything is wrong with that treaty. For one thing, the Vittmians will have commercial access to all of our planets and will have consulates on every one of them, but we can only go to Earth 89, their home planet."

"Keeping us out of their occupied planets," Ori finished the thought. "That sounds suspicious to me."

"And that's not all," Metchavork continued. "The two parties have declared a neutral zone into which none of the parties can go. It includes the sector in which Earths 45 to 49 are located."

Ori was shaken. "Doesn't the High Commission have to approve the treaty first?"

"Yes, and that is why I am heading to Omtvumx," Metchavork said. "Leaders from the whole planet are gathering to vote on what Earth 19's position will be. I plan to rally for the rejection of the treaty. If Earth 19 votes no, and if six other planets join us, the High Commissioner will not have a three-fourths majority and the treaty will not be ratified."

"Certainly, the treaty won't be ratified," Ori predicted. "It is obviously flawed. The leaders of the Confederation aren't stupid."

"One would hope," Metchavork agreed. "But some of the statements I read in the press give me pause. Some of the commissioners appear to be real Dummkopfs."

"Did you say Dummkopfs?" Ori asked.

"*Jawohl!*" the former Prussian Oberst replied with disdain. "Cowards! *Richtige Dummköpfe!*"

Ori decided not to break the news to Unni. He figured the High Commission would sort it out and make the right decision. In any case, he did not want to spoil the joyful moment for his family or give his wife anything to worry about while she was recovering, especially not something that was not likely to ever occur.

Two weeks later, the new family took a train ride to Olistoss to visit Ori's mother. Ori's mother mellowed at the sight of grandchildren. But the constant crying of the newborn baby seemed to be wearing on Ori's stepfather, so Ori and Unni cut short that leg of the trip, spending only one night. The family arrived back in England on December 20.

It was a joyful time in the Svavapass home. But would it last?

27.
Neutral Zone

Ori never told Unni about the neutral zone in the treaty. He intended to, but she found out on her own from the news on the trip home. It was only after they were back in London that Unni asked Ori what would happen to their mission.

"The High Commission will certainly reject that provision of the treaty," he assured her.

But they did not. On his next trip aloft to Station 48-3, Ori was informed that the treaty was ratified by a vote of 23-4. It was little consolation to him that Earth 19 cast one of the dissenting votes. The High Commissioner was already on her way to Earth 89 for a formal signing ceremony in the Vittmian capital.

Hours later, Ori received a call from Subdirector Vlaris.

"I cannot believe the High Commission ratified such a misguided treaty," Ori declared. "Can't anyone see that the Vittmians are using this to get us to lower our guard? You can be sure they will break this treaty within fifty years."

Vlaris did not disagree. "I am personally opposed to the treaty myself. I began to suspect something like this was coming down when I could not get funding for new space stations for Earths 47, 48, and 49. But the way the Director explained it to me was that the Confederation is stalling for time to rebuild our fleet with larger and better vessels."

"You don't doubt the other side is doing the same thing, Sral?"

"In my position, I have to watch my tongue, Ori. In any case, it is what it is, and we need to begin withdrawing our personnel. I am sending over detailed instructions how to accomplish this."

"Withdrawal? Sral, don't you remember the history of our own planet, Earth 19, back in the days when the nations and economic systems rivaled each other? The nations were always spying on each other, and that did not stop in times of peace. Just because there is a neutral zone doesn't mean we stop gathering intelligence."

"Maybe so, but I have my orders, Ori. The treaty explicitly says that neither side may have a presence in the neutral zone. You and your team have to leave Earth 48. I'm sorry."

"This is insane," Ori protested. "You don't seriously believe those bloodthirsty Vittmians will keep their end of the bargain, do you?"

"That's not my call," the Subdirector replied.

"And what happens to all of these agents?"

"They will be reassigned to one of the seventeen planets under surveillance that are not in the neutral zone," Vlaris explained. "I am working on that now. Of course, they will have to come back to training and learn different languages and cultures."

"But the field agents on my team are all of the white race, selected because they resemble Europeans," Ori pointed out. "You know that the natives on the leading continents of the other surveillance worlds are of a different appearance."

"I am afraid I do not have any spots in the field for them. I suppose I can find them desk jobs."

"Desk jobs for trained field agents?" Ori was beyond disappointment.

"Any day now, it will be announced that the Interplanetary Intelligence Service will be opening a third branch, the Bureau of Counterespionage. There will be Vittmian diplomats on all of our worlds, and some of them will be spies. Under the circumstances, Earth 19 will have a fine group with which to build their security team."

Ori did not respond. He did not know what to say.

Vlaris could tell Ori was very unhappy.

"Look, Ori. I could send you to Earth 17. The team leader there is getting ready to retire in two years. I could assign you there. By the time she leaves, you would be fully up to speed. And it's an easy job. Earth 17 is at Technology Level 11, Cultural Level 8."

Ori still did not reply.

"And they are getting a new space station, Ori. Think about it, a new space station with simulated outdoors where your children would have a place to play."

Finally, Ori broke his silence. "I suppose I need to gather the agents to Space Station 48-3 for a meeting."

"Yes, Ori. And sooner is better. I've been told we need to be out of there in five months."

Ori did not immediately call for the general meeting of his field agents that Vlaris ordered. Instead, he decided to go back to the surface and think about it. He also wanted to go to the one person in whom he could freely confide: his wife.

On the trip back to the surface, there was no one on the transport except Captain Squeem. "It's just you and me," the pilot said with his usual smile. "Why not come up here and sit in the copilot's seat?"

The first quarter of the trip was marked by a steady stream of chatter by Captain Squeem. Then Ori abruptly changed the subject.

"Captain, I recently rented a spacecraft. I flew in interstellar space from Earth 36 to Earth 19. It was my first solo flight, and my first flight of any kind since the Academy."

"Not bad, Special Agent Svavapass. Not bad at all."

"I got there safely, but I was wondering about a few things." Ori then began to ask Squeem one question after another about flying a small spacecraft. The lighthearted Squeem suddenly became very serious and began to explain to Ori some of the finer points of piloting. Ori learned a lot.

"As I was docking at the spaceport, I funny thought struck me," Ori said. "How would you land one of these things on the surface of a planet?"

"Once you enter an atmosphere, all of the rules change," Squeem replied. "Instead of flying perpendicular to the plane of the decks, now you want to fly parallel to the deck. These vehicles are built to minimize wind resistance and are very maneuverable in the lateral direction. That's why they shape them like shallow bowls, or saucers, as the natives say."

"So, you would be using the laterals, then," Ori surmised, pointing.

"Yeah, but let me show you. See this button here? It transfers the laterals to this stick. So, with your right hand you control your descent, and with the left one you maneuver. But don't pull that red lever at all. That one is only for emergencies; it strongly accents your lateral maneuvers if, say, a native jet fighter fired a missile at you."

Ori kept asking questions about flight within the atmosphere. Squeem suddenly offered to let Ori land the spacecraft.

"Are you sure?" Ori asked.

"Don't worry. My hand will be on the duplicate set of controls, and I will override your station if we are in any danger."

Ori took the pilot up on the offer. Once they were in the atmosphere, Ori began to move laterally, cutting the air with the edge of the "saucer."

"If we were landing on a Confederation planet, the coordinates of the landing pad would be showing up. But we are coming down on an alien planet, so I loaded the coordinates manually," the pilot instructed Ori. "We prefer to land on farms. They are flat, and usually the crops absorb the telltale markings of a landing, rather than the hard ground. That way, the circular indentations aren't permanent."

Ori recognized the geography below as the eastern part of North America. Shortly, they were over the Atlantic Ocean.

"You are coming in a little steeply," Squeem said. "If this were Earth 45 or 46, half the alien air force would be on your tail by now."

"I suppose I should have selected a shallower arc?"

"Right. But not too shallow or you would overshoot the target. You are aware that with a very shallow arc during reentry and the wrong orientation of the spacecraft, we would burn up. Of course, my hand is on the stick, and I would never let that happen."

Soon they were nearing Europe and Ori slowed the vehicle down and guided it to England, to the selected spot next to London. Ori hovered over the landing site and carefully set the spacecraft down.

"And that was your first time?" Squeem marveled. "That was great for a first time! And in the dark, no less."

"I had a good flight instructor," Ori returned the compliment.

Ori had decided to walk to the edge of town and hire a coach. He wanted to think. But it was not a pleasant walk. He had not anticipated the snow.

It was well past midnight when Ori finally reached the townhouse. He found Unni awake. "Leonard has been keeping me up at night. He has not been sleeping very well."

Ori had no heart to tell Unni what Vlaris had said. He waited two days. Then, in the privacy of their bedroom, Ori told Unni everything.

"Is there some way we could stay behind?" Unni asked.

"That would achieve nothing, except getting us thrown in prison. We have transponders in our bodies. Even if we got Dr. Stanton to remove our chips, they would notice and come after us."

"But we can't just let the Vittmians take this place," Unni insisted.

"I know. And I have been thinking of a plan," Ori said. "Perhaps we cannot stay, but we could come back after everyone is gone. After the Confederation has totally withdrawn from the Neutral Zone, they would have no way of tracking us."

"I like what I am hearing," Unni said. "But how do we get here? There won't be any starships going anywhere near here."

"Oh, that's the easy part," Ori assured her. "We can rent a spacecraft at any major spaceport, like I did when Leonard was born."

"They will notice we are missing. They will certainly guess where we went."

"Not if we are dead," Ori replied with a devious smile. Unni raised an eyebrow.

"What if we rented the ship near here, say, Earth 40 or 44? We told people we were going to Earth 19 to visit relatives. The we hooked around to Earth 48, landed in England, and sent the ship on autopilot to Earth 19. As the ship enters the system, we send prerecorded messages to your parents and to my mother, as if we will be there soon. We would tell them we are landing in Omtvumx instead of docking. It is faster, you know, even if it costs a little more. But the ship will be programmed to enter the atmosphere at the wrong angle and orientation."

"The ship would burn up and any pieces would be strewn over the ocean," Unni finished the thought.

"If there are any pieces. The accident would be attributed to my inexperience as a pilot. We would be officially pronounced dead."

"A bit unrighteous, though. The lies, the cost of the ship to the insurance company."

"So you don't like my idea?"

"I love the idea!" Unni hugged Ori. "It is not half as unrighteous as handing over billions of natives on five planets to slavery and extermination. I suppose our unclaimed estate would cover the cost of the lost space vehicle. The best decision I ever made in my life was to marry you."

Leonard woke up and needed to be fed. While he was feeding, Unni suddenly remembered that Ori said that was the easy part. She asked what the hard part was.

"That would be getting Earth 48 ready for the invasion," Ori replied. "We can't just announce it to the world or people will think we are insane. We would have to start feeding the natives advanced science and technology. It's not like we would be bound by any protocols anymore."

"To me, the key would be the diplomacy and the politics," Unni remarked. "Earth 48 would not be part of the Confederation at the time the Vittmians come. No doubt, the violation of the Neutral Zone would provoke a war. But could Earth 48 hold out alone before the High Commission got a fleet out here?"

"I am not sure," Ori admitted. "Even if they did, millions would die. But Earth 45 is already at Technology Level 12, and Earth 46 should at least reach Level 11 by then. Earth 48 could make an alliance. Better still, we could form our own little confederation while we wait for the big one to act."

"Wait a minute, Ori, wait a minute. Earth 45!" Unni's eyes became large and earnest.

"What about Earth 45?"

"Earth 45 has been on the brink of being contacted for years now."

"That's right. Some sort of technicality has been holding up the Exploration Commission from a decision on admission," Ori recalled. "Some kind of cultural issue."

"Right, but if the Vittmians were about to form a neutral zone, wouldn't that have gotten the Commission to make their move? But they have not. Certainly, there is some provision in the treaty that would still allow Earth 45 to join the Confederation. It might apply to Earth 48 if this planet suddenly reached the needed level of culture and technology. We need to take a look at that treaty."

"It is hundreds of pages long or I would have printed a copy for you," Ori said. "Too bad I had to return that holographic communication device when they reactivated the space station."

"The next time the transport lands, I am coming with you," Unni declared. "I want to read that document. There may be a clause in there somewhere that allows planets in the Neutral Zone to still join the Confederation if they reach certain criteria."

"What about Leonard and the girls?"

"Hire a nanny," Unni replied.

Less than a week later, Ori and Unni sat in his team leader office on Station 48-3 with the door closed. Unni was reading the treaty at her station and Ori was at his, planning the dismantling of the team he had so diligently assembled.

"Look at this, Unni," he said. "My third job offer. This time it is with the Bureau of Counterespionage as an office chief on Earth 20."

"I've gotten a few myself," she replied. "The best one was from the Diplomatic Commission in the Vittmian Embassy on Earth 89."

"Sounds exciting," Ori agreed sarcastically. "I don't suppose they would want me along in Security."

"Actually, they did. You'd be a "diplomatic attaché.""

"A fancy word for spy," Ori said. "So that's four job offers."

About an hour later, Unni found what she was looking for. "Ori, look at this!"

Article XVI, Section 223 stated that any planet in the neutral zone that requested to join the Confederation or the Vittmian Empire could make a formal request to do so. The party to whom the request was made was obligated to inform the other party in this treaty of the said request. After that, the annexation could be made after five months. The second paragraph stated how the border of the Neutral Zone would be altered by the annexation, and other technical details.

"This means we do not need to arm the natives on Earth 48 and risk them using the weapons on each other," Ori surmised. "All we need to do is get them up to a technical and cultural level that matches other admissions in the past and have them send a signal to another member of the Confederation."

"So our original plan is the one that we follow," Unni said. "We need to train Leonard because he is the one who will ultimately lead the British Empire to technical and cultural excellence."

The following week, Ori summoned all of the field agents to give them the news that they were all being withdrawn. There was great disappointment. Ori gave the agents the official line, dictated from Vlaris. They had no choice but to accept.

Ori did not want to stir the imagination of the natives. All disappearances were to be explainable.

Agents in Prussia were to say they were moving east to cities Prussia gained from the partition of Poland. France had just captured Algiers in 1830 and was determined to conquer the whole of Algeria. The agents in France and their families were to say that they were moving to Algiers. American agents were "moving west." The Erdiseks were to tell people they were bound for India to assist in the project to build railroads there.

These moves were to occur in the springtime, consistent with the concept of the natives. They wrote letters back "home" stating that they had arrived safely with dates in late May and early June that agent Mlai could post to their respective destinations from Posen, Algiers, St. Louis, and Bombay.

One by one, the families were transported to a starship bound for Earth 40, from which they were dispatched to their new assignments by the Interplanetary Intelligence Service.

Ori went to the starship and personally thanked each member of each family as they came aboard. Some of the wives and children were relieved. Some were frustrated. Some were without words or emotion. Some were sad, and there were tears. The reaction that most shocked Ori was that of Beempu Erdisek. Ori heard him say to his mother, "But I don't want to leave. I like England. Isn't there some way we could stay?"

His mother Mlee tried to comfort him. "When we get to Omtvumx, I will buy you any holographic game you like. How is that, Beempu?"

He replied in English. "My name is not Beempu. It's Will Anderson, and I don't play any bloomin' bloody holographic games!"

After the agents were gone, the space station had to be decommissioned. Ori saw to the removal of all property of the Interplanetary Intelligence Service. He left the rest of the work of shutting down the station to the military.

Ori and Unni waited until the beginning of May before informing Charlotte and Sherry of their departure from London. They could not tell the girls of their plan to return for fear they might divulge it. They took baby Leonard and the girls to Green Park, to the spot where they had gotten engaged thirteen years before.

"Our assignment on Earth 48 is over," Ori told his daughters solemnly.

Charlotte and Sherry were in tears. "We don't want to go back to Earth 2," Sherry sobbed.

"We don't fit in there," Charlotte added. "This is our home."

"We aren't moving to Earth 2," Unni said. "We are going to Earth 43."

All things being equal, Ori and Unni would have preferred to move to Earth 19, their home planet where their relatives lived. Ori had an opportunity there with the Bureau of Counterespionage. But if the Svavapass family lived on Earth 19, they could not have an apparent accident trying to visit that planet. It was Unni that got the job offer in an office that worked with defectors from occupied Vittmian planets. Ori applied for a transfer to Counterespionage on Earth 43 and was hired. It was not in a leadership role, but Ori did not care. He and Unni had their special goal.

After the girls were in bed, Ori and Unni had a private word with Shelby. They told him the whole family was going to Canada for a business pursuit. They asked him to keep charge of the house in their absence. A trustee at the bank would pay for him and the cook, plus expenses for maintaining the townhouse.

Of course, Vlaris would have no way of knowing that Ori had not terminated the Weatherby aliases. In a year, they would be secretly back in London.

Ori and Unni hoped the Reform Bill would be passed by then. Violence was increasing by May 1832, as segments of the populace began to become angry at the obstruction in the passage of a bill that would greatly increase the number of men eligible to vote, eliminate "rotten boroughs," and provide more seats for cities that had grown with the Industrial Revolution. Ori was unhappy with his benefactor, the Duke of Wellington for his skillful role in blocking a bill that the people so greatly desired.

The United Kingdom was as close as it had ever come to a revolution at that time. This violence would come to be known as the "Days of May." Shelby wondered if the Weatherbys were really going to Canada for their own safety. Shelby and Mrs. Morris knew that their employer was a political ally of Wellington's and were secretly worried that the townhouse might be targeted by the crowds.

In the midst of that time of unrest, the Svavapass family boarded a coach bound for the landing spot west of the city. It was the early morning of May 7, 1832. Soon they were aloft, leaving a troubled England far below them.

28.

Verification

The Svavapass family reached Earth 43 four days later. After a few more days, the family settled into their apartment in downtown Ropalb, the principal city on the planet. Unni enrolled Charlotte and Sherry in a private school where all classes were taught in Grellish, rather than in the local language of Earth 43. Unni's office at the Bureau of Protective Action was close to their home on the east side of town, but Ori had a longer commute downtown to his office with the Bureau of Counterespionage.

The Vittmian Treaty stipulated that the Neutral Zone was to be evacuated by 37543.8.6. According to the treaty, a Vittmian ship and a Confederation ship were to travel together to the five inhabited planets on a mission of mutual verification. Vlaris was one of the Confederation officials selected to make the trip. The Krajorts were the last ones out of the Neutral Zone on 37543.6.27, departing Earth 47 fourteen days after the Svavapass family left Earth 48.

Vlaris was on a small starship with a crew of only fifty. The ship met up with a Vittmian vessel of approximately the same size in the middle of the Neutral Zone. Together, the two ships visited each of the five worlds, scanning to verify the absence of signals from transponders to demonstrate that all agents were gone.

They also verified the removal of all space stations and satellites. Only one satellite was allowed per inhabited planet to monitor radio and television transmissions from the surface, and all data were to be shared. Of course, only Earths 45 and 46 were transmitting; it would be a long time before Earths 47, 48, or 49, invented radio or television.

It is much more difficult to prove that something is not there than to prove that something is, and the Vittmians were very slow and thorough at Earth 46 and 47. Since they were spending several days in each solar system, Vlaris decided to take a trip to the surface of Earth 48 and visit his old fields of service one last time. He had deliberately drafted Col. Hortu for this trip just in case he had a chance to visit Earth 48. He also brought native attire.

As they descended toward London, Vlaris told Hortu his story. "I spent forty years of my life with this planet, twenty on the surface as a field agent and twenty in orbit as team leader."

"I spent nine years here myself," Hortu said.

"I was in Paris most of the time acting as a diplomat for King Louis XVI. Most of my diplomatic work was with the Holy Roman Empire, whose capital was Vienna. There was a major revolution while I was in Paris, and the team leader had me flee to Vienna, or rather, stay there on my next official trip and not return. When the team leader position became vacant, I was appointed in part due to my seniority, and in part because I was fluent in French and German, two important languages down there.

"Paris and Vienna are both primitive Technology Level 8 cities, but they are very beautiful, more lovely than any city on my native Earth 19."

"Then why are you going to London?" Hortu wanted to know.

"I intend to eat a fine meal in Paris today and watch a concert in Vienna this evening. But I need a way to pay for these pleasures. This planet still uses hard currency, even metal coinage."

"And how will you obtain such money in London?" Hortu asked.

"My records show that Special Agent Svavapass never closed his bank account in London. Since I actually opened the account years ago, I should be able to access it. I will have some of the gold in the safety deposit box converted to French and Austrian currency."

Vlaris arrived at the bank just as it opened. He asked in his broken English if there was someone who could help him in French. When the teller saw the account number and realized how large the account was, they immediately sent forth a banker who was passable in French.

"*Le droit cette voi, monsieur Valerie,*" he directed his wealthy client.

There was a significant amount of gold in the deposit box. Gold was an asset that the Bureau could use elsewhere. He was a little disappointed that Ori had not withdrawn the gold to return it to the Interplanetary Intelligence Service.

Out of curiosity, he asked for a statement for the account. The attendant showed him a ledger. The account was quite healthy. Svavapass had left behind a large enough sum for an Englishman to be independently wealthy. Vlaris supposed that the money meant little to Svavapass, since he was leaving Earth 48 forever. Vlaris converted a small sum to the French and Austrian currency he needed.

While he waited for the bank attendant to give him his money, he began to read the ledger. Who was this Mr. Alistair Shelby? The withdrawals were rather regular. Vlaris surmised that Shelby was a household servant. But why was he still withdrawing money? There were two withdrawals since the Svavapass family had left.

He knew Ori had owned that townhouse for sixteen years. Perhaps Ori had left a pension for his loyal servants. But the amount seemed a bit high.

The attendant handed Vlaris his money. Now Vlaris had a choice. He could go to the townhouse to check things out or he could hurry back to the transport to get on with his plans to visit Paris and Vienna. As he left the bank, he decided not to go to visit the townhouse. His English was not good enough to converse with this Mr. Shelby. There was probably a good explanation for what Ori had done, and to find that out it would cost him his last chance for a fine French meal.

Hortu hated daytime flying on an alien planet. He took off in the direction of the sun to make it difficult for natives to distinguish the spaceship.

Vlaris spent the rest of the day in Paris, and met Hortu at sunset. "Careful, Colonel," Vlaris cautioned his pilot as they lifted off. "I believe I may have overeaten."

Hortu informed Vlaris that the starships had left earth orbit to look for hidden satellites in orbit of the gas giant planets in the outer solar system.

"I do not wish to spend the night weightless in orbit, not after what I've eaten. Let's go to Vienna. I will show you Vienna at night."

"It is against regulations to leave a space vehicle on an alien planet unattended," Hortu reminded his distinguished passenger. "Besides, I am black and this is a Cultural Level 6 world; Vienna is on a white continent."

"Fine. I will see you in the morning. I will spend the night in a nice native hotel."

Vlaris hired a coach from the outskirts of the city. He arrived at the concert hall barely in time to catch the beginning of a performance. Vlaris had brought some "shillings" to record whatever he could. He was in luck: that night the orchestra was performing Mozart's 41st Symphony. On his way to the hotel, Vlaris could not help but notice a poster for a performance the next day of *Die Zauberflöte*, an opera by Mozart.

The next morning, just before sunrise, Vlaris checked in on Hortu. The pilot told him that the starships would not be back for at least twelve hours. That would give Vlaris ample time to go back to London to check out this Mr. Shelby.

But Vlaris opted for Mozart. Vlaris knew he had other ways to check up on the devious Svavapass family.

Five months after their arrival on Earth 43, the Svavapass family took a vacation. Ori rented a spaceship and took off from the surface of Earth 43 bound for Earth 44, which was loosely in the direction of Earth 48.

Ori tried his best to give his family a comfortable ride, but inside the atmosphere, he was not as smooth as he wanted to be.

"Who taught you to drive, Daddy?" Charlotte asked. "Captain Squeem?"

"Yes, as a matter of fact," he replied. "He did teach me how to fly a spacecraft."

"It shows," Unni jested. The girls laughed.

They visited an amusement complex on Earth 44 for three days, beginning on the eleventh day of the first month, which was November 12 on Earth 48. The family had decided to celebrate the children's birthdays on November 12 because Sherry's birthday was a week before Leonard's and a week after Charlotte's—by the Earth 48 calendar. But with the Mraznian calendar it was awkward. Charlotte's birthday was 5.29, Sherry's was 4.15, and Leonard's was 1.33, and now they were celebrating all three on 1.11. And this was all because Earth 48 whizzed around its sun in only 365 days instead of 380 like Earth 1. Charlotte was now twelve, Sherry was eight, and Leonard was turning one, at least in England.

Ori and Unni took turns sitting with Leonard as the other partook of activities with the girls.

After three days, the family boarded the rented spaceship and flew to Earth 19. Ori chose to land at the spaceport in Urgst rather than dock at the commercial spaceport in orbit. They spent six days with the Vlaytorks. It was during this time that Leonard took his first steps.

The Svavapass family took another vacation beginning 3.25. This one was shorter, but the pattern was the same. Ori rented a spaceship and flew it himself. They went to Earth 42 for two days to a scenic park. Then they flew to Earth 19 and landed on the surface in Urgst.

By then, Leonard had learned to run. The older Vlaytorks had never baby-proofed their dwelling; it was fortunate that Leonard did not break anything.

When it was time to leave, Unni got choked up. Ori was very concerned that her emotional goodbye might leave an impression. Unni realized what she was doing and used her training to control her emotions. It was when they boarded the spaceship that Unni let her tears drop.

"Why is Mommy crying?" Sherry asked.

"Because Mommy never likes to see vacations end," Ori explained. "But don't worry, Sherry. We have another vacation planned in a little over two months."

As the spaceship left the atmosphere, Charlotte observed that they had visited an amusement complex on Earth 44 and a park on Earth 42. "What will we visit next time?"

"It will be a surprise," Unni said, trying to get her mind off Yoilafa and her family.

"My favorite surprise would be to go to England," Sherry remarked.

Vlaris sat at his desk, going over his budget and listening to the latest additions to his music collection. Suddenly, his holographic device chimed to indicate an interstellar call. He saw the caller was Captain Urelt Sraymlat of the Planet Patrol.

"Well, Sral, I followed Ori and his family the whole time they were away from Earth 43," Sraymlat told his former boss.

"What did you see?" Vlaris asked.

"The same as last time," Sraymlat said. "He headed in the direction of the Neutral Zone, this time to Earth 42, and took his family to a popular tourist destination. Then after two days he headed for Earth 19 and spent six days. Again, Ori chose to land on the surface rather than use an orbital commercial spaceport. He booked a suborbital flight to Yoilafa and spent six days there, presumably with Unni's parents. Then he took his family back to Earth 43."

"Any chance you were seen?"

"No chance at all, Sral," Sraymlat assured Vlaris. "The Planet Patrol has ways of stalking our prey without being detected; otherwise, how would we ever catch smugglers?"

"What did the crew of your patrol vessel think of your interstellar voyage?"

"I gave them the same line as last time, that we were tracking contraband," Sraymlat replied.

Vlaris paused for a moment. Then he told his friend, "Thank you for this huge favor. I owe you. I owe you double."

"What next, Sral?" Sraymlat asked.

"Nothing. They have made two trips, and both times they were found to be legitimate. There is no need for you to track Svavapass any further. You have verified some things for me. I am fully satisfied."

"Very well, but I may call in the favor someday," Sraymlat concluded the transmission.

Vlaris may have been fully satisfied, but Urelt Sraymlat certainly was not.

29.
The Surprise

The Svavapass family had encased the trunks Mr. Shelby had helped pack the year before in synthetic containers. Now the containers were loaded onto a rented space vehicle. The family was leaving on another vacation. Only Ori and Unni knew that this time, the trip was one way.

The family set out on 37544.5.30. Ori accelerated the vehicle into interstellar drive and followed a course outside of the plane of the ecliptic, but within the influence of Earth 43's sun. "Sherry, I have a surprise for you," Ori told his daughter. He changed course and dropped the vehicle into orbit of a gas giant planet in the solar system of Earth 43.

The planet had a spectacular system of rings. "Almost all gas giant planets have rings, but very few planets have a system of rings this beautiful," Unni explained to the girls.

"Mommy told us that Saturn has rings too," Sherry told her father.

"The sixth planet in the solar system of Earth 48 is another example of a planet with an elaborate system of rings. When I arrived in that solar system for the very first time back in 37525, the captain of the starship made a brief stop there to show us those rings. I will never forget that vista."

"I've seen them twice," Unni commented. "This planet is the closest I have ever seen that could compare."

"Could we see Saturn's rings, Daddy?" Charlotte asked.

"Saturn, like Earth 48 is in a solar system that is in the Neutral Zone," Ori told his daughter. "I'll tell you what, if everyone returns to their seats, I'll take us out of the plane of the ecliptic and give you a view from this planet's north pole."

The girls hurried to their seats. Unni moved up from a seat near the rear of the main cabin to the copilot's seat. She had been seated next to Leonard, whose seat had an adaptation device made for toddlers. With a lurch, Ori moved the spacecraft into a position that afforded a view of the rings from the top, with a portion darkened by the planet's shadow.

The girls expressed their amazement. "What a sight!" Unni exclaimed. "This is simply unforgettable."

Ori used this position to set course for the Neutral Zone. He accelerated to interstellar drive and placed the ship into automated control. On its present course, the artificial gravity was no longer caused by the ship's acceleration, and was only 0.36 g, a situation that was uncomfortable at first.

A few hours later, Unni put the girls to bed in a cabin on the lower deck. Unni had formulated a sleeping and waking schedule to get the family onto English time in three days.

"When shall we tell the girls where we are really going?" she asked.

"Not before we cross into the Neutral Zone," Ori replied.

"Are you sure we won't be spotted by the security buoys?" Unni asked.

"Those things are programmed to look for larger starships, warships. To spot something as small as our ship, someone would have to know in advance we were coming and be looking for us. Just to be on the safe side, I am steering a round course between the two buoys between us and Earth 48."

"Have you programmed the return trip to Earth 19 yet?"

"I'll have a lot of time on my hands tomorrow," Ori replied. "I plan to do it then."

The following day went as planned. Ori programmed the ship for the second phase of its journey.

At dinner time on the second day, the family gathered in the galley to eat. The children were giggling, and everyone was playing with their food, even Charlotte. Everything behaves differently at 0.36 g. The mess Leonard was making was going to be challenging to clean up.

"We've played with our food enough, now we need to eat it," Unni admonished her merry children.

"Are we going to Grandma and Grandpa's house?" Sherry asked.

"No," Ori answered. "Where we are going is a surprise."

"I thought the planet with rings was the surprise," Charlotte said.

"We have another surprise," Unni said.

"Is it that famous mountain peak on Earth 37?" Sherry asked.

"You'll see," Unni said. "We don't want to spoil it."

Ori woke up three hours before the rest of the family so that he could manually navigate around the buoys. Every time he changed course, the decks of the small ship pitched. Sometimes he could hear chatter from the girls below.

Ori's final maneuver took place after Unni and the children were up. They were trying to dress into their day clothes when they were pulled sideways. Sherry climbed up to the upper deck and ran to her father, half in her night clothes and half in her day clothes.

"Daddy, what is happening?" she asked. "The ship never rocked like this in interstellar space in our other trips."

"That was a midcourse correction," he explained. "My last one, I might add, so go downstairs, dress, wash up and I will be joining you for breakfast."

Sherry was a little puzzled, but she did as she was told.

Later, as the family was seated at the breakfast table, Ori and Unni's eyes met. They nodded.

"Now is the surprise," Unni announced. "Do you know what day it is today?"

Charlotte answered, "Today is 37544.5.32."

"For some people, yes, today is 37544.5.32," Unni agreed. Then she switched into English. "But for us, it is May 3, 1833."

"And, henceforth, we will only speak English in our home," Ori added. "And we will only use our English names. We are the Weatherby family."

"That's the surprise!" Sherry exclaimed. "We are going back to Earth 48!"

"And the name of that planet is not Earth 48," Unni corrected her daughter. "It is simply Earth."

The girls began to cheer. Leonard also cheered although he did not understand why.

"And when we land on Earth," her father continued, "we will live as any English family and forget about spaceflight, electricity, other earths, ten-day weeks, thirty-eight-day months, and everything else that our fellow Englishmen do not know about."

"Now let us all change out of these ghastly clothes and into our English clothes," Unni commanded with a measure of joy. I placed a set on your beds when you came into the galley. We will be landing in London in about ten hours."

The girls finished their breakfast and skipped off to their shared bedroom with glee. A moment later, they emerged dressed as typical English girls. They climbed up to the upper deck and approached their father, also in English attire, seated at the controls.

"Daddy, could you show us Saturn?" Charlotte asked.

"It will set us back a little," Ori replied. "Let's wait until Mommy comes up."

Unni brought Leonard up to the upper deck and strapped him into his child seat.

"Unni, the girls want to see Saturn," Ori told his wife.

"That's Jenny, remember Robert?" she corrected her husband.

"Right, Jenny."

"It will set us back, but we have time, and this is probably the last space-flight the children will ever take," Unni said.

"Saturn it is," Ori announced. "Everyone to your seats and strap in."

Unni took a seat in the back next to Leonard. Sherry sat in the copilot's chair.

The ship lurched as Ori adjusted its course. Soon, the small half-illuminated disk of Saturn became visible through the forward window with part of its rings darkened by the planet's shadow.

"Is that Saturn's north pole?" Sherry asked.

"No, that is the south pole," her father answered.

As the ship got closer, the planet grew larger in view.

"I say!" Sherry exclaimed. "This planet *is* more beautiful than the other one we saw."

"I would have to agree," Unni said from the back.

"Can I see? Can I see?" Charlotte called out. "It's my turn to sit in the front."

"You can see plenty well from the back," Sherry said.

"Let your sister have a turn," Unni exhorted her younger daughter.

The two girls traded seats, bouncing as they walked in the diminished gravity.

Ori brought the ship into the plane of the ecliptic into a moderately inclined orbit. For the next hour, the family watched in awe. They saw the rings edge-on. They also got a view of the upper cloud deck of the gas giant itself.

Ori then reoriented the spacecraft so that the lower deck pointed at the planet. Now it could only be viewed by the monitors. He began the acceleration on an arc-shaped course toward Earth 48. Gravity began to increase to nearly one-half of a g.

As the small vessel pulled away from Saturn, the girls chattered excitedly. The family had enjoyed a special moment together.

But their joy was about to end. The next surprise was not at all pleasant.

30.
Confrontation

Suddenly, a familiar voice came over the ship's radio.

"Orishackt Svavapass, this is the Planet Patrol. Cut your engines and prepare to be boarded."

Unni hastily took the seat next to her husband, which Charlotte relinquished without needing to be asked. A number of questions swiftly ran through Ori's and Unni's minds. How could the Planet Patrol be all the way out here? How were they found? Why was that voice so familiar?

Ori could see that he was traveling toward the patrol vessel. He rapidly reversed course back toward Saturn. Charlotte was not strapped in and hit a wall and the ceiling before landing on the floor. She quickly strapped in after that, sore, but too afraid to complain.

Ori was thinking quickly of a reply.

"This is Captain Urelt Sraymlat of the Planet Patrol," the voice repeated. "You are both under arrest. Surrender at once!"

"I should have known," Unni said with disgust.

Ori pressed the button that allowed him to transmit. "On what charge?"

"A whole litany of changes, Ori. How about entering the Neutral Zone for starters?"

"You don't have permission to be here either, Urelt." Ori replied. "So we are even."

"We are not even, Ori," Sraymlat said. "But I am about to get even. I have dreamed of this moment for thirteen years, thirteen long years."

273

Unni pressed the transmission button. "What is it you want, Urelt?"

"I want to see you both in prison! And your children in orphanages."

Unni was visibly angry.

Ori was moving at a high rate of speed, but the patrol vessel was gaining on them.

"What do we do?" Unni asked.

"Their vessel is faster and more maneuverable than ours. They will eventually catch us, haul us into a forced docking and boarding."

"Can't we go to interstellar drive? We'd be equals at interstellar drive."

Ori grimaced. "That's right, but we would run out of fuel before they do. It would just put off the inevitable. I am afraid we will have to surrender."

"No, Robert, please don't!"

Ori pressed the button to transmit. "You will never get away with this, Urelt. You have no jurisdiction here, and the courts will see this sham for what it is, a personal vendetta."

"You are overlooking one important point, Ori. In the improbable scenario that the courts acquitted you on that technicality, your mission to Earth 48 would be forever over," Sraymlat argued.

"Is that what you want, Urelt? To give this place over to Vittmian atrocities?" Unni countered. "Didn't you once collaborate with us for this mission?"

"Enough chatter!" Sraymlat burst forth. "My vessel is armed. Yours is not. Surrender now or I will fire!"

"Why would he need to fire at us?" Unni asked her husband. "He has us, doesn't he?"

Leonard began to cry, and it was impossible to hear what Sraymlat said next. Ori and Unni donned headsets.

"…and so, Ori, the choice is yours: prison or death!" they heard Sraymlat finish.

Unni shook her head. She gestured to Ori not to surrender to Sraymlat.

"I have missiles, Unni," Sraymlat continued. "I'll use them if I have to. Think of your children."

Ori pointed to the monitor. Unni could now see that the patrol vessel was slowing. That could only mean that Sraymlat was going to fire and that he wanted some distance.

Leonard quieted and the two removed their headsets.

Ori changed course southward, as if to go under Saturn's south pole.

"Gravitational slingshot?" Unni asked.

"Right." Ori confirmed.

"I mean it, Ori," Sraymlat continued his harangue. "I'll shoot."

Just then, Sraymlat fired a missile. Ori and Unni both saw it on their monitor.

"Robert!" Unni cried.

"It's just a proverbial shot across the bow, Jenny."

"No, it isn't!" she exclaimed. "It's closing."

Ori realized that his wife was right. Suddenly, he remembered what Squeem had told him about the red lever for accenting maneuvers. He wondered if it also worked outside the atmosphere. Ori grabbed the lever with his left hand and the stick with his right.

"Closing!" Unni cried out.

"Hold on!" Ori shouted as he pulled the lever and swerved hard to starboard. The missile missed. Unni cheered like a schoolgirl. For an instant, there was hope on the faces of Charlotte and Sherry.

But Sraymlat fired again. Another missile sped toward the little spacecraft.

Again, Ori executed an evasive maneuver, this time to the left and northward at the same time, subjecting his children to a great acceleration stress.

The missile missed, but it exploded when it was nearest to the spacecraft. Ori and Unni saw a great flash of light on their monitor. A moment later, the spacecraft was pelted with some sort of particulate mass.

The engines failed. The lights went out and the red emergency lights came on. The ship was on a northward trajectory under the planet and heading into its south polar region.

Ori knew he had to act quickly or the ship would enter the planet's atmosphere and burn up.

He noticed the ionic propulsion system was still on line, and he fired the six thrusters hard, using them as retros to break the fall. Two of them had been damaged, and the ship began to roll. The children were screaming.

Somehow, Ori managed to slow the roll by getting the computer to pulse the functioning thrusters of the ionic propulsion system. The ship had lost much of its velocity, but Ori managed to insert the ship into a low equatorial orbit, not far from the inner ring.

The sound of the engines was gone. The ventilation blowers had stopped. They were weightless. A deathly quiet fell over the family.

"What happened?" Unni asked.

"I managed to prevent us from crashing into the planet, but the engines are offline, and our ionic propulsion system is spent and not recharging. We are in orbit, and unable to move much."

"So, it's over," Unni said softly.

"Yes, it is. The ship is crippled. I think we need to give up," Ori conceded. "For the children."

Unni did not say anything.

In resignation, Ori flipped a switch and activated the distress signal.

The silence was broken by Sraymlat's gloating voice over the radio. Unni was not sure if it was a good thing that the radio was still functional. "So, you give up, Ori?"

"Our vessel is crippled, and our life support system is faltering," Ori replied. "We request assistance."

"Assistance?" Sraymlat mocked. "I'm not taking my ship into there. You are inside the rings. Who knows how many moonlets and chunks of ice are in there? I'm not going to chance it for you."

"Honestly, Urelt! You are the Planet Patrol," Ori pleaded. "Certainly, your helmsman is skilled enough to handle situations like this."

"Well, you see, Ori, I handpicked my crew," Sraymlat said in a light-hearted, cynical tone. "But I chose them for loyalty, not skill. So, I'm afraid you and your little wife are on your own."

Unni clenched her teeth in anger. "He's still the same coward he was at the Ortees trial."

Ori took the cue from his wife. He pressed the transmission button and broke into English. "It seems you are still the same coward you were at Waterloo. Only this time, there is no infantry square to keep you from running, and no bleeding captain to hide you from Wellington's glare. It is you who are on your own, Lt. Greenhill."

"No, that's not true!" Sraymlat shouted back.

"Maybe you're right, Bill," Ori agreed. "At least about not being alone. When you get back to port, you will still have your old friend, the bottle."

"I ought to fire another missile and finish you off, Svavapass, but I prefer you die a slower death," Sraymlat shot back. "You need to suffer as I did when you robbed me of a marriage and a career!"

"The patrol vessel is leaving," Unni said, pointing at the monitor.

Ori pressed the button to transmit, but Unni put her hand on his. "Never mind, Robert. The patrol vessel is jamming our signal. We are stranded."

"Well, look at the bright side, at least will not have to fake our deaths," Ori quipped.

"Are we going to die, Daddy?" Charlotte asked.

"Not if I can help it," her father replied with a resolute voice. "Jenny, I am going below to look at the life support system."

Ori floated out of his chair to go to the lower deck.

"Mommy, I think I am going to throw up," Sherry said.

Ori removed the panel and surveyed the life support system. To his relief, everything looked to be in order. So then, why wouldn't it work? He spotted the problem. The system was still hooked up to the main power core. The relay to the emergency power needed to be thrown manually. He wondered how long emergency power would last with the life support system taxing it. But he had no choice but to throw the switch. They had to breathe.

Ori did not have time to go up to give Unni a progress report. He thought the sound of the ventilators would be enough of a signal.

Ori proceeded to the power core. Here was the main problem. If he could get this working again the ship would be able to run. Ori went for a tool kit and proceeded to work. The power core had six cells. One was a total loss. When it failed, it brought the others down with it. Three of the six appeared to be reparable. A fourth one would take more work. When he got the first one going, the lighting came back on, and the auxiliary power cells began to charge.

Ori surveyed the rest of the damage. Two of the six pillars of the landing gear were jammed. The food synthesizer was only partially operational. The water purifier was damaged. Only some of the ionic thrusters were operational, and they were going to need to recharge. But thankfully, the main engines were intact.

Just then, Unni swam down.

"How is it coming along, Robert?" she asked.

"The bad news is that the rental company will certainly remove us from their preferred customer list."

Ori's quip removed some of the worry from Unni's face.

"I could fix a lot of this," Ori said. "The question is whether we have time. The food synthesizer is not working. We only have enough food for one or two days. The water purifier is down, and the purified water in the tank would only last us three days. This means that we need to get moving. I have to be strategic in what I fix and what I don't fix."

"Can you get the engines going that quickly?"

"Yes, because the engines are fine. It is the power core that is damaged. Only one cell is working, and we need about four of them to run the engines at a great enough speed to reach Earth before our water is gone."

"And you know how to repair a power core?" Unni wondered.

"I had to work all sorts of jobs as a teen in order to afford school," Ori reminded his wife. "I worked a year assisting a repairman."

"Couldn't you perform some of the repairs while we are moving?"

"Yes, but not the power core," Ori replied. "My father died doing something like that."

"There is another reason we need to move soon. I think our orbit is unstable," Unni informed her husband.

"Will it last even six hours?"

"I think so. I'll keep my eye on it while I watch the children." She floated back upstairs.

The girls were unaware of the problems their parents were facing. They felt like the crisis was over and had blind confidence in their father to work the problem out. They got out of their seats and went to the forward window to take in the spectacular view of Saturn's rings edge-on. Then they began to play in the weightless conditions. Ori could hear their giggling upstairs as he toiled downstairs.

Unni floated back downstairs three hours later.

Ori looked up from his work on a power cell. "Is this about the orbit, Jenny?"

"No, that is holding steady, sort of. It's about the children. They say they are hungry."

Ori grimaced at his "upside down" wife. "I found out that the food synthesizer is offline because the water intake is dry. All we have for water is what is in the primary tank."

Unni swam over to the galley and took an inventory of the food. There were leftovers and a few packaged items they had taken along. She planned the rationing of the food.

"I nearly have three power cells ready," Ori told his wife. "It all comes down to this: do I stop with three cells, or do I stay and try to get the fourth one. With four, we are certain to make it to Earth orbit. But if I try and fail to fix the fourth one, I will have squandered a day that we still had food."

"Why do we need so much power?" Unni asked.

"Because we have to make most of the trip at interstellar drive."

"Inside a solar system?" Unni asked. "Earth is about ten astronomical units away. We could be there in less than three days at only two percent the speed of light."

"Using conventional power, it would take us months to get there even at three gravities of acceleration," Ori explained. "We have no choice but to use interstellar drive to avoid the effects of the accelerations.

"Of course, we would only be traveling at a fraction of full interstellar speed, just as we were when I took the us to see the gas giant by Earth 43. The course I have plotted will take us out of the plane of the ecliptic in an arc and drop us back in the plane two days later about six earth radii from the surface. After that, we brake all the way using conventional engines."

"But, Robert, it only took us a few hours to reach the gas giant by Earth 43," Unni reminded Ori. "Why do we need two days?"

"We were on six power cells back then."

Two hours later, Ori floated to the upper deck. "Everyone strap in," he commanded. "We will be moving soon."

"Mommy, I'm hungry," Sherry complained.

"We will eat once we are moving," Unni replied. "Better not to eat before we have gravity."

Ori started the engines. The lights flickered. Ori held his breath. He maneuvered the ship southward out of the plane of Saturn's equator. Once the ship was sufficiently distant from the planet, Ori went into interstellar drive. They were on their way.

The family then went down to the galley on the lower deck to eat a late dinner, their first meal since breakfast. The gravity was weak, just about one quarter of normal. Ori leveled with the girls about the food and water shortage. "We barely have enough to last for the two days. I hope to reach England late in the evening, the day after tomorrow or early the next morning."

"That would be May 5 or 6, right, Daddy?" Charlotte said.

"That's right. And in the interim, it would be good to spend time napping or sleeping, not to burn energy."

After the children were in bed, Ori and Unni went to the upper deck.

Ori was very somber. Unni put her arm around him. "You were a real hero today, Robert, the way you handled Sraymlat and the miracle you performed on the engines."

"We are still going to need one or two more miracles if we are going to make it," Ori admitted. Landing is going to be very difficult. Once we enter the atmosphere, I will be trying to navigate with one third of the ionic thrusters damaged. I am still a novice at flying in the atmosphere as it is. Next, there is the landing gear. Two out of six landing pillars are jammed, so our landing will probably be very rough. After that there is the question of how to hide the ship after we arrive."

"I suppose we tackle these problems one at a time," Unni replied. "You've pulled off enough engineering brilliance for one day. Tomorrow is another day."

The couple went to bed. They were exhausted.

31.
Crash Landing

Less than three hours later, the Svavapass family was awakened by an alarm. Ori jumped out of bed, and nearly stumbled, forgetting that the gravity was lower than normal. He ran up the ladder to the pilot's seat. The panel indicated that the alarm was about the engines. They were not getting enough energy from the power core.

Ori immediately shut down the engines. The artificial gravity created by the interstellar drive ceased. Unni quickly floated to the upper deck. "Robert, what is happening?"

"The engines were overtaxing the power core. I had to shut them down to protect the power core from damage."

Ori looked at some figures on his holographic terminal and did some quick mental math. In the meantime, Sherry and Charlotte appeared on the top deck.

"The three cells are not up to the task of maintaining the engines at this speed for the forty more hours we need. We will need to power down and hope that the cells hold."

"Power down?" Unni asked.

"Go get Leonard and bring him up here," Ori said without explanation.

Ori realized that he would need to chart a different course at a lower speed. He also knew that they could no longer afford to run the life support system on both decks. Unni strapped the children into seats on the upper deck. She then moved the remaining food in sealed containers. She detached the primary water tank and brought it to the upper deck. Then she sealed the hatch between decks.

By then Ori had a new course. He dialed the life support system to half the normal rate and diverted all of the air to the upper deck. Then he switched to emergency lighting. Only then did he restart the engines.

Unni strapped herself into the copilot's seat. "Robert, how much slower are we going?"

"This adds a day and a half to our travel time," he said grimly.

The next two days were miserable. They had little to eat, could not wash, and had only dim red lighting. They could not sleep well either. Ori and Unni had to take turns staying awake to watch the energy levels. Ori was afraid the cells were not fully stable.

Leonard was very upset because he did not understand what was going on. His mother was either taking her turn at the controls or trying to rest. Fortunately, Charlotte and Sherry rose to take care of their little brother.

With the bottom deck inaccessible, any repairs of the two damaged thrusters of the ionic propulsion system or the landing gear were out of the question, but repairing those devices was out of Ori's skillset in any case.

On the morning (English time) of May 7, 1833, the small vessel dropped out of interstellar drive at a location and trajectory very close to the one Ori had hoped for. He saw a welcome site, the half-illuminated Southern Hemisphere of the planet he now called "Earth." Ori began the deceleration using conventional drive at nearly 9.8 meters per second-squared. The ship now had relatively normal gravity.

Ori switched on the normal lighting; conventional drive used less power than interstellar drive. He also reactivated the life support system on the lower deck. The family went down the ladder to the galley to eat what was left of the food.

Ori was painfully aware of the fact that this could be their last meal in more ways than one. He leveled with the family as to the risks, including the two ion propulsion units that were not operational and the landing gear.

After they had eaten, Ori told his wife and children how fortunate he felt to have had such a family. There were some tears and hugs.

Sherry expressed her confidence in her father. "If anyone can land this broken spaceship, it is Daddy."

Ori wanted everyone seated in the rear of the upper deck, the spot on the ship that would be the safest in a rough landing. Unni resealed the lower deck in case of a hull breach during reentry. Then she sat down next to her husband at the controls. He urged her to move to a seat in the rear, but she insisted on sitting with him.

Ori pointed out that the trajectory was what he had planned. "It will be near sunset in England when we land, and we are coming in from the west, so it will be hard for the natives to see the ship clearly."

Reentry went without a mishap. The ship entered the atmosphere over the South Pacific.

It was only when Ori took the stick in his hand and began to navigate laterally that he realized there was something very wrong.

"Jenny, the thrusters aren't responding. Without them, I won't be able to steer."

"They must have been working before we entered the atmosphere. How did we navigate so well to our reentry point?" Jenny pointed out.

"The computer did all of the calculations," Ori replied. "Maybe if I entered the coordinates of that farm west of London, the computer could control the thrusters."

Ori entered the location. Nothing happened. He tried again with no result. Ori wiggled the stick. There was no result.

"The ionic thrusters are totally off-line," Ori informed his wife. "We are just like a cannon ball, moving on our momentum."

Unni produced a holographic globe from the computer. It had the natural geography of the planet but none of the cities or political boundary lines, which were classified information of the Interplanetary Intelligence Service. Unni plotted the ship's trajectory on the globe. A dashed line appeared pointing northeast, crossing the equator and ending fifteen hundred miles short of Mexico.

"We are going down in the ocean," she said. "Does this ship float?"

"I don't know," Ori replied. "It doesn't matter. We are out of food and water, and it could take weeks to wash ashore."

Ori pulsed the main engine to see if he gained altitude. He did, and the line lengthened.

"Robert! Look! When you added altitude, you lengthened our path."

Ori did it again, and the line reached land. Ori realized that the he still had control of one parameter: where along his trajectory he would land. Of course, wind resistance was against him; he could not do it indefinitely.

"You don't speak Spanish, do you?" Ori asked.

"A little, but not much" Unni admitted.

The computer now had enough data to fill in Mexican geography. Ori saw how mountainous the terrain was and feared landing there was too risky. He began to thrust again and the trajectory extended into the Gulf of Mexico.

"Robert! What are you doing! We will overshoot the land"

"Jenny, there were too many mountains. I couldn't risk it."

He fired a few more thrusts and the line extended back onto land.

"Well, Jenny, how does New Orleans sound to you?" Ori asked.

"I'll take it!" she exclaimed.

"Good, because we will be there in a few minutes."

Unni performed a quick calculation and a red dashed line appeared that crossed the southeastern portion of Upper Canada. "Is there any chance we could make it to Canada?" she asked, pointing.

"That would help us explain how we got there," Ori said. "I was telling people we were going to Canada last year when we left."

"And it is part of the British Empire," Unni agreed.

"And some of the officers in the garrison there are from my old regiment," Ori added. "Shall we try for it?" Ori asked.

"Why not?" Unni affirmed.

Ori fired the engines a few more times. The line lengthened more than five hundred miles.

Ori groaned.

"What's the matter? Unni asked.

"Wind resistance. There is a finite limit to the number of miles I can add to our trajectory. Do the girls still remember those American rebellion songs?"

"Oh, Robert!"

"I think that large river down there is called the Ohio River."

The black part of the dashed line fell short of the river. Ori fired the engines, and the line crossed the river, but not by very much. Ori was getting fewer and fewer miles of extension with each firing.

"We've lost too much momentum to atmospheric resistance," Ori said. Quickly! Move to a seat in the rear!"

"But…" Unni protested.

"Now!"

Unni quickly moved to the seat between Sherry and Leonard in the back. As she ran, the ship's floor lurched in response to Ori's last desperate bursts of the engine, trying to get out of the forested area onto flat ground.

No sooner had Unni clicked her seatbelt than Ori shouted, "We're going down! Tree tops!"

The wounded spaceship scraped the tops of the trees and rode through the top of the forest, cutting a swath of broken branches and tree trunks and finally scraping the bottom of its bruised hull on the ground, coming to rest before three trees into which it had crashed.

The lights went out. Sparks were flying. Only part of the pilot's console was still operating.

On impact, the front of the vehicle had buckled, and some of the pieces of siding had come forward, crushing the seat where Unni had been sitting only minutes before and striking Ori's right leg. He was not sure if it was broken, but he could see it was bleeding.

The girls were frightened but quiet. Leonard was crying.

Ori knew they had to leave the ship at once. One of the sensors on the operational part of the panel indicated that the power core was destabilizing.

He saw something even more disturbing on the monitor. Just two hundred feet away was a woman holding a basket, and three children were with her. They had turned and were heading for the crash site.

The cabin began to fill with a foul odor. The life support system was beginning to bring in a fine smoke. Ori turned off the life support system and opened the air lock and the outer hatch of the upper deck. He tried to stand, but the pain in his leg worsened. He had to sit back down.

Ori powered down the engine, but the reading on the power core sensor began to rise to critical. He reactivated the engines on idle, and the reading dropped somewhat. He realized that the power core was going to explode, and he was trying to vent the excess energy.

Unni came up behind him. The girls were unstrapping their seatbelts and coming forward to their injured father.

"The ship went down before we reached Lake Erie. We are in American territory. I saw a map when I worked down in Ordnance. This territory is part of an American state called Ohio."

"Ohio," Unni repeated.

"What you need to do is take the children and leave here. Get as far away from the ship as possible. There is a clearing to the southwest. I saw a log cabin a half mile from here. We can meet there."

"You are staying?" Unni asked.

"The power core is about to blow. I am playing with the flow, trying to vent off energy. Once I see that you are at a safe distance, I will fire the engines to release some of it and make my escape. I hope to be far enough away when it blows."

"But what about…"

"And another thing. There is a native woman with three children approaching from that direction." Ori motioned to his left. "You have to warn them to get away from here."

Charlotte turned toward the hatch to the lower deck.

"No, Charlotte!" her father cried out. "Stop!"

"You said we needed to leave."

"But not the usual way. The lower deck is not safe. You have to go out this hatch." Ori pointed to his right, to the open airlock.

Unni went into the airlock and looked down. "It is a ten-foot drop," she observed.

"Right," Ori said. "There is a rope in the cabinet next to the door. You will have to climb down. Have you girls ever climbed rope before?"

"Yes, we did, in Adaptation Hall. Miss West taught us," Sherry replied.

Unni found a backpack with the rope. She placed Leonard into it. Charlotte helped her put it on. He was a heavy boy for eighteen months.

"Sherry, watch this gauge," Ori commanded his daughter. "If it goes over 145, let me know immediately."

Ori hopped on one leg to the airlock and tied the rope securely to two pipes. He kissed Charlotte affectionately. "You be a big girl and a helper to Mommy."

"Yes, Daddy." Charlotte hurriedly turned to hide her tears and went down the rope.

"Daddy, it's already back up to 142!" Sherry exclaimed.

Ori shuffled back to his seat, collapsed into it, and pressed some buttons. The monitor backed off to 133. Sherry bent down to kiss her father. Then she turned toward the door noticing the trails of blood from her father's leg to and from the airlock. She slid down the rope where her sister was waiting.

Unni then went over to Ori. His fine English clothes were torn. There was a cut on his face. Blood was coming through his pantleg. His hands were still filthy from his repairs four days before.

She stooped to his chair. They kissed and hugged. It brought Unni back to the day fourteen years before at Green Park when they kissed for the first time.

"I love you, Unni. I know you will take good care of the children. Now hurry, Jenny! And if you hear a rumble, fall face down!"

"You're not going to make it, are you?" she realized.

"It's like I said in South Zarfixu," Ori replied. "Your life is more precious to me than my own because without you I would not have any real life to live."

Unni fully understood what Ori meant. She kissed him one last time and went down the rope with the heavy burden of Leonard on her back, and a heavier burden in her heart.

Unni followed Charlotte closely as she and her daughters made their way through the thick forest to the clearing. Unni could barely see through the tears in her eyes.

She thought she saw a boy through the brush about twenty feet away to her right running toward the ship.

"What in creation is that?" the boy called out. "Mary, look at this!"

Very shortly, they sighted the woman with the basket and her two daughters, also going the opposite way.

Unni shouted, "Turn back! Run away!"

Charlotte and Sherry joined their mother in warning the woman.

The woman waved in acknowledgement. Then she shouted, "Jimmy! Get back here! Now!"

Convinced that the woman understood the danger, Unni and her two daughters continued their hurried walk away from the ship.

"Mehetabel! Mary!" the woman called. "Catch your foolish brother! We need to get away!"

The woman and her daughters continued to shout Jimmy's name. Then the shouting stopped. Unni assumed they must have found him.

Ori set the monitor on his family. When he was convinced that they were out of range, he fired the engines in the hope of lowering the levels in the power core. The last reading that he saw was 106 on the monitor. Now was his best chance. He made his way for the door and the rope. He painfully began to flee from the ship, badly hobbled.

Then his heart sank. A boy about seven years of age ran up to him. The front of his clothes and his face were stained orange from Ori's last engine burst. "You are in danger, young man! Get away from here!" Ori shouted.

The boy followed Ori away from the ship for a few steps. Ori said, "No! Don't wait for me. Flee!"

The woods were less dense now, and Unni could see the sunlight from between the trees. Unni heard a rumble. She hurried to remove the backpack. Unni fell forward with Leonard under her. Get down!" she shouted. The girls immediately complied.

The ship was incinerated. In a brief instant, the fireball consumed Ori, and in succession, Jimmy, Mary, Mehetabel, and their mother.

Unni felt the sting of intense heat over her legs, back, and neck. After the fireball passed, she looked back and saw a mushroom-shaped cloud. "Quickly!" she shouted. The girls got up and ran into the clearing.

Unni spotted the log cabin Ori had told her about. It was about thirty by twenty feet in size. Beyond the cabin was an agricultural field. In the distance, she could see a pioneer farmer and a boy of about ten years of age toiling there.

The farmer was a large man, six feet tall, and stocky. He heard the rumble. He looked toward the woods. He saw a blindingly bright light. For a moment, he could hardly see.

"Fire in the forest!" he cried.

Forest fires were common in the warmer weather, and they could destroy large tracts of woods, as well as pioneers' cabins and crops.

"Tom, where is your mother?" the farmer asked.

"Mom went into the woods to pick berries with Mehetabel, Mary and Jimmy," the boy told his father. "I think I see them over there."

The farmer and his son's eyes were still adjusting from the bright burst and could only see shapes.

Charlotte ran ahead toward the log cabin and encountered them. As she approached them, Tom declared, "Fire in the forest! Some kind of lightning bolt!"

"Yes, we…" Charlotte was interrupted by the pioneer.

"Thank goodness you are all safe!"

Unni and Sherry with Leonard were making their way to the field. The pioneer took a minute to convince himself of the danger.

"It is certainly coming this way," he said with anxiety. "I'm afraid it will make trouble for us. Mehetabel, run to the house with my axe and bring me the shovel."

Charlotte was emotionally spent from the ordeal her own family had just been through, but she was too shaken by the events of the past few hours to point out the mistaken identity. She simply took the axe and ran to the house.

"Where would an American pioneer keep a shovel?" she thought. But the log cabin only had one room, and she quickly found the shovel and put it into the hands of the farmer.

Unni reached the pioneer just as Charlotte returned with the shovel.

The farmer, still blinded by the flash, said to Unni, "We must fight it, Eliza, or only ashes will be left of our home at sundown."

Unni, dazed by the crash and still coming to grips with her sudden widowhood, did not know what to say. She knew this man did not have time for any kind of explanation. She quickly mustered a response.

"I fear as much. These forest fires are terrible."

"Mehetabel, you and Thomas follow me," the farmer commanded. He and his son ran across the house lot to the edge of the woods to prevent the fire from attacking his home. Charlotte looked at her mother. Unni signaled with her eyes in affirmation. Charlotte ran after the two.

As Charlotte ran toward the two natives, Unni saw her back. The back of Charlotte's dress was ruined, and her hair was badly singed. Unni placed Leonard in the smallest bed in the cabin and stepped outside to watch the pioneer fight the fire.

Unni saw Sherry's back. The back of her dress was also ruined and much of her hair on the back of her head was gone. Unni touched the back of her own head and her own back. She also had been singed by the fireball.

Unni stood outside the log cabin trying to fathom her situation. She should be arriving by coach to her townhouse in London with Ori just now. Instead, she was stranded in the wilderness on an alien planet, in a foreign country without a husband, without a home, without any native currency, without clothes, without food, without anything.

Certainly, Sraymlat and his minions would cover up their dirty deed. As a result, no one she knew would ever have any idea where she was.

Her situation was worse than anything she had ever dreamed of. On the positive side, she knew what a longshot it had been that she should even be alive. If Ori had not evaded the missiles, she would be dead. If Ori hadn't known how to fix the engines, they would have fallen into Saturn. If Ori had not made so many correct decisions on the voyage, they would never have made it to Earth. They could have sunk into the ocean, crashed into the mountains of Mexico, or landed in a country where they did not know the language; they could have died in the explosion. But she and Charlotte and Sherry and Leonard were alive.

Unni watched the farmer battle the blaze, fighting for a family that was mostly dead. Only hours before, Ori had done the same for her and the children. As she watched the pioneer struggle, she thought of Ori. She said, as if her husband could hear, "You know, Orishackt Svavapass, the two of us are just alike. The problem with us is that we were sent to watch, but we could not simply stand by and watch a catastrophe befall an unwitting world."

Unni realized one critical truth: she now owed it to Ori to survive and to make sure that all three of her children survived.

And toward that end, she was ready to do whatever it took.

32.
The Ultimate Alias

Unni watched Charlotte from a distance. The pioneer's retinal fatigue had certainly worn off a long time ago. She wondered if they had realized that Charlotte was not Mehetabel.

Somehow, Unni had to get her children to Lake Erie, cross into Upper Canada, and find a way to convince someone that she had money back home to let her family sail to England. She could take up her place in the townhouse in London. She could tutor Leonard, and perhaps he could still become a British leader someday.

But she had no means at all to get to the lake, much less cross it. She was not only without food or money, but she had to somehow do this with a small child.

Unni, the trained intelligence agent, began to let her imagination take over. The similarity between this pioneer family and her own was not lost on her. Mehetabel had been about the same age as Charlotte. She did not get a good look at Mary, but she seemed to be close enough in age to Sherry. Eliza had been about the same height and weight as Unni. As a trained spy, Unni began to consider the possibility of assuming the identities of the natives consumed when the ship exploded.

Of course, it was just wishful thinking. Leonard presented a problem. Jimmy was seven and Leonard was only eighteen months old. Unni put her hand on the inside of the front of the dress. She pulled out her emergency medical kit. She found one hypno-wipe!

291

Unni could use it on Tom or on that farmer, but not on both. She decided it was futile to try to change places with the dead.

On the other hand, she felt responsible in part for the farmer's loss. She felt she owed him something. What if she told the truth, or at least something he could believe? She could say she had just been widowed by the same fire. He needed a wife; she needed a husband. He had lost three children, and she had three.

Whether she assumed the role as wife by truth or by stealth, Unni would still have to know what kind of man he was. She did not even know his name. Was he someone she could love?

These thoughts went around and around in her mind. There was no easy solution, but the problem was dire. Unni knew she had to do something, and she had to do it immediately.

Unni went into the house to check on Leonard. He was sleeping. The family Bible caught her eye. Curiosity and her training as a professional spy got the better of her. She opened the Bible and found some of the family records.

The farmer's name was Abram. His wife's maiden name was Eliza Ballou. They were married on February 3, 1820, less than three months after Ori and Unni. Mehetabel was born on January 28, 1821; she was only three months apart from Charlotte. Thomas was born on October 16, 1822, making him ten years old. Mary was born on October 19, 1824, just a month before Sherry. But James B. was born on October 31, 1826, making him five years older than Leonard.

Abram had only moved the family into the wilderness three years earlier from Zanesville, Ohio. They were in Orange in Cuyahoga County. There was a distance of miles to their nearest neighbor.

Looking around the house, Unni could see the real poverty of this family. The log cabin was made of notched, unhewn logs. The gaps between the logs were filled with clay mud. The floor was made of logs that had been split in half and hewn smooth with an axe with the flat sides up.

The house only had three small windows and a door made of a single plank. The windows had no glass, just greased paper. There was a fireplace on the side with a chimney made of wood and mud. In the rear of the cabin was a loft with a permanent ladder. The children slept on the floor of the loft on straw beds.

Unni wondered how the girls would take to a place like this after living in a London townhouse with three servants and in a modern home in Ropalb on Earth 43 full of electricity and conveniences.

She stepped outside. Abram was still fighting the fire. Charlotte had come back now.

"They keep calling me Mehetabel," Charlotte told her mother.

"So they have not noticed that you are not?" Unni asked.

"They are too busy fighting the fire to care," Charlotte replied. "I think Tom is starting to get wise, but he is confused. He said their nearest neighbors are miles away. So, he must be thinking, if I am not Mehetabel, who could I be, and where is the real Mehetabel?"

Unni wanted to open her plan of switching places with the dead family members, but Charlotte insisted that they start preparing dinner. "They will be hungry when they get in," Charlotte pointed out.

Unni did not know how to prepare a meal with the available tools. But Charlotte and Sherry did, even drawing water from the well, and locating the vegetables and salted meat, building the fire, and making the soup.

"Where did you learn all of this?" Unni asked in amazement.

"Adaptation School on Earth 2, during the months that our teacher was Miss West," Charlotte replied.

That was the second time Miss West's name was mentioned that day.

"Thank goodness for Miss West!" Unni declared.

"Thank goodness for Beempu," Sherry added.

"His name is Will," Charlotte thought to herself.

Unni opened her idea about adopting the names of the dead Eliza, Mehetabel, and Mary as aliases.

"Do we need to do something that extreme?" Charlotte asked.

"Extreme measures are going to be needed if we are to survive," their mother explained.

"I am not sure if that is right," Charlotte said. "But if your plan has any chance of working, you are going to have to rid yourself of that English accent. You need to speak like an American."

From that moment on, Charlotte and Sherry brought back their American accents.

When the fire was out, Abram and Tom returned to the cabin. Dinner was not ready, so Abram went outside and sat on a stump. He was overheated, covered with perspiration, and exhausted. A cool, refreshing breeze was blowing from the west. Unni did not see that Abram had exposed himself in his overheated and wet state to the breeze until she came out to call everyone for dinner. It was too late by then. She was concerned that he could have gotten himself sick.

It was dark inside the cabin and the sun soon set. Abram and Tom did most of the talking at the table, and Unni kept Leonard out of view. Thus, the subject of her identity was avoided for the short term.

After dinner, the family retired to bed. The girls were afraid to say anything about the straw beds. Unni slept on the edge of her bed, trying to stay as far away from that huge stranger Abram as she could.

She tried to think of what to say the next day, but too many emotions convulsed her soul: intense grief, fear, and anger. Unni grieved for Ori, feared for her children, and seethed in anger toward Urelt Sraymlat, whom she held responsible for Ori's death and for the deaths of four innocent natives. But she was too exhausted from the ordeal of the day, and she fell asleep.

But just a few hours later, Unni was awakened by the writhing of the huge farmer next to her. He was in great pain. He complained that his throat was congested.

As the sun rose, Unni dispatched Tom to fetch a doctor.

Unni tried to control his fever by placing cloths soaked in cool water on this forehead. She slipped an antibiotic from her emergency medical kit into his water and gave it to him to drink. Later, she gave him another pill from her kit to control his fever. Abram kept thanking her and calling her Eliza.

At first, he seemed to begin to improve. Then two neighbors arrived. One was Amos Boynton. The other claimed to have some medical knowledge. Unni felt no choice but to turn Abram over to this man's medical care. But he aggravated the illness, and Abram's condition began to deteriorate.

Abram asked Unni to gather his children around him. It was only then that Unni brought forth Leonard. Abram looked at Unni. "Eliza, I have planted four saplings in these woods; I must now leave them to your care."

Unni thought those words might match Ori's sentiments as well.

Just moments later, Abram expired. Unni felt so empty. In a way, she had been widowed twice in as many days.

There were only four families within a ten-mile radius, and they soon came. The neighbors wept with the fatherless children and Unni, who was still grieving for Ori. They helped her put Abram's remains into a rough box and bore him out the low door of the cabin to a corner of the wheat field, where they buried him. There was no pastor or sermon or spoken prayers.

The neighbors departed. The last to leave was Amos Boynton. He kept eying Leonard.

Just before he left, he finally spoke his mind. "You keep calling this boy Jimmy, but he can't be Jimmy. Five years ago, Jimmy was two. He should be seven by now."

Unni searched for words. It was Charlotte who finally spoke up.

"Jimmy died shortly after that. When our family had another boy, we also named him James."

"With a different middle name, I gather," Mr. Boynton surmised.

"Yes," Unni replied. "This boy's middle name is Abram, after his father."

Mr. Boynton nodded in approval. He departed to his farm soon after.

Under the aliases of Eliza, Mehetabel, Mary, and Jimmy, the Svavapass family was able to survive. Through the hypno-wipe, Tom accepted them as his real family. As it would turn out, Tom was a selfless, hardworking young man. His dedication and labor were a critical factor in the family's survival, as was Unni's tenacity and strong will. Unni soon learned the skills of life in the wilderness.

Her young son Leonard was her pride and joy. She would often gaze at the handsome young man and wonder what might have been. He could have been a wealthy, well-connected gentleman named Leonard Weatherby. Instead, he was just a poor farm boy named Jimmy.

Epilogue

By the middle of the summer, Shelby began to worry as to the fate of the Weatherby family. They were months overdue. He wrote to their only known relative, Jenny's mother Abigail Carter. But he received no reply. He wrote to the War and Colonial Office to see if they could locate the Weatherby family in Canada. They could not find any such record. Shelby also tried Scotland Yard, but to no avail.

The Weatherby family became a great missing persons case and the subject of speculation. Even the Duke of Wellington paid interest to the case. The entire family was eventually declared legally dead in 1839. By that time, Shelby had found other employment, not an easy feat without a reference from his former employer.

The Weatherby Estate became a ward of the state because Robert Weatherby had died intestate with no known heirs or relatives. All of his property was to be auctioned off.

As the clerks were boxing Robert's and Jennifer's possessions, they came across a very odd seashell. It was pink, perfectly formed, and large, the size of a hand.

One clerk held it up and examined the shell. "I 'ave never seen the likes of this, 'ave you?"

"What d'ya tike me for? Some kind of ocean scientist?" the other replied.

"Don't ya think we should 'ave someone look at it? This might be valuable."

"Ow g'on. It's just a shell."

March 4, 1881 was a cold day, and the ground in Washington, D.C. was still partly covered by snow. Unni sat on the platform on the front forward-facing row, as her son Leonard was about to be inaugurated as the twentieth President of the United States.

Unni looked around the platform. On one side, she saw her daughter-in-law Lucretia and her grandchildren. On the other side was the outgoing president, Rutherford B. Hayes, who seemed relieved that his term was over. Below, the U.S. Marine Corps Band was playing a march that was written specially for her son, composed by its conductor who was only twenty-six, a certain John Philip Sousa.

Unni looked with pride on her son. He grew up to be the very image of the father he never knew. The look in his eye, his height, the way he bore himself, and the timbre of his voice reminded Unni of her husband Ori. Leonard had even grown a beard and trimmed it the same way. And he had the same indefatigable personality.

Her other children were not present. Charlotte had gotten married in 1837 at the age of sixteen, just four years after the crash. Sherry had been an excellent helper caring for her little brother, and the two became close. Sherry married in 1845, when she was twenty-two. Thomas had been an indispensable pillar in the family, forgoing his chance to go to school so that he could work to maintain the farm. He worked extra jobs just so that his little brother "Jimmy" could have shoes to go to school. Tom had gotten married in 1849 at the age of twenty-seven and had later moved to Michigan. Tom's personal sacrifices and labor of love had made it possible for Leonard to reach this moment in his illustrious career.

And Leonard's accomplishments and talents were many. He had been a college professor by the age of twenty-four and became the college president the following year, and he would entertain friends by writing with both of his hands at the same time. He was a brilliant orator. He was an ordained minister and developed a preaching circuit in several neighboring churches. With no military training, Leonard was commissioned as a colonel in the Union Army in the Civil War and captured Paintsville, Kentucky. Leonard was a co-planner of the highly successful Tullahoma Campaign that rid central Tennessee of rebels in 1863. Leonard's heroic ride at Missionary Ridge prevented a Union disaster at the Battle of Chickamauga. He rose to the rank of major general.

Leonard had published a proof of the Pythagorean Theorem. He served as an Ohio state senator, a nine-term representative in Congress, and chairman of the House Appropriations Committee, and was elected to the United States Senate. It was from this platform that Unni expected her son to forward her agenda to advance Earth 48. She never expected him to be elected president, at least not this early in his career. But Leonard delivered a speech at the deadlocked 1880 Republican Convention for one of the candidates that was so brilliant and full of content that he inadvertently caused the convention to nominate him for the presidency.

Unni had been out of touch with interstellar news for forty-eight years and had no idea how long it would be before the Vittmians would reach this planet. But she had satisfaction in knowing she had done her part.

"How proud Ori would be!" Unni said softly in Grellish, her words drowned out by the Marine Corps band. "I did it, Ori. *We* did it. Mission accomplished!"

Unni's old friend and mentor, Saibert Ortees, had been right after all. It was clear to Unni, a former analyst of the Interplanetary Intelligence Service, that it was the United States of America that would become the dominant power on Earth 48 in technology, strength, and culture. Although the Germans did unite behind Prussia into a powerful state a decade before as Metchavork had predicted, and although the British Empire might arguably have been still in the lead as a world power, all of the momentum was with the United States.

And the United States was about to receive a huge impulse of acceleration that would lead the planet forward. On the inaugural platform stood the political equivalent of Leonardo da Vinci. While laboring on the farm, spinning at the spinning wheel and even splitting rails, Unni had found the time to tutor her son and had grounded him in the principles needed to send his nation forward. Unni was going to move into the White House to be with her son and advise him as needed.

Leonard was bristling with plans to improve agricultural technology, improve education and make it universally available, ensure voting rights and civil rights for African Americans, and overhaul civil service. He was also prepared to implement an activist foreign policy that would allow this planet to bypass the world wars that his mother knew would otherwise convulse this planet as they had nearly all of the other Earths at this stage of their development.

The press hailed Leonard as one of the only men in the country who understood all of its issues. Unni considered it ironic that a man so knowledgeable did not know his real name.

Finally, the moment arrived. Chief Justice Morrison Waite stood up to administer the oath of office. Unni was almost overcome by the emotion of satisfaction.

Leonard placed his left hand on the Bible.

The Chief Justice said, "Raise your right hand and repeat after me: I, James Abram Garfield, do solemnly swear...."

The son of Unni and Ori Svavapass responded, "I, James Abram Garfield, do solemnly swear...."